Murder on the Prairie

A North Florida Mystery

ISBN 1-59113-665-2

Printed in the United States of America.

Booklocker.com, Inc.
2005

Murder on the Prairie

A North Florida Mystery

M.D. Abrams

M. D. Abrams

For Dorie, my muse and greatest fan!
In memory of Audrey and Al, always in my heart.

Acknowledgments

I owe the discovery of my retirement passion to the *Writing the Region* annual writers workshop, and to five women I met there—my weekly writers group—a resource essential to my writing life. Thanks to Lindsay Newman, Dorothy Staley, Katy Tonnelier, Vicky Woods, and Margie Zander!

Choosing to write a north Florida eco-mystery evolved from an appreciation of the region's fragile natural beauty gained from working with Florida Defenders of the Environment under Marjorie Carr. My focus on Paynes Prairie was inspired by Lars Andersen's book: *Paynes Prairie: A History of the Great Savanna* (Pineapple Press, 2001). Thanks to preserve biologist, Jim Weimer; former park manager, Jim Gillian; staff at the Visitor's Center; and poet Stetson Kennedy's permission to use his poem, *Paine's Prairie*. The Alachua County's Matheson Museum and Joanne Gillikin enhanced my research. I hope those who know the Prairie will forgive dramatic liberties taken in describing some of the area's specific locales.

My actress protagonist, Lorelei Crane, and I thank those behind the scenes of this mystery: Gainesville's Hippodrome State Theatre—special thanks to Lauren Caldwell, Artistic Director; Tamerin Dygert, Dramaturg; and Sara Morsey, actress and professor. Thanks to deputies in the Alachua County Sheriff's Office, especially Detective Joseph Branaman and Lt. Clare Noble. Former city commissioner, Bruce Delaney, helped with land use issues, and Sharelle Turner with property crimes. Friends Dr. Marsha Bierman, Gail Grossman, Mary Giella, Barbara Tewell, and nephew Michael Canning all contributed. Profound thanks to Chris Flavin for her dedicated editing. I hold all blameless for any inaccuracies. Finally, I thank my uncle Harold T. Berc (*Short Sea Sagas*, Athena Press, 2002), for his encouragement and example—he has been my lifetime mentor and inspiration.

Gainesville, Florida
February 2005

Chapter One

The Prairie marsh basin had flooded. Water was lapping over one lane of Highway 441, and there were a dozen or so alligators lined up at the road's edge. Cars and trucks crawled along as drivers gawked at the prehistoric reptiles and the vast flooded marsh. It was only the first of the day's extraordinary events.

I had never seen Paynes Prairie like that before, though some north Florida old timers still called it Alachua Lake. The appearance of the alligators was even more astonishing. Apparently, the cold-blooded creatures had been forced by the high water to do their warming on the dry surface of the road.

I shuddered as I passed them, and irrationally powered my car windows halfway up as I, just as irrationally, whispered "Go Gators!" It was the mantra of University of Florida football fans and used so ubiquitously, it tended to seep into one's DNA.

I continued into Gainesville past the old Brown Derby Restaurant. It was the former scene of so many celebratory and clandestine meetings, and ironically, I thought, was now an Islamic Center. As I drive by, I occasionally have the flicker of a memory of Jeffrey, and a dark, uneasy feeling. Jeffrey, my former husband and I, would often rendezvous at the Brown Derby. Sometimes, I'd even stop there for a drink alone—until the murder.

A young woman college student who also may have stopped by for a drink, or to meet someone, was beaten to death. Her car was in the Derby parking lot. Her battered nude body was found, across the street, in a shallow grave. It gave me the creeps when a friend asked me to go hiking with her in that area. I refused. Not like I was afraid of ghosts, but...

My close encounter with the alligators, and the white-washed serenity of the once notorious restaurant somehow felt connected. Cold-blooded gators. Cold-blooded murder. I shivered at the thought.

As I drove up 13th Street near the University, I was once again caught in a snarl of traffic. Cars, mopeds, bikes, and sandal-footed, head-phone wearing students, all in a hurried jumble. In Gainesville, it is not the weather but the tide of thousands of students that signals the change of seasons. Fall semester was beginning.

Though I was more than twenty years from my own undergrad days, I could still feel the air prickle with the excitement of fresh starts. I flirted with the appealing idea that the day might bring me something new and exciting. Little did I suspect it was a wish I would come to regret.

I stepped into our office, the Center for Earth Options, and announced, "Hey, can you believe it? I just saw a dozen alligators sitting roadside on the Prairie. The whole place is flooded. It's an amazing sight."

My boss, Diana Demeter, gave me a quick anxious glance before bringing her hands up to her mouth, and shaking her head. Her large-brown rimmed glasses gave her an owl-like look, and her severely tailored appearance reminded me of my elementary school librarian.

Dropping her hands, she said, "This just can't happen. Heaven knows, we cannot let it happen!"

"What's up?" I asked, and walked further into the office. "What can't happen?"

I looked at Diana and then at Becky, our office manager, who sat behind the reception desk. Diana gave me a wan smile. Becky sat erect, and was tapping her pencil back and forth on the desk. She looked as though she would burst into tears at any moment.

Diana finally explained, "Apparently the south Florida Valdez Development Company has plans to build a high rise housing project on the rim of the Prairie."

I was stunned by the news. "But how can they get a permit? I mean, what about the county's land use plan, for God's sake? Isn't the Prairie rim on preservation status or something? There are single family homes out there, but… surely they can't allow a whole damn high rise development, can they?"

Becky responded, "That's what we thought, but Dr. Ames, from the Sierra Club, just called and told Diana that Valdez has an old permit. And," she paused, her heavy dark eyebrows shooting up dramatically, "it has no expiration date. They're basically good to go."

"Dalton said they are already on the agenda for the next County Commission meeting. They're really moving fast," Diana added, touching Becky's hand to stop her repetitive tapping.

"Jesus," I said, walking over to my desk and plopping down in the chair. "I can't believe it!"

"Neither did we—at first," Diana said, giving me a sympathetic look. "We were devastated by the news."

I sat in stunned silence, and watched as the two women hovered over Becky's desk, murmuring to one another, and shuffling through various papers. I thought about the diverse backgrounds that had somehow landed us together.

There was twenty-something Becky, fast-talking, and filled with zeal over many issues. Her family lived in Boston. And, Diana, a soft-spoken widow in her forties with a son she described as a "troubled teenager." I looked at her, and felt a wave of affection as I recalled our first meeting, my job interview. We clicked right away, and shared some of our personal history. She and her husband had been Georgia farmers until he was killed in a farming accident. She said it made her into a "steel magnolia." And then there was me—living out my mother's dream to be an actress—raised as an only child, in south Florida, by a mother and father who owned an orange grove.

How comical it would be if Becky, Diana, and I were lined up together? I'd be the tallest, Becky the squarest, and Diana slender and petite. Yet, despite all of our differences, it was certain that the news of the Valdez plan would ignite our shared passion to preserve this wild land.

After several minutes, Diana sat down and started to speak to us in her slow Georgia drawl. "I think you should know something about who we're up against," she said. "Valdez is run by two old University buddies: Jimmy Valdez and Crawford Keezer. I first met them at an Environmental Permitting Conference in Sanibel a couple of years ago. Those two boys couldn't be more different from one another, but both of them are pretty slick in their own way. They build developments big as a whole town, and they start out by just scraping the land of everything on it. If they do get this thing going, I guess we can expect the same." She shook her head sadly and looked away from us.

Becky suddenly jumped from her chair. As she began speaking, her long wiry brown hair seemed to bristle with the intensity of her tone.

"But that's not going to happen," she said, and pounded her fist on the desk. "That's why we're here. Right, Diana? And I've got lots of other friends who'll know how to stop this thing, too. "

I guessed Becky was referring to the rag-tag group of grad students she hung out with. They were all members of a radical environmental group called EcoSave!.

"Okay," I said, and sat down again. I put up my hands in a gesture that signified I had heard enough. "We obviously need to stop their project. Diana, how can we get the County Commission to overturn the permit?"

"I'm not sure," she said. "So far, Dalton says that there's not much the Commission can do since the permit is still valid."

My anger flared thinking about some of the other fights we'd had with our largely pro-development Commission.

"Or won't do if Commissioner Judson Sparks and his friends are in on it," I said.

"Well, you can be certain of one thing, ladies; we'll give them one heck of a good fight." Diana stood up, and faced us with renewed confidence.

"Becky, please get me all the old coalition files. We're going to call an emergency board meeting and round up the faithful."

Becky headed to the file cabinets that lined one whole wall of the office.

Diana stood up, straightened her back, put her hands on her hips, and said, "We'll get something going pretty quickly. I just hope we can head them off before deals get firmed-up. And you're right about Judson Sparks, Lorelei. We'll need to keep our eye on him. I heard that Sparks, Valdez, and Keezer all belonged to the same fraternity in college."

"What can I do?" I asked.

She looked at me for a moment, "How about preparing an action alert to email to our members? And also a news release. Something about an environmental coalition forming under Dalton Ames direction. I'm sure he'll approve it."

Without awaiting a response, Diana walked back into her office. I felt emotionally jarred, and aware that my neck and shoulders ached. As soon as Diana went back in her office, Becky stopped rifling through the files, and turned to me as I leaned back in my chair for a long stretch. Her mouth was working as though she wanted to say something but hadn't decided how.

Finally, she announced, in a whisper, "I think we need to get Jeff Waterman up here." She looked from me to Diana's office door and back.

I broke my stretch at the sound of Jeffrey's name. How weird; I thought, I had been thinking of him again, on the drive in. Remembering the times we sat at the Brown Derby bar. The same bar where the murdered girl had sat.

Becky rushed over to my desk. She bent down, and said very quietly, "Remember how good he was at organizing the whole Jonesville protest? What do you think, Lorelei? I know you could talk Diana into asking him."

Ask Jeffrey to come back here from Orlando? What an outrageous idea, I thought. "Why do you even think he'd be interested?" I asked and realized my mouth had gone dry. "He's been gone so many years."

"Oh, we're still in touch. Of course he'd want to be involved. He loves the Prairie."

"I don't know, Becky." I appeared to give the idea some consideration. "Bringing Jeffrey Waterman up here would make things more stressful than they already are." Now that's an understatement, I thought, and I found my heart beating rapidly at the mere thought of seeing him again.

Diana stood at her office door and glared at Becky. "Did I hear Jeff Waterman's name? That loose cannon? Forgive me, Lorelei, but thank goodness he's not around to declare war."

I shrugged, seeming to be indifferent to her comment.

She said, "I'm still trying to overcome the damage he did our reputation because of his tactics at Jonesville. Where are those files, Becky? We need to get going."

Looking defeated, Becky returned to the file cabinet.

"I'm going home to work. I need some fresh air and time to think about all of this," I said gathering my mail and stuffing it into my handbag. "Keep me posted if you hear anything else."

I approached Becky on my way out the door, and whispered, "Becky, you'll just get Diana more riled up if you call Jeffrey in on this. Really, like I said, it would complicate things right now. Please. Just don't do it."

Becky didn't look up from the files, and gave me a non-committal grunt as I left the office.

I drove back home on automatic pilot. I was reflecting on Valdez, and on the threat to my peace if Becky failed to heed my warning about calling Jeffrey. Micanopy is just 10 miles south of Gainesville, and I soon re-crossed the Prairie basin. The gators had withdrawn or the Park Rangers had somehow managed to get them off the road, and the traffic was moving more quickly.

My feelings began shifting as I took a deep breath, and was calmed by sight of the tall pines, moss draped oaks, and dense shrubs that shaded both sides of the highway. I lowered my car windows to experience the forested air made fresher by the tropical storm that had touched the Gulf coast and crossed the North Florida peninsula.

"Lorelei, whatever will you do if Jeffrey shows up?" I said, sighing deeply.

I recalled Bill's question, before we went to sleep last night. He had asked, "Honey, how are we going to celebrate our 10th anniversary? You know it's coming up next month."

I had put him off. Celebrate? I thought. What's to celebrate? A house, a cat, and occasional love-making? That's all we'd come to share as Bill's professorial life and my so-called career as an actress had caused our schedules, and our lives to diverge. And now, I worried, what impact would Jeffrey have if he were to suddenly appear on the scene?

Chapter 2

Two hours of yoga helped me to get centered, and push back my tangle of thoughts about Bill, Jeffrey, and Valdez. I took my laptop out on to the screened patio that adjoined our kitchen, and spent the afternoon working on press releases and an email campaign.

The whirr of the ceiling fan and the warm air made me drowsy as I paused to study the beauty of the woods, and the yellow sulfur butterflies that flitted among the shrubs. As I was envying their lightness of being, I experienced a stab of dread. It felt like a premonition of something terrible—something that would arise from the morning's events.

After a light supper, I went upstairs and spent the night in bed. I distracted myself by studying a book of Chekhov plays in preparation for our upcoming production. I was already asleep when I felt Bill crawl into the bed beside me.

"Long first day of classes," he murmured in my ear. He lightly kissed my shoulder, and turned over to his side of the bed.

By Tuesday morning, the feeling of dread had subsided. I headed out the door still preoccupied with thoughts about Jeffrey and about the Prairie development, and I stumbled over our calico cat, who Bill had named "Maynard" after the economist, John Maynard Keynes. Maynard let out a protesting squeal and fled toward the kitchen before I could pick him up and apologize.

On the drive in, the threat of a ruinous development on the Prairie's edge made me slow down to inspect the basin more closely. It was a sheet of water dotted with intermittent patches of tall shrubs and small trees. The sun bounced off of it with quick flashes of light. The water apparently was draining back into the Alachua Sink, the opening to the aquifer on the other side of the basin.

Yesterday's flooding made it easy to imagine its colorful history as a lake with boats and steamboat traffic when it was plugged up as recently as the late 1870's and 80's. Harder to grasp was that the Prairie basin was a more than 17,000 acre giant sinkhole caused by the collapse of underground limestone caverns, and that this geo-hydrologic activity was still continuing. What a unique place, I thought, and how worthy of our fight to preserve it.

I parked the car and entered the Center office.

"Diana's not in yet this morning. At the Sheriff's office," Becky replied, without her customary cheerful greeting.

"Oh no," I said. "Is it her son, Hank, again?"

"Dunno," she said, without looking up.

Okay, I thought, as I moved toward my desk. Becky's in a mood and Diana's going to be distressed. Gloom ahead. Definitely a Chekhovian day.

"Is that the one and only Lorelei Waterman? The famous actress?"

My head jerked up in the direction of the voice, and I felt a shock wave slam into my body. There he was: lean build, long straight black hair covered by a baseball cap, and the familiar cocky smile on his tanned face. He bowed, with his arms outstretched, and rose to complete the theatrical cliché with a "Ta Da!"

He started walking toward me and said, "Hey, babe. Surprised to see me?"

"Jeffrey? What are you doing here?" My low pitched, almost raspy voice came out sounding shrill.

"Didn't Becky tell you?" He stopped and turned to look at Becky.

I shot her an angry look, but her head was down. She was carefully ignoring both of us.

"I left Orlando last night," he said. "After I talked with her. Sounded like you guys needed some help." He moved closer, sat on the edge of an empty desk, and folded his arms across his chest as he looked down at me with a self-satisfied grin.

I noted the wisps of gray in his sideburns. "In case your brain has failed you, my married name is Crane. Lorelei *Woodington* Crane."

His appearance still had me stunned. Despite his still youthful good looks there was something dissipated about his face, and he looked thinner than I remembered him. He was dressed in hiking boots, cargo shorts, and a faded t-shirt that said "Don't Worry; Be Hopi."

"I know. I know," he said. "Just wanted to get your attention…in case you didn't remember me." He gave me his fakey boyish look, but I resisted responding to it. "So, aren't you glad to see me? It's been quite a while."

"Of course, I'm surprised to see you." It was a lie, and I glared at Becky. Yet, at some level I had fully expected to see him, maybe ever since I had thought of him yesterday morning. "Bill asks me, from time to time, if I've heard from you."

"I'll bet," he said. "How is the great professor? Still training kids to run the corporate kingdom?"

I ignored his taunt. I tried to regain control of my labored breathing and hoped he didn't notice it.

"How did you manage to leave Orlando so quickly? Aren't you working?" I asked.

He made no reply, and walked around the area as if he were looking for something. He picked up items from each of the desks, studied them for a moment, and then dropped them back in place. I followed his movements with fascination, and remembered how much kinetic energy he possessed. He never could sit still.

Finally, he faced me and said, "You didn't answer my question."

"And you didn't answer mine," I replied sharply.

"Fair enough," he said. "First mine. How are you and Billy boy? Becky keeps me up-to-date with my Gainesville buddies but…"

"Bill and I are doing just fine," I said. Saying Bill's name made me relax a little. I took a couple of deep breaths and my heartbeat slowed down to almost normal. "He travels a lot but…"

"And leaves you all alone?" He gave me an appreciative glance and said, "You still look like the hottest old lady I've ever met."

"Cut the old lady stuff, Jeffrey. You're only six years younger than me. And frankly, you look like you're catching up fast."

He shrugged.

"It's my turn now, why are you really here?"

"I had to come," he said. "You know how I feel about the Prairie. I couldn't resist. Just the thought of the two of us in the good fight again. We were great together, you know." He gave me a meaningful look and moved to the side of my desk.

I stood up defensively, stepped behind my chair, and held onto it. At 5'7", I was only a couple of inches shorter than he. We stood facing each other with the chair as a buffer. My breathing had become shallow, and my bravado quickly faded. I became swept up by the fragrance of his favorite bath soap, and the soulful look in his large black eyes.

"What are you so nervous about, Lor?" he said softly. "It's just me." He gave me a sweet smile, but a hint of sadness crept into his eyes.

I gripped the chair back more tightly, took another deep breath, and searched for something to say that would break the spell between us.

"So you're here to pull another Jonesville stunt?" I said it harshly, as a taunt. "Things are different now." I looked down to see that my knuckles were white and my hands felt clammy.

"Okay, I get the picture." He raised his hands in surrender, giving up more quickly than I had expected. The moment of intimacy had been shattered.

He stepped back, leaned against a desk, and eyed me before saying in a lighter tone. "How about let's start with lunch and you can fill me in? Where can we get a slice of pizza and a cold brew? I haven't had good pizza since I left Gainesville—what, 8-9 years ago?" He looked over to Becky for confirmation. She was still working as though she was alone in the office—playing like the proverbial three monkeys.

I sat back down, put on my glasses, and started to rifle through the mail. "Pizza and beer? I swear, Jeffrey. You still haven't grown up, have you?"

"I've just kept the boyish charm you used to like so much," he said.

I rolled my eyes and sighed, "Get serious. This Valdez thing is huge. I'd pretty much do anything, short of murder, to stop them. Correction, I think I could commit murder…I'm so damn mad at the thought of it. So, as long as you're here, I hope you have some brilliant ideas to put into the pot."

"Speaking of pot, Red, any good "Gainesville Green" still around?" I blushed at his use of this familiar name. He was the only one, since my childhood, who called me by my hair color.

Becky and I both giggled at his question as the front door opened and Diana walked in. She didn't seem to notice Jeffrey.

"I have to take Hank to Teen Court," she said in a flat tone, as she checked the in-box on Becky's desk for phone messages. "He got caught with marijuana at school and maybe worse. I don't know yet. He's not talking much." She was speaking to Becky, who had finally looked up from her computer. Then Diana turned and paused a moment as she gave me and Jeffrey a look of disbelief.

"Jeff Waterman? What are you doing here?" Diana stood rigid, placed her hands on her hips, her disbelief turning to anger. "Not in my wildest dreams did I think you'd have the nerve to show your face in my office again. I want you out of here. Right now!"

She slammed her hand flat down on Becky's desk knocking over a pen holder. Becky immediately crouched down to pick up the scattered pens and pencils, leaving me and Jeffrey in Diana's line of fire.

Now, wait a minute, Diana." Jeffrey hunched over in a placating stance and slowly approached her. "I know I have some explaining, apologizing even…"

"Explain? Apologize? Indeed. How do you explain completely derailing my negotiations with those Jonesville developers? It took me a long time to rebuild the respect our organization has always enjoyed."

"Okay. Point taken. Me and my buddies—yes, we pulled some dirty tricks—messed up their construction site, and things got out of hand. But at least it put the issue and the Center in the news. You've got to admit…"

"No. It wasn't sensational publicity, but the persistent efforts of our Board of Directors and volunteers that finally won that battle. Not you and your hooligan friends in EcoSave!"

Jeffrey looked down for a moment, folded his hands contritely, and glanced from me to Becky as if trying to enlist our assistance.

Finally he said, "Please. That was almost a decade ago. I've changed. I think I can really help you now. And you know I have a special feeling for the Prairie. Hell, I don't want to see it ruined."

"Oh, really?" She said. "And just how do you think you can help?"

Her face was set in a scowl.

Jeffrey turned again, and looked pleadingly at me. But I averted my eyes, and sat back down at my desk. This was between the two of them, and I felt relieved by the break from his intensity and my own unruly emotions.

"Diana, I think I know a way to beat back Valdez. It's why I came up here."

Diana paused and eyed him suspiciously. "And just what might that be?"

"There have been some serious rumors about Valdez in Orlando." Jeffrey started to pace back and forth while he talked. "Well, more specifically, about their financial situation. And of course, they're still notorious for the big fracas in Miami. But this time..."

"Rumors? How do you think rumors will help us?" Diana asked.

"What if we could pin them down, and dig up some serious shit—I mean dirt—wouldn't that be to our advantage? To totally discredit them?" He stopped pacing and looked at the three of us.

"Yes, it could give us some leverage," Diana conceded. I saw her considering the idea. Her body relaxed, and she gave Jeffrey an interested look.

"So, what do you think? Can I work with you guys on this?" Jeffrey asked.

Diana paused before responding. She looked him over, and I wondered if she too was noticing the ways in which he had aged.

"Okay," she said. "But it must be our way: with facts not...dirty tricks. Do you understand?"

Jeffrey ducked his head at her reference. "Yes. Your way," he said. "I want to rebuild the trust we had, and maybe pay you back for the trouble I caused."

"I sure hope you have changed. We have built good working relationships with the development community. For the most part, our local developers are sensitive to ecological issues. And when you and your EcoSave! gang pulled those stunts at Jonesville..."

"I'll have to go back down to Orlando to do a little snooping around," Jeffrey said as he rested his elbow on a nearby file cabinet. "For starters, I have a very good friend who works at the water management district.

"Swift-Mud?" Becky said.

"What?" Diana asked. She looked like she was already absorbed in the implications of Jeffrey's plan.

"Our little joke," Jeffrey replied. "The Southwest Florida Water Management District...we call it Swift-Mud."

"Yes, of course," Diana said absently.

"Anyway," Jeffrey continued, "my friend Louisa is the one who told me about the rumors. I'll call her now. Is there a phone in that little office?" He pointed to our storage area cum office at the back of the room.

Becky nodded, but Jeffrey looked to Diana for approval.

"Go ahead, you can use it," she said.

When Jeffrey left to make his call, Diana said, "You know, if Jeff can come up with something really serious, it might give the Commission a basis to revoke their permit."

The phone rang. Becky answered and handed it over to Diana, "It's Dr. Ames."

Diana took the phone. "Hello, Dalton, any news?" She listened, nodding in agreement.

After she hung up, she looked squarely at Becky and me, smoothed the waist of her skirt, and announced in her business-like voice, "That's it. Dalton says that Crawford Keezer is scheduled to make a presentation tomorrow afternoon at the County Commission meeting. He suggested that we pack the meeting room with our people. He wants the Commission to know that we're watching this thing very closely."

"Why would Keezer even go before the Commission if he already has a permit?" I asked.

"Probably because he knows this project is a public relations nightmare and he's trying to do damage control up front." Jeffrey reentered the room as he spoke. "Anyway, I couldn't find my friend. She's at some meeting in Tallahassee and not answering her cell. I'll try her again tonight."

Diana started to make some notes at Becky's desk.

"Jeffrey, you mentioned something about Valdez in Miami. I don't think I ever heard the particulars," I said.

Jeffrey rubbed his hands together, took a deep breath, and said, "Here's the short story: It seems that the Sierra Club and some allied groups created a publicity campaign to stop Valdez from getting a land use variance for a pet project of theirs. The land was at the edge of the Everglades. Sierra got a bit too passionate, and printed some personal stuff that made Jimmy Valdez look bad. Sierra also got some high powered attorneys who ultimately succeeded in stopping the project. Valdez retaliated with a law suit for slander, etcetera, etcetera."

"And tell her about the fire," Becky said.

"Oh yeah, a couple of months after the whole thing had settled down, the Sierra Club's office was burned to the ground. It was arson, but they never proved who did it."

"Wow," I said. "Sounds like the Valdez Company is scarier than I thought.

Diana looked up and made a dismissive gesture. "Some of that's nothing more than rumor. In any case," she turned to Jeffrey, "we need your information quickly. Keezer only has to meet with the County's Development Resources Committee before Valdez begins major land clearing. That's only a week or two away." She went into her office.

"So, Red…" Jeffrey walked over to me.

"Look, Jeffrey. Unlike you, who apparently is not currently employed, I have a job to do here. And I've got to leave in about a half an hour to get over to the theater. So please, just do whatever it is you do, and leave me alone. And you, you little twerp," I said, pointing at Becky. She appeared genuinely contrite.

"Lorelei, I promise you. I didn't tell him to come. I only…"

"We'll talk about this later," I cut her off and turned to my computer screen, ignoring both of them.

"Anyway, about lunch?" Jeffrey asked. "I really could use a beer right now."

"Not with me. Not today," I said and started to close down my computer.

He looked disappointed, and turned to Becky. "How about you, Beck? You do get unchained for lunch, don't you?"

Becky stopped working, leaned back in her chair and stretched out her arms and legs. As she jumped to her feet she said, "Definitely, Jeff. Cool. Let's go over to Charley's. Some of your old buds will probably be there around now."

Becky stood by her desk, and completed her stretching. She was dressed in her usual attire: clunky shoes, hip hugger jeans, and a short blousy top. When she bent down, you could see a scroll of flowery body tattoos across the base of her spine.

"Lorelei, will you tell Diana I've gone?" Becky said, waving her hand toward me as the two of them left the office. I realized how hungry I was, as I rifled through my desk drawers until I found a stale bag of salted peanuts. I ate the peanuts, but resolved to bring better snacks into work.

I gathered my stuff to go, and on my way out, I stopped in Diana's office. She was talking on the telephone, staring out the window with her back to me, and unaware of my presence. I scribbled a note on her desk and left.

Driving back to Micanopy, I inadvertently turned off onto Archer Road and found myself in Shands Hospital traffic. My mind was spinning with memories of Jeffrey. We had lived in a townhouse off of Archer near the University until I got pregnant.

I pulled onto a side street and parked the car to regain my composure. Dammit, I thought, what's he doing back in my life? When Jeffrey first appeared at the office, I had the same excited feeling as when I first met him at an environmental rally a hundred years before.

"Get a grip, Lorelei." I said aloud, and I turned back onto SW 13th street. I made a quick stop at the theater to pick up the Chekhov script, and headed for home. On the way, I reviewed my plan of attack in studying the play, and pushed back thoughts of Jeffrey. I reasoned that, with any luck, I wouldn't be in the office often enough to run into him.

Chapter 3

There was a line of traffic backed up at the southbound entrance to the Prairie basin. I saw the whirling lights atop Sheriff's cars and the yellow crime scene tape. Someone attacked by a gator? Or maybe even a suicide. The Prairie was known as the site for all sorts of dramatic events. It was so wild and vast, and so easy to hide anything. As I drew nearer to the scene, I let my window down to talk with a Deputy who was directing traffic.

"What's going on, Officer?" I asked.

"Some joker robbed a bank in town," he replied. "We gave him a chase and he threw his weapon out the window here before we caught up with him. Our dive team is going down to look for it."

"What about alligators? Is it safe down there?" Gators were always my first concern on the Prairie.

"Safe as can be," he replied. "It's their job." He motioned me to move ahead and directed the car behind to follow me.

At home, I walked into the dark kitchen, and just as I switched on the light, the phone rang.

"Honey?" It was Bill. "I'm glad I caught you. I won't be home until after nine, maybe later. I agreed to meet with some doc students after class tonight and..."

"Oh, Bill. I'm so glad to hear your voice. You won't believe what happened today."

He sound rushed as he continued, "Just wanted to let you know. We'll talk later. The Department budget meeting's starting, and it's really important. Bye, sweetheart."

"But, Bill..." The phone was dead.

What a life, I thought, as I finished opening a can of cat food and placed it in Maynard's bowl.

"Thank God, we have only you, dear Maynard. What if we did have children? We simply wouldn't have time for them." *Jeffrey*, I thought. No, don't go there, I warned myself.

I popped a Lean Cuisine into the microwave. Maynard jumped into the wooden bowl on the oak table and began to wash himself. I started making a salad.

"Can you believe it, Maynard? Jeffrey just showing up like that? Ouch!" I cried, stared at the blood spurt from my finger, and dropped the paring knife. "Dammit, Lorelei, how can you be so clumsy?" I rushed to the sink, ran cold water on my hand, and pressed the cut until it stopped bleeding.

I read *The New York Times* theater section while I ate dinner. Afterwards, I called my young fellow actress, Cassie Woodruff. We agreed to meet for a quick lunch the next day since I had to come into town for the County Commission meeting. I grabbed some fruit and went upstairs to read the script revisions I'd picked up at the theater.

Bill got home about 10:30. I told him about the Valdez project, and Jeffrey's unexpected appearance.

"So Waterman showed up, like the Calvary, huh? Interesting. It's been a lot of years since we've heard from him, right?" He looked at me, waiting to judge my response.

"C'mon, Bill. You know Jeffrey was passionate about Paynes Prairie. I should have expected him to be here."

"Well, I hope that's the only passion he's arrived with," Bill said, as he got up and entered our large walk-in closet to undress.

I was taken aback by this hint of jealousy, and a bit pleased to hear it.

"We have a real crisis on our hands. Diana says…"

"Crisis? A little dramatic, isn't it?" Bill returned, buttoning his pajama top, and sat down on my side of the bed. "Look at it from a different angle. Everyone knows we need more housing here. The whole state's population just goes on growing. What is it now? About a thousand people a day moving into Florida? It's inevitable that developers will want to build on whatever land they can buy at a decent price. What's wrong with that?"

"Save the business rationale for your students! We're talking about the rim of Paynes Prairie—not just some piece of property. It's a place that's unique in the entire world."

For a moment, Bill looked shocked by the intensity of my response. He didn't reply, but impassively shrugged his shoulders, got up, and walked into the bathroom. I followed him in, and we stood, side by side, in front of the mirror at our double sinks.

"Lorelei, remember when you first came here, and we took a tour of the Prairie? The guide told us it had been a cattle ranch for hundreds of years until the State bought most of it in 1970, and started to restore it as a historic marshland. A few buildings sitting at the edge isn't going to change anything so much is it?" He started brushing his teeth.

"You still don't understand, do you?" I asked.

"Honey, really, I'm not trying to make light of your concern. I just think you should lighten up a bit. You make everything sound so—well, so dramatic."

"Well, I am an actress you know," I said, my anger dissipating. I teasingly bumped him with my hip. "You said my dramatic flair was exciting when you seduced me in New York. You proposed only three weeks later."

I saw his lips curl into a smile. "I guess I did find that part of you pretty attractive. Still do," he added, with a wink.

As I creamed my face, I studied him in the mirror. Bill was just over six feet tall and a bit flabby—he thought exercise a waste of time. His handsome squarish face, broad forehead, and perpetually thoughtful look gave visible truth to his student's nickname for him, "Cranium Crane." A lock of blonde hair hung over his forehead, distracting from his receding hairline and making him, at 54 years old, still appear oddly boyish.

"What?" Bill asked, pushing the hair back off his forehead.

"Do you still find me attractive?" I asked, staring at my own reflection with satisfaction—almond shaped hazel eyes, a youthful complexion, and shoulder length red hair hung in shaggy layers around my face.

He moved behind me, rubbed his hands up the sides of my nightgown, and rested them on my shoulders. "Honey, you look as good to me as any of those glamorous stars on the award shows you always watch on TV."

"Right answer," I said.

"So, will you be working with him?" Bill was watching my reflection in the mirror. His face became suddenly serious.

"Jeffrey? I shouldn't have too much to do with him. I work away from the office most of the time. Really, darling, don't worry."

I returned to the bedroom, and propped myself up in bed waiting for him to join me. As he left the bathroom, I said, "Naturally, I can't help thinking about what happened between me and Jeffrey all those years ago. But then it did turn out for the best, didn't it? If not for that last terrible year, I might never have had the courage to go to New York and..."

"We might never have met," Bill replied.

"Yes, of course." But I was thinking more about the chance it gave me to try out the life of a professional actress.

"And, of course, there was your career," he said, as if reading my mind. He picked up a stack of business journals from the floor, and sat down on his side of the bed.

I studied him, in his characteristically rapt attention, as he reviewed the contents of each journal, and carefully inserted post-it notes in the articles he wanted to read.

I remembered how he had come into my life at just the time when I was desperately trying to survive as an actress in New York. It was my third year there, and I felt increasingly alone as most of the friends I made through acting class had already given up and returned home. The darkness of the winter days had become unbearable, I started to have flashbacks to the accident, and later began to experience panic attacks.

Bill and I met at an Academy of Management conference. I was working as a temp at the registration table. We dated every night during the conference. He seemed fascinated by everything about the theatrical world. When he returned to Gainesville, we talked on the phone every day, and in three weeks he flew back to New York and proposed.

I found Bill attractive, even sexy in a way. Although my overwhelming feeling toward him was gratitude. He became my childhood knight in shining armor who would carry me back to sunny Florida, and to a stable married life. If Jeffrey had been immature and impulsive, Bill was his opposite. He was older, established, and predictable to a comforting degree.

"Ready to turn off the light?" he asked, breaking into my reverie.

"Yes, darling," I replied, snuggling close to him.

"You will tell me if Jeff starts coming on to you, won't you?"

"Yes, darling," I said.

"Good," he said, as we both turned off our lights.

I lay in Bill's arms, and already felt trapped in a lie about Jeffrey. The past couple of days had taken such weird and improbable turns—all the startling events on the Prairie, the threat posed by the Valdez Company, Jeffrey's reappearance in my life, and in a final ironic twist, our production of *The Cherry Orchard*—a play about cutting down trees. Life imitating art imitating life? It all felt so crazy, I thought, as I drifted into sleep.

Wednesday morning, I got an early start at Gainesville Health and Fitness. After my workout, I showered and changed into a pair of black slacks and my favorite Chico's emerald green striped shirt with a matching jacket. I drove downtown, parked in the garage, and made my way to the new Asian restaurant where I was meeting Cassie.

She waved to me from a small table in the corner of the dimly lit room. As I approached, her beautiful classic face broke into a dimpled smile. Cassie could have been a cosmetics model. She had lustrous blonde hair, blue eyes, and a complexion women spent fortunes to achieve. Yet, despite her beauty, there was something childlike about her. She was modest and unfailingly kind, two traits said to be a rarity in our competitive profession.

I bent down and gave her a hug before seating myself at the table.

"I've just come from the gym, and I'm famished," I said.

"Here, Lor, have some of my salad," she shoved the dish toward me, and motioned for the waiter. I took a few bites before he came for my order.

"I'm so glad to see you," she said. "I've been a wreck about this play. I don't know if I can do it. I mean I've never done anything as serious as Chekhov."

"Yes, I'm a bit intimidated myself," I said. "There is something terrifying about doing a classic. Everyone has their own idea as to what it should be like."

"But, you've done major roles, even Shakespeare. I've always played the ingénue. I mean frothy little roles, you know?"

"Hey, don't complain," I said. "You'll still be getting parts when I'll be lucky to play an occasional granny. Did you ever see Julie Harris?" She looked at me blankly. "A great actress with looks like yours. And she still got roles as young women when she was in her 50's."

"Okay, I get the point. But still it frustrates me that—well, here's *The Cherry Orchard.* Guess what they're going to give me?"

"Anya, of course," I replied. "You're a natural for it."

"Right, the young daughter—self-centered, frivolous—the usual. See what I mean?"

"You'll be wonderful," I said, and looked up to see the waiter serve the ginger tofu stir-fry I ordered. "And it's a major role. Imagine! Meryl only got to play the maid when she did *The Cherry Orchard* in New York."

Both Cassie and I adored Meryl Streep.

Cassie smiled. "The part isn't my real concern. I'm used to being type-cast." She poked her fork in the air to make the point, "it's with Chekhov—he's so damn morbid, and the characters are always so bored with their lives. Who's going to want to see a play about the Russian revolution, the aristocracy, serfs, and all that period stuff?"

"We'll see," I said. "The play notes say some directors stage it as a farce...you know, the heavy sighs and long pauses. In fact, Chekhov himself thought it was a comedy. It'll be interesting to see Renee's concept."

We speculated further on the casting, and agreed I would probably get the role of Cassie's mother, Lyubov Ranevsky, owner of the estate. I had been given leading roles in the last couple of productions.

After lunch, Cassie and I parted with promises to meet again after Sunday's first read thru. I walked over to the County Courthouse for the commission meeting, and met Diana and Jeffrey at the elevator.

We entered the commission chamber, and nodded greetings to a number of fellow environmentalists already seated on the long polished wooden benches that lined the room. We found seats on an aisle in the middle row. I sat next to Diana and Jeffrey climbed over the two of us in order to sit next to me.

It was the first time I had been to a commission meeting. I looked around the dimly lit wood paneled room with its raised platform where the commissioners sat. There was a buzz of conversations, people being greeted as they entered the chamber and some simply standing and talking to one another. It reminded me of a courtroom before the judge appeared.

"I hope more people show up," I whispered to Diana as I pulled my jacket closed. "At least it would warm the place up. Why do public buildings have to be so cold?"

"To keep the commissioners awake," Jeffrey quipped.

"Did you reach your friend at Swift-Mud, as you call it?" Diana asked leaning toward Jeffrey.

He shook his head and said, "I'll keep trying."

He leaned back, and put his arm on the bench behind me. I gave him a look, but his attention was innocently focused on the podium.

Diana got up to greet Dalton Ames at the door. He was a short, muscular man with heavy dark eyebrows that always appeared to be knit into a frown. He reminded me of a gentle gnome. Dr. Dalton Ames, a retired distinguished professor who established the Center for Environmental Policy, was the charismatic dean of the environmental community.

"So, what was Bill's reaction to me being in town and working with you?" Jeffrey asked, as he moved closer to me.

"Bill? Oh, he's fine with the idea," I said, and felt the warmth of Jeffrey's body next to mine. "By the way, where are your staying while you're here? You never said."

"With Becky," he replied. "She has the room and invited me for the duration. Why?"

I felt my face flush, and I moved slightly away from him, hoping he wouldn't notice my reaction. Fortunately, at that moment the seven commissioners and staff filed in to take their seats, and the conversations diminished to a murmur.

Diana returned to her seat, and I slid back against Jeffrey to make room for her. As I did so I felt his body tense, and I glanced sideways at him. His attention was riveted on the dais. He looked as though something had grabbed him by the back of his shirt and pulled him straight up in his seat.

Chairman Sparks struck his gavel. He was a wiry looking man with a black goatee. His face wore an anxious look as he peered out at the crowd, and he fidgeted with papers until there was silence.

The meeting began with an open forum for public comments. Several people went to the speaker's podium to present ideas or request the commission's action on one thing and another. There were knowing laughs from the audience when one of the petitioners announced he wanted the commission to revoke all the rental permits from student houses in his neighborhood.

"These kids act like they were raised in a barn," he said. "There's garbage and broken furniture in the front yards, and on the weekends the whole block reeks of beer. Talking to them does no good. They have no respect."

The chairman referred him to his neighborhood association for advice, and moved the agenda to the scheduled speakers.

Another half hour passed before Crawford Keezer was called up. I turned to see him as he strode to the podium from the rear of the room. I could almost feel the air vibrate with energy as he passed our row of seats, and I caught the strong aroma of a musky men's cologne. Keezer was about 6'2" with the build of a football player. He had salt and pepper white hair that was long in the back, and he wore chino slacks and a casual tan jacket.

"Mr. Chairman, my name is Crawford Keezer, and I'm here for the Valdez Construction Company of Boca Raton." His voice was deep with an appealing Southern drawl.

Diana poked me in the ribs and whispered, "Now, remember what I told you: Keezer and Sparks were college fraternity brothers. Let's see what shenanigans they're going to pull."

"Oh grand," I said, and nudged Jeffrey, "we're about to have a bit of theater." But when I turned to him he just nodded, and kept staring at the platform.

"Mr. Chairman and Commissioners," Keezer continued. "As you probably know, some of you being in the real estate business, the Valdez Company owns a large parcel of land here for which we have long held a building permit."

Judson Sparks nodded absently, but the other commissioners were paying close attention.

"We are ready to activate that permit," said Keezer.

Some members of the audience let out a low hissing sound, and Mr. Sparks hit his gavel to quell it.

Keezer continued. "Now I realize we really don't need the commission's approval to get started, but..." he paused and turned to face the audience. He had a wide bent looking nose and thick white mustache that narrowed at the edge of his lips. He flashed an engaging smile at the audience before turning back to face the platform.

"As I said, we could begin building pretty soon, but we came here today to let you and the community... " He stressed the word, and paused for emphasis as he spread his arms out in an embracing gesture, "We want all y'all to know what our intentions are with this project. We think you'll be very pleased with what you hear."

"Yes, but please be brief. We have a long agenda." Sparks sounded inexplicably irritated, and began to bite on a hang nail as he listened to Keezer's pitch.

"Now this here is going to be a model low to medium income housing development," he said.

There were snickers in the audience at the word model.

"We've applied for a federal grant, and are following some projects that have already been successful in California."

A heckler from the rear shouted, "Bet they didn't build 'em in their state parks."

The Chair rapped his gavel, "Please, give Mr. Keezer a chance to tell us about his project."

There was more talking in the audience, but everyone finally quieted down.

"As I was saying…well, let me tell you about some of the features. First of all, we're making it easy for folks to move in, there'll be flexible leasing agreements, and furniture rental. Next, we'll have supervised recreation for teens, including a state of the art computer lab so students have a place to do their homework. For the young'uns there'll be a low-cost on-site day care center."

"Sounds too good to be true," said one of the people sitting on the front row.

Keezer continued, "But it is true. And here's the last innovation I want you to know about: the development will have a resident chef and catering department to prepare take-out lunches for the children and dinners that can be purchased by families. Now, they do that in California," he said, turning to look at the audience. "And ain't that something we'd all like to have? This is going to be a truly caring community."

"Too good to be true usually isn't either," said a woman in the front row who stood up to face Keezer. "Your so-called caring community will destroy of one of the most pristine places in all Florida."

"Madam," Keezer said, unperturbed by her comment. "Valdez assures you that this will be an exemplary development in every way. That means we will protect the fragile environment, and may even improve it."

"What a snow job," Jeffrey finally turned to Diana and me, "It makes me want to puke." He sat back, took a deep breath, and finally seemed to awaken from his silent watch.

"Excuse me, Commissioner Sparks, but I have a question for our county manager." It was the newly elected commissioner who spoke.

"How is it possible for the Valdez Company to exercise a building permit on land that is now a state preserve?"

There was a buzz of approval in the room as the question lingered in the air for several moments. All eyes turned to the county manager. He cast a worried glance at Sparks, and slowly replied that the permit had been granted with no expiration, and thus, he said, took precedence over the state's designation.

The commissioner who raised the question said to Sparks, "I'm not convinced he's right. And, I think this is of sufficient importance to warrant further investigation by the manager and our attorney."

Several commissioners nodded their heads in agreement, and the audience broke into applause.

Sparks rapped his gavel, glared at the audience, but finally gave his approval for the investigation.

"The county manager is instructed to report back to this commission, in no later than two weeks' time, affirming the legitimacy of the Valdez permit," he said. He then turned to Keezer. "Thank you for coming here today, Mr. Keezer. Your project does indeed sound like a needed addition to our housing community. I'm certain the matter of your permit will be resolved quickly. In the meantime, you will, of course, be clearing all of your plans with the appropriate county boards." He hit his gavel, and called for a 10 minute break.

Keezer immediately approached the podium, and engaged in an animated conversation with Sparks as the other commissioners filed out for the break. The room began to empty.

"You see that?" Diana said to Dalton Ames who was now standing next to us. "I think that's in violation of the Sunshine Law. They shouldn't be talking privately like that."

Dalton nodded agreement, and took a small notebook from his pocket to write in. "Well, no need to hang around now," he said. "At least we know how they plan to lure the community into supporting their plan. Model development, indeed. I'd be surprised if they provided half of what he's described."

"You're right, Dalton. We've got to stop them," Diana said.

"It's an ecological disaster in the making," Jeffrey added.

Dalton reached out and pressed Diana's hand in his. "We'll do it. Don't you worry," he said, and gave her a quick smile before moving away to talk with other activists in the back of the room.

Diana, Jeffrey, and I began to leave the chamber, and I looked back to see that neither Sparks nor Keezer were still in the room. When we reached the elevator area I saw Sparks walking down the hallway in the opposite direction from us. Diana called out to him. Sparks turned and, instead of looking at her, stared directly at Jeffrey. At first he looked puzzled, and then frightened. He quickly lowered his head and pushed through the crowd into the commission's private offices.

How strange, I thought, and turned to see Jeffrey's reaction.

"What was that about?" I asked him. "Do you know Sparks?"

Jeffrey paused before responding. He frowned, and his face took on a cold, closed look. It was one I had never before seen on him. "Well...not really," he replied. "He just reminds me of someone, that's all."

I didn't believe him.

Diana chuckled and said, "Sparks probably was scared off at the sight of three environmentalists closing in on him. I was going to dig him about his conversation with Keezer. But we'll catch up with him another time. I need to get back to the office and ready for tomorrow's board meeting."

The three of us walked together to the parking garage. Jeffrey and I stopped at his truck, and Diana continued up the ramp to her car.

Jeffrey said, "How about going for a drink with me, Lor? We could beat the crowd at Lillian's."

"Sorry, Jeffrey, but I've got some errands to run, and then I'm meeting Bill. He's working late tonight and..."

"Are you avoiding being alone with me, Lor? That's the message I'm starting to get. If it's true, I'll just stop asking." He stood so close to me that I could feel his breath on my face.

"No, no, really." I said, stepping back from him. "It's just that I'm busy. Honestly, Jeffrey." He didn't look convinced, but I wasn't ready to be alone with him. "I'll take a rain check, but I've got to go now. Maybe I'll see you tomorrow—at the office."

I started walking to my car, expecting he would be persistent and follow me. Instead, when I turned, he was still standing in place. His shoulders drooped, and he had a half sad, half confused look on his face. I raised my arm and waved, and quickly walked on without turning again.

Once inside my car, I turned on the ignition, and the air conditioner shot out a blast of cold air that bathed my face and shocked away the tears that had begun to well up in my eyes. What is happening to me, and what am I going to do about you, Jeffrey? I took several deep breaths.

I was startled to hear the tinny musical phrase coming from the cell phone buried in my handbag. I searched for the phone and answered. It was Bill.

"Hi, sweetheart. How was the meeting? Anything earthshaking?"

"Oh, hi, Bill. I'll tell you about it when I see you. We're still meeting downtown at Starbucks, right?"

"I'm afraid I can't make it today, sweetheart. My grad assistant is here and we're still working on my conference presentation. You know I leave for the coast on Friday."

"Right," I said, and hit the end button on the phone.

Grad assistant, again? I thought. Sometimes Bill seemed to spend more time with them than me, his wife. And I had forgotten the trip to San Francisco that he'd marked on our kitchen calendar.

I tossed the phone back into my bag. I hated the damn thing, and often pretended not to own one when people asked for my number. I only carried it because Bill insisted. He worried about me driving home from the theater late at night.

I pulled out of the garage, and headed for home. There was so much to think about—the afternoon's commission meeting, and Jeffrey's strange reaction. His encounter with Sparks was an enigma. I tried to think why Jeffrey would lie about knowing Sparks, and why Sparks looked so fearful seeing Jeffrey. I realized I really didn't know much about Jeffrey's life since he left Gainesville, and I decided that it might be time for us to have that luncheon date after all.

Chapter 4

"Absolutely not, Jeffrey. I will not go out with you to the Valdez site. It'll be wet and mucky, and...there's gators crawling all around. No way."

It was mid morning and I was standing in the office kitchen, a hot mug of Chai tea in hand, when Jeffrey and Becky approached me with the idea.

Jeffrey frowned. He said, "Really, Lor, for someone who said she'd do anything—even murder—to stop this development, don't you even want to go out there to see what you're saving?" He struck a disbelieving pose before turning to fill a paper cup with water from the cooler.

"C'mon, Lorelei," Becky said, picking up the sales pitch. "It'll be okay. Gators are shy as long as you don't actually step on them. Their mating season is over so even the bull gators won't be aggressive." She gave me a once over, and added, "You do have other shoes in the car, don't you?"

"Oh, all right," I conceded. "I'll go with you. But no tricks, you hear? No scaring Lorelei, just for fun. Promise?"

They nodded. Jeffrey looked barely able to conceal his amusement at my response.

"Okay, it's set. We'll leave in about an hour," he said. "Afterwards, we can pick up some hoagies and eat at the park pavilion."

"Count me out, guys," Becky said. "I have to get back here, and prepare for this afternoon's board meeting."

"How about you, Red. Join me? I haven't been on the Prairie in so long."

I was unsettled at the idea of lunch alone with him in an isolated setting. "Are you sure you can't have lunch with us, Becky?" I asked, stalling as I tried to imagine how it might go.

"No, I really can't. I'll drive my own car out to the Valdez site. The two of you can ride together."

Her suggestion made me wonder if Becky's lunch excuse had been pre-arranged.

"Then it's a date," Jeffrey said, looking pleased. He rubbed his hands together, and returned to his small office before I could protest.

I started checking the news releases on my desk, and thought Jeffrey might not be so pleased if he knew the only reason I accepted his lunch plans was to learn more about his life. I especially wanted to know why he lied about Judson Sparks.

"Becky is everything arranged for the board meeting?"

"Everything's under control," she said. "Do you mind if I go to the Valdez property with Jeff and Lorelei? I'll be back in plenty of time for the meeting."

Diana looked surprised. "Lorelei, you're going onto their site?"

"It was Jeffrey's idea," I said. "He thought I should see it before the board meeting. Do you want to come with us?"

"No, Dalton and I have hiked around there many times. It just wouldn't have occurred to me that…" She smiled.

"That I'd get my feet dirty?" I said. "Well, you know me, Diana, I love the earth; I just don't like getting it all over me."

"I'm glad you're going." Diana said, and she returned to her office.

I was used to the reactions I got from the three of them. I was the odd ball in the office and often the butt of good natured jokes. After all, who would expect to find someone in the Center for Earth Options who didn't hike, camp, bird watch, or do any of the outdoorsy things environmentalists like to do? My adventures were confined strictly to the stage."

"Lorelei, can we talk?" Becky said, sitting down at my desk.

"Sure, Becky, what's up?"

"Well, I just want to apologize."

"Apologize?"

She glanced at the small room where Jeffrey was, and said softly, "For Jeff. His coming up and all. After you told me not to call him. You definitely made it clear you didn't want him here."

"I'll admit I was royally strung-out when he just appeared. And quite angry at you, by the way."

She dropped her head and nodded contritely.

I patted her hand. "But I've gotten over it, I guess," I said, with more ease than I felt.

"I really didn't tell him to come up. He just—you know Jeff, Lorelei."

Oh, yes, I thought. It was also obvious Becky had a crush on him. His name appeared on her job references, and I guessed she had been one of his protégés while she was an undergrad. She obviously remained in touch with him though she had never mentioned it to me.

Becky continued, "He didn't give me a chance to tell him not to come. In fact, he reacted so fast, it was like he was almost waiting for something, you know?"

"Hmm," I said. "What's he been doing in Orlando?" I couldn't resist prying just a little.

She made a non-committal shrug. "Something with developers, but he's not been happy there," she said. "He told me he wanted to come back to Gainesville—to start over."

"Start over what?" I asked. "Never mind. It's fine with me, Becky. Please don't worry. No one has control over Jeffrey's actions, and I'm sure he would have found out about Valdez from another of his buddies."

"So, you're not mad at me anymore?"

"No, Becky. We're okay."

"Thanks, Lor. You're so cool," she said, getting up to return to her desk.

Cool? I thought, and shivered. It's freezing in here. As I slid my arms into the sweater on the back of my chair, I shouted, to no one in particular, "Can't we turn down the damn air conditioning?"

Becky didn't even look up at my habitual complaint, and I returned my attention to the news releases. I wasn't able to concentrate. I kept thinking about our trip to the Valdez property and lunch with Jeffrey. I opened my email, and stared at the screen as I tried to listen in on Jeffrey's phone conversation in the other room. His voice was muffled by the noise of the air-conditioner.

Finally, it was time to leave. I went out to my car to change into my athletic shoes, and recalled that when I first met Jeffrey, he used to spend most weekends camping and hiking with his buddies. Early in our relationship, I tried several camping trips with him, but they always seemed to be a disaster. It either rained, was bitter cold, or something unpleasant happened, like the final outing when I acquired a long lasting case of chiggers. That put an end to it for me.

Jeffrey and Becky came out the front door, and he called to me, "Okay, let's get going and take a look at what the bastards think they're going to destroy."

We drove down 13th Street, past the University, and out of town. Despite the fact the car windows were down, the interior of Jeffrey's camper truck had the unpleasant aroma of French fries and stale beer. The back was piled with camping gear, and an assortment of containers that made it look like he lived out of his vehicle. Before getting into the truck, I had noticed the rear window plastered with travel decals, and a bumper sticker proclaiming, "Not all who wander are lost."

We didn't talk much on the way to the Prairie. He asked me a few questions about the plays I had appeared in. I asked him about his travels out west. Now that we were alone, there was an air of formality between us.

At the approach to the Prairie basin, Becky was standing on the roadside waving to us as Jeffrey made a u-turn across the median and parked. There were several other vehicles parked along the roadside.

"Well, this'll be interesting," he said, as we got out of the truck. "I'll bet they're not expecting company."

He inspected the large silver Hummer with a grunt of disgust. There were also a couple of trucks parked nearby. One of them had the name "Gator Security Service" on the door of the cab.

"Maybe we shouldn't go out there right now," I suggested.

"Hell no," Jeffrey said. "We've got a right."

He motioned Becky to follow as we started marching into the moss-draped live oak forest. The path was strewn with broken limbs and crushed underbrush as though a heavy vehicle had driven through. Large saw palmetto palms lined the sandy pathway. It felt significantly cooler, and my nostrils were filled with the pleasant woodsy aroma. Becky and I hurried along the path trying to keep pace with Jeffrey. The only sound was the crunching of forest debris underfoot. Then a plaintive bleating of a crow in the trees above was followed by the loud chilling whine of chain saws cranking up.

"God dammit," Jeff muttered. "They're already taking down trees." He quickened his pace, and Becky and I half-ran to keep up with him.

We approached a small clearing in which a large red truck was parked. Three men were standing facing the open back hatch. Two of the men seemed to be arguing. One of them was Crawford Keezer. A third man, dressed in fatigues and wearing a Florida Gator cap, stood by and watched. Large sheets of construction plans were lying scattered on the open hatch. The men looked up when they became aware of Jeffrey heading toward them.

"Good morning, gentlemen, cutting a little firewood?" I heard Jeffrey call out in a loud voice.

"What the hell?" exclaimed Keezer. He turned to face Jeffrey, and barked, "Y'all looking for something? This here's private land."

The man in fatigues started toward us, but Keezer motioned him back.

"Well, that may be," Jeffrey said coolly, standing with his hands on his hips and his legs planted wide apart. "But you aren't permitted to begin clearing this land just yet." Jeffrey pointed in the direction of two workers with the chainsaws. "Tell your men to stop cutting, or I'll call the Park Ranger." He took a cell phone from his pants pocket.

Keezer stepped up to within inches of Jeffrey, and demanded, "And just who in hell are you, son?"

"I'm the environmental consultant for the Center for Earth Options, and these ladies are my associates," he said. "We know for a fact that your permit to build on this land is under review. Now stop the damn chainsaws." He held the cell phone up as a threat.

There was a moment of silence as Keezer looked back to the man with whom he had been arguing. The man was about five nine, dressed in dark slacks and a short-sleeved embroidered white shirt with a tuft of gray chest hair sticking out at the neck. He appraised us, smoothed his fingers over his pencil thin mustache, and walked forward. He wore black alligator shoes that were dusted by the sand.

"Excuse me," he said, "but this land is owned by the Valdez Company. I'm Jimmy Valdez. It's my company." He extended his hand to Jeffrey who ignored the gesture by pocketing his cell phone instead. Valdez shrugged and continued, "We're only making a bit of a clearing here. And we're in the middle of a meeting. I would appreciate it if you and your friends would leave."

"We're not leaving until the damn chainsaws stop," Jeffrey said.

Jimmy Valdez glanced at his expensive looking watch, and looked up at us with a fixed smile. The sinister look in his eyes gave me chills. He reminded me of a description I'd read about the actor Jack Nicholson—eyes like a cobra and a dazzling smile, or something like that. Valdez had those eyes, but not the smile.

Becky moved closer to me, and whispered, "Did you check out the muscle guy. What a hunk."

I did. He wore a tight tee shirt with a Gator logo and his company's name. Despite his ice blue eyes, and menacing gaze, Becky was right; he had good looks worth staring at. His hair, showing under his cap, was salt and pepper gray, and I guessed he was in his forties.

Valdez studied Jeffrey for a moment, nodded to the man in fatigues, who walked back toward the chainsaw gang.

Keezer said, "Are you satisfied now?"

"No. Not by a long shot," Jeffrey replied. His face was set, and he was staring defiantly at Keezer. It looked like a stand-off scene from an old western movie. "This is still a state preserve. You damn well know that what you're doing is illegal."

Keezer pointed his finger within inches of Jeffrey's face and shouted, "That's it. I've heard enough from you, boy. Now just get out of here or else..."

The security man came running back, and stopped next to Keezer. "You heard the man, buster. Shove off before you have some real trouble."

"Like hell," Jeffrey persisted, ignoring both of their threats. He looked at Keezer and Valdez. "We know what you guys are doing, and I know your reputation. Shoddy construction. Payoffs to subcontractors. The whole nine yards. I'm sure we'll find even more dirt when we look around a bit."

"Jeffrey, let's go," I said, grabbing his arm. He jerked away from my grasp. I hated it when he got so stupidly belligerent.

Valdez gave the security man a look. The guy, who looked much taller and stronger than Jeffrey, grabbed Jeffrey by the shoulders, spun him around, and gave him a shove. "On your way, amigo," he said.

"Wait a minute," Becky yelled, trying to help Jeffrey as he stumbled. "You can't do that."

"Becky, Jeffrey, let's just go!" I said, walking back toward the path.

I felt relieved as Jeffrey began following me. Then he stopped at the edge of the clearing, and turned back. "You mark my words," he yelled. "We'll make you guys crawl out of town before you get a chance to put your crappy housing on this land."

"Enough, Jeffrey," I said, trying to pull him along with me, and motioning Becky to grab his other arm.

"Save your threats," Keezer shouted back. "We've dealt with you tree-huggers before. Now you get off this land directly, or I'll treat you like a damn trespasser." He jumped onto the running board of his truck, and reached up to the back window. I noticed it held a full rifle rack.

"Jeffrey, c'mon." This time it was Becky's plea.

He pointed a finger at Keezer, and said, "Don't worry, you old Geezer. We're gonna stop you all right."

Keezer stood on the running board of the cab and glared at Jeffrey. His hand rested on one of the rifles. The security man watched us as he cracked his knuckles. Valdez walked to the back of the truck, and the harsh din of the chain saws had stopped.

We retreated from the clearing. Becky and I urged Jeffrey to hurry, but he resisted and mumbled, "Assholes. We're going to blow them out of the water. You'll see."

I said, "Oh, yes, we've seen, haven't we, Becky? Now, you understand why I didn't want him up here. He hasn't changed a bit. He's still the hot-head he always was."

Jeffrey's breathing was labored, and he grunted at my words.

Becky looked dazed. She may not ever have seen Jeffrey in his full plumage of righteousness, but I already knew this encounter would come back to haunt us.

Chapter 5

"What in hell were you thinking?" I exploded at Jeffrey when we got back to the side of the road. The three of us were standing next to his truck. "You could have been shot. Keezer was obviously just one insult away from grabbing his rifle."

Jeffrey was leaning against the fender. His face was still flushed with anger. "Oh, that was nothing. Guys like him are used to confrontations. They're always yelling at their contractors or somebody. I work with them all the time."

"Well, I was worried there for a minute," Becky said, and looked adoringly at Jeffrey. "But you were really rockin'." She turned to me and said, "He got'em to stop the chainsaws."

"Don't be naïve, Becky," I said impatiently, feeling annoyed by her blind admiration. "That was Mr. Valdez's doing to get us to leave. And by the way, did anyone else feel that he was a little creepy? Rubbing his mustache all the time, and those eyes…"

"Yeah," said Jeffrey, "I suspect he can be one mean dude."

"Look you guys, I've got to get back to the office," Becky said. "The board meeting and all. See you later." She hurried off to her truck.

"So, now to lunch?" He held the truck door open, and gave me an ingratiating smile. "That is, if you're not still pissed at me."

"Angry? No. I always have enjoyed watching your theatrical tantrums. I just hope they don't get you killed some day."

"Tantrums? That's your opinion? What's happened to your passion, Lorelei? Or are you still saving it for the stage?"

"Not fair," I said.

"Well then, why was I the only one madder than hell at those guys?" He was still holding open the door as I slipped in and made no response to his question. He banged it shut.

We didn't talk to one another until he stopped in Micanopy at Pearl's Country Store and politely asked what I wanted for lunch. I went in with him to get my own sandwich.

A couple of miles up the road, we entered Paynes Prairie Preserve State Park, and drove to the pavilions near the camp grounds.

"Here, you'd better put some of this spray on you," he said, handing me a can of bug spray after pulling into the deserted parking lot. "The mosquitoes can be pretty aggressive around here." He reached behind his seat, and grabbed a pair of binoculars which he hung around his neck.

We walked down the boat ramp to the edge of Lake Wauberg. My attention was captured by a large sign that read, "Caution Alligators." It depicted the universal symbol for no swimming, and showed a picture of a large alligator snout. I decided not to comment at the risk of Jeffrey's teasing me about my fear of alligators.

But, he saw me staring at the warning sign, and grabbing my hand he pulled me to the water's edge yelling the football cheer, "C'mon Gators, let's go!"

"Dammit, Jeffrey," I said, jerking away from him as I jumped back from the lapping water.

"Shssh." He made a sweeping gesture toward the lake. "Just look."

The water sparkled as if it were bursting with little sunlights.

Jeffrey pointed to a great blue heron standing regally on top of a fallen log down stream from us. He raised his binoculars.

"There," he whispered. "Up there." A large bird was flying high over the trees on the other side of the lake. "It's a southern bald eagle. Here, take a look." He stood behind me and held up the binoculars while I watched the bird languidly cruise the treetops. I was aware of Jeffrey's body pressing lightly against me.

"Hmm, beautiful," I said, and side-stepped.

"Did you know eagles mate for life? Would be nice to know their secret, wouldn't it?" Jeffrey said, giving me a meaningful look. "Jesus, how I miss this place."

"Yes, I'll bet you do," I replied.

He grinned, and wagged his finger at me. "But, I see you're still the old scaredy cat you used to be. You think some gator is going to rush up this ramp to swipe our lunch?" He grabbed the lunch bag from me, and dangled it over the water's edge.

"Jeffrey, stop clowning around. Let's go somewhere and sit down. I'm hungry."

"You always were hungry. I'm glad some things don't change."

I turned, and started back up the ramp toward the pavilion picnic tables.

He caught up with me. "You know, Lor, gators can run at a pretty fast gallop, but I don't think they'd leave the water for your sandwich. It's a wonder I ever got you to go camping with me. You're so skittery-jittery."

"Oh, can it, Jeffrey. It's natural to fear alligators, and...snakes."

"And bears," he continued as we walked toward the pavilions "And let's see, oh yes, you're also afraid of crawling insects of any size, rodents, buzzards, large turtles, even wild turkeys...?"

"Except the kind you can drink on ice," I countered, and we both laughed. It was an old game we played, naming things in nature that repulsed or scared me.

Despite the beautiful afternoon, we were the only ones in the pavilion. The warm breeze, soft sounds of distant birds and insects, and the fresh smelling air were slowly melting away my earlier feelings of hostility. It felt good to be here, with Jeffrey, in his world.

"God, it's hot," he said, and placed his binoculars on the table. He took a red plaid handkerchief from his back pocket, leaned over a grassy area, and poured some bottled water over the cloth before tying it loosely around his neck.

"Here, come sit next to me, Lor." Jeffrey said, patting the bench. He tore open the bag and set our sandwiches side by side. We ate in silence.

Finally, he glanced at me and said, "Actually, you should be a bit afraid of gators around here. Prairie gators are among the most aggressive in the state. Did you know that?"

"Oh great, Jeffrey. Thanks for sharing."

"No kidding," he paused, taking a bite of his sandwich. "Until recent years, all the so-called nuisance gators—the ones who found their way into swimming pools or threatened people or their pets—those were caught and deposited here, on the Prairie."

"Didn't they just shoot them, like they do now?"

"Oh no. They couldn't shoot them back then. They were an endangered species. But the gator population's been restored, and now there are lots of them. Too bad for the poaching trade—and for the gators. Now any poor old gator that happens to mistake someone's dog for lunch gets promptly dispatched."

"And you don't think they should? Wouldn't you want to do away with a wild animal if it attacked you or your pet?"

"Really Lorelei. Use your brains. Like it's the gators' fault? We're in their territory, you know. You don't see them walking down our Main Street like we do theirs. Hell, gator hunters will shoot a bunch of them if they can't tell which one was the attacker. Is that fair? I hate to see animals killed because of our stupidity," he said. "Basically, we have no respect." He turned and gave me a tight smile. "Oh, what the hell. It's such a beautiful day. How's your sandwich?"

"Hmm, it's wonderful," I said, giving him sidelong glances as we finished eating in silence. His face was set in a scowl.

"Jeffrey, life hasn't gotten any better for you, has it? What have you been doing in Orlando? I want to know how you are—how you really are—no b.s."

"Right. Well, I have an apartment in Winter Park. I've been working as a free-lance environmental consultant." He rolled his eyes in self-mockery. "I have clients like these Keezer and Valdez guys. Only out for the quick bucks—Florida's version of the old Vikings...pillage, burn, and pave."

"What is it you do exactly?" I asked.

"Mostly I survey development property for wetlands mitigation, that sort of thing. Oh, and I spend a lot of time looking for gopher turtles. That's fun."

"So you enjoy what you're doing."

He shrugged. "I like being outdoors, but truth is I'm fed up with whole scene down there. I hate Orlando, and somewhere along the line my life's taken a wrong turn...in a lot of ways." He got up and started pacing along the edge of the pavilion.

"Have you given any thought to coming back to complete your doctoral degree? You mentioned that Dr. Curtis..."

"Not really. I can't leave Orlando just yet...I have commitments."

"Is it your mother, or is there someone else?" I thought about the woman, from the water management district he'd been trying to reach. "How about your friend, Louisa?"

He stopped pacing, and smiled at me. "No, Mom's doing fine on her own, and Louisa and I are just good friends."

"So," I persisted, "what about your love life?"

The question evoked a snicker as he grabbed the binoculars from the table, and walked back to the edge of the pavilion, scouting the area. After several minutes of silence, Jeffrey turned, motioned me to join him, and in an excited voice said, "Lorelei, I think we have company. And you'll never guess who it is."

"Who?" I hurried to his side. He handed me the binoculars and pointed in the general direction of the parking lot on the other side of the boat ramp. "Isn't that the same red truck we saw at the Valdez site? I can almost make out who's in it...looks like a man and a woman. What'd you think?"

"It wasn't here when we pulled in. I'll bet it's old Keezer himself," Jeffrey responded and rubbed his hands together. "Maybe they're having a little love tryst."

"I wonder who the woman is." I said, struggling to get a sharper focus with the binoculars. "Diana told us he's married and has a family down in Boca. Oh, this might be juicy. I'm going to try for a closer look."

"Be careful, Lor. He's a mean old snake, and we've already poked him once today. I'll wait for you in the truck—with the motor running."

I left the pavilion and moved closer to the red truck by walking along the edge of the parking area. Masses of large scrub palmetto shrubs kept me protected from being seen. When I found a good vantage point, I raised the binoculars to peer into the truck. The windows were darkly tinted, but I could tell the couple was absorbed in an argument. She was jabbing her finger at him and I saw him grab her wrist. I wasn't able to hear what they were saying because of my distance and the loud noise of the motor running for the air-conditioner.

The woman abruptly turned her head facing the side window as if she sensed being watched. I ducked down into the scrub, and could see her more clearly. She had long black hair, a round and somewhat chubby face that was pinched up in anger. Her head swung back to Keezer, and in a moment the door of the truck opened, and he was standing on the running board, looking straight in my direction.

"What are you doing here?" he shouted. Apparently, I wasn't as well hidden as I thought. "Are you spying on us? You'd better have a damn good explanation." He slammed his fist on the top of the cab, jumped down, and started striding toward me.

Jeffrey was honking the horn, and waving his arm at me to hurry. He started backing up the truck in my direction, as I ran back along the edge of the shrubs. We met and I jumped into the vehicle.

"Safe!" I said, feeling my heart beating wildly.

"Yeah, are you happy, Ms. Snoop?" Jeffrey asked, as we drove through the tree-sheltered campground area and onto the main road leading out of the Park. His tone was gently derisive. "To quote a friend of mine, 'you could have gotten us shot.'"

"Hardly. I almost caught him with his pants down," I replied with a salacious giggle.

"So what did you learn playing junior detective?"

"You know, Jeffrey. You're not the only one who can get some dirt on these developers. Keezer and that woman have something to hide—meeting out there like that."

"Lorelei, a little adultery isn't exactly big news. Anyway, someone could say the same thing about us."

While his remark had the intended effect of making me uncomfortable, it was an opening for my question. "Okay, smart guy, how about some of those secrets of yours?"

"What secrets?"

"For starters, what's with you and Commissioner Sparks?"

"What'd you mean?" Jeffrey's hand tightened on the steering column, and his face assumed that withdrawn look that I had seen at the courthouse. "I told you before. He just looks like someone I once knew, in Orlando."

"C'mon, Jeffrey. You were never a very good liar."

"Lorelei, just leave it alone." His voice was firm. "Haven't you had enough adventure for the day?"

"I'm not letting this go, Jeffrey. You're lying to me, and I want to why."

"Jeez, Lorelei. You sound like my mother."

He obviously remembered that old accusation was an effective argument stopper and it worked again. I rapped him on the arm, and said, "Okay, I'll let it go for now, Mr. Waterman. Just take me back to the office. But I do deserve to know more about your life in Orlando. You've forced your way back into mine and..."

"Forced my way? That's an interesting choice of words," he said. "But yes, there is a lot more we have to say to each other." He glanced at me with a dead serious expression on his face. "A lot more, Mrs. Crane."

We drove back to the CEO office arriving just in time for the board meeting. As I was getting out of the truck, Jeffrey said, "I know Diana doesn't want me to show my face at the meeting, so I'll just go on my way. Can we have another lunch or dinner together sometime?"

"I'm going to be very busy, but I'm sure we'll be seeing one another again. Just try and stay out of trouble, will you?" I said.

Annoyed with myself for sounding like his mother again, I abruptly turned away and walked into the office.

"So, how was the field trip?" Diana asked as I came through the door. She didn't look up from setting out agendas on the long meeting table.

"Didn't Becky tell you about it?" I asked.

"She said you saw some of the Valdez crew there so you didn't stay long."

I exchanged glances with Becky, who was cleaning off her desk and stuffing things into her backpack.

The president of the CEO board came in, greeted us briefly, and immediately followed Diana into her office.

"You didn't tell Diana about Jeffrey and Keezer, did you?" I asked.

"No. Gee, Lorelei, Diana just made up with Jeff. I don't want her mad at him again. Besides, I thought you'd fill her in."

"I'm sure you did," I replied. "What's the hurry? Where are you going?"

"Home to Boston…for the Jewish holidays. Jeff's driving me to the airport."

"Oh, I'd forgotten about it. Have a good trip."

"Thanks," she replied, pulled open the front door, and nearly collided with board member, Wiley Evans.

"Whoa, young lady, who or what's chasing you out of here?"

"Oh, hi, Wiley. Jeff Waterman's picking me up to take me to the airport."

"Jeff's back in town?" He looked at me quizzically. "I always liked that boy. Has spunk, that one. And a damn good biologist. I worked with him some when he was doing research on the Prairie."

Becky flashed a smile, waved goodbye, and left.

Wiley walked over to where I stood at the meeting table, and asked, "So you called Jeff up here to give us a hand with this thing?"

"No, he just decided to show up and volunteer."

"Betcha Diana was none too pleased," he said, as he leaned over the table, and began reading the agenda. I caught a slight scent of pine as he passed. Wiley was a retired forester whose rugged outdoor energy was palpable. He stood well over 6 feet tall, a square built man, solid like a tree trunk. I liked his directness.

"Wiley, I'm glad you're here," I said. "You've been a park ranger. What's your reaction to this Valdez project?"

"Project?" he spat the word, and sat down at the table. "It's more like a catastrophe. I just hope this board meeting will amount to something, Lorelei. People have to get off their butts and stop this one. It could set a bad precedent. The whole prairie rim could be bought up and paved over before the dang fools realize the damage that's been done."

The front door opened. Several board members came in, and one by one, they greeted me and sat down at the table.

"Where's Diana?" Wiley asked with a note of impatience in his voice.

"I'm here," she said coming out of her office just as several other board members arrived.

Some immediately helped themselves to refreshments; others simply sat down and began studying the agenda.

The President called the meeting to order, thanked everyone for showing up on short notice, and asked Diana to describe the reason for the emergency meeting. She recounted what had happened at the county commission meeting, and what was known about the Valdez Company.

"...so, you see," she concluded, "the board needs to decide what we want to do about this serious threat. The legitimacy of the Valdez permit may be determined as early as next week."

"How do you think it will turn out?" asked one of the members, a young nature filmmaker, who always wore a light meter around his neck like a medallion.

"That's easy," said Wiley, "they'll uphold the permit. It's no secret that Valdez will have Sparks in their pocket. And Sparks has the county manager in his."

"I think we need to get more facts before we can decide anything," the board's treasurer asserted. "We can't just go off half-cocked. Do we even know what the state's position is on upland development? What can we expect them to do about this?"

"Yes, I have to agree," said another board member. "We can't make any assumptions here. Our reputation is at stake. Furthermore, from what I've heard so far, I don't really see the crisis. The housing project seems sound enough, and if they went to the trouble to appear before the commission, Diana, maybe you've overreacted a bit."

Good heavens, I thought, Diana should just give this guy a good slap. But, he was too rich, and she was too genteel for that. She once told me: "Politeness is our family vice."

"You've got to be kidding," blurted Wiley. When he stood, his plaid shirt bulged at the waist. He pounded his fist on the table, and said, "Sometimes, I wonder why I bother with you people. You don't have the sense of a rattlesnake. Can't you see that if this Valdez development isn't stopped, we'll have other south Florida developers buying up the rest of the uplands? And then what? The Prairie basin will be one big retention pond."

One of the woman board members raised her hand and said, "What about negotiating with them? Find a way to get them to scale down their project."

"Negotiate? For heaven's sake, woman." Wiley sat down, turned briefly, and glared at her. He said, "They'll soon be dumping thousands of tons of concrete on that land. Can't you imagine the impact? Damn fools," he muttered, pushed his chair back from the table, and sat with arms crossed. It wasn't clear if he was referring to the board members or Valdez.

"Okay, okay. We all need to settle down a bit here," the president said. He got up and walked over to the refreshment table for a bottle of water. "We obviously have different points of view. And that's good…even though it feels frustrating at times. Diana, you're the one who works with Friends of Paynes Prairie, and meets with all the state and university experts. Tell us your take on this." He remained at the snack table.

"I agree with everything that's been said here," she slowly stood up and paused before continuing.

I was glad Harry had reminded them of Diana's expertise. Her soft-spoken and usually modest manner often caused even some of our own board members to underrate her ability and influence.

"Yes," she said. "This project will appeal to many interests in our community—our own commissioners have never fully understood the significance of Paynes Prairie."

"I'm with Wiley," the filmmaker blurted. "We've got to stop it, period."

"Just a minute, I haven't finished," Diana said. "If their permit is still good, I expect they'll start clearing the land within a week. And soon after…"

"Once the trees are down, and the animals have fled…it'll be like Humpty Dumpty," said one of the members, and others murmured their agreement.

Diana smiled at the nursery rhyme analogy, and continued, "All other considerations aside, the Prairie watershed will be in jeopardy by large-scale development, and we all know one thing: water is what makes the Prairie what it is."

"So do you have a recommendation, Diana?" The President asked, looking at his watch.

Diana paused again before speaking. "I say it is imperative that we act, and act quickly! Dalton Ames has begun putting together a coalition of citizens groups to educate the community about the Prairie, and to better insure its protection from this and future threats. Given our large and distinguished membership and corps of volunteers, he wants us to take a leading role in the coalition."

At the mention of Dalton Ames, several board members nodded their heads approvingly. Even those who were usually skeptical nodded approval.

Diana added, "Dalton says that this is the proverbial line drawn in the sand in north Florida."

"Right on," said the filmmaker. "What's his plan?"

"A key strategy will be to rally the whole community. We'll need to make a more dramatic and emotional case for preserving Prairie land than we've done in the past. You know as well as I do, most people still think of it as empty land they speed across to and from Gainesville."

"Lord knows that's true enough," said Wiley, with renewed interest in the proceedings. "If we could only get them out on the trails, let their hearts be lifted by the sight of waves of marsh marigolds, or a pond where storks and herons and cranes all stood feeding together…they'd be standing shoulder to shoulder to stop anyone from destroying it. And that's a fact."

"Yes, yes, Wiley. We all know your passion for the Prairie," said the woman he earlier criticized. "But did you ever think that in 10 years or so we'd look back, and see this development as a good and necessary thing? Florida is growing, like it or not. And people do have to live somewhere."

"If everyone could live on a 15 acre estate like you do, madam, I guess they'd be less concerned too," Wiley said, looking away from her with disdain.

The President said, "I think everyone's had a chance to express their point of view. So, I'd like to put it to a vote. Will anyone make a motion?"

"I will," said one of the members who had not spoken previously. "I move that the Center for Earth Options stand against the development on Paynes Prairie, and join the Sierra Club coalition. I also move that a sub-committee of the board, headed by Diana, meet to develop an action plan. "

The motion passed, and the meeting was adjourned.

Diana stood at the door, saying goodbye to each of the departing board members, and then went into her office. Several people lingered by the refreshment table, engaged in excited conversations about the upcoming Gator football game against Auburn.

"Oh, the traffic," complained one man as he started helping me clear the table. "When 80,000 Gator fans descend upon us, it's like the invasion of the Visigoths. I just retreat into my garden for the weekend."

"Hey, watch out," said one of the board members. "You know what the bumper sticker says, 'If you ain't a Gator fan; you're Gator bait.'"

I started carrying things into the kitchen, and just as I turned to say something to Wiley, I saw Diana come out of her office. She was ashen.

"Dalton's dead," she declared, and leaned against a desk.

There was a chorus of gasps.

"They found him—at the Sierra Club office. They say it had been vandalized."

The room was totally silent.

Chapter 6

"Dalton dead? I don't believe it. I just spoke with him last night. We were planning..." Her voice trailed off, and Diana dropped into a chair near the meeting table. Her body slumped, and her hands covered her face.

Board members, who had just been in noisy arguments over the upcoming Florida football game, stood in a shocked silent tableau. There were a burst of questions: Who called? When was Dalton found? How did he die? Who would have ransacked a Sierra Club office? Could it be connected with the Valdez project?

"I don't know. I don't know." Diana slowly shook her head. "Mike Smith called me...Dalton's Vice-President. He just heard about it. I think he said the police are still there."

Mention of a connection with the Valdez project made me think about the feud between Valdez and the Miami Sierra Club, but I wasn't going to talk about it now. I was more concerned about Diana. I sat down next to her, and put my arm around her shoulder. I held her close to me.

"Oh dear. Diana, I am so sorry. This is shocking. I know you and Dalton were close, and now..."

She looked up with tears running down her face. I reached for a tissue on Becky's desk and handed it to. As she dabbed at her eyes, she said, "Dalton was a friend. He was there for me when my husband died, you know." She looked up at the group of concerned faces surrounding her. "He even helped me get this job. Heaven knows what we'll do now...without him."

"Do you think it was a heart attack?" One of the members asked.

"Heart attack?" Diana said. "Yes, it could be. He was taking medication for that." She broke into a sob.

Several board members moved to form a close circle around Diana as though shielding her from any further shock. They murmured words of sympathy. I looked up, and noticed Wiley had stepped away from the group.

"Well, I guess there's nothing to be done for now," someone said. "We'll have to wait until the police can tell us what happened."

Another person gently touched Diana's shoulder and said, "Would you like me to drive you home? I don't have a class until this evening."

"Oh no, thank you. I can manage. I just need to—catch my breath. I'd feel better driving alone," she said.

People began talking to one another in pairs and small groups as they prepared to leave. Diana stood up, shaking her head as though trying to rid herself of the shock. She scanned the room until she saw Wiley Evans staring out the front window. She walked over, and stood silently beside him. He turned and took her hands in his, and they joined in a brief consoling embrace.

Diana returned to the front door and the departing board members. Her voice sounded ragged as she said, "We must still go on, you know. Now more than ever. Remember, the action committee will meet on Monday, as planned."

Everyone slowly began to file out of the office. One by one they hugged, or sympathetically touched Diana as they left.

"Lorelei, let's get Diana to go for a drink with us. Give her a chance to talk." Wiley said, after we watched Diana retreat into her office.

"I'm sure she's still in a state of shock," I replied. "Maybe she just needs to be alone for a while. It's all been so sudden," I said.

"Yeah, guess you're right. I think I'll just hang around in case she needs to talk or something."

"Good idea, Wiley. I hate to leave, but I've got to get home to see my husband. He's leaving for a conference in San Francisco tomorrow, and he'll be gone for at least a week.

"You go on ahead."

Diana came back out; looking grim but composed, and said she was ready to close up.

"You sure you don't want me to drive you home?" Wiley asked. "I don't have any plans."

"No, that's very kind of you," Diana replied. "I need some time alone." She looked around the office, held the door open for Wiley and me, and turned out the lights.

Wiley said goodbye, and I walked Diana to her car.

"I think you should stay home tomorrow. Work out in your garden," I urged. "It's always so nourishing for you."

She shook her head, and tears welled in her eyes. Without saying a word she gave me a long hug, got into her car, and left.

On my way out of town, I realized how shaken I was by the announcement of Dalton's death. My mind raced with scenarios about how he might have died so suddenly. The timing fueled my paranoia and, in light of what Jeffrey had told us, I again considered the role of Valdez in the event. I knew my instincts about Jimmy Valdez were right. His eyes gave him away.

Impulsively, I stopped at a gourmet shop and picked up a couple of ready to eat dinners, Bill's favorite wine, cheese, and an irresistible chocolate mousse pie. Despite the day's events, or maybe because of them, I felt a compulsion to make our last night together a festive one.

Driving across the Prairie in the late afternoon was a totally different experience than coming into town in the morning. A bright haze washed out the distinctive hues, and made it seem more like just an open space. I encountered a lot more traffic: large semis, cars, and SUV's charged across the basin like an angry stampede of cattle. I joined the rush, eager to get home. My thoughts tossed between the day's happenings, and plans for an evening with Bill.

A light rain began as I pulled into our driveway. I hurried into the house, calling Bill's name on my way to the kitchen. Maynard was nowhere to be seen.

"I've fed him already," said Bill. I jumped as he came up from behind, and put his arms around me. "What's for dinner? My last night, you know." He nuzzled my neck.

I turned, gave him a perfunctory kiss, and shoved him away.

"That's not very promising," he said. "Maybe you need a little warming up before dinner."

"Bill, Dalton Ames died today."

"How?" he asked.

"We don't know yet, but it's really shocked everyone, especially Diana."

"I'm sure it has. Is she all right?"

"I don't know. Anyway, it's been an incredible day. Give me a chance to settle in, and I'll tell you all about it."

"Okay," he replied. "Take your time. I'll go upstairs, and finish packing. Holler when you're ready."

"Fine," I said. "Meet me on the patio in thirty minutes."

I hurriedly set up the cheese tray, placed the dinners in the oven to warm, put the wine in a bucket with ice, and set the patio table. I looked at my watch, and was about to call to Bill when he appeared.

"Now that's more like it," he said, as he walked around the candlelit table, surveyed the hors' oeuvres, and checked the wine label. "Hmm, nice. Very romantic."

He embraced me, and I stood wrapped in his arms listening to the rhythmic beat of a light rain on the tin roof of the patio. At last, the world had stopped whirling, and I relaxed.

"What's with the deep sigh?" he asked.

"I think it's my first deep breath of the day."

"Sounds like some day. Tell me about Dalton." He poured us each a glass of wine, and we sat down at the table.

I held the glass up to the candlelight, and looked at Bill through the pale rosy glow of the Zinfandel.

"Remember how I always used to wear rose colored sunglasses?"

"When you played in *Breakfast at Tiffany's*. Sure I do."

"Holly Golightly. How I loved that role. I'd love to live that role!" I took another sip of wine. "When did we lose all the gaiety? I want to feel that light hearted again."

"What's this about, Lor? It's not just about Dalton, is it? I didn't think you knew him all that well."

"It's not just Dalton…it's everything else," I said, and took a long gulp of wine.

"Well, let's start with him. You said they didn't know how he died. It wasn't foul play was it?"

"We don't know yet. Probably a heart attack from what Diana said. They found in the Sierra Club office. The crazy thing is that it had been vandalized."

"That's certainly strange. Do you think there's a connection?"

"Who knows, but..." I repeated the story that Jeffrey had told us about Valdez, and the fire at the Sierra Club office in Miami."

"Why would the Valdez Company want to vandalize the Sierra Club in Gainesville? I'd let that one go, if I were you," Bill said, getting up to pour more wine in my glass.

I nodded thanks and said, "The police are investigating. We'll probably hear more about it on the news tonight. It's all so distressing."

Bill held up his wine glass, studying the candlelight's reflection in it. In repose, his face looked younger, more vulnerable. "You're right," he said finally. "We never do know when or how our time will come, do we?"

Panic seized me as I thought about Bill's long airplane flight to the coast. Anything could happen. It could be our last night together.

As though sensing or even sharing my thoughts, Bill came and crouched down next to me.

He brushed the hair away from my face. "Don't worry, sweetheart. Nothing's going to happen to us. We both have too much left to do."

I leaned down and kissed him, and he got up and returned to his chair.

We sat in silence for what seemed a long while before I rose to clear the table.

"What else happened today? Did you see Waterman again?" Bill asked as I returned to the patio.

I ignored the obvious probe and said, "We had our emergency board meeting, and the board voted to join a coalition that Dalton was organizing. We were all so energized...and then, boom! Diana must have checked her voice mail, and got the message from Mike Smith."

"I can see you're upset by all this. Was Waterman at the meeting?"

I took a sip from the glass of wine, and said off-handedly, "No, but before the board meeting, Becky, Jeffrey, and I went out to see the Valdez property."

Bill's eyes narrowed, and he looked at me closely. "I thought you weren't going to have much to do with him."

"I needed to see the property, Bill. We went out there, and met up with Mr. Valdez himself, along with Crawford Keezer, and their security man. Jeffrey got into a fracas with Keezer."

"So what's new? From what you've told me, whenever Waterman is around there seems to be some disturbance." He stared at the candlelight, and his face had the pouting look he got when he didn't want to talk about something he found unpleasant.

"Bill, this trip of yours. I'm going to miss you." I reached across for his hand just as he started to get up from the table.

"Let's eat, shall we? I'm starved." He went into the kitchen, and called out, "Is this stuff in the oven ready?"

"Yes, just put it out as is."

Bill returned to the table with the chicken dinners that had been warming in the oven. He emptied the wine bottle into our glasses, sat down, and began eating in silence. I was ravenous, and quickly finished my dinner.

I sat back and watched him eat. The rain had stopped, and moonlight was shining through the trees into the surrounding woods. I took several deep breaths of the fresh night air. For the first time that day, I was beginning to feel peaceful. The soothing hum of katydids enveloped me in the protective cloak of evening.

"I really will miss you," I said. "Please don't get upset about Jeffrey." I stood behind his chair, and began to gently massage his shoulders. I could feel him relax, and when I bent over to look at his face, saw it no longer held that distant look. I whispered seductively in his ear, "There's chocolate mousse pie for desert…your favorite."

Bill grabbed my hand, stood up, and said, "Let's have it for breakfast." He blew out the candles, and led me upstairs to our bedroom.

After Bill left for his trip to the coast, I spent the rest of Friday studying for the play. Now, Saturday morning, I was sitting at the kitchen table sipping a cup of Chai tea. The table was strewn with research materials provided by the theater's Dramaturg.

I began studying the script to review the plot line: Lyubov Ranevsky, the leading character, returns to her family's Russian estate after a five year absence. She learns that unless a large sum of money can be raised, the family property will be sold to pay debts, and her beloved cherry orchard will be cut down. She and her brother, who resides on the estate, ignore the impending crises, and persist in their aristocratic indulgences and nostalgia for the past. Lyubov's young daughter, caretaker stepdaughter, a cast of servants, and other distinctive characters, all of whom variously depend upon the family, move around the crisis in their own tragic-comic dramas.

It occurred to me, we might be like Chekhov's passing aristocracy: nostalgic for preserving the old Florida despite the compelling modern reality of population growth and its exigencies. Maybe even housing developments, like those built by the Valdez, were demanded by changing times. I hoped not.

I read and re-read the script, and, at various times during the day, found myself struggling to intensify my focus. My mind drifted back and forth between the play and my present day drama in my own world.

By late afternoon, I realized I had consumed too much coffee and too little food. I grabbed a box of crackers, some cheese, and moved out onto the patio to think about the character of Lyubov, whom I was certain to play. Upon first reading, this 19th century woman appeared utterly frivolous, and distracted. But, when I deconstructed her history, I had an epiphany: Lyubov Andreyevna Ranevsky and Lorelei Woodington Crane had shared a journey.

I, too, had fled my home and my marriage, and I knew that to play the part I would need to draw upon my own heartache. It was a deep pain that, only since Jeffrey's return, had begun to leak, like an underground river rising up to the surface.

The afternoon showers reminded me of that rainy night long ago.

"Jeffrey, are you sure you're sober enough to drive?" I had asked.

"Sure, I barely had anything to drink," he had replied, but I didn't believe him. During the party, he was out of my sight for long periods of time.

The rain was coming down in great sheets as we drove the narrow road from the lake house in Hawthorne. I strained to see out of the windshield.

"Do you think you should pull over?" I had begun feeling anxious about the low visibility.

"No, if we keep on driving, I'm sure it will let up. Don't worry."

"Don't worry," were the last words I heard him say as I saw the headlights looming in front of us.

"Oh, my God," I screamed, as we skidded. "Jeffrey!"

In what seemed like slow motion, everything was turning upside down, I felt my head hit a hard surface, and I was falling out of the car. The next thing I remember was awakening in the hospital.

"Thank goodness you're all right," Jeffrey said, standing at my bedside. "I was so worried about you." His face was bruised and the hand that was holding on my own was covered with a bandage.

Coming back to the present, I wiped my tears away with my hand. But, I hadn't been all right. It was after the two weeks I spent in the hospital that our relationship began to deteriorate. The accident had changed everything. His guilt and my distrust gradually spawned a distance between us. We no longer talked about the accident, or our feelings. Jeffrey started drinking again, and then my father died. He, too, was an alcoholic.

After the divorce, mother urged me to get away. She financed my move to New York to attend acting classes. Until the winter when Bill rescued me, I thought I had successfully submerged my pain by being someone else on stage.

The thought of my own losses made me wonder how Diana was getting along. I wanted to give her time to grieve, but I was worried about her.

When she answered the phone, her voice sounded stuffed up, like she'd been crying, but she insisted she was "managing all right."

"Have you learned anything more about Dalton's death?" I asked.

"The police have pretty much ruled out foul play," she said, and there was a long pause before she added, "they'll know more after the autopsy, but they're pretty certain it was a heart attack."

"Could it have been caused by the shock of coming into the office like that?"

"Yes, I suppose it's possible. We'll never know, will we?"

"What about the break-in?" I asked.

"Mike Smith told me all the computers had been taken. So they've lost their membership databases, and, well, you know."

"What a mess," I replied. "Could it get any worse?"

"I don't think so, but we've got to push on. I've called everyone to make sure they show up for the planning committee on Monday. You'll be there won't you?"

"Of course I will. And Diana, if you feel like talking anytime..."

"Thank you, Lorelei, but I'm dealing with things in my own way. I hope your Sunday rehearsal goes well."

I moved all of my Chekhov materials from the kitchen to the patio table. It was very humid outside, but I hoped the fresh air and chirping birds might lighten my spirits.

The phone rang, and I ran in to the kitchen to get it. I thought it might be Diana calling back, or my mother. I hoped it was my mother. She would talk about the play, and I would get back into it. I reached the phone just as the answering machine picked up the call.

"Lorelei, pick up. I know you're there." It was Jeffrey shouting over the recorded message.

"Wait a minute," I said until the recording stopped. I noticed the answering machine had a message on it. Bill, I thought. He must have called while I was in the shower.

"I've been waiting for you to return my call." Jeffrey sound peevish.

"I wasn't answering the phone."

"I got that," he said. "I really need to talk with you, Lor."

"You know I'm preparing for my play."

"Oh, yeah. I forgot. You go into deep freeze when you're in a play."

"Deep freeze would be a relief about now," I replied, feeling sticky from sitting outside.

"Have you heard from Diana? How's she taking the news about Dalton?" he asked.

"She's seems to be getting along. They're pretty sure Dalton had a heart attack." I wanted to end the conversation as quickly as possible. "What's on your mind?"

"Ames was a good man. A bit conservative for my taste. Anyway, I called to see if you'd have a couple of drinks with me since Bill's out of town…he is, isn't he?"

"How did you know that? Never mind, I think I know." Becky, I thought. "No, Jeffrey, I appreciate the offer but let's just keep our meetings at the office."

"This is important business. I need your help. It has to do with the Valdez thing, really."

"Can't do it, Jeffrey. I've dedicated this weekend to Chekhov, not Valdez."

"Well, I know you'll need a break sometime. I mean, Chekhov? Yeah, you'll need a break. Here's a plan: you work hard for another hour or so, and meet me at Charley's. We can grab a bite, and I'll fill you in on the plan Wiley and I cooked up."

"I said no. I need to stay focused on the play."

"Okay, Lor. But if you won't come out to meet me, I'm just going to get some pizza and come over there. I know you don't eat well when you work on a play."

It was too unsettling to think of Jeffrey showing up and demanding to be let in. He'd make a ruckus, the neighbors would come out, and Bill would eventually learn that Jeffrey had been here.

"Okay, okay. I'll meet you for just an hour. That's all."

"Let's say about 6:30." He paused, and added, "And Lor, be sure to dress real casual. Just jeans and sneakers…and, oh, wear something with long sleeves."

"What? Since when do you tell me what to wear?" I said, puzzled and annoyed by his instructions.

"Well, you know what a dive Charley's is. And, if I remember correctly, you always complained about air conditioning. See you in a little while." He hung up.

There was a dull throb in my temples as I sat down at the kitchen table and rested my head on my arms. I listened to the hum of the refrigerator, and experienced a feeling of profound desolation. It was my empathy with Lyubov's anguish over all things once beloved by her and now lost.

I regretted my decision to meet Jeffrey. I felt too tired and vulnerable. Maynard rubbed against my legs telling me it was time for him to eat. After I fed him and brought my play materials back into the kitchen, I went upstairs. By the end of a fifteen minute set of yoga routines, I felt a little better, took a shower, and got dressed to leave.

Chapter 7

I entered Charley's, and stood by the door until my eyes adjusted to the dark interior. Jeffrey was right; it was as cold as a cave. There was an unpleasant aroma of beer and stale smoke. Two pool tables were positioned in the center of the room, and dark wooden booths ran around the perimeter. The lighting was low, except over the pool tables with their phony stained glass hanging lamps. At one of the tables, two women were playing pool.

"Lorelei. I'm really glad to see you," Jeffrey said, as he approached me. He took my elbow, and guided me to a booth at the far end of the room.

"Wow, I don't remember this place being so skuzzy." I said looking around as we settled into a booth. There was loud laughter at the crowded bar. The football game was over, and the patrons ignored the blaring TV's at either end. About half of the booths were filled mostly with college kids.

"Let me get our pizza order in. Still heavy on the cheese?" He asked.

"You remembered," I said. "And some ice tea, no sugar, please."

Jeffrey left the booth, and I continued studying the familiar bar. It still had the usual Gator football photos lining the walls. There was a juke box, with a small worn linoleum dance floor in front it. I could just make out the words of the country song that was softly playing.

Jeffrey returned with our drinks and asked, "So how's the play going? Will I like you in it?" He asked.

"Truthfully? So far, I find it depressing…for a lot of reasons. And imagine, of all the plays to produce right now—one about cutting down trees for development."

"Yeah, I remember. Funny coincidence."

"Speaking of funny coincidences," I said. "How about the theft at the Sierra Club office? It made me think of the story you told us about Valdez and them in Miami."

"Interesting, huh? One of my buddies works for Gainesville P.D. He told me they really trashed the place. They think Dr. Ames may have walked in on them, and..."

"Caused his heart attack? That's too wild for Gainesville. Our developers fight their battles in the political arena. Maybe just as intimidating, but it's less violent."

"I told you this Valdez outfit played dirty," Jeffrey said. "But, enough about Valdez." There was an awkward silence, he took in a breath, and a sweet smile came across his face as he looked at the juke box. "Hey, remember that old Willie Nelson song?" The next record that had begun to play was: *You were always on my mind.*

"Lorelei, do you ever wonder... what if?" He reached for my hand, but I withdrew it.

"What if...?" I repeated, and felt my stomach knot up. If he only knew the distress I had felt that morning as I remembered. "Jeffrey, please, don't," I said, and looked at my watch. "You'd better get the pizza. I only have an hour, remember?"

Looking rebuffed, he withdrew his hands, took a long swig from his bottle of beer, and absently began to play with a peg-board game that was on the table.

"Now tell me, what was so important that you had to drag me here today?" I asked, trying to keep our conversation on business.

He looked up, and pushed the game aside. "Drag you? All right, I heard from my friend at the water management district. Louisa says that Valdez and the district are in a wetlands dispute on one of their current projects."

"That doesn't sound like such a big deal."

"She also told me she thinks there may be a really big financial scandal, but she doesn't have the details yet. I may have to go back down there to help her dig around."

"Sounds promising," I said. "But you said you needed my help with a plan you and Wiley cooked up. What's that about?"

Jeffrey sat up straight, and his face brightened at the mention of a plan. "Wiley and I met last night. Right here, as a matter of fact. He told me about the board meeting. We had a few brews, and decided the only way to get the Valdez thing in the public eye is to hold a large rally right near their property. Let people actually see what we'll be losing."

"That's a wonderful idea, Jeffrey. A rally can generate a lot of great publicity. It's got to be done before they break ground and start clearing trees."

"I know, we've got to work fast."

"So I assume the thought was to plan the rally with Diana's committee on Monday, and then take it to the other groups. Dalton already had some lined up?"

"You got it."

"But if Wiley's going to talk about it on Monday, why did you need to see me today?"

Jeffrey didn't respond right away. He looked at me with what I used to call his "soft eyes." I pretended to be busy putting sweetener into my iced tea.

"I'll tell you in a minute. But, there's something I have to say…I don't want to upset you, but I need to get it out of my head. Then I promise, I won't mention it again."

I could sense it was going to be a painful confession. Something I definitely didn't was to hear. I squirmed nervously in my seat and glanced toward the door, and escape. But he looked so pathetic, so unlike him, my resistance melted. I nodded, and mutely agreed for him to continue.

"In all these years…," he spoke haltingly. "I've met a lot of attractive people, you know. Truth is, I think I'm afraid to love anybody. That I'll screw it up like I did with us." He averted his eyes, and began to fidget with the game pegs.

I dared not respond with my own, already ragged, feelings. I looked away and watched as a young college couple got up to dance. Finally, I turned back to him and said, "Jeffrey. Let's not dig at the past. I'm sorry that you haven't found anyone else, but…"

"No, I've got to tell you." He looked up at me again, ran his hand nervously through his hair, and took another swig of his beer.

"Ever since I came back and saw you again, Lor, my mind is just…well, crazy. I'm so confused. I know I was definitely stupid in a lot of ways. Don't think that I will ever, ever forgive myself for the accident, and our baby girl."

"Please don't," I said, feeling a sharp pain in my chest.

"You don't still blame me, do you? I've got enough guilt..." He gave me a pleading look, and his eyes brimmed with tears.

"Jeffrey, stop it." My throat constricted, and I felt like I couldn't breathe. "Please, stop or I'm going to leave. Right now." I started to slip out of the booth. "I don't need this."

"Okay, I'll stop." His body collapsed into a defeated slump, and I sat back down. "I just had to get it all out. We can still be friends, right?"

Before I could reply, the bartender called his name, and Jeffrey got up to get our pizza. By now, I felt more like throwing up than eating. I needed fresh air. I needed to get back to the safety of my home and even the melancholy comfort of a 100 year old story with its fictional doom.

He returned with the pizza.

"Listen," I said. "I need to get out of here, and I don't feel much like eating anymore." I rose to leave.

He said, "Good. We'll take the pizza with us. I was going to tell you, I've got to go out to the Prairie. Wiley and I think we have the perfect spot for the rally, and I need to check it out."

"The Prairie? You're going there now?"

"Yes, I need to scout a place, near the Valdez site. I told Wiley I'd do it this weekend, before your Monday meeting, and that I'd get you to go with me so you can..."

"You told him what? That I'd go traipsing around the Prairie with you? You must be crazy," I said, suddenly energized by the outrageousness of his plan. I glared at him as he stood holding a tray with a large pizza. "I get it now; you had this whole thing planned without even asking me. That's why you told me what to wear. Gee, Jeffrey, why do I keep thinking you've changed?"

He put the pizza tray on the table, tried to take hold of my hands, and when I rebuffed his gesture, he said, "Lorelei, you do want to stop this development don't you? Or maybe you just want to write little publicity blurbs, study for your play, and stay on the sidelines."

Sarcasm was always his fall back mode in an argument, and as usual, it hit the mark.

"This is a high stakes game," he continued, grabbing my arm in a tight grip. "Either you're a player, or you're not. Decide!"

I was taken aback at the sudden reversal of his mood. Now here was the old Jeffrey, I thought. This is the man whose in-your-face righteous determination swept me up into the environmental movement, and later, into marriage.

"Okay, okay, I'll go with you." He released my arm. "Do me a favor though, in the future, don't try to manipulate me like this. We always agreed to be honest with one another, remember? No games."

He got the pizza boxed to go, and we left Charley's. I followed him in my own car. The arrangement gave us both a chance for our emotions to subside.

We parked on the roadside just north of the Valdez site. As I walked up to Jeffrey's truck, he already had the pizza box open on the hood, and was devouring a slice. He pushed the box toward me, and I took a piece.

"Here's the deal," he said, still chewing. "The actual rally will be here." He pointed towards the woods. "And see, the Valdez site is just a bit south. By a sheer stroke of luck, Wiley knows the owner, and has already arranged for us to use the property."

Cars whizzed by with Gator fans heading home after the game. One of them honked, and the driver waved exuberantly at us. Jeffrey waved back with a slice of pizza, and yelled, "'Go Gators!' It was an awesome game, Red, you should have seen it." Apparently, Jeffrey had forgotten about my total lack of interest in football.

"Let's make this fast, shall we?" I said. "I have to get home. Bill will be calling from the coast."

"Yeah, Bill, of course." He rolled his eyes. "Okay, what we have to do is find a place for the rally somewhere on this property. It has to be a spot that's clear enough for a large crowd. And preferably near the edge of Valdez site."

"Why?" I asked, and we both reached for the last slice of pizza at the same time. I took it, and he gave me a fake hurt look, until I said, "Hey, I've earned it, haven't I?"

He cracked a smile, carried the empty box to the rear hatch of the truck, where he unloaded a bundle of wooden stakes tied with red ribbons.

"C'mon," he said. "Just follow me, and don't worry. By the way, did you know alligators love the scent of pizza? I'd watch myself if I were you."

I stuck my tongue out at him for teasing me, but continued eating the slice of pizza. "You didn't answer my question," I said, running to catch up with him. "Why do we need to be near the Valdez site? And, what's with the stakes?"

He stopped walking and said, "Maybe I shouldn't tell you. But if you promise not to go blabbing to Diana..."

"Uh oh," I said. "This doesn't sound like something I want to hear, but tell me anyway."

Jeffrey rested the stakes on the ground, and said, "You know some of us believe in taking action rather than just talking about things. We plan to stage some activities at the Valdez site during the rally. And since the media will already be there..."

"Oh no, Jeffrey. After you promised Diana you wouldn't."

"It's not going to be me exactly. Some Greenpeace folks already heard about it, and may show up. They've been working the oil rigs in the Gulf. Then, of course, there's EcoSave! And maybe some others. You know how it is: word travels fast, and this is a high profile fight. I'm just making sure whoever's here has good press."

"C'mon, Jeffrey. This could be another Jonesville disaster."

He frowned and said, "Seems to me disaster is how everybody described the development project. Fire with fire, and all that."

"And Wiley approves of all of this?" I asked, incredulous.

"Lor, don't you get it? Wiley's as passionate about this as we are. Now, let's move along." He picked up the bundle of stakes, and continued walking into the woods. He stopped every so often, and hammered one of the ribboned stakes into the sandy ground, and said he and friends would come back during the week to clear a path.

"Why didn't we do all this while it was still full daylight," I complained, after I tripped on a tree root, and realized my blouse was sticking to me, wet with perspiration.

"Didn't want to run into any Valdez people again," he replied, stopping to pound another stake into the ground. "Here you can carry the rest of them."

At last we reached a large natural clearing. There was a fire pit in the middle that made it look like an abandoned campsite. Jeffrey walked around, and kicked some empty tin cans. "Homeless," he said. "Probably Viet Nam vets. Some of them live out here in the woods."

"If they're lucky," I said. "You know a lot of homeless people have been kicked out of the woods around Gainesville."

"It needs to be cleaned up a bit," he said, looking at small mounds of trash around the perimeter of the clearing. Wait here while I check to see how close we are to the Valdez property line. Be right back." He disappeared into the brush.

I dropped the stakes, and was too afraid of chiggers and snakes to sit down on one of the fallen logs. It was dusk, the woods were growing darker, and my senses heightened. A strong breeze came up, and brought the scent of rain. I heard a noise behind me, and I swung around—my heart pumping with fear. It was just the palmetto shrubs rattling in the wind. I wished I had stayed back at the road, but Jeffrey would have teased me unmercifully if I had suggested it.

The sound of a gunshot cracked through the air, and I jumped. I felt barely able to breathe, and my heart was pounding violently, as I screamed, "Jeffrey!" I ran to the edge of the clearing. "Where are you?" I shouted again.

A hand grabbed my arm and I was roughly pulled to the ground. It was Jeffrey. He crouched beside me. "Stay down, you damn fool," he hissed, his fingers biting into my arm.

There was another shot. It sounded closer.

We froze, huddled together for what seemed like an eternity. My breathing was labored, and my underarms felt sticky with nervous sweat. Then I saw a man standing at the edge of the clearing opposite us. He wore heavy boots, camouflage pants, and carried a rifle casually slung over his shoulder.

We stood up, and when he saw us, he blurted, "What the fuck? Don't you know you could get shot bein' out here this time of day?"

"Take it easy, buddy," Jeffrey said. "Don't you know it's a felony to use a gun on the Prairie? What the hell were you shooting at, anyway?"

"None of your fuckin' business, mister." He looked around nervously, and dropped the gun barrel so that it was pointing to the ground, easily lifted to aim and shoot.

Jeffrey touched my arm and said, in a low voice, "Stay here." He approached the man at a casual pace. "So what were you after? Rabbit? I see you got a full pouch on your belt." Jeffrey's voice was more conversational than before as he moved closer.

The hunter looked to be in his 20's, he wore a Tampa Bay Buccaneers cap, and his arms were tattooed with elaborate dragon designs.

"Buddy," Jeffrey said, standing a few feet from the man, "you know you really could get in a lot of trouble bringing that rifle out here. There's no hunting on the Prairie. It's a preserve. I should report you to the park rangers."

"I'm not here to hunt. I'm guarding property over there," he said, nodding his head in the direction of the Valdez land.

"That's odd, you seemed to be coming from the opposite direction," Jeffrey said. "I'll be you were after some big deer, weren't you?"

"Look mister," he said. "It gets pretty boring just sittin' around all night. And even if I was shootin' at some buck, and I didn't say I was, the rangers wouldn't care. I'd be doin' them a favor. They ain't allowed to thin the herd out there." The man looked past Jeffrey at me and said, "Hey ain't you that actress that came with the theater group to Santa Fe High School a couple of years ago?"

I was startled by the incongruity of his sudden recognition. "Yes," I replied.

He walked up closer, and gave me an appraising glance. "I recognized you by your red hair; never figured old lady Macbeth to be such a pretty woman. Your actin' was real good, too," he said. His face softened, almost boyishly.

"Thank you," I said, feeling confused by the sudden turn in what had been a threatening situation.

Jeffrey slowly walked back to my side and said, "You'd better get back to your job, boy. I know for a fact that the rangers cruise this area at dusk."

"Mister," the man replied, and a sneer came over his face, "the only cruisin' goin' on around here is by the fuckin' queers. I find a little gunshot keeps 'em away."

Jeffrey stiffened, and pointed at finger at the young man. "Well, right now son, you're trespassing on private property. So get the hell off!"

The man's lips curled in an angry sneer.

"Fucking poacher," Jeffrey muttered, picking up the stakes, as he turned to leave the clearing.

Instead of raising his gun, the young man made an obscene gesture at Jeffrey, gave me a curt bow, and vanished back into the woods.

"That was scary," I said. "Those shots were close. Didn't anyone ever tell you not to argue with someone holding a gun? For God's sake, let's get out of here. He may have a partner."

"No, not likely," Jeffrey said taking my arm, as we walked away from the clearing. "I know the type: a good old boy, probably working for peanuts, and the chance to be out to the Prairie to go hunting at night. He hopes to get lucky, and run into a large buck—he's right about them being protected so they get to be pretty big out here."

"How would he get a big deer home by himself, and without being noticed?" I asked.

"Oh, he'd call a buddy on his cell phone, and get it picked up at night. Some of these boys even go professional, and get into cattle rustling."

"Cattle rustling on the Prairie? Like in the old west?" I said. "You've got to be kidding."

"Oh, you'd be surprised. There's lots of cattle roaming the Prairie, and no way to patrol 21,000 acres. So, guys come in, pen up some of the herd, then come back in the middle of the night, and load them onto a truck. I've even heard of them using GPS systems to give their pals the exact location of the pen."

"Fascinating," I said, amazed once more by Jeffrey's knowledge about the Prairie. I stayed close to him on the walk back to the road, and when I heard the sound of traffic was relieved to be nearing the highway. The woods were intimidating enough in the daytime, but at dusk it was a shadowy and dangerous place.

Jeffrey put the left-over stakes into the back of his truck, and said, "Okay, Lor, you can go home now. I'll get Wiley and some of my buddies to come back out here and set things up. You can tell Diana and the others that we found the place for the rally. Oh, and remember your promise. Don't need to mention anything about why it's close to the Valdez site."

I nodded agreement, surprised to find myself conspiring with him.

"Friends?" I asked, feeling more relaxed now that we were out of the woods.

"Yes, we can be friends," he said softly as he raised his hand to touch my hair, but stopped midway. "Your hair still looks like a fall sunset. I hope Bill appreciates what he's got." He flashed a crooked smile, and shook his head. "Thanks for coming with me. You always were a good sport."

"To be honest, Jeffrey, I always did find your little trips rather exciting—a little too exciting this time."

I waved to him, returned to my car, and was aware of the aroma of the newly mowed roadside grass, and the tall trees silhouetted against the twilight sky. Crossing the Prairie basin, there was a thin streak of crimson on the horizon where the sun had set, and a quarter moon hung in the east. I felt surprisingly serene. I looked forward to Bill's call, and my return to *The Cherry Orchard*. Yet, I had a lingering feeling of tenderness at Jeffrey's familiar gesture in reaching out to touch my hair.

Chapter 8

It was late Saturday night when Bill called. I had dozed off while reading in bed, and was startled awake by the phone ringing. He asked me about my day, and sleepily I recounted everything I had done, including a brief mention of my meeting with Jeffrey.

"So Jeff got you out on the Prairie again?" Bill said. His tone sounded petulant.

"He needed help, Bill…for the rally," I replied feeling defensive, and fully awake.

"Gee, Lorelei, I thought you were afraid to go into the woods. You always insist that you're such an urban creature."

"Yes, but…"

"You wouldn't even go with me to that conference at the rainforest resort in Costa Rica. Remember?"

"Well it all has to do with the development. I can't very well defend the place if I act afraid to go out there, now can I?" I heard myself using Jeffrey's argument.

"I guess," he replied, but I sensed he still felt unsettled.

"Now, enough about me, Bill. How about the conference? What's the weather like out there? The humidity's like an outdoors steam bath here. I couldn't even do my yoga on the deck without being drenched."

"I haven't been out of the hotel since I arrived," he said, his tone lightened as the subject veered from Jeffrey. "It could be snowing for all I know. I've been at pre-conference workshops all day. Oh, you'll never guess who I ran into…"

He talked about dinner with former colleagues. He mentioned a management consulting job he agreed to do while he was in the Bay area, and warned he might be working too late for him to call me.

We talked a few minutes longer before saying goodnight. I called Maynard up on the bed, and snuggled back in to read. I decided to take a break from Chekhov, and picked up a book from my night table. It was a Sharyn McCrumb mystery—*If I'd Killed Him When I Met Him*. I always enjoyed her stories about Appalachia, and I didn't put it down until midnight. It took me a while to fall asleep since I had my usual attack of anxiety prior to the first night's read thru.

I was awakened at dawn by a morning thunderstorm, and decided to begin my Sunday early for a change. I had a leisurely breakfast, and called my mother.

"Are you excited about rehearsals? I used to dread the first play reading."

Mother was an actress, prior to her marriage, and she derived vicarious pleasure from my career.

"I'm excited, and nervous, Mother. Just like you used to be."

"You don't ever get over it, do you dear?"

"No, I hate first cast meetings. I have such irrational fears—that I'll have a coughing fit, or be struck dumb, or something equally catastrophic."

She laughed. "I know just what you mean. But somehow you'll get through it all, won't you? Just take one sentence at a time."

We chatted for a while longer about the play, and then gossiped about some of her neighbors. She mentioned she had driven by the orange grove property we once owned.

"You just wouldn't believe it, Lorelei. They've built an enormous development on it. You can't even recognize where you are anymore in Davie. When will all this building mania stop?"

"I know, Mother. Florida just seems to be filling up, doesn't it?"

When she asked about him, I told her about Bill's trip to San Francisco.

"I know it's important to accept every role you're offered, but don't you think you should go along with Bill every so often? A man on his own…well, you know."

"What about a woman on her own? By the way, Jeffrey is in town." I should have bitten my tongue instead of blurting this particular piece of news.

"Jeffrey? I haven't heard his name in a long time. How is the dear boy? He isn't still drinking, I hope."

"I don't know. As you said, it's been a long time."

"If only he had been more…"

"Mature?" I knew this conversation by heart.

"Yes, that's right. He never could have provided for you as well as Bill, you know. Did he come up there just to see you?"

"No, Mother. Jeffrey is here to work on an environmental issue. We just happen to be working together on it," I said.

"Does Bill object?"

"No, he's fine with it." I said, knowing it was an outright lie.

"Well, things did turn out for the best, didn't they?" It was a conclusion that pretty much characterized my mother's take on every difficult situation in life.

"Do tell Jeffrey I asked about him. And be sure to give my love to Bill when you talk with him again."

We ended the conversation. As I hung up the phone, the echo of her comment about our old orange grove struck me as yet another resonance with *The Cherry Orchard*. I remembered how sad mother and I were the day we closed on the sale of the property. Its loss, along with my father's passing, was like a double death.

I threw myself back into Chekhov, and spent the day studying the script. I read aloud, and tried different voices for the characters. Later, I watched a video of Michael Cacoyannis' film production of the play. I was eager to see how he handled it for a contemporary audience. Charlotte Rampling's stunningly haunting performance of Madame Ranevskaya only served to increase my insecurity about playing the role.

By late afternoon, I was ready to call it quits, and I put a frozen dinner into the microwave. Thoughts of Jeffrey kept edging their way into my mind. I recalled that Becky would be home from Boston, and I decided to call and fill her in on the board meeting. I wondered if Jeffrey would pick up the phone, but he didn't.

"Welcome home. How was the trip?" I asked, when she answered.

"Lorelei? Oh, really, really cool. I love going home in the fall, and I got to see a lot of friends and family."

"So you had a good time?"

"Oh, yes. Rosh Hashanah is my favorite holiday. Hey, what a bummer about Dalton Ames. Jeff filled me in on what's been happening."

"It's been a dramatic few days, to say the least."

"Really. Jeff told me the two of you scouted a place to hold a rally. That's going to be awesome."

"Did he also tell you about the planning meeting tomorrow?"

"No, Diana did. She called earlier, and asked me to pick up sandwiches and drinks on my way in. Dalton's memorial is going to be held in the afternoon."

"I guess we'll all go over after our meeting. Is Jeffrey around?" I asked. I didn't know what I would say, but I felt an urge to talk with him.

"He isn't here. I kind of thought he was with you."

"Me?" I said, surprised by her assumption. "No, I haven't seen him. He didn't go back to Orlando did he—to check out the Valdez rumor?"

"No," she replied, "actually, if he didn't go to see you, I'm not sure where he is. He was acting kind of in a hurry when he picked me up at the airport. Jumpy like. You know how impatient he gets."

"Did he tell you his plans?"

"He didn't. All he told me was about the rally and stuff like that. Then after we got home, he said he was going out...that he had to meet someone."

"Did he say who?"

"I asked him, but he wouldn't say. He said was the meeting could be important for our cause. He seemed like all tensed up."

"Hmm. Could he be meeting one of his buddies, Wiley maybe?" I pursued the question of Jeffrey's whereabouts feeling sure that something was amiss.

"No, Lorelei, he'd of told me if it was Wiley. Come to think of it, there was something really weird about him."

"Weird?" I asked.

"Yeah, he came out wearing his hiking clothes, but he nearly knocked me over with his cologne—CK, I think—and he changed into a new shirt."

"That's strange. I thought he hated men's colognes."

"Me, too. I even kidded him about having a hot date."

"What did he say to that?"

"He gave me a funny look, but he didn't say anything." She paused for a moment. "Lorelei, I was just kidding about the date. You don't think he has a girlfriend in Gainesville, do you?" Becky sounded worried.

"You should know since he's staying with you. I wouldn't be concerned about it, Becky." Jeffrey's behavior not only evoked my curiosity, but I now felt a spike of jealousy. Did he have a girlfriend neither of us knew about?

"Do you want him to call you when he comes back?" Becky asked.

"No, no. I'm off to the theater. In the meantime, don't worry, Becky. You know Jeffrey. He likes to be mysterious."

By the time I left for the theater, my agitation about the first read through had overshadowed thoughts of Jeffrey. I was consumed by my empathy for the character of Madame Ranevskaya, and my desire to play her.

The Tuscawilla Players Theatre was located in the south Main Street area in a renovated two story building. While I had played the Tuscawilla for about six years, I still experienced goose bumps every time I entered the house. Theater was my passion, and this was the home in which I felt most aroused.

I went directly into the rehearsal hall. It was sparsely furnished with a large sturdy table, the kind used for cutting fabrics. The table was also used by the costume designer whose racks of costumes lined the wall opposite the windows. Multi-colored sequins, a red and gold sash, and some shoes lay scattered on the floor beneath the racks.

An assortment of chairs had been set up around the table. Another table, at the opposite end of the room, contained basic snack items: a microwave, Mr. Coffee machine, mugs, and assorted fixings.

I was the first actor to show up for the meeting. Chester, the Stage Manager, was busy preparing his handouts: rehearsal schedules, cast contact sheets, and the like. After a perfunctory greeting, I sat down and started drawing doodles on the inside cover of the script. I felt out of sync, and irritable. Jeffrey's mysterious rendezvous nagged at me again.

One by one, other actors and staff members drifted in. As the conversational buzz grew louder, I looked up and saw my friend Cassie Woodruff standing in the doorway. She was talking on her cell phone, and motioned to me to save her a seat.

At 6:30 sharp, Chester started the meeting. The director, Renee Scalia, sat off to the side. She was hunched over, elbows resting on her knees, and staring into space. This petite former New York actor was rarely so immobile. She had an electrifying, highly energetic presence, and was widely respected for the quality of her productions.

Though most of us knew one another, we were asked to introduce ourselves. It helped break the ice. Chester reviewed the handouts, and gave us a pep talk expressing confidence in our success.

"Now the moment you have been waiting for," Chester said, as he handed out the cast assignments.

I scanned the list of the fifteen principal characters, and quickly saw I had been not been given the role of Madame Ranevskaya. I was to play the adopted daughter, Varya. Cassie, as we had predicted, was cast as the younger daughter, Anya.

"Are you disappointed?" Cassie whispered as everyone applauded the casting selections, and listened to the set and costume designers as they showed some mock-ups of their plans.

"A little," I whispered back. I didn't look up—pretending to still be studying the list—since I found myself close to tears. I had counted on having the leading role, and had already envisioned myself playing the beautiful, and tortured Lyubov Ranevskaya. I was beginning to understand her.

"Really?" Cassie asked.

"Really," I replied, finally able to look at her. She was scrutinizing my reaction.

Certain I looked convincing—I was an actress after all—I repeated, with greater emphasis, "Yes, I'm actually relieved."

Things always happen for the best, I could hear my mother's voice saying. And, it came to me there were good reasons to be glad for the casting. The role of Varya would be less pressure with everything else going on in my life: the Valdez project and, of course, Jeffrey. Varya was also a major character, complex and quirky. She would be a challenge to play.

My disappointment subsided as we started the script read-through. After a while, the smell of burned coffee permeated the room, and scraps of pastries littered the table. When the last line had been read, the director began pacing around the table as she described her vision for the production.

"Everyone wants to do Chekhov," she concluded, waving her arms in the air. "But believe me, it will not be easy. As actors, you will have to be very involved. Stanislavski directed Chekhov's works, and we'll try to emulate his methods for this production. I ask you to go deep, and find the motivation and intention of your character. I want you to know the character's life story and be able to live in it. Also, be aware of the delicate balance in this play: it see-saws between farce and tragedy, and that's what makes it an incredible challenge. But I'm excited by the challenge and I know you are, too. Together we will bring it to life," she concluded with a dramatic flourish.

After Renee's comments the actors expressed their feelings and ideas about the play. By 10 o'clock, everyone started to leave, and I walked out to the parking lot with Cassie. We gossiped for a few minutes about the cast assignments, hugged one another goodbye, and parted.

Maynard met me at the door when I arrived home. I dropped my bag on the bedroom stairs, picked him up, and walked into the kitchen. The blinking light on the answering machine caught my attention. I slung Maynard over my shoulder, and hit the play button. Bill's voice explained he'd be in meetings all evening, and would call again the next night.

I put Maynard down near his food dish, and stood for a few moments watching him, while I tried to decide if I had enough energy to make myself something to eat. I didn't, and instead, trudged upstairs feeling hungry, exhausted, and disappointed to have missed Bill's call.

By the time I showered and got into bed, I could barely keep my eyes open. I drifted into sleep trying to visualize myself as Varya: prim and repressed, but instead there was the image of Jeffrey reaching up and running his fingers through my hair.

Chapter 9

The phone ringing woke me. It was Becky. I was still in a semi-dream state, and it was the urgency of her tone as much as what she said that caused me to become instantly alert.

"Jeffrey? Shot?"

"Yes," she said. Her voice was breathless. "He's here at County General. In intensive care."

"How bad?" I asked, pushing back the bedcovers. I jumped up, and looked around the room to get my bearings. The numbers on the digital clock flipped to seven seventeen.

"I don't know. He was shot in the head. They found him on the Prairie. They're taking him into surgery in an hour."

"Shot in the head…on the Prairie? I can't believe it."

"I'm totally freaked. Can you come over, Lor?"

"Of course," I said. "I'll be right there. Becky, take some deep breaths."

I hung up, hearing the echo of my own advice, and tried to take several slow, conscious breaths. I quickly dressed, and was out the door of my house in a matter of minutes.

I drove to the hospital on autopilot. My mind kept flashing images of Jeffrey, reminding me how everything had changed since he reappeared in my life just one week ago.

The sun was coming up as I crossed the Prairie. Its rays spread out in startling shards of light through a misty haze—as if from a heavenly opening. I felt shivers, and then a peculiar calm. An inner voice said, *Jeffrey will be all right.* I heaved a deep sigh, and, felt release in the tears that spilled from my eyes.

On the other side of the Prairie basin, I was surprised to see sheriff's vehicles parked alongside the road. Several were near the entrance to the Valdez property; others were at the spot Jeffrey and I marked for the rally. Yellow crime scene tape fluttered loosely near both entrances. I slowed the car and considered stopping to see what I could learn, then sped up again. I was anxious to get to the hospital.

I entered the gray stone County General building, and Patient Services directed me to the Surgical Intensive Care Unit on the 5th floor. When I got out of the elevator, I rushed down the corridor to the nurse's station hearing only the slap of my sandals on the polished floor. The odor of a pine disinfectant lingered in the air as I passed a cleaning crew.

"I'm Lorelei Crane, Jeffrey Waterman's former wife," I told the nurse stationed at a desk near the SICU. "How is he?"

She looked down at a chart, and said, "He's in critical condition."

"Can I see him?"

"He's being prepped for surgery right now."

"What exactly is his condition?"

"I can only tell you he's in critical condition," she said.

"Nurse, please, I already know he's been shot. Can't you tell me anything more? Was there any mutilation?" I asked, dreading her reply. My secret worry was that alligators might have gotten to him while he was lying out there. Alligators were always my concern on the Prairie, and especially now after all the rain.

The nurse's eyebrows shot up. "Mutilation?" she repeated, but before she could respond Becky rushed up and threw her arms around me.

"Lorelei, I'm so glad you're here. I'm really scared," she murmured.

We held onto each other for a few moments. I said, "I know. I'm scared, too. How did you find out about him?"

"A friend from EcoSave! is a nurse here," she said. "He called this morning when he came on duty, and heard Jeff was admitted last night."

I turned back to the desk nurse.

"If Jeffrey's been here all night why is he just now going into surgery?"

"He's been unconscious since they brought him in," the nurse said, suddenly willing to give us some information. "They had to stabilize him. He lost a lot of blood."

"Oh, God." I was having trouble breathing, and grabbed Becky's hand until I regained control. "Nurse, I want you to tell us the truth. What are his chances?"

She gave us an appraising look before she said, "Look darlin's, I'm sorry, but there isn't much to say right now. Why don't you go into the SICU waiting room?" Her tone was gentle. "We'll let you know when it's over."

"I want to see him," I said. "He's got to know I'm here…that we're here with him. Please."

"Honey, like I said, he's in pre-op. It won't do no good for you to see him now. He's not even conscious. Just wait. I'll let the surgeon know you're here," she promised. "He'll come see you after the surgery. It'll probably be a couple of hours."

The phone rang. She answered it and turned her back.

"Jeez, Lorelei. What'd you think? Will he be okay?" Becky's eyes were red-rimmed, and she held onto my hand as we walked away from the nurse's station.

"We'll just have to wait and see. C'mon, let's go down to the cafeteria. We both could use something to eat, or at least some coffee. She said it would be a couple of hours."

We went through the cafeteria line, and settled at a table near the front of the brightly lit room. I began to quiz Becky more closely about Jeffrey's activities the previous night.

"And you have absolutely no idea who he was going to meet?"

"No, Lor, honest. He just was not going to tell me."

"And at night on the Prairie of all places. It's so dangerous out there. " I said, and told her about the police cars I saw on my way into town.

Becky was staring down at her plate, as she absently pushed her fork around the untouched scrambled eggs and grits.

"Are you going to eat that?" I asked. I had only gotten an English muffin and coffee, and the aroma of food made me realize I was still hungry. She pushed the plate toward me.

"He couldn't of been meeting a woman," she said. "At least not there. I mean, it doesn't make sense."

"None of it makes any sense, Becky." I was rapidly consuming the food she'd given me. "Have you called Jeffrey's mother?" I hoped for an affirmative reply. Jeffrey's mother had said hurtful things to me when she learned about the divorce. We had not been in contact since that time, and I had no desire to be the messenger of this bad news.

"I tried to call her when I first got to the hospital but there was no answer. Then I remembered Jeff mentioned she was driving across country with a friend. Going to visit his sister, Janine, I think."

"Do you have Janine's number?"

"Gee, Lorelei, I don't know it. I'm not even sure where she lives. Jeff only mentioned Oregon."

"I thought she was in California."

Becky shrugged, and was watching the doorway as a shift of nurses arrived.

I sighed deeply, and began rubbing my neck which was aching with tension.

"Well, maybe the police found some emergency ID on him," I said.

Becky made no reply, and we sat in silence sipping our coffees.

"Why'd that damn fool go out on the Prairie at night?" I heard the familiar voice along with the scrape of the chair he pulled out at our table.

"Wiley? How did you find out?" I asked. He sat down, and slapped his hands on the table top. I drew back as my coffee sloshed dangerously near the edge of the cup.

"Oh, I forgot to tell you, Lor. I called him as soon as I heard," Becky said.

"Just got over here, but they won't let me see the boy," he said. "Talked with some detective up there in the waiting room," he said, jabbing a thumb at the upstairs.

"What did he say? Do they have any idea who did it?" Becky asked. Her shoulders heaved, she started to cry, and I placed my hand over hers until she stopped. "Who would want to shoot Jeff?"

"That's a good question, Becky." Wiley frowned. "The detective—McBride's his name—asked me the same thing. Fact is he asked me quite a few questions, but he didn't give me any answers."

"Wait a minute," I said. "I know someone at the sheriff's office. Maybe she'll be able to tell us something." I was thinking about Delcie Wright. Years ago, we took theater classes together, and still remained friends.

"Oh, you'll get a chance to talk to McBride," Wiley said. "I wouldn't be surprised if he was already at the Center office waiting for you. I told him you'd both be there today."

"Guess we better get back upstairs. I don't want to miss the surgeon," I said, and we all got up to leave.

Becky and I returned to the SICU. While Becky called Diana, I went back to the nurses' station to inquire about Jeffrey's personal effects.

"No, m'am, there was no ID on him when he was brought in," said a young male nurse. "Are you family?"

"I'm his closest relation. I'm his ex-wife, Lorelei Crane," I said.

Becky rushed up to me from the waiting room. "Diana's upset about Jeff, but wants us back at the office as soon as possible," she said. "She needs us at the meeting this morning, and Dalton's memorial is this afternoon."

"Damn, I almost forgot about the meeting," I said.

Becky frowned and pursed her lips. She said, "I'm sorry, Lorelei, but I'm not leaving here until I know Jeff is all right. Somebody's got to be here when…well, whatever happens."

"I feel the same way, Becky. Still I understand Diana's urgency: there's so much at stake. Maybe the surgery will be over soon." We sat down in the waiting room.

By the way, do you know Jeffrey's friend Louisa?" I asked.

"Louisa Monterosa? I don't know her personally, but she and Jeff are really tight. Just friends, you know."

"Yes, but I'm thinking she might know how to locate his sister, Janine. Let's give her a call as soon as we get back to the office. Right now, I'm going to try and reach my friend Delcie."

I placed the call from the waiting room phone. The sheriff's office reported that Delcie was in Jacksonville until Wednesday. I couldn't think of anything else to do, so I sat alongside Becky as we both rifled through the worn pages of magazines. The waiting room was frigid. I looked around for a thermostat, and saw the TV monitor mutely showing a weather report. Another storm front was moving toward North Central Florida.

Finally, the surgeon came into the room. He was clothed in blood stained scrubs.

"Mrs. Waterman?" He looked first at Becky, and then settled on me.

"Crane," I said, and stood up. "He's my former husband."

"Well, Mrs. Crane, I can't give you anything conclusive yet. He lost a lot of blood. Head wounds are like that. The bullet hit the frontal lobe so there may be deficits in the optic nerve."

"Are you saying he's blind?" I felt my breathing grow shallow.

"We won't know for a while how much damage has been done. We're going to keep him on Pentothal, in a drug induced coma until…"

"A coma? I don't understand, Doctor." I felt Becky's body heat as she practically welded herself to my side, intent on getting the doctor's news.

"With a wound like this, it's sometimes advisable to keep the patient completely immobile. The drug slows down his metabolic function so the brain tissue has time to heal."

"How long will you keep him that way?" I asked.

"We'll start with a week, and then take some tests to see what's happening. We can't tell how he's recovering while he's in the slowed down state."

"And your prognosis?" I asked the dreaded question.

"Too early to say, really." Becky and I gave each other worried looks. The surgeon patted my arm. "Don't worry. He's a young man, and seems to be in pretty good physical condition. He could easily pull through." He looked up at the clock, and his tone was suddenly businesslike. "Any more questions?"

"No, not right now, doctor. Thank you."

"When can we see him?" Becky separated herself from me, and seemed revived by the doctor's upbeat assessment.

"Give it another day." He started to leave, and then turned to look at me. "Does he have any other family?"

I mentioned Jeffrey's mother and sister.

"I'd be sure to notify them. Just in case...you never know for sure with head wounds like this," he said, and left.

Becky and I gave each other a worried look. Finally, I said, "Well, I guess there's nothing more we can do here since we can't see him. Let's get over to the office. Maybe the detective will be there, and we can find out what happened."

As Wiley predicted, when we walked into the Center there was a man standing in the doorway to Diana's office. He immediately turned as we entered. He was middle aged, stocky with a square ruddy face, and close cropped brown hair.

"Crane? Lorelei Crane?" he asked. I nodded. "And you must be Becky..." he looked down at his small pocket notepad before struggling to pronounce her last name. "Hamowits?"

"Haimovitz," she corrected irritably.

"I'm with the Alachua Sheriff's Office, and I'd like to talk with you girls— separately—it won't take long."

"'*Girls*?'" I thought, chafing at the word, but I let it drop.

Becky said, "Girls?" She gave me a look.

I stepped in front of her, and said, "Well, I'm actually eager to talk with you, Detective...?" We looked one another over. He wore slacks, an open necked shirt, and a fitted tweed jacket. He had cool hazel eyes.

"Sorry," he said. "I should have introduced myself before. McBride, H.T. McBride." He flashed his ID, and I noted it said Homer T. McBride.

Diana came out of her office rubbing her hands together. She looked fretful. "I'm so sorry to hear about Jeffrey," she said. "We're all quite shaken by it. And so soon after Dalton..." her voice trailed off, and her face took on a distant look.

"We've just come from the hospital," I said. "He's out of surgery, but they have him on heavy drugs. We can't see him until tomorrow."

"Oh my," she said, "I certainly hope he'll be all right."

McBride cleared his throat, and Diana nodded in his direction. "Lorelei, I told the detective that he could use my office to talk to you. He promised he wouldn't be too long. Detective McBride knows we have an important meeting in just a little while." She took Becky's arm and gently ushered her into the back kitchen area.

"After you, Mrs. Crane," the detective said.

We entered Diana's office, he closed the door, and I sat in my usual seat. He moved into Diana's chair with such an air of self-assurance that I half expected him to lean back and put his feet up on the desk. I remained silent while he flipped through the pages of his small red notebook before giving me a detached look.

"What happened to Jeffrey, Detective McBride?" I said, unable to remain silent any longer.

"Don't know just yet. Crime scene boys are still out there. But, I'm sure you can help us. I just have a few questions for now."

"Of course," I responded, and settled back into the chair.

"Let's start with your relationship to Mr. Waterman." He glanced again at his notebook. "According to Mrs. Demeter, you and he were divorced about 12 years ago, right?"

"Yes, that's correct. I remarried, Dr. William Oakley. We're coming up on our tenth anniversary."

"Ten years? And Mr. Waterman has just recently come back into your life?"

"Yes, we're working together, but what has that to do with anything? I want to know what happened to him. How was he shot?" I persisted.

"That's what we want to know, Mrs. Crane. Please be patient. These are just routine questions, but I must ask them. If Waterman doesn't pull through, we're looking at a homicide. Serious business."

"Murder?" I was shaken.

"Yes, murder. We hope he'll make it, but in the meantime it's my job to pursue an investigation."

I nodded, and he continued, "Where is your husband now, Mrs. Crane?"

"My husband? He's in San Francisco. At a conference."

"Hmm. And what did your husband think of you working together with your ex?" He gave me a curious look.

"Why…nothing. He didn't think anything of it." I sputtered, surprised at the direction of his questioning. "I mean, Jeffrey just came up here to help with our campaign… to save the Prairie from development." I was feeling defensive, and I didn't like it.

"So your husband's not the jealous type?"

"What are all these questions about?" I asked. "Surely you don't think my husband had anything to do with Jeffrey's shooting? That would be absurd." I leaned forward, sitting on the edge of the chair.

"Well, m'am, when there's a crime of violence like this, first thing we do is check out the spouse and relatives. More times than not, they—or someone else known to the victim—turn out to be the perpetrators."

"Well, this isn't one of those times."

"Okay, let's leave your relationship with Mr. Waterman…for now. I need to establish the exact sequence of events that led up to the shooting. Tell me about the last time you saw your ex."

I told the detective about my dinner with Jeffrey, and I began to relax as I described our experience going out on the Prairie, and our encounter with the security man whom Jeffrey thought to be a poacher.

"Did he at any time raise his gun to Mr. Waterman?"

"No. Jeffrey said he was all bravado, and I think he was right." I pictured the young man, and the quaint bow he gave me before disappearing back into the woods.

"So who was Mr. Waterman meeting there last night?" he asked abruptly.

"I have no idea. Becky and I have been trying to figure that out. She said he dressed up like he was going on a date. He even put on cologne, and Jeffrey never wears cologne."

"If it was a date, would it have been with a man or a woman?" he asked.

"A woman, of course!" I said, feeling angered by the detective's question.

He leaned forward, "You probably don't know it, but lots of gay boys meet out there on the Prairie."

"Are you implying that Jeffrey? Oh no, detective. Positively not. I would certainly know, wouldn't I?"

"Okay, Mrs. Crane, I believe you." He looked at me sympathetically and said, "And it's been how long since you've seen him. Twelve years?"

"That's right. I moved to New York after our divorce, married Bill, and by the time I returned to Gainesville, Jeffrey was living in Orlando. Our paths haven't crossed until now."

"That's more than a decade since you've known your ex. Lots of things can change in that long a time, don't you think?"

"Just what are you getting at?" I asked.

"There may be things about your ex-husband you don't know." He jotted something in his little book. "Anyway, that'll be all for now. I'm sure I'll have other questions for you later."

His questioning made me feel irritable and uneasy. I was relieved the interview was over. My hands were clammy.

McBride stood up as I started to the door.

"By the way, Mrs. Crane, one last question. Do you have any idea at all who might have taken a shot at your boyfriend, anyone who wanted him out of the way?"

Boyfriend? I was momentarily stunned by the word, and I saw he was watching to see my reaction. Finally, I heard myself blurt out, "Keezer. Jeffrey had a fight with Crawford Keezer, the developer."

"Oh, really?" McBride took my elbow, and led me back to my chair. "Sit down. Tell me about the fight."

"Listen, detective. What I just said is ridiculous. Jeffrey couldn't have been meeting Keezer. The way he dressed up…it just doesn't make any sense."

"We'll see. Tell me about the fight with Mr. Keezer."

Feeling a wave of fatigue, I recounted our visit to the Valdez site, meeting Jimmy Valdez, Crawford Keezer, and their security man. I related the encounter between Jeffrey and Keezer, and

Keezer's threat to use the rifle in his truck. I also described our subsequent encounter with him and the unknown woman at the Prairie marina. He listened quietly, taking notes, until I had completed my story.

"You have quite an eye for details, Mrs. Crane," he said. "So you're saying Mr. Keezer's threat wasn't serious?"

"I don't think it was," I replied. "Yes, he was really angry. As for the gun…I'm sure it was his way of trying to scare us off. Jeffrey pushed him a bit much. He does that."

"Does he? Enough to get himself shot?"

I didn't respond.

"Okay, Mrs. Crane. That'll be all for now." He handed me his card. "Here's how you can reach me. Call if you think of anything else."

"I will."

Once again, he got up and opened the door for me to leave.

"Please send in Miss…what's her name?" He said, glancing down at his notebook.

"Becky Haimovitz."

She was not at her desk, so I went into the kitchen where Diana was using the copier.

"You were in there quite a long time," she said. "Did you learn anything?"

"No. I'll tell you about it later. Where's Becky? The detective wants to see her."

"Oh, I sent her out to get lunch stuff for our meeting. We're running so late. Wiley called, and I told him not to come until noon."

I returned to Diana's office, and told the detective that Becky was out on an errand, and would return soon. He looked at his watch.

"I've got to run. Sorry she didn't wait." He frowned, and his voice was harsh when he said, "Tell her I need to talk with her, and look over Waterman's things. Tell her I'll be at her house at seven tonight…sharp." He gave me another one of his business cards.

He left, and I stood in the empty office not quite sure what to do next. A few neck rolls eased some of my tension, but I decided fresh air was what I needed.

"Diana, I'm going out for a little while," I shouted, over the noisy air-conditioner, in the direction of the kitchen.

I went outside and sat in my car with the windows down. It was quiet except for the harsh cawing crows in the nearby trees. A murder of crows, I thought, remembering the group term for them. How strangely apt considering my encounter with Detective McBride and his disturbing questions. Who was Jeffrey meeting? More importantly, who would want to shoot him? It was baffling. He had only been here a week. Maybe it was someone who followed him up from Orlando? Click! The idea made sense, and I knew the one person who might provide some missing information.

As I returned to the office, a blustery wind came up, and the shrubs started blowing wildly. A storm was on its way. Once inside, I looked around Becky's desk until I found a listing for the water management districts. I picked up the phone, and nervously placed a call to Louisa Monterosa at the Southwest Florida Water Management District or, as Becky had called it, "Swift-Mud."

Chapter 10

Louisa Monterosa's assistant told me her boss was out of the office but would be calling in later that day. I explained that a good friend of Ms. Monterosa's was in an accident, and asked that she call me as soon as possible for the details.

Diana walked back into the main office, and I started telling her about my conversation with McBride. I had just begun to describe the confrontation between Jeffrey and Crawford Keezer when I was stopped by the arrival of several board members.

Diana greeted them, and Wiley, who was the first to come in, immediately asked, "Lorelei, how did the surgery come out? I called over there, but they wouldn't tell me anything."

Everyone turned to hear my response. Apparently they had all heard about the shooting.

"The surgeon said it went okay, but they won't know anything certain for awhile. They have to keep him on heavy medication so the brain tissue will heal."

Becky arrived, and started distributing sandwiches and drinks as Diana beckoned everyone to sit down.

"Of course, we'll all pray for Jeffrey's recovery," Diana said. "In the meantime, the best thing we can do for him, and for poor Dalton, is to get a plan to stop the Prairie development. We've got a lot of ground to cover, and not much time. Dalton's memorial starts at two."

Everyone started eating, and reading copies of the handout Diana had placed around the table. I followed Becky into the kitchen, and gave her McBride's message and his card. She looked at the card, and stuffed it into the pocket of her hip huggers.

"I bet he was pissed that I left…before he could talk to me, right?" Her voice sounded strained. "I just couldn't hang around, Lor. I hate the pigs."

"Becky, he seems like an okay guy. And we do want him to find out who shot Jeffrey, right? Just tell him what he wants to know and try to overlook his..."

"Sexism? I don't know if I can do that."

I sighed, and felt envious of her youthful ability to see everything in such black and white terms. "C'mon, Becky, let's eat," I said, and led her back into the other room.

"And we had a detective here to question us about the shooting," Diana said, as Becky and I joined them at the table.

"Why'd he come here?" Bob asked.

"Because Jeffrey had started working with us," I explained. There was no need to add my relationship to Jeffrey.

"Wow. So you think it's connected to the project?" Bob said.

Everyone looked up to see my response, but I simply shrugged and continued eating my sandwich.

"Speaking of connections, Lorelei, did you ask Mr. McBride if they've found out who broke into the Sierra Club office?" Diana said.

"I didn't get anything from McBride except a headache," I muttered, and took another bite of my veggie wrap.

"Oh, my goodness, I almost forgot. Before you all got here, Lorelei started telling me that Crawford Keezer and Jeff Waterman had some kind of a confrontation. Tell them about it."

I gulped down my food, and was sorry Diana brought it up. "Okay, here's the short version: Jeffrey, Becky, and I went to check out the Valdez property last week. We ran into Keezer and Jimmy Valdez, and one thing led to another..."

"They were already starting to cut down trees," Becky interjected.

"Anyway, there were some words, and Keezer threatened to shoot Jeffrey if he didn't get off their property."

"Keezer...threatened to shoot Jeff? This is the first I've heard of it, Lorelei," Diana said. "Why didn't you tell me about this before?"

"That's all there was to it, really. Just a threat. I guess there was so much going on that day that..." My voice trailed off, I continued eating, and avoided Diana's glare.

"I think Keezer would have shot him," Becky said. "You guys should have seen him, he was really, really mad."

"Wouldn't that be something," Wiley said grimly, "if that old bear Crawford Keezer was the one who shot our boy?"

Diana didn't respond. She was no longer staring at me, but looked deep in thought with her hands pressed together and clasped against her mouth. She dropped her hands and said, "Even if he's just a suspect it will bring a lot of notoriety to Valdez. Without sounding callous about it, this whole thing with Jeffrey could work in our favor."

"Diana!" I said nearly choking on a piece of apple.

"No offense, Lorelei. I truly am sorry about Jeff's condition, but don't you see? The publicity is going to get people's attention about why he was in Gainesville in the first place."

Wiley stood up. "Well, with Dalton gone, and Jeff in the hospital, it's on our shoulders now." His large meaty hands clutched the back of the chair. "I talked with Mike Smith, at Sierra, about our plan, Jeff's and mine. He thinks it's a good one, and he wants Diana and me to get the coalition's approval."

"The coalition meeting is right after Dalton's memorial," Diana explained. "Everything needs to be done very fast, you know. The legitimacy of the Valdez permit may even be decided today. Wiley, go ahead and tell everyone what you and Jeff came up with."

Wiley continued standing as he spoke, and held up the handout everyone had received. "This is an outline of our plan for a big rally on the property right next to the Valdez site. Lorelei here scouted the area with Jeff last weekend." He paused, gave me a sympathetic look, and waited to see if I wanted to say something before he continued. "The space is available to us, and thank goodness, the rally will be scheduled for a Saturday the Gators play Auburn. It's an away game."

"Otherwise, we'd have to hold the rally outside the Swamp!" Bob said, referring to the Ben Hill Griffin stadium where the Florida Gators played at home.

"Then we'd have a crowd for sure," Wiley said, with a brief laugh. "Anyway, this'll be our chance to tell folks about the Prairie, and the awful mess this development will cause. If we get enough people aroused, maybe some politicians will get off their duffs and help us."

"The coalition will have conservation, labor, and civic groups participating," Diana added. "It could be huge."

"And don't forget the students," Becky said. "Jeff planned to have lots of pizza. And he thought the Sister Hazel band might be willing to play. They sometimes do local benefits."

"The media will have a field day," Wiley said. "Hell, we'll make it such a big event they'll hear about it in Tallahassee."

I was sitting next to the woman board member who had not yet spoken. She had been making flower doodles throughout the discussion. She pushed her paper aside, and said, "Yes, a rally is a great idea, but will it be enough to stop them? After all," she warned, "if the permit holds, then all the talking and hollering in the world can't legally keep them from beginning construction."

No one spoke. It felt like the air of excitement had been sucked from the room. Out of the blue, I had a mental picture of Jeffrey lying in a coma at the hospital. He had been so confident that information about a Valdez scandal would be a powerful tool to use against them.

"Wait a minute, there's another strategy we haven't mentioned," I said looking at Diana.

"Oh, yes. Tell them, Lorelei."

All heads turned toward me. "Jeffrey said there were rumors of a big scandal about the Valdez Company in Orlando. He has a friend who was going to help him find out about it."

"Yeah," Becky perked up, "You're going to contact Louisa, aren't you, Lor?"

"I've already called her and left a message."

"Hey, why don't you just go down to Orlando in Jeff's place?" Becky proposed. "I'll bet Louisa will work with you. Jeff told me she's a really an amazing lady."

I was momentarily startled by Becky's suggestion. She was a step ahead of me, but her idea was reasonable enough.

"Could you do it?" Diana asked. "What about your rehearsals?"

"I guess I could do it in the middle of the week. Maybe just for a day or so," I said, thinking about Friday night's rehearsal.

Wiley, who had been slouched in his chair, sat straight up, slapped his hand on the table, and said, "If we could actually get something juicy on them... maybe something big enough to break in the press right before the rally. Now that would help, wouldn't it?"

"I must admit," Diana said, "for the first time in a week, I feel a ray of hope. I always feel better when we have more than one plan. I think we've come up with a couple of ways to at least slow them down." She looked at her watch. "Oh, my goodness, we need to get to the church for Dalton's memorial. I'll keep you all posted."

Everyone got up, cleared their luncheon debris from the table, and drifted out of the office. The aroma of tuna and pickles followed me all the way across the room to my desk, and I was gathering up my things when the phone rang.

"Lorelei, it's for you. Louisa Monterosa," Becky said excitedly.

"Mrs. Crane? This is Louisa Monterosa." Her voice was deep and silky. "My assistant just told me of your phone call. Please, tell me about Jeff. How is he?"

No point in dancing around it, I thought. "Jeffrey had surgery this morning, and the doctor thinks he has a good chance to recover," I said bluntly, and with more optimism than I felt.

"A good chance?" she repeated. "What happened? Were you with him?"

"No, I wasn't. It happened in the woods...last night. He was shot in the head."

"Who on earth would do such a thing?"

"All I know is that Jeffrey had a run-in with the Valdez people, but I really don't think..."

"Valdez? Jimmy Valdez's company?"

"The argument was with Crawford Keezer," I said. "Anyway, the important thing is that Jeffrey is in good hands now."

"I know Keezer. He has quite a temper. Like Jeffrey."

"The police are investigating, and hopefully they'll find out something soon."

"Mrs. Crane—may I call you Lorelei? Jeffrey has talked to me about you so often."

"Yes, of course," I replied, surprised by her comment.

"Thank you. Lorelei, tell me honestly. How serious is his condition? Should I come right up there? This is terrible news."

"No, no. They have him on very heavy drugs—so his brain can heal. He's in a coma, and will be for a week or more. It wouldn't do any good."

"But I feel so helpless…isn't there anything we can do?"

"Actually, Louisa, there is something you can do."

"Tell me. Anything."

"First of all, do you know how to reach Jeffrey's sister? The doctor advised us to let the family know in case…"

"His sister, Janine? No, I don't know. I think she lives somewhere in Oregon. I could check though. Jeffrey has another friend here, and he might know."

"Good. There's another way you can help. Jeffrey told you we needed information to use against Valdez's proposed development here."

"Yes, and I told him I'd help track down the rumors."

"Would it speed things up if I came to Orlando?"

"Yes, definitely," Louisa said. "In fact, there is someone who can help, but he has to be very discreet. It would be best if you could meet him yourself, in person. He might be persuaded to help you."

"Would this Wednesday be convenient?"

"Yes that's a good day. I can arrange the meeting by then, and I think you should stay in Jeffrey's apartment," she said. "I have a key, and you'll be comfortable there."

I was taken aback by her suggestion, and didn't respond immediately. It was an intriguing idea, and my first thoughts were it would give me a chance to find out more about Jeffrey, and look for Janine's number to call her. Yet at the same time I felt an undertow of dread.

"Is it settled then? You'll stay there?" Louisa asked.

"Yes."

"Good. I'll let the apartment manager know, and fax you the directions."

We hung up, and I related the gist of the conversation to Becky who was hovering over my desk.

"Great, Lor," she said. "You're all set. Gee, I wish I could go with you."

I left Becky to lock up the office.

Before turning on the ignition, I sat in my car for several minutes, taking some deep breaths, and trying to digest the day's events: being awakened with the news of Jeffrey's shooting, the frantic drive to the hospital and waiting for the surgeon's report, back to the office for a disturbing interview by Detective McBride, and his implications. All that plus the spur of the moment decision to go to Orlando.

"Great Caesar's ghost," I said aloud, using one of my father's favorite expressions. I should be a total wreck. Instead, I felt oddly energized and alive. I started the car, and headed for the Presbyterian Church and the memorial service for Dalton Ames.

During the still dark morning hours, I found myself staring at the ceiling above my bed. I was trying to analyze what Bill had said—and not said—in our conversation last evening.

He called, and soon realized we couldn't talk over the background noise of a party he was attending. When he moved to a quieter place I gave him a run-down on the dramatic events of the day. He was shocked to learn Jeffrey had been shot, and asked me more questions than I was able to answer. Finally, he let it go, and focused on his concerns about my trip to Orlando. I could still hear the echo of our conversation.

"Is it really necessary for you to dig into Valdez's affairs?" he had asked.

"Yes, absolutely," I replied.

"But you may be getting involved in something that's way out of your league."

"I have to do it, Bill," I insisted. "We need to slow them down. We heard that the county attorney didn't find cause to invalidate their permit."

"Well, please be very careful," he said. "Sometimes you get a bit too assertive for your own good. Prying into people's financial affairs can be outright dangerous. You know what I mean."

"Yes," I said. "I'll be careful."

"Good, that's my girl." After a long pause he added, "Lorelei, I'm going to stay here over the weekend. You'll be busy with rehearsals anyway, and it will give me a chance to catch up on some loose ends."

"Oh, Bill, I was looking forward to seeing you this weekend. What loose ends?"

"I told you before," he said, sounding defensive. "I have this consulting job, and I need the weekend to wrap it up. It's just a couple of days."

"But, Bill..." I had searched for the right words to ask him more without exposing what, until that moment, had been a latent suspicion.

"Gotta go, sweetheart," he said, cutting me off. "I'll call when you're back from Orlando. Take care of yourself. And don't worry; I'm sure Jeff will recover. Love you."

After he hung up, I had held onto the receiver feeling emotionally unsettled. Impulsively, I hit the button keyed to his cell phone number, but he didn't answer.

Now, early Tuesday morning, I wondered: was he or was he not having an affair? If he was, I guessed it would be with the perky young grad assistant who accompanied him to the conference. They had often worked late hours together. But then I chided myself for being paranoid, and maybe even projecting my own stirring feelings about Jeffrey.

I had slept very little after the call, troubled by thoughts of Bill's possible infidelity, Jeffrey dying, and my apprehension about going to Orlando. Feeling frazzled and wide awake, I got up, dressed, and went downstairs to sit out on the patio with a mug of tea. As I listened to the birds announce the dawn, I tried unsuccessfully to sort out my night's anxieties. The one thing I could do, I thought, was go to the hospital, and see for myself if Jeffrey was okay.

It was almost 6:30 when I hurried down the silent corridor toward the Surgical Intensive Care Unit. The nurse on duty let me into the SICU with the warning: "You can only stay for 10 minutes."

"How is he?" I asked, as she led me past several rooms through the stark ward with its glaring light. I caught glimpses of patients: an old man as white as the bedding on which he laid, a woman with multiple tubes connected to her face and arms, and others similarly crowded amid machines. The small cubicles looked like experimental pods in a sci-fi movie. It was quiet, except for the hum of equipment, and the air was frigid.

"He's unchanged," the nurse said, in reply to my question. "Of course, that's to be expected in a comatose state."

I followed the nurse into the room where Jeffrey lay. An alarm went off; the nurse quickly silenced it, and checked the monitor wires attached to his body.

"Ten minutes," she reminded me, and left.

I moved next to the bed and studied Jeffrey. His head was bandaged, and there was a respirator tube securely tied to his mouth. Except for the rise and fall of his breathing, his body was motionless. His hands had been neatly placed at his side, atop the covers, with a taped IV drip needle, and the finger monitor in the one nearest me. A Foley catheter tube was hooked to another stand.

"Oh, Jeffrey," I groaned at the stark reality of his condition. My eyes filled with tears, but I tried to hold them back. I remembered that people in comas were sometimes able to hear what went on around them, and I didn't want him to hear me crying.

I sat down on the chair next to his bed, and touched his hand. I was surprised to find it warmer than my own. I scanned the room looking at the array of monitors; their multicolored graphs and moving lines were unintelligible to me. The sounds of the pumping respirator and beeping monitors contributed to the eerie and unreal atmosphere.

"You're going to be all right, Jeffrey. The surgeon told me you're in good physical condition and you will recover. You just need to rest…to heal."

I spent several minutes with my eyes closed, and visualizing him surrounded in healing white light.

I leaned close to him, and said, "I'm going down to Orlando tomorrow to meet with your friend, Louisa, just like you were going to do. When she heard the news, she wanted to come right up here to see you, but instead she's going to help me get the dirt on Valdez."

I glanced at the clock on the wall and saw my time was almost up.

"Don't worry, Jeffrey darling." Darling? Where had this swell of emotion come from? Once again, tears blurred my vision, and I squeezed his shoulder.

"I have to go now. They won't let me stay any longer. I'm sure Becky will come to see you later."

I bent down and lightly kissed his wrist. As I raised my head, I saw his hand move, ever so slightly. He knew I was with him, I thought. I silently prayed, dear God, please make him well again.

I nodded to the nurse as I left the unit and reentered the warmth of the hospital corridor. It was still quite early, but I decided to head into the office.

Diana arrived a few minutes after I did. She had dark circles under her eyes, and she had obviously been crying.

"Lorelei, I didn't expect to find you here so early," she said flatly.

"I had trouble sleeping, and thought I'd get to the hospital early to see Jeffrey."

"How is he?" she asked.

"Alive," I said, with relief. "Beyond that I really couldn't tell anything. He's hooked up to so many damn machines and drugged into oblivion. All I can say is that at least he's breathing!"

"Well I'm sure he'll pull through," she said, turning away and walking into her office.

I was a little surprised at her abrupt departure, and followed her in to see what was going on.

"How about you?" I asked, and sat down across from her. "You look like you had a pretty tough night, too. It's Dalton, isn't it?"

She waved a hand, and said dismissively, "Oh, you know. How could I sleep knowing he's really gone? Dear soul. How I'll miss him. I wonder how his wife's taking it."

"She seemed quite cool at the memorial service," I said.

"Well, they've been separated so many years," she said, and began to fidget with papers on her desk.

After a few moments, she sighed deeply, and said, "And if Dalton's death weren't enough, there's this business with Hank."

"What about him? I thought you just had to take him to teen court."

"Uh huh. I thought so, too. But last night Detective McBride called. He wants to meet with us this evening. He wouldn't tell me anything on the phone, but I'm worried that Hank may be in more trouble."

"McBride? That's curious," I said. "Goodness, Diana, no wonder you're having such a hard time."

"They say the Lord doesn't give you any more than you can handle," she said with a mirthless laugh. "To top it all, I've been worried all night about them getting that damn permit. It makes it almost impossible." She shoved the papers aside, and buried her face in her hands.

"Don't get down yet," I said. "The rally could still help, and I'm determined to find out something when I go to Orlando."

"Of course, you're right." She looked up and gave me a weak smile. "I'm not giving up. I guess I'm just a bit worn to the bone right now. Raising a teenage son without a father, and trying to save some of Florida for my grandkids. You know, I often think about what my friend Joe, down in south Florida, used to ask, 'Just how many times do we have to save the Everglades?' We do seem to keep fighting the same battles over and over again."

"Yes, it does feel that way," I responded.

"And now, with Dalton gone. Well, it's almost more than I can bear." She took a sharp intake of breath, her shoulders heaved, and I saw she was trying hard to stifle a sob.

More than she could bear? I was surprised by the intensity of her emotion over her former colleague. Yet she looked so distraught, I went over and gave her a hug. I wished she would tell me more about her relationship with Dalton. Right now, it might have helped us both to have a confidante. But Diana was a private person, and I left her alone with her grief.

By mid-morning, I had cranked out a series of press releases and some flyers about the rally. I wanted to finish my work before the hordes of volunteers descended upon the office, and made it impossible to do any thinking. They were an enthusiastic group of students and seniors who would operate a phone bank, and work on preparing and distributing the promotional materials for the rally. Normally, I found their presence an enlivening change in the tone of our office, but today I couldn't deal with their high energy.

Around eleven, I got a call from Delcie Wright. Del had already heard about Jeffrey's shooting, and that McBride had been assigned to the case.

"Listen up, girl friend," she said. "You don't realize it, but you've got a real bulldog on your tail, and he especially likes to give women a hard time."

"You mean Detective McBride?" I asked, surprised by her comment.

"Trust me, we definitely need to talk." She told me she was on her way back from Jacksonville and could meet me for lunch by noon. We agreed to meet at the Noodle Bowl on SW 13th Street.

Diana's door remained closed all morning, and Becky had not yet come in to work. Before leaving the office, I stopped to check on Diana.

"Are you all right?" I said through a half-opened door. "I'm leaving now. Is Becky going to bring you some lunch?"

"No. She's on her way in from the hospital, but I'm just going to have some of the pizza we've ordered for the volunteers. We're okay," she said, looking more composed than earlier.

I left the office and drove south to meet Delcie. Despite a brief slow-down near the University, it was a quick trip to the restaurant on the other side of town. It was one of the things I loved about Gainesville. As long as you stayed on the east side of town, avoiding the heavily developed west, you could be across town, downtown or in the countryside in ten to fifteen minutes. Quite a difference from sprawling south Florida…at least so far, I thought grimly.

Chapter 11

As I pulled into the parking lot of the Noodle Bowl, I reflected on my friendship with Delcie. She was the only friend with whom I laughed a lot. Long ago, we made a pact not to take life too seriously, no matter what happened. It was a youthful gesture we tried to keep alive even as we aged. I wondered how I could make her laugh today, and was struck by a whimsical idea. I would surprise Delcie by wearing the black wig that I got from the Tuscawilla costume department.

When Renee asked that I dye my hair for the role of Varya, I convinced her to let me first try wigging. They let me take one home to try out for a couple of days, but it looked so wacky I put it in the car to return.

I grabbed the wig from the back seat, adjusted it in the mirror, and entered the restaurant. I stopped at the bar for a glass of wine before taking a table on the back deck overlooking a small lake. The thermometer, with a picture of a gator holding a can of Japanese beer, showed it was 92 degrees. I guessed Delcie and I would have privacy since few customers would venture out into the heat.

My eyes burned from sleeplessness, I closed them, and leaned back in the chair. The warm breeze, the mesmerizing buzz of insects, and the wine made me afraid I'd fall asleep. I sat up again, and stared across the green blue lake at the dense vegetation that encircled it.

"Lorelei, is that you? Lordy girl, what happened to your hair?" I looked up to see Delcie. She stood, hands on hips, giving me a wide-eyed laughing look before bending down to kiss my cheek.

I reached up to touch the wig that I had almost forgotten. "It is a shock, isn't it?" I giggled. The wine and the heat were having its effect.

"Well, I guess. You look like someone from *The Adams Family.*"

"I thought so, too," I said, chuckling as I stood up to give her a hug. "I'm so glad to see you."

"What in the world is my favorite actress up to?"

"I'm playing in Chekhov's *The Cherry Orchard*," I replied. "How's my favorite sleuth?"

She whistled, "Chekhov? Heavy stuff."

Delcie removed her light gray blazer to the back of her chair before sitting down. With fashion model good looks, she made an unlikely looking cop. A waiter appeared and took our orders, which were always the same at this restaurant: summer rolls and a super veggie sushi tray.

"I'm afraid your favorite actress is up to her teeth in real life drama," I said.

"I know. I've heard all about it."

At the sight of her, I felt a relaxed and girlish light-heartedness. I observed how little the years showed in her beautiful dark-skinned face. Had she persisted with her theater major, she would now have many opportunities to act. So many more roles were given to African-American actors today than when we went to school.

"Yes, it was pretty shocking to hear your ex was back in town, let alone that he got himself shot." She looked me over, assessing my reaction. "What's it like to have him back in your life again? Any sparks left?"

"I'll let that pass," I said, and more seriously, "Tell me what have you've heard about the shooting? I need to know what happened. It's all so crazy."

"In a minute. First, how is he? I'm sure you've been to the hospital."

I recited the surgeon's report, and told her about my morning visit to see Jeffrey.

"And you?" She studied me closely. "How are you taking all of this? You once told me that if anything happened to Jeffrey, you wouldn't want to live. Course, a lot of water has flowed over that dam, but still…"

"I'll admit, I'm more than shaken by it all. It scares the hell out of me to think that he may..." I couldn't say the word. "But, you still haven't told me—what do they know about the shooting?"

"The shooting," she said, and paused as though about to begin a recitation. Delcie turned her chair, and stretched her long legs out to the side of the table. She gave me one of her half-lidded appraising looks, before continuing to speak. "Well, after I got your message, I made some inquiries—not to McBride mind you—we aren't exactly buddies."

"Really?" I said.

"Yeah, really. Anyway, the crime scene analysis is underway. It's going to be a tough one with the woods, the rain, and all. They got footprints, a shell casing...I don't know what all else. Forensics is still out there. And they've started interviewing people in the neighborhood."

"On the Prairie?"

"Oh yes, and around the highway: store owners, residents...anyone who might have seen cars parked on the road or heard shots. Funny thing, you'd think there would be more homicides out there. It's so large and wild."

"What about the college girl found murdered across from the old Brown Derby?" I asked. "They never found out who killed her, did they?"

"Didn't you read about it? The prosecutor's office thought they had the guy just a few years ago. He was in prison up in Wisconsin for kidnapping a college student there. His cellmate told police the man confessed to the Gainesville murder, and the girl's family fought for years to get him extradited back to Alachua County. They finally succeeded just a few years ago. Unfortunately, the case was dismissed for insufficient evidence, and the guy was returned to Wisconsin. The case is still open."

"But why are we talking about murder?" I said with a shiver. "Jeffrey's not dead, Delcie."

"Of course." She touched my arm, and gave me a reassuring smile. "You've never been involved in a potential murder investigation. Let me warn you: it can get nasty…and personal, you know."

"You're wrong about my inexperience," I responded, momentarily recovering my good humor. "Don't you remember? I murdered my first husband."

Delcie looked puzzled, then laughed, and slapped her hand to her forehead, "Oh, right. I forgot I was talking to old lady Macbeth."

"Speaking of the investigation, what about Crawford Keezer?" I asked. "I told McBride he had threatened Jeffrey. I guess that makes him a possible suspect."

"Don't know about him. These investigations take time, Lor. It could be weeks before they gather all the evidence and…"

"Weeks?"

"Sure. The whole thing is much more difficult being out of doors…and with this weather. By the way, another front's moving in later today."

"We don't have weeks," I said. "We've got to get something on Valdez sooner than that or they'll have the whole place cleared."

"I know about their project on the Prairie, but what do you hope to get on the developer?"

"I don't know. Somehow…I just have this feeling that it's all connected."

"What are you talking about?" Delcie looked puzzled.

"Jeffrey, Keezer…" The ideas were only beginning to take form. "Did you know that Dalton Ames died?"

"Yes."

"Everybody was shocked. It was so unexpected. Now I think they've forgotten that the Sierra Club office was ransacked on the same day. Do you know anything about that?"

Delcie gave me one of her intense, half mocking looks before asking, "What are you getting at, Lor?"

"Do you think there could there be some conspiracy? I mean here's Jeffrey Waterman with a reputation for aggressive anti-development fights, and Dalton Ames, president of the Sierra Club, and leader of a coalition to stop the Valdez development. Dalton drops dead on the same day his office is ransacked, and Jeffrey gets shot a few days later...see what I mean?"

"Sweet Jesus," Delcie said rubbing the tips of her fingers across her forehead. "When you put it that way...and you think these events are related to Valdez?"

"Holy shit," I shouted, jumped out of my chair, and pointed to the water below. "See that gator? He's climbing up here."

Delcie stood up, put her arm around my shoulder, and exploded into a deep-throated laugh.

"You know, Lorelei, I dearly love you. But you are the biggest chicken I know. Of course, he won't climb up here. He's jus' looking for a sunny spot to take a nice afternoon snooze. Look," she said, and pointed to the water's edge, "he's got a couple of friends coming to join him."

Two other alligators, with half-lidded watery golden eyes seemed to appraise us as they skimmed just under the surface, and climbed up on the grassy shore.

"Go Gators!" Delcie shouted, cupping her hands over her mouth.

"You are so bad," I said. "Let's go inside. It's too hot out here anyway."

"Yeah, right," she said, and laughed again.

We went indoors and took a table next to the window. I could still see the gators below, but at least there was a barrier between us. The waiter delivered our order, and we started to eat.

"Back to your idea," she said, munching on her summer roll. "So you're suggesting that these Valdez folks may be playing hard ball?"

"Maybe. Do you think I should talk to Detective McBride about it?"

"He has the same facts you do, Lor. You could tell him, but don't be surprised if he dismisses your idea as some wooly woman's intuition. He can be very patronizing. Bottom line, you really need to wait until all the evidence is in, and hope for a miracle. An eye-witness to the shooting would help."

"I guess you're right. It's just a feeling I have."

I told her about my trip to Orlando, and she gave me the name of a woman detective she knew there.

"If you need the cops," she said, "call Syd. She's good people. Just mention my name and she'll give you a hand." She took out one of her business cards, and wrote the name and phone number of the Orlando detective on the back of the card.

Between bites of food, the conversation bounced around from work, to love life—none for her, mine glossed over—and finally, landed on our favorite subject: the theater.

"Quite a coincidence you doing *The Cherry Orchard* right now," Delcie said. "My most vivid memory of it was the sound of the axe at the end of the play. It was chilling."

"Yes, it's pretty dramatic, isn't it?"

She stared out at the water, looked at me thoughtfully, and said, "You know, I envy you sometimes. Law enforcement? It gives me the security I wanted, but..."

"And you meet a lot of handsome felons, right?"

"Oh yeah, that's definitely a perk," she laughed. "Seriously, I wish I had an occupation with more regular hours so I could do some acting...other than what I do in front of judges. It would be a relief to get into another role for awhile."

"I haven't heard you say that before, Del. What's going on?"

"I don't know, maybe an age thing. You know, you hit your forties and start taking a serious look at your life. Like, where's it going, and was this really my dream? You know what I mean."

"I know, only too well. I think I'm going through the same thing myself right now."

"Are you? Then again, maybe I'm beginning to feel overwhelmed by the stuff I've seen. I couldn't begin to tell you what it's like being a cop. Lordy, what people do to one another...but, we've had this conversation before."

"It's amazing you've lasted in the job this long," I said. "For me its like, am I ever going to be more than just a home town actress, and a professor's wife? Is this what I gave up having kids for? Remember the line in the Peggy Lee song?"

"Is that all there is?"

"That's it," I said.

"As for kids, don't even go there. My mama is still at me about that."

Delcie's cell phone went off, she got up, and walked back out onto the deck to take the call. I watched her through the window, and thought: this woman should be moving gracefully across a theater stage, not standing out in the heat taking down notes about crimes. I continued to observe her as she flipped the phone closed, put it back into its case on her belt, and returned to our table.

"Sorry, sweetie. I've got a hot date with a break-in over at Haile. It's at one of the fancy houses on the golf course, and they want me over there an hour ago." She reached for the check but I grabbed it first, and put down a bill to cover it.

"This is on me. Please do me a favor, Del, and see what you can find out about Jeffrey's case. I'll be back in town on Thursday. I'll call you."

"Okay. Now you be careful down there, and remember to call Syd if you get in a jam."

"I will," I promised.

She bent down, brushed her lips against my cheek, turned, and strode out of the restaurant.

I ordered another glass of wine and took it back out to the deck. The gators were gone. As I stood at the deck railing, I thought about what Delcie had said: we needed a miracle, like an eye-witness to Jeffrey's shooting.

The thermometer gauge now hovered near 95 degrees, and the air was densely humid and dead still. The sky had clouded over, and there was a suffocating calm. The kind you get before a storm. I began forming an idea that both frightened and excited me. I took a last sip of wine, set the glass on a table, and headed back to the hospital to see Jeffrey.

Hospital life was in full swing, as I swiftly walked down the corridor to the SICU. Food aromas permeated the air as lunch carts sat outside patient rooms awaiting return to the kitchen. Visitors lingered in the hallway talking in hushed tones. Those associated with patient care—doctors, nurses, aides, medical technicians, dietary staff—were all woven into the texture of activity on the hospital floor.

Just as I pushed the button to the intensive care unit, the doors opened, and Becky came rushing out.

"Lorelei, thank goodness you're here," she spoke breathlessly. "I've got to talk to you. Please. Don't go in yet."

"Why? What's happened?" My stomach gripped in a knot of panic. "Is he all right?"

The door swung closed behind her.

"That's just it. No one will tell me anything. I've been in and out of his room all day. He doesn't move, Lorelei! They even have a machine breathing for him."

"I know. I saw him early this morning," I said. "You've never been in an intensive care unit before, have you?"

She shook her head. "Can we go somewhere and talk? I've just got to talk to someone," she said miserably.

I looked around and saw the waiting room was crowded. I took her arm and walked with her to the end of the hall. We stood next to a large window. The midday sun radiated enough heat to give me some warmth in the otherwise cold corridor.

"Okay, Becky, but before we talk about what's bothering you, did you go back to the office at all? I'm concerned about Diana, and she was expecting you."

"Diana?" she said, with a bewildered look. "Oh my goodness, Lor. Yes, I did call her, and said I was coming back, but then…"

It was obvious Becky had only one person on her mind: Jeffrey. I could identify.

"Okay, so you haven't gone back yet. Just call her. Now, what's going on with you?" I asked.

"Lorelei, I'm terrified he's going to die. He looks dead already." Her hands covered her face, and she began to sob.

"Becky, he's not going to die." I put my arms around her, and felt the shuddering sobs.

After several moments, I stepped back and said, "Listen, honey, he looks the way he does because he's on heavy medication. It's healing him. What he needs is our support and *positive* thoughts. That's important. Do you understand?"

She nodded; her mouth was still trembling, but she caught her breath. "Lorelei, there's something you don't know." She turned away from me, and faced the window. "I'm in love with Jeff," she blurted the words. "You don't mind, do you, Lor?" She looked at me, her eyes were red and swollen. "I was afraid to tell you, but now..."

"No, I don't mind. I've guessed how you felt about Jeffrey. You worshiped him. A lot of girls did."

She sniffled, and nodded. "That's just the trouble. I'm not a girl anymore, and he still treats me like his kid sister." Her eyes filled again with tears. "This time, I was hoping he'd see me differently. He was just starting to open up to me...when this happened." She looked back toward the SICU, with a despondent sigh.

"So, you've been seeing Jeffrey since he left Gainesville?" I asked.

"Oh yes. He's been up here, and stayed with me a few times. But he's always so distant. You know, everything's a big secret with him. Just like that meeting on the Prairie."

I was surprised to find Jeffrey in yet another lie. First his denial about knowing Judson Sparks, now learning that his claim not to have been in Gainesville for many years was untrue.

"So what are we going to do?" she asked, angrily.

"Do?" I was startled by the sudden reversal in her mood.

"You know. We've got to find out who did this to him," she said. "The cops aren't going to do it any time soon. That detective doesn't care about Jeff. It's just another case to him."

"I don't know about that, Becky," I said. "But I am concerned about the fact that my friend, a deputy with the sheriff's office, just told me the investigation may take several weeks or more."

"See, we can't just sit around and wait, Lorelei. I want to find the sick dude who shot Jeff, don't you?"

I shared her sense of urgency about finding Jeffrey's attacker. I wanted to see if my hunch was correct about the Valdez Company's involvement. If Keezer or someone connected to Valdez was even indirectly responsible for Dalton's heart attack, the mess at the Sierra office, and Jeffrey's condition, it was essential to know about it sooner rather than later. I decided to tell Becky about the idea I conceived after my lunch with Delcie, and enlist her help.

"There is someone who might have information about Jeffrey's shooting," I said. "But I'm afraid he's not likely to come forward because it might get him in trouble."

"Who?" She asked, eagerly stepping closer to me.

"You remember hearing about the security guy we ran into when we found the site for the rally?"

"Yeah, I do."

"Well, he recognized me from when a Shakespeare scene I once did at his high school."

"How will that help?"

"He works a night shift patrolling the Valdez site, but he admitted he also did some hunting around the area where Jeffrey was shot."

Becky's eyes widened, as she said, "So you think if we can find him, he might have seen something?"

"It's only a chance, but miracles can happen," I said, echoing Delcie's comment.

"Let's go find him, Lorelei. When?"

"It's got to be this afternoon. I'm leaving for Orlando tomorrow, and I'm busy the rest of the week."

Becky thought for a moment, and said, "If he's working the night shift at Valdez, he's not going to be out there before dusk. How about around seven? There'll still be a little light."

"That's good," I said. "Oh, but the police will be all around the area. I saw the crime scene tape when I drove into town yesterday."

Becky considered the situation for a few moments before responding, "No problem. Meet me in the parking lot of the massage school. It's right on the edge of the Prairie. We can hike along the rim from there without running into the cops."

Becky seemed to have recovered from her earlier distress. Both of us were emotionally strengthened by purposeful action; we were going to find a witness to Jeffrey's shooting.

"Now Lorelei," Becky said, as we started walking back to intensive care. "Be sure to bring a flashlight. Do you have hiking boots? No, of course not. Well, at least wear sturdy shoes. It'll be wet out there. Maybe even bring a slicker. You know a storm front is moving in."

"I know. And I'll bathe in bug spray."

Becky's drill was familiar. It was similar to what Jeffrey told me before we met for dinner the night he surprised me with the Prairie visit. Jeffrey and Becky treated me like I was some fragile dodo, and maybe it was time for me to stop playing that role.

Becky left, and I went in to see Jeffrey. He looked exactly as I had seen him earlier. Once again I sat by his bed, and placed my hand on his arm.

"It's me, Jeffrey, Lorelei. Everyone at the Center is very upset that you were...hurt. They all asked me to tell you they're praying for you."

I sat with my hands folded in my lap, and watched the steady, slow, and mesmerizing movement of his breathing. Soon my own breathing synchronized with his, and Delcie's words came back to me: how I once said I couldn't live if anything happened to Jeffrey.

But at that time nothing bad had happened to him; it happened to me. I was the one who wound up in the hospital when we had the car accident. It was Jeffrey who sat at my bedside. Jeffrey who cried when the doctor told us I had miscarried. And even now, it was Jeffrey who still mourned the loss of our child. And apparently, that of our life together. My scars were intact. At least, I thought they were...until now.

I bent toward him, and in a rush of emotion, I whispered, "Oh, Jeffrey. I've been so selfish and mean to you." I felt as though my sense memory of the hospital room had finally released some of the horror of my own brush with death, and long buried feelings. "I know you still feel guilty about our baby, and I can't even explain why I wasn't more honest with you. I was terribly confused and depressed."

I sat up, grabbed some tissues from a nearby tray, and dabbed my eyes while I struggled to regain composure. The rhythmic sounds of the machines, the stark white room, and the motionless body suspended me in its dream-like state until I experienced a flash of truth. I hesitated before uttering the words that had been unspoken before.

"Jeffrey, I have a confession to make," I whispered. "I didn't want our baby." Tears were streaming down my face as I continued to speak, "I know now that I never wanted to be a mother. All I wanted was to be wildly and passionately in love, and to be an actress. Those were my dreams."

I pressed my fingertips to my temples. I can't believe I've finally acknowledged the lie I allowed to live in both Jeffrey's mind and my own. How had I let him carry the blame for the miscarriage, and for our divorce? How could my true feelings have remained so repressed? Did I want to retaliate for his drinking and cold silences after the accident? Did I have the same streak of cruelty I had witnessed in my mother when she became exasperated by my father's drinking?

"Time's up," the nurse said. She placed her hand on my shoulder. "He is healing, you know." It was a kind reassurance, but she was ignorant of the real reason for my grieving.

"I hope so," I replied wiping my face dry of tears. I hope we both can heal, I thought.

I touched Jeffrey's hand, and told him I was going out of town, but would be back to see him again in a day.

"I'll keep you in my thoughts, dear." And, then I was surprised to hear myself say the parting words that Jeffrey, even in a coma, might enjoy: "Go Gators." The nurse chuckled as she readjusted his pillows and checked his IV as I left the room.

My body screamed for exercise—too many aches in too many places. I drove over to the gym and brought my script in to study while I worked on the treadmill. By the time I finished my workout, showered, and dressed, it was late afternoon. Thinking about my rendezvous with Becky, I impulsively decided to buy a pair of hiking boots, and drove to the store owned by Commissioner Spark's wife. I was curious to meet her. Jeffrey's reaction to Sparks continued to puzzle me.

The young woman who waited on me said Mrs. Sparks wasn't in the store. I tried on a couple of pairs of boots, smiling at how funny they looked with the billowy Chico's pantsuit I was wearing. *You look so totally out of character, Lorelei,* I thought. I settled on a pair of the least chunky shoes and also picked up a small backpack.

I re-joined the busy rush hour traffic around the university and headed home to rest before my meeting with Becky. Somehow, my confession at Jeffrey's bedside made my spirits lighter, as if speaking the truth—even to myself—had lifted a long-held burden. I had a feeling of adventure about the plans Becky and I had made. Like me, Chekhov's Varya would have been too frightened to go into a wild place at dusk. But I thought she, too, might do it if it would help her family and their land.

I glanced at the shoe box and back pack on the seat beside me and experienced an indefinable boost in confidence. The hiking shoes had been a brilliant idea. They were an icon representing some new aspect of myself. Even the darkening sky that enveloped the Prairie failed to disrupt my mood.

Chapter 12

It was almost seven o'clock when I pulled into the parking lot, and spied Becky's truck.

She approached, glanced at my shoes, and said, "Wow, cool hikers." She gave me a smile of approval. "Let's get going. We've only got an hour or so of light."

We struck out along the path that led into the woods. The wind picked up, and there was the fresh smell of rain in the air.

"I hope we don't get caught in the storm," I said, as I looked up at the steel gray sky, and began having second thoughts about our expedition.

"Don't worry," she said, following my gaze. "I've hiked here a thousand times. We'll be in and out before it hits."

At the edge of the Prairie basin, we turned south to walk along the rim. I followed Becky, and listened to the soft crunch of wet leaves and twigs under our feet. The trees and shrubs were swaying back and forth to the harsh uneven rhythm of the wind, and thick palm fronds rattled like the flapping of window blinds.

There was a piercing howl, and Becky stopped abruptly. "Coyote," she said. "He's trying to scare other males away from his territory."

"I'm not male, but he scared the hell out of me," I said.

She caught my anxious expression, and said, "Don't worry, critters will keep their distance. Jeff told me they don't like the way we smell." She laughed, and started walking again. "Our guy might not be easy to spot as it gets darker, but he'll see us. Even if he's hunting, he'll see two women, and won't be scared off; he'll be curious."

In a few minutes, Becky stopped again. "Wow, look over there," she said, pointing in the direction of an opening through the trees onto the basin below. "Did you ever see such a light show? Prairie lightening storms are awesome," she murmured, and stood transfixed by the dramatic jagged flashes in the distance.

Great, I thought, there's lightening and we're in the woods. "C'mon, Becky, let's get going," I said.

Further along, she stopped again and surveyed where we were. "I think this is about where you and Jeff were when the guy met up with you, but closer in towards the road."

We stood there as the wind gusts became stronger, and I felt the sudden drop in temperature that closely preceded a storm.

"We're going to be in for it sooner than I thought," she said. "It'll save time if we split up. I'll go directly ahead, to the Valdez site, and you walk in toward the clearing. That way, we'll cover more ground."

"Okay," I agreed, hiding the nervousness I felt at being on my own. "If you see him, tell him Lady Macbeth wants to talk to him."

"Good idea," she said. "And if you're not back here when I return, I'll follow after you. Okay?"

I nodded, and we started off. I held onto the flashlight since it looked darker in the woods ahead. After walking for several minutes, I approached a narrow muddy track at the edge of a steep sinkhole. This isn't so bad, I thought, as I looked for landmarks to find my way back. I shined my light on various colored fungus, and admired one in particular that was arrayed like rows of pink seashells.

Despite the growing darkness, and erratic winds, I began to feel confident about my solitary trek. I had even begun enjoying it when, all at once, the wind velocity increased. It was immediately followed by a torrential rain that dumped sheets of water so thick I couldn't see ahead.

There was a loud screeching sound to my left and I turned to look. That's when my right foot hit an exposed tree root. I stumbled and lost my balance. The flashlight dropped out of my hand, and I made a grab for some tree vines to break my fall. As I tried to catch myself, both feet slipped from under me, I landed on my back, and found myself sliding feet first over the edge of the sinkhole.

"Oh, my God," I thought, skidding down so fast I was almost aloft. My feet kept skimming the drenched earth as I slid down a muddy ravine. I frantically tried to grab hold of fallen tree limbs and shrubs without success. I tried to dig the heels of my hiking shoes into the mud, but the earth quickly washed away, and sent me further down the mucky gulch.

Great sheets of water kept falling. I felt a stab of pain in my arm as I scraped against something. The torrents of water were washing me down the side of the sinkhole like so much debris as I slid over ferns, leaves, and decomposing trees.

Finally, one of my boots landed on an outcropping of rock about two feet wide, and I was able to dig my other heel into a tangle of shrubs alongside of it. At last, I had stopped falling. I was heaving, gulping for air. I froze in my position, afraid to move. My eyes stung and remained shuttered by the force of rain pouring down the slope, and covering me as though I were part of the landscape.

My whole body seemed to be shivering, but I made a concerted effort to slow my breathing. I assessed the situation, and knew I needed to turn and face into the slope to gain a better footing. My fingers explored the soil alongside me, and found their way to limestone rock. I used the rock as ballast, and very carefully shifted my weight and feet until I was securely facing into the side of the sinkhole. Panting from the exertion, I pressed my forehead against the wet fresh smelling earth, and tried again to take slow breaths. "It's all about the breathing," my old guru used to say.

My arms were outstretched clinging to the rocks, my heart was still pounding wildly, but I forced myself to turn my head and look down. It was only about 20 feet to the green pond at the bottom of the hole. Just as carefully, I looked up and was barely able to discern the tree-lined top of the sinkhole. It looked like I was closer to the bottom than the top.

Idiotically, I pictured myself climbing the long flight of stairs at the Devil's Millhopper sinkhole. But there were no stairs here, and I wondered how long I could continue clinging to the wet slope? I briefly considered that if I fell to the bottom, there might be an alligator there to eat me alive—in the dark.

The rain let up, and I hoped Becky might now be in the area. "HELP!" I screamed toward the top of the hole. "HELP!"

There was someone standing in the shadowy darkness at the top of the sinkhole. Who was it? Becky? Was it him? Or, just a trick of my mind?

"Help me," I screamed again more hoarsely. "I'm stuck down here. Please, help me."

The figure move slightly closer to the sinkhole, and suddenly disappeared. Why didn't he answer me? Maybe he went for help, I thought.

Minutes passed, as I listened to the sound of the water rushing down over the limestone channels. My hands gripped the rocks like frozen claws. How did they do it? Those people who survived for days on the edge of sheer cliffs or floating in the ocean. How did they handle the fear and the pain? They must disassociate from their bodies. Like the rock climber who cut off his own hand to free himself from a boulder.

That's it, I thought, I am not my body. My body is just like a role I play. I can transform myself. I've done it so often on the stage. Okay, Lorelei, you've got this role, so how do you want to play it? Victim or victor? What does your character want here? Courage, right? So just go for it. Take the action; risk the fall. Climb your way out of this God awful slimy hole. You can do it!

I took one last deep breath, and silently asked for help from whatever spirit was listening. I started climbing, digging my numb fingers into the soil, and clawing at roots and vines. I shoved my feet upward in fast crab-like motions—moving at an angle from the ravine—not staying in any one place long enough to slip, grabbing at rock outcroppings and trees to force my way up. I was like a machine, unthinking, moving mechanically, and relentlessly up, up, up.

At last, with vision blurred by mud and water, I felt myself lying on level ground. "Thank you," I whispered as I lay panting.

"Lorelei, is that you?" I turned my head at the sound of Becky's voice.

"Oh my God, Lorelei, what happened? You fell! Are you okay?" She bent down to help me up.

"No, leave me here a minute. I've got to get myself together."

Becky stooped beside me, and took my arm, gently urging me to sit up.

"I slipped and landed down there." I nodded in the direction of the sinkhole. "I'll tell you about it later." I allowed her to help me to my feet.

"Careful. It's slippery; I don't want both of us to wind up in the sinkhole," she said, and handed me the flashlight I had dropped.

"Let's get out of here, Becky. I think I saw him, but he vanished. Did you see him? He's out here, I'm sure."

"No, I didn't," she said, putting her arm in mine. "Right now, the best thing we can do is to get you out to the road and home."

We picked our way around the sinkhole to the broader terrain of the woods.

"Whoa, ladies." A man's voice yelled and a large beam of light blinded us until it was lowered.

It was a sheriff's deputy wearing an orange slicker with a rope slung over his shoulder.

"So you're the ones out here in the storm," he shouted, trying to override the rain which was pouring down again. "Was it one of you calling for help?" The officer pointed his light at me, and said, "From the looks of you, it must have been you I was comin' out after. Follow me."

We went a few hundred yards, along the perimeter of the crime scene tape that wound around the clearing.

"Watch you don't step over the tape," he shouted. "Here." He led us to a large bus that said "Mobile Command Center." We stepped under its awning. He hung his lantern from a cross pole. It swayed back and forth in the wind, putting the three of us in a ghostly, flickering light like that of an old time movie.

"Now, tell me," he said. "What are two women doing out here in all this mess?"

"Actually, officer, we were just hiking when the storm came up," Becky said.

"Don't any of you hikers listen to a weather report?" He gave me the once over. "You must have taken a heck of a spill, lady."

"Did you see anyone else out here?" I asked.

"Yeah, there was some guy who came up and reported hearing a call for help...down at the sinkhole. I was just on my way down there."

"Was he about five nine, early 20's, wearing camouflage?" I asked, picturing him from our earlier encounter.

"That's him," he said. "You saw him then? He told me I'd need a rope to pull you out. You're mighty lucky, lady. That's a deep hole out there."

"Did he give you his name?" Becky asked.

"Oh, I got his name all right," the deputy replied, and patted the pocket of his slicker. "I have to report anyone who comes near the crime scene, including you two." He reached into his pocket and took out a small notebook.

I gave Becky a look of relief, and we provided the information he asked for.

"Any chance you could give us the man's name?" I asked. "I'd like to thank him for trying to help me."

"Sorry, m'am. I can't do that. But if you call the Sheriff's Office, and ask for Detective McBride, he might give you the fellow's name."

He pointed to the path that led back to the highway, and we stepped back out into the rain. I glanced at the area roped off by the crime scene tape, but was unable to see anything related to Jeffrey's shooting. My legs felt leaden, and the cuts and bruises I had gotten were starting to act up. I knew I was a mess. We trudged silently through the woods until we reached the highway.

"Better not walk on the pavement," Becky said, and pulled me closer to her. "Cars can't see you through this downpour."

Numbly, I allowed myself to be led. I felt 100 years old. I realized that I was shuffling along like Firs, the ancient servant in *The Cherry Orchard*. And like him, all I wanted was a place to sit down. Finally, I felt myself being gently helped into Becky's truck. I slumped against the door, sighed deeply, and waited to be carried home—to safety and my own warm bed.

Becky drove me home from the Prairie, and I immediately went upstairs for a long shower and a dose of Tylenol. The scent of food drew me downstairs where she had prepared plates of scrambled eggs with onions, tea, and toast. I devoured everything on my plate without speaking, and then slumped in my chair sipping a cup of soothing chamomile tea.

In a complete state of exhaustion, I found Becky's rambling monologue to be comforting. She talked about our excursion, enthused about my success in crawling out of the sinkhole unaided, and speculated on the identity of the man we sought. As soon we finished eating, she put the dishes in the dishwasher and left. I returned upstairs to bed.

The next thing I knew, I awoke to find Maynard lying on my chest and licking my chin. It was 8:47 a.m. Wednesday, and I had slept for almost ten and a half hours. I lay in bed, conducted an inventory of my body aches, and then slowly got up to tend to my scrapes and bruises. I packed a few things for the trip to Orlando, dressed, and went downstairs to the kitchen.

There were messages on the answering machine, and I listened to them while I filled two large bowls of cat food to last Maynard while I was gone.

"Lorelei, this is Louisa Monterosa. I hope you find it easy to follow the directions I faxed you. I've left my key to Jeffrey's apartment at the manager's office. She'll be expecting you. I've told her Jeffrey was in a minor accident. Call me at work when you arrive, and I'll come over." Pause "And Lorelei, if you see Jeffrey before you leave, please tell him that we're praying for him. Safe trip. See you soon."

We're praying? Louisa's use of the plural was as curious as the fact that she had a key to Jeffrey's apartment. I placed a cup of water and a tea bag in the microwave, as I listened to the next message.

"Hi, honey. Sorry I missed you again. I called last night about 10:30. Surprised you weren't home. Anyway, good news. My business is wrapping up sooner than expected. I'll be home Friday evening after all. Can't wait to see you. I love you sweetheart."

Friday? I wondered what happened to the "loose ends" that were going to keep him longer in San Francisco. Had I wrongly suspected him of infidelity? He sounded so eager to see me.

My next door neighbor obliged by giving me a lift to pick up my car. I drove to the hospital, spent a few minutes with Jeffrey, and then stopped at the Center office to pick up the directions Louisa had faxed.

As I traveled down I-75 to the Turnpike, my mind kept reliving the sinkhole experience. It seemed ironic that it happened just as I was beginning to overcome my fear of the woods. Becky had been generous to describe my action as courageous; it was merely survival instinct. Yet the incident must have had some effect since I was feeling less apprehensive about my trip to Orlando. I thought, what could possibly be worse than what I had experienced yesterday?

It was almost one thirty by the time I drove through Orlando to the picturesque town of Winter Park, and found Jeffrey's apartment building. Palm Terrace Apartments was a two story 1950's era structure with exterior walkways, and lushly landscaped grounds. I felt a pang of nostalgia for my south Florida youth when I saw familiar shrubs, pink and red hibiscus flowers, giant crotons, and the variety of graceful palm trees that shaded the parking lot.

The apartment manager was on the phone, but paused to give me the key and directions to Jeffrey's apartment on the far corner of the second floor. I felt suddenly self-conscious about going into his home, and I hesitated for a moment before entering.

Finally, I opened the door to a dim interior. It smelled musty the way old Florida houses do when there is no air-conditioning. I went straight over to the AC unit and turned it on. The living room was spacious with comfortable looking overstuffed furniture and one of those extra-large screen TV's. In one corner of the room was an assortment of camping gear stacked in a more orderly fashion than what I had seen in his camper truck. I wandered around picking up his books, and touching small items on the end tables as though I could make a familiar connection with the man I had once known.

Next I went through an alcove dining area to the kitchen. I automatically inspected the refrigerator. It held the usual condiments, a six pack of beer and an open can of soda. I took the soda out and dumped it in the sink, remembering how typical it was for him to leave open containers in the refrigerator.

I rifled through the cabinet drawers looking for an address book or something that would lead me to Janine's phone number, but had no luck. Finally, I called Louisa.

The soft voice answered, "Louisa Monterosa speaking."

"Hi, Louisa. It's Lorelei. I'm here. At Jeffrey's"

"Oh good, Lorelei. Have you had lunch yet? I was going to stop and get something. I can bring you a sandwich. Yes?"

"That would be great," I said. "Just tuna on whole wheat and an unsweetened tea."

"Okay. I'll be there in a half hour," she said.

I hung up and scanned the notes and photos on the cork board next to the phone. There was one of Jeffrey with his arm around a dark haired handsome man who looked to be in his late twenties. They were both grinning happily. Another photo showed a woman with a young man in a graduation gown. I recognized the woman as Jeffrey's sister, Janine, and guessed the boy was her son. I read the Post-It note reminders and smiled at a business card that read PIZZA: 24/7.

I returned to the living room, and walked through the door to Jeffrey's bedroom. I could barely see my way to the windows where I pushed open the heavy drapes. An unmade king size bed with a burgundy quilt dominated the small room. A tall chest, with several framed photographs on the top, stood next to the bathroom door. I was drawn to the pictures. In the center was one of Jeffrey and the young man whose photo I had seen in the kitchen, another of Jeffrey waving wildly from a heavily packed canoe, and I was startled to find a small framed snapshot of our wedding. I picked it up and examined it closely. Such a handsome couple, I thought, and so filled with hope and passion. With a pang of regret, I replaced the picture.

Next, I sat down on the bed next to the night table, and absently browsed through the magazines that lay there. Under a couple of issues of *TIME* there was a magazine called *OUT*. Its cover pictured a handsome bare-chested young man, and a feature story headline, *The Gay Naked News Advisor*". Underneath *OUT* was *The Advocate* billed as *A Gay and Lesbian News Magazine*.

The magazines caught me completely off-guard. Jeffrey's sexual tastes had always been pretty traditional. I wondered if he now needed gay magazines as a turn-on.

I looked over at the other night table expecting to see a *Playboy*—which used to be his favorite—but there was none. My mind raced through the possibilities, yet kept coming back to the same conclusion: the magazines weren't the typical fare for a straight man.

Initially—when Detective McBride first raised the question—the idea of Jeffrey being gay or bi-sexual seemed preposterous. But now...click! My eyes were drawn back to the chest of drawers and the photo of the handsome young man. Was it so impossible? I assumed I still knew him well, but now a small voice in my head whispered, *what about the lies he's already told you?*

There was a knock at the front door. I hurriedly got up and left the bedroom, closing the door behind me.

Louisa looked as beautiful as her voice. She was tall, slim, and dark-skinned with shiny long black hair. Her coloring accented the splashy tropical print of her dress.

"Lorelei," she murmured warmly as she hugged me. "At last I meet Jeffrey's long lost love."

"Lost is probably the right word," I replied as she entered the apartment and walked directly to the dining alcove.

She took a bag of sandwiches from her large shoulder bag and placed them on the small table. "Let's eat and talk. There is so much to discuss," she said, and we both sat down.

I studied her face, and was mesmerized by the unusual coloring of her eyes. They were like dark-rimmed emeralds set against a sea green background.

"So, I finally meet the famous Lorelei Crane," she said smiling warmly.

"And I get to meet Jeffrey's friend. Tell me Louisa, how did you meet Jeffrey?"

She stopped eating and looked away for a moment before responding. "Actually, we met while he was doing a job for a development firm here. We liked one another instantly, and frankly, I found him quite attractive, and charming."

"Did you date?" I asked

She eyed me curiously. "Oh, we went out a couple of times. We're better as friends," she said, and continued eating her sandwich.

There was an awkward silence, and then I said, "I haven't found Jeffrey's address book. But in looking around the apartment, I did find something that...well, to be honest, took me by surprise." I stopped, and glanced at the cork board that held the photo of Jeffrey and the smiling young man. Suddenly, I was unsure if I should pursue the question of Jeffrey's sexuality so quickly.

"I take it Jeffrey didn't mention Eduardo to you?"

"No, he didn't. I had no idea."

She nodded her head toward the cork board. "He's in that picture by the phone. In fact, I introduced him to Jeffrey. His sister and I are sorority sisters, from college. Handsome isn't he?"

"Well, yes he is," I said, staring once again at the picture. "So he and Jeffrey...?"

"They don't live together. They have an arrangement; an 'open relationship.'" She gave me a questioning look. "He's so bad," she said. "When he told me he was going to Gainesville to help you, I assumed he would tell you about Eduardo," she said.

"No, he didn't."

"Please don't let Eduardo know that. It would hurt him very much."

"Tell him? Will I be seeing Eduardo?"

"Oh, yes. He's eager to meet you," she said.

"I see." I was feeling confused, and barely able to digest the implications of this new Jeffrey.

Louisa said, "When Jeffrey told us that he was going back up to Gainesville, Eduardo became very jealous. He knows Jeffrey still sometimes goes out with women, and he knows about you."

"What's he like?" I asked.

"Eduardo? He's a sweetheart. Intelligent, very kind, and as you see, quite handsome." She looked up again toward the kitchen cork board.

"What does he do?"

"He's an accountant with a large law firm. He's also a wonderful photographer. You see." She pointed to the framed photographs that lined a wall of the alcove. They were all nature scenes: wetlands, a field of sunflowers, and a cypress pond.

"Does he know what happened to Jeffrey?" I asked.

"Yes, of course. I called him as soon as I found out. He wanted to drive right up there, but I told him what you told me…that it would be no use."

"So he didn't go?"

"I couldn't stop him. He was very emotional. He drove up that same night after work. I'm surprised you didn't see him there."

"No, I didn't."

"He came home very depressed."

"I'm sure he did," I said.

"But, he's overwhelmed at work right now so he says he just calls the hospital everyday. He may even drive up after work—he wouldn't tell me—it's four hours both ways. He knows I'd be worried about him. He's so stressed out."

"I want to meet him, Louisa," I said impulsively.

"Yes, yes," she said. "You need to meet him. It's Eduardo who can tell you about Valdez."

"What does he know?" I was surprised at this twist.

She finished the last bite of her sandwich, and wiped her hands on the napkin. Before answering she looked at her watch and said, "Okay, here's what I know. When Jeffrey first called me from Gainesville, he said he needed information that would help to stop Valdez from their development there."

"And I thought you were the one who had the information," I said. "By the way, what exactly is your position with the water management authority?"

"I'm an environmental scientist. I told Jeffrey all I knew were things that might only be embarrassing to Valdez...illegal treatment of wetlands, that kind of thing. Nothing all that uncommon around Florida."

"How does Eduardo fit in?" I asked.

"Actually, it's Eduardo who has the most sensational information. His law firm is handling a private matter for the Valdez project director."

"Not Crawford Keezer?" I began to get excited at the prospect.

"Eduardo will have to tell you himself. It's complicated. But trust me, it's very, very illegal."

"Now I'm even more eager to meet Eduardo," I said.

"Ever since Eduardo found out about this Keezer matter he's been upset. He didn't even tell Jeffrey about it. And now, he's a total wreck." Louisa sat back down, and took a cigarette out of her handbag. She offered one to me, and when I refused, asked, "Do you mind?"

"No, go ahead."

She took several short puffs of the cigarette before continuing. "At first all he told me was that he had an ethical dilemma at work. He uncovered something he thought he should tell his sister, but telling her would violate his professional ethics. He asked my advice. Hypothetically."

"His sister?" I was beginning to feel almost dizzy trying to follow the bizarre interconnections Louisa was weaving.

"Yes, his sister's husband, Eduardo's brother-in-law, has relatives who work for Valdez in Boca, and well, you know how it is with family...especially Cuban family."

"So Keezer was doing something the company didn't know about?" This was becoming more and more curious.

Louisa went on, "When Eduardo learned about Jeffrey, and the possibility that it was this same Crawford Keezer who might have shot him? Well, that pushed him over the edge, and now he's ready to talk about what he knows."

"When am I going to meet him?" I asked. My excitement was growing at the opportunity to meet my ex-husband's lover, and get information that might stop the Valdez project.

"Tonight."

"Tonight?" I asked, "Why wait. Can't we go to his office?"

"Oh, no, no," she said forcefully, putting her hands up to stop the idea. "This is very confidential. He could be fired if his company suspected he was violating client confidentiality. No, we'll meet him this evening at the Candlelight. It's a gay super club. Is that a problem for you?"

"No problem. I have gay friends in the theater." And now, I thought, a gay ex-husband. "I've been to clubs before."

Louisa's face suddenly collapsed into a sorrowful look, and she said, "Tell me the truth, Lorelei. You've seen him. Will Jeffrey fully recover?"

I hesitated before replying, and reflected on the surgeon's prognosis. "They won't know anything definite until he's out of the coma. But I feel he'll be all right. What he needs right now are our positive thoughts and prayers."

"Yes, prayers. That's what I told Eduardo." She glanced again at her watch, and got up from the table. She regained her cheerfulness.

"I'm so sorry, Lorelei, but I must get back to Brooksville. We're having an important mitigation hearing today, and I have to be there. It may drag out into the evening."

"Okay," I said, and walked her to the door. "What time will we meet?"

"I'll pick you up at ten o'clock. Will you be all right until then? There's a good Cuban restaurant around the corner from here."

"I'll be fine, Louisa. Don't worry. I'll meet you in the parking lot at ten. In the meantime, I'm going to scour this place until I find an address for Jeffrey's sister. His family doesn't know anything yet."

"Maybe Eduardo knows where she lives," Louisa added helpfully as she stood in the doorway, ready to leave. "You can ask him this evening." She brushed her cheek next to mine, turned, and walked quickly down the breezeway to the stairs.

I shut the door, leaned up against it, and closed my eyes. There was so much to think about. I went into Jeffrey's bedroom, and briefly considered crawling into his bed. Instead, I dragged the quilt back to the living room couch, kicked off my shoes, and stretched out. My mind was a jumble of thoughts: Jeffrey has a lover named Eduardo; Eduardo's sister has ties to Valdez; Keezer's involved in something illegal—"very, very illegal"—according to Louisa. My body began to ache again, but I quickly drifted off into a dreamless sleep.

Chapter 13

I had slept deeply, and awakening in the dark room made me momentarily disoriented until I remembered I was in Jeffrey's apartment. I showered and changed clothes for the evening. Then I continued to rummage through Jeffrey's things in search of Janine's address.

Finally, I found an unopened letter from his sister that was among a pile of other mail on a shelf in the entertainment center. The return address was Cherry Grove, Oregon, and the envelope included photos taken at Epcot. The short note referred to the picture of her son's graduation. It was the same photo I had seen on Jeffrey's cork board.

I calculated the time difference on the west coast, and decided to have dinner before trying to reach Janine. I grabbed my handbag and headed out to the Cuban restaurant Louisa had mentioned. I needed fresh air and a distraction.

I was seated at a small table, and ordered a glass of sangria wine, and the house specialty: red snapper in green sauce, plantains, and yucca seasoned with enough garlic to keep the werewolves at bay. Under other circumstances, I would have relished such a delicious dinner, but I was preoccupied with thoughts about Jeffrey's secret life, and my conversation with Louisa. I also felt surprisingly nervous about meeting Jeffrey's boyfriend later that evening. I finished with a café con leche, signed the credit card receipt, and left the restaurant.

When I returned to the apartment, I got Janine's phone number from information. When I called, a young man's voice answered the phone.

"This is Lorelei Crane...in Florida. Is your mother home?"

"Yeah, just a minute," he said. I heard him call out, "It's for you. Some lady from Florida."

The sound of hurried footsteps, clicking across a tiled floor, made me suspect that Janine was probably already anxious about receiving a phone call from Florida.

"Yes, who is this?" she asked.

"Janine. This is Lorelei."

"Lorelei?" She repeated my name as though she was unsure she had heard it right.

"Yes, Janine, Lorelei. I'm in Winter Park, calling from Jeffrey's apartment. That's where I found your number."

"You're at Jeff's? Is he there?" She asked sounding puzzled.

"No, I'm afraid not, Janine," I said. "Actually, Jeffrey is in the hospital in Gainesville."

"What? Hospital? What's happened to him?"

"He's going to be okay," I said.

"Why are you in his apartment? I thought you said he was in Gainesville? Please, Lorelei, tell me what's happened!"

I described the shooting, the surgeon's hopeful report, and the status of the police investigation.

"My God," she gasped. "This is a nightmare. I can't believe it. What will I tell Mom? She's due here in a couple of days."

"Well, maybe by then…"

"Your Uncle Jeff's been shot." I heard her voice turned away from the phone as she was obviously talking to her son. "Yes, shot."

"Janine?" I called into the receiver.

"Can you give me the number for the hospital?" she said.

I had it in front of me, and gave it to her. There was a long silence, as I let her absorb the news.

"But I still don't understand, Lorelei. Why are you in my brother's apartment? Don't you still live in Gainesville?"

"Yes, I'm down here on business, and his friend Louisa suggested I stay at Jeffrey's. It gave me a chance to look for your phone number. He didn't have it in his belongings up there, and no one down here had it either."

"I'm glad you found me. Jesus, Lorelei, how will I ever tell my mom about this? I don't know what I should do," she said, half talking to herself. "Of course, I'll need to fly out there, but I can't leave until she arrives."

"He's still in a coma, so you have a few days before you'd even be able to talk to him," I said.

I reassured her that Jeffrey was in good hands, that friends in Gainesville checked on him daily, and that Eduardo and Louisa would probably go up to see him this weekend.

"All right, Lorelei. I guess there's nothing much I can do for now. I'm so damn far away. And you said they don't know who shot him?"

"Not yet, Janine. The police are still investigating. If you'd like, I'll call you again when there's something more definite."

"Yes, I would appreciate it. At least until I get there."

"I'll do it," I promised.

"Okay," she said sounding resigned to the arrangements, "thanks for letting me know, Lorelei. I'll call the hospital right now. Alachua County, you said."

I hung up the phone feeling stressed, but relieved to have done my duty by notifying Jeffrey's family.

At ten o'clock, I left the apartment and stood at the foot of the wrought iron stairway where Louisa could easily spot me. Moments later, a late model sedan pulled up, the side window rolled down, and I saw it was Louisa behind the wheel.

"Hi, Lorelei. Everything okay?" She asked, as I opened the car door and got in.

"I finally found Janine's address." I buckled my seat belt. "She lives in a town called Cherry Grove, Oregon."

"You called her?" Louisa pulled out of the parking area onto the main thoroughfare.

"Yes. Naturally, she was shocked."

"I'm glad you were able to reach her. I wouldn't have wanted to make that call myself. Was the mother there?"

"No, she hasn't arrived yet, so Janine can't leave until she does. By the way, have you met Jeffrey's sister?"

"Yes, we've met. She and her son came here to visit Jeffrey…and Disney, of course." Louisa turned and smiled at me. I noticed how white her teeth were against her dark skin.

"Does she know about her brother and Eduardo?" I asked.

The car turned onto a busy street called Orange Blossom Drive. It was lined with clubs, restaurants, and some seedy looking bars.

"Oh, yes. They got along very well. But then, who doesn't fall in love with Eduardo?"

"Right," I said, and was beginning to feel almost weirdly jealous over Jeffrey's boyfriend.

We drove for another 15 minutes or so before pulling in at the front of a dimly lit restaurant, The Candlelight. Dense foliage almost hid the entrance. At the reception area, Louisa told the Maitre d' that we were meeting Eduardo Sanchez.

"Ah, of course," he said giving Louisa an admiring smile. "Yes, I remember you. Mr. Sanchez told me to expect you. He's in the lounge."

We walked through the reception area past a table with an enormous bouquet of flowers whose reflection ricocheted endlessly in the dimly lit mirrored walls. We passed a large, candle-lit dining room, and entered the lounge. Pop music was being softly played on a baby grand piano by a blonde haired man with an old looking face. He flashed a beaming smile, and waved to Louisa as we walked by.

I followed her around a horseshoe shaped bar, decorated with twinkling Christmas lights, to the leather booths on the other side. She raised her hand in greeting to a man in seated in the last booth. He immediately rose to meet us.

"Louisa, como esta?" he said in a deep, velvet smooth voice. He embraced her, but all the while looked directly at me. At first his looks made me think of the actor, Antonio Banderas. He had black hair, slickly combed back from a lean face with chiseled features. His dark eyes, accentuated by heavy lashes, held a hint of sadness. When he stepped away from Louisa, I saw he wore an expensive looking suit, an open-necked white shirt, and a gold braided necklace that showed off his glossy tan.

Louisa made the introductions, we smiled and nodded politely to one another, and he gave me a long and frankly appraising look.

"Please, sit down," Eduardo said, ushering us into the booth. "You are more beautiful than your picture."

"And you're more handsome," I replied feeling somewhat giddy by his intensity, and the festive surroundings.

He took our drink orders and he left for the bar.

"Whew, I see what you mean," I said to Louisa. "I've think I've got the vapors! He's gorgeous. And that voice. Why are all the best looking guys...?"

"Gay?" Louisa completed my sentence and laughed. "I don't know, but I fall in love every time I come in here."

Eduardo returned to the booth, and slid in next to Louisa. "The waiter will bring our drinks in a moment." He looked at me, and said in a slightly cool tone, "So this is Lorelei, the one who lures sailors to their death."

"Eduardo!" Louisa said, and gave him a reprimanding look.

"Sorry," he said, looking unrepentant.

"That's okay," I replied, "but for the record, mother named me after her French grandmother, and not the German myth."

I get it, he's feeling a little jealous, too. And, he probably blames me for Jeffrey's condition.

"I guess that was uncalled for, but you can understand how upset I am about Jeffrey."

"I do understand, Eduardo. It's very distressing."

The drinks arrived; he took a sip, and began flipping his stirrer back and forth on the table. He stared at me again until I became uncomfortable and looked away.

He whispered harshly, "Tell me something, Lorelei...why now? Why did he join up with you again, and on this stupid quest to protect some piece of land in Gainesville? It may cost him his life. What is that about? Can you explain it to me?"

I was beginning to feel warm, either from the drink, his confrontational posture, or both. "I didn't ask him to help, believe me. He just showed up. It's complicated my life, too."

"Okay, now both of you..." Louisa said, spreading her hands over the table as if trying to smooth out the agitated air between us, "we're all here because we care about Jeffrey." She turned to Eduardo. "You know very well why that Prairie is important to him. And you told me you were willing to tell Lorelei about this man Keezer. Especially now that he's a suspect in Jeffrey's shooting."

Eduardo nodded, and wiped his face with his hands as though to erase his anger and hostility.

"Eduardo," I spoke gently, "before you tell me anything about Keezer, I want you to know that I'm happy that Jeffrey has found someone who obviously cares for him as much as you do."

"He's taught me so much," Eduardo said, his tone softening. "Before I met him, I never really looked around me." He stretched out his arms in a broad gesture. "You know, at all the natural beauty. Then Jeffrey started to take me camping with him."

"I've seen some of your photos," I said, recalling the landscapes on Jeffrey's dining room walls. "They're beautiful."

"Thank you. He was the one who encouraged me to buy a better camera and start taking my photography more seriously. He's not only my lover, but my teacher as well. If it was up to me, we would be living together," he said, and giving me a severe look, added, "but he insists he's not good marriage material: 'Tried it once and failed,' he keeps telling me."

It was my turn to shrug blamelessly.

Louisa placed her hand on his arm, and he stared moodily at his drink. She said, "Eduardo, tell her about Crawford Keezer."

He nodded, and huddled closer to us as though he feared someone might overhear what he had to say. It seemed unnecessary since the noise level in the bar had increased since the pianist initiated a sing-a-long of old show tunes.

"First, you must promise never to tell anyone that I gave you this information."

"Okay," I said. "I promise."

"Understand, I could lose my job, and my reputation. Confidentiality is very, very important in my profession," he said, and quickly glanced around the bar.

"Eduardo, I promise. I will not reveal you as the source of anything you tell me."

"And, it's not just because of my job. My family is involved."

I nodded, and waited patiently for him to reveal his secret. Louisa gave me a worried look, while Eduardo continued to study his drink as though still considering whether or not to expose what he knew.

The silence lasted longer than I could bear, and I said, "Please, Eduardo, just tell me what Mr. Keezer did that is so illegal. If I have some details, it'll give me a chance to check it out from other sources that won't implicate you."

Eduardo looked up, and sighed before speaking, "You know I'm telling you about this only because of Jeff. If I hadn't heard that Keezer might have been the one…" His eyes filled with tears, and in an effort to regain his composure, he lowered his head and cupped his hand over his eyes.

I reached across the table, and touched his other hand. "Eduardo," I said. "Telling me about it is the right thing to do. I don't know if Keezer shot Jeffrey, but I do know Jeffrey wanted the information you have. It was important to him."

He looked up, and nodded. "You're right, of course. That's why I agreed to meet with you."

I relaxed back into the booth and waited.

"Okay, here's the story," he said, sat up straight, and rubbed his chin before continuing. "There are a few attorneys in my law firm who will do almost anything to increase their billing hours. One of them handled a matter for Mr. Keezer that came to my attention because there were tax issues involved, and I'm a tax accountant."

"Yes, Louisa told me you were."

"The lawyer is the registered agent for a shell corporation set-up with Keezer as president and some woman named treasurer. No other officers. When I looked at it, the corporation had already received a funds transfer of over a million dollars. It came from a big land clearing company that was recently awarded a contract by Valdez."

He paused to sip his drink.

"And so?" I said, urging him on.

"The funds purported to be in payment for services by this shell corporation. But basically, I believe the money was skimmed off from a bank loan made to Valdez for their new land development project in Central Florida."

"Skimmed off? You mean Keezer's stealing it? How can he get away with that?" I asked, looking at Louisa who appeared equally incredulous.

"On the surface, it all looks legitimate," he explained. "Keezer must have someone at the land clearing company willing to create dummy invoices showing they have sub-contracted with his bogus corporation."

"And they don't do any work; they just get the money, right?" Louisa asked.

"Oh, they might arrange for some expenses just to make it appear legitimate, but the corporation is just a legal entity. It has no assets: no employees, no equipment, and the like. It's just a name."

"You make it all sound so simple," I said. "Won't Valdez find out?"

"Legally, it's very hard to follow money through this type of corporation."

"Wow," I said, surprised at the seeming simplicity of the scam. "But what happens when Jimmy Valdez finds out that a huge chunk of their development funds vanished?"

Eduardo shook his head, "The bank made the loan in good faith, and Jimmy Valdez probably had to personally sign-off on it, so he'll have to cover it somehow."

"You said there was a woman named as treasurer. Who was that?" I asked.

"Someone named Sparks," he said.

"Chelsea Sparks?" I exclaimed in disbelief. Could it be that the wife of our commissioner was in cahoots with Crawford Keezer? Or maybe both Judson and his wife were in on it? It was too bizarre.

"You know this woman?" Louisa asked, seeing my reaction.

"Know her? She's just the wife of our county commissioner. She and the commissioner have known Keezer since college."

Suddenly, I flashed back to the image of Keezer and the mystery woman with whom Jeffrey and I saw him on the Prairie. Could that have been Chelsea Sparks in the truck? But according to the pictures I'd seen, Chelsea Sparks was a blonde. The woman I saw had black hair.

"Lorelei," Louisa touched my hand. "It sounds like this could be a much bigger scandal than any of us imagined."

"And dangerous when it all explodes," Eduardo added. "Which is why you and I need to stay out of it. If you want to discredit Keezer in Gainesville, you will have to find a way for his scam to be discovered by someone else."

"But who?" I asked.

Eduardo gulped the rest of his drink and rubbed his hand across his forehead. "I don't know, maybe something will come out during the police investigation of Jeffrey's shooting."

"You mean, if Keezer is a suspect?" I said.

He nodded, and wrapped both hands around his glass, "The way I feel right now, I could kill the man myself. My lover is lying in a hospital bed. Who knows if and how he'll recover, and this...this bastard is walking around free, and a million bucks richer!"

"Please, Eduardo," Louisa said softly, "you're just getting yourself more stressed. We don't know for sure he's the one who shot Jeff. Right, Lorelei?"

"No, we don't," I replied. "But back to the million dollars, I still don't get it." I looked at the two of them: with their dark good looks they could have passed for brother and sister. "Why would Keezer do something like this to Jimmy Valdez? They aren't just business partners; they're supposed to be old friends."

Eduardo leaned back against the banquette, and lifted his shoulders and hands in the universal shrug that said, "Who knows why people do things?"

Louisa touched Eduardo's sleeve and he looked up at her with a weary smile. She said, "What a coincidence you were one they chose to handle this."

"More like a curse," he said. "I've been so torn about what to do with the information. First, because of the family, and now..."

"I must be really naïve," I said, still mulling over the whole fantastic scheme. "I didn't think it was that easy to steal such a large sum of money."

"Ever heard of Enron?" He gave me a sardonic smile. "Anyway, unless something happens pretty soon, Jimmy Valdez will get royally screwed, and Keezer and his girlfriend will be drinking *Coco Locos* on some Caribbean island."

"Have you considered going to the authorities?" Louisa asked.

He gave her a look of disbelief. "Are you kidding? Valdez won't want this to be made public. I told my sister about it this morning. She'll know what to do. I also let her know I was going to meet Jeff's ex-wife, and tell her what I found out. She got very upset with me. But I don't care. I had to do something for Jeff."

"Why would she be upset? Didn't she understand how you felt about it?" I asked.

"Why? Because, she knows the family will want to deal with this in their own way. The Valdez Company wouldn't want a public scandal with all the repercussions. Jimmy Valdez is a respected leader in the community. He also has many connections. You understand what I'm telling you?" He gave me a wary look.

Louisa, too, looked at me with alarm. "You see, Lorelei, you must be very careful. This is dangerous information."

I was still digesting Eduardo's warning. "What are you implying?" I asked.

"He's connected to a lot of different organizations, and to some people you wouldn't want to meet on a dark street," Eduardo said. "Let's just say, he's not someone to cross."

I realized I had the information I came to Orlando to get, but I was totally at a loss about how to use it without violating my promise to Eduardo, and risking harm to myself. "I'm still thinking about what you said about getting someone else to expose all of this. Any ideas?"

Louisa looked thoughtful and, after a few moments, said, "Didn't Jeff tell me your husband was a business professor at the University? Does he have any connections in Orlando with anyone who might investigate this?"

I nodded, suddenly picking up the thread of her idea. "Yes, maybe Bill could make inquiries through some of his colleagues or former students. Good thinking, Louisa. I'll talk to him about it."

"I have to be at work early," Eduardo said, looking at his watch. He turned to me and asked, "Are you going back to Gainesville tomorrow?"

"Yes, first thing."

"Good," he replied. "I'm hoping the doctors will know something more about Jeff by the end of the week. Did Louisa tell you that we're going to drive up this weekend?"

Louisa added, "Maybe we'll see you…at the hospital."

"Yes, maybe," I replied. "I'm going to be busy all weekend with rehearsals, and the rally Saturday afternoon. You both should come."

"I don't think so," Eduardo said, looking at Louisa to see what she thought about the idea.

"It might do us good," she said, giving him a decisive nod. "Jeff would like it. You could see why he found it so important to go to Gainesville."

We walked out to the parking lot together. Eduardo extended his hand, but I reached up and hugged him. His skin had the familiar aroma of CK cologne. It was the same fragrance Becky said Jeffrey had worn the night he was shot. I thanked him for his help, we exchanged warm goodbyes, and Louisa and I left.

It was after midnight when Louisa dropped me back at Jeffrey's apartment. I stood at the bottom of the stairway and waved goodbye as she pulled away. As I turned to start up the stairs, someone roughly grabbed me from behind. I let out a scream, but it was abruptly cut-off when a hand clamped over my mouth.

"Sssh" a man's voice whispered hoarsely. "Don't make noise or I'll kill you."

He roughly pulled me into the bushes. I felt one of my shoes slip away, and my bare foot scraped through the branches of a shrub. Before I knew it, I was lying face down on the grass and his knee was on my back. With my face pressed into the ground wet with dew. I suddenly felt like I was back in the sinkhole. I began making grunting noises as I tried to squirm loose to push him off, but he only pressed harder into my back until I was afraid he'd break it. He had succeeded in tying my hands behind me.

I turned my head to see his darkly clothed body kneeling next to me. I tried to scream again, but he grabbed my hair, pulled my head back, and quickly stuffed a handkerchief into my mouth. I gagged.

"Breathe through your nose," he ordered.

My heart was beating wildly. I quickly found a breathing rhythm that brought a steady stream of air into my nostrils. Thank God for yoga, I thought.

A car pulled up alongside the grass, and another man came up and bent over me. He wore black slacks and a light-colored guayabera shirt.

"Vamos, vamos," he said, as the two of them roughly lifted me into the back seat of the car.

The driver's door slammed shut, the car pulled away, and the man in the back seat crushed me to him.

I struggled, and made protesting noises through the handkerchief. At last, he pulled it out of my mouth. I bit his hand.

"Bitch!" He spat and slapped my face hard. "Quiet or I'll put you down on the floor." He sucked his hand where I bit him, and wrapped the handkerchief around it.

My face stung from the slap, and I automatically moved my tongue around my mouth to see if I tasted blood, or any teeth had been loosened. My head started to ache, and it didn't help that the volume from the rear stereo speakers blasted some bass-driving rap music in my ears. It was so loud, no one could hear me even if I yelled through the closed car windows

"What do you want from me?" I shouted, almost choking on the grass and dirt that filled my mouth. "I need water."

"Shut up," he snapped.

I tried to spit on him, but my mouth was even too dry for that.

We were driving on I-4, going very fast, and I knew there'd be no chance of jumping out. I realized I was totally at the mercy of these two thugs. I was enraged and terrified at the same time. The adrenalin rush I felt silently shouted, *fight*!

"What the hell do you want?" I demanded again, pulling away from him. His body reeked from a mixture of sweat and nicotine. His face was pockmarked, and his pupils appeared distended. I prayed he wasn't on any nasty drugs.

The driver glanced back at us, and nervously shouted something in Spanish to the man.

"Talk English, man," the thug shouted back. "The bitch is fightin' me here."

The driver didn't respond.

I slid across the seat to get away from him, but he roughly pulled me back holding me tightly against him. He felt like a mass of bulging muscles, and I wondered if he was a body builder.

Putting his mouth to my ear, he said, "You know something about Valdez. We want you to forget what you know."

"Forget what? I don't know anything."

So that's what this is about, I thought? My heart was beating violently—boom, boom, boom—the sound merging with the repetitive bass of the speakers. How did they already know about my conversation with Eduardo and where I was staying?

"We ain't gonna hurt you—this time," he said, releasing me from his grasp. "Long as you say nothing about what Sanchez told you tonight, you understand?" He grabbed my chin and turned my face to him. "You're an actress, right? If you want to keep your pretty face, do as I tell you!" He grabbed a handful of my hair and jerked my head away from him. He had a crazy, leering smile on his face, and his blonde pony-tail shook back and forth with every motion of his head. "You understand, right?"

"Ouch, you're hurting me. Let go, you fuck!"

The more I struggled, the more painfully he gripped my hair. This guy could rape me right here in the back seat of the car, I thought. Hell no, I'm an actress; I can play against this maniac. I thought of Delcie's advice: don't panic, stay calm, and you'll be all right. I stopped struggling, and let my body go limp. He let go of me.

"That's better. Now shut up and you won't get hurt," he said. "If you tell anybody what you know, we'll find you again. Get it?"

"Yes, I get it." I looked up at him submissively. "Now please just take me back to the apartment. I promise to do what you say."

Apparently he was convinced I was sufficiently terrorized and compliant. He told the driver to turn around and go back. We exited the highway and returned in the direction from which we came. My head was throbbing, and my scalp ached where he had yanked my hair.

Nothing more was said, and the car pulled up at Jeffrey's apartment building. The hulk took out a pen knife, shoved me forward in the seat, and cut the cord that bound my hands. I instinctively began rubbing my wrists to restore the blood flow. He opened the door, and as I started to climb out, he whispered gruffly, "Remember, say nothing!" He gave me a final push, and I stumbled onto the ground where I sat dazed, and watched the car speed away.

Chapter 14

After the thugs had sped away, I got up and limped over to the foot of the stairs. I was wearing only one shoe, and I held onto the railing to get my bearings. I looked around, until I spied my other shoe at the edge of the sidewalk where I had been pulled into the bushes. I put it on, and very slowly started to climb up the stairs.

I was grateful to be out of the car, and away from the grasp of the sweaty body that pinned me next to him in the back seat. He could have cut me with his knife or worse, and I shivered as I recalled his leering look. I numbly clung to the railing for help as I half crawled, half stumbled upstairs.

It seemed an eternity before I finally entered Jeffrey's apartment. I went directly to the bathroom, and feeling a rising wave of nausea, I slumped down in front of the toilet just in time to retch. The stench of garlic from the yucca I'd eaten earlier threatened to make me sick again. I grabbed a damp towel, wiped my mouth, and leaned back against the bathtub...completely exhausted.

The sting of hot tears, and a feeling of childlike vulnerability made me wish there was someone around to comfort me. The shock of the abduction following on the heels of yesterday's sinkhole ordeal, made me feel like I was in the middle of a nightmare. Yet, my aching body told me it was all too real. Could it have been only a week ago that I was longing for more excitement in my life?

"Leave it to me to find the high drama," I mumbled, as I forced myself to get up and look in the mirror. My hair was disheveled, my face was smeared with dirt, but there were no marks indicating the hard slap I had received.

I viewed myself objectively. "More like a Russian peasant than a member of an aristocratic family," I said, and swept my hair back, held it in a pony tail, and tried picturing myself as Varya.

How he frightened me! My heart's simply throbbing, I recited the line, with a hand over my heart. Yes, I could empathize with her fright at the unexpected confrontation with a menacing-looking vagabond.

Relating the experience to my role in the play somehow steadied me, and I came back into the bedroom to call Louisa. It was a little after one o'clock in the morning. I was relieved to hear her soft voice answer the phone.

"Louisa? This is Lorelei. I've been mugged."

"What?"

"After you dropped me off. Two men. They grabbed me."

"My God, Lorelei. Are you all right?" She sounded breathless. "What happened? Tell me everything. I just walked in the door."

I told her everything that had happened: how one Spanish speaking man and a sadistic Anglo thug had driven me around and threatened me to remain silent about Keezer's theft of the Valdez money. I described the men to her, what they did, and how they had finally dumped me out of the car back at Jeffrey's apartment. I also told her that I thought Jimmy Valdez was behind the threats.

"I wonder how they found out about me, and that I was with Eduardo," I said.

"They mentioned Eduardo? Oh my," she replied, in a worried voice. "Lorelei, are you sure that you're not hurt? Do you want me to come over there?"

"No, no. I'm getting my second wind. I just needed to talk to someone. What'd you think? How did they know? They even knew I was an actress, and threatened to mess up my face." Instinctively, I put my hand on the cheek that he had slapped.

Louisa paused for a moment, "I think you should call the police and report it," she said firmly. "It was a kidnapping, you know. I knew this was dangerous, but so soon?"

"They didn't really hurt me; they only threatened. And dammit, I didn't get a license number for the car. I'm not even sure what make it was. What would I tell the police? Two guys abducted me and then set me free."

"It doesn't matter. You should report it." Louisa insisted. "I'm sure you were terrified. I would have been."

I remembered Delcie had given me the name of a woman detective in Orlando. It was in my handbag somewhere.

"Okay, Louisa. There is someone I can call here, but not until I return to Gainesville. I can't afford to get tied up with the local police today. I have too many things to do at home. I'm leaving first thing in the morning."

"Please be careful, Lorelei. Now you see why Eduardo was so reluctant to talk about what he learned."

"Come to think of it, shouldn't I call Eduardo and tell him what happened to me? He could be in danger too."

"No, no," she said. "I'll tell him tomorrow. He's worried enough right now."

"Okay, Louisa," I said. "You better watch out, too. You know as much as I do."

"Don't worry. Just get some rest. You've had a terrible ordeal. I'm so sorry," she said, softly with feeling.

I hung up, still baffled by how it had all taken place. Then it hit me, as it must also have occurred to Louisa who was too loyal to express it: the informer was Eduardo's sister. He said he had lunch with her, told her about my being in Orlando, and that he was going to meet me. He also said she was against it. So, she must have passed the information on to the family, and they in turn told Jimmy Valdez.

I hung up, feeling less alone, but emotionally drained. I desperately needed to sleep. I started leaving the bedroom to return to sleep on the living room couch. Instead, I dropped back onto Jeffrey's bed. Feeling utterly weary, I pulled off my clothes, and crawled under the cool top sheet.

"What the hell," I muttered, briefly picturing Jeffrey and Eduardo cuddled together in the same bed.

The clock displayed 3:07 when I awoke with a start. Was there someone out on Jeffrey's balcony? What woke me? I began to shiver, but I knew I couldn't just hide in bed and wait. My whole body strained to listen for a sound, but there was only the air conditioner cycling on and off. My mouth was dry as I lit the lamp on the night table, got up, and grabbed a shirt out of Jeffrey's closet.

I cautiously moved into the living room, eyeing the balcony drapes as though I expected a man to suddenly jump out at me. I peeked through the drapes, but no one was there. Finally, I turned on all the living room lights, and tried to fall asleep with the quilt over my head. It didn't work.

I got up again, and turned the TV on to the Weather Channel. The placid drone of the commentators, as they described the unpredictable with certainty, was somehow reassuring. I stretched back out on the sofa and began to relax. I must have dozed, because when next I looked, it was light outside. I took a long revitalizing shower, and fortified myself with aspirin and a can of Nestea I found in the refrigerator. I was more than ready to leave.

I dropped Jeffrey's key into a message box attached to the manager's door, and started driving back to Gainesville. I stopped to have breakfast at the Turkey Lake Service Plaza, and two hours later, I exited I-75 at Micanopy.

I pulled into my driveway, and sat in the car with the windows open, absorbing the relaxing warm air and the sound of chirping birds. Thank God, I'm home, I thought. I looked around, and felt a burst of love for my woodsy Micanopy retreat. There was a gentle, almost mystical centering effect I always experienced in this place. I liked to think it was the spirit bequeathed by the early Native American settlers who lived here.

Micanopy is believed to be the second oldest town in Florida, after the coastal city of St. Augustine, which was the first Spanish settlement. Timucuan Indians were early settlers in this inland area. Then it was a Seminole Indian village called Cuscowilla at the time the famous naturalist William Bartram visited in 1774. Later, some referred to it as "Micanope," after the Seminole Indian chief.

As I finally dragged myself out of the car, I felt badly in need of a massage, a sauna, and a nap. Yet, I knew that once I entered the house there would be phone calls to make, and I wondered how to describe my experience in Orlando in such a way that would honor my pledge to Eduardo, and insure my own safety.

Maynard must have been waiting at the door when he heard the car pull up. As I opened the front door, he started meowing, walking toward the kitchen, and looking back to make sure I was following him. The answering machine was blinking, but I ignored it, and checked to make sure there was food left in the cat's bowl.

I carried him upstairs, dropped him on the bed, and resisted the urge to crawl in alongside him. Instead, I did some restorative Yoga postures and Shavasana—the totally limp position known as the "corpse"—and I fell sound asleep on the floor of my bedroom.

By noon, I felt revived and able to begin making phone calls. The first call was to my hair salon for an appointment to get my hair dyed before Friday night's rehearsal. Next, I called Delcie to ask her about reporting the incident in Winter Park. Thankfully, it wasn't voice mail, but Delcie who answered her phone. I told her what had happened to me.

"You have to report it, Lorelei. It's a criminal act. I'm not sure about Winter Park and whose jurisdiction it's in, but you'd be safe to call the Orlando police. You have the detective's name I gave you."

"Yes, but I can't give them any real details about the guys," I said. "Except for the bozo who sat on me in the backseat."

"Think about it, Lor, what if they pull the same stunt on the other woman?"

"Louisa?"

"Yeah. And what if they do more than just threaten her?"

"Oh, they wouldn't harm Louisa." I was thinking about the fact that she was best friends with a Valdez family member.

"You don't know what they'd do, Lor. When people get desperate to hide something, they can even commit murder."

"Okay, okay. You made your point. I'll call, what's her name again? I've got it written on the card you gave me." I reached down to the floor for my handbag and emptied it out on the bed next to me. I found the card.

"Syd. Detective Sydney Black," she said while I was looking at the card, "Tell her every detail, you hear? And by the way, what the hell did you poke your pretty nose into, Ms. Jessica Fletcher?" I laughed at her allusion to the old TV show, *Murder She Wrote*.

"I'm afraid I can't tell you, at least not yet. I was sworn to secrecy."

"Well, given what you've been through, it's best not to go blabbing what you know. But, Lorelei, if it's wearing that much trouble, maybe you need to tell a law enforcement officer. We can protect you, you know."

"I guess I could give you a general idea about it. It has to do with Crawford Keezer and Chelsea Sparks."

"THE Chelsea Sparks?"

"Yes, and maybe the commissioner as well."

"Mercy girl, you really have stepped into it, haven't you?"

"What I learned has to do with the embezzlement of a lot of money. The problem is I can't go public with it because my source swore me to secrecy."

"Ah huh, so that's where the thugs came in. To make sure you didn't break your promise."

"It's more complicated, but you've got the general idea," I said.

"I hope this business doesn't follow you up here. It's all the more reason to be careful. Don't trust anyone, that is, except for me… and Mc Bride. He's got to know"

"I can't tell him much. As I said, I'm sworn to secrecy."

"Talk to McBride. The men who abducted you mean business. Next time they might go after Keezer, or even you again," she added.

Me again? I shuddered at the thought. I didn't want to consider any "next time." I was safe at home. The whole incident was already beginning to seem far away, and not as threatening.

"What have you heard about Jeffrey's case?" I asked, wanting to change the subject. "Has McBride turned up anything yet?"

"I mean it, Lor," she said. "You need to tell McBride what you learned. Even if you can't prove it. It may have bearing on Jeffrey's shooting. Especially since Keezer's name is still on his list."

"But I can't imagine…"

"No matter what, Keezer is up here. The whole mess could follow him. You get it?"

"I guess so. Anyway, what have you heard?"

"About Jeff? They've got a few things so far. They got an ID on the cars parked near the crime scene, and a picture of the guy who made the 911 call."

"No kidding, how'd they get that? Who was it?" I asked.

"He called from a pay phone at a 13th Street gas station that had an outside camera. Hard to tell who he is, but it's something."

"So do they think they know who did it yet?"

"Lorelei, I told you not to expect anything that quick. Sometimes it takes months just to get the blood samples analyzed by FDLE...Florida Department of Law Enforcement."

"You mean, with all the modern technology you guys have, you can't come up with anything faster than that?"

I heard her intake of breath. "This is a tough case: out-of-towner, shot in the woods at night, during the stormy season no less. But your friend Keezer's still in the picture. They matched the shell casing to the type of rifle that Keezer has in his truck, and his alibi is a bit airy."

"Then it really could have been Keezer," I said, less astonished at the thought than I would have been two days ago.

"Hey, I saw a deputy report with your name and Becky's on it," she said. "What in hell were you two doing out at the crime scene?"

"Just hiking."

I heard her laugh in disbelief. "Hiking? C'mon, girlfriend, we don't do hiking. What's the deal? Tell me."

"Okay, we were looking for the guy Jeffrey and I had met up with. Remember, at lunch, you told me we needed to find an eye witness?"

"That's interesting. They also found a recently decapitated buck near the scene."

"A deer?' I said. "What does that have to do with anything?"

"Lots. For one, forensics can connect the time the deer was killed with the estimated time that Jeff was shot. That tells them they probably have a witness, or maybe even the shooter himself."

"Delcie, who would take a deer head and leave the body?"

"Some of those country boys who love to hunt. Bringing out a big rack proves their skill…it's a trophy. Also, it gets them a few thousand dollars from some other dude who wants a wall hanging."

"So you're saying the guy who killed the deer might be a witness or even the one who shot Jeffrey?" I thought about the young man we had met, but couldn't picture him being the one.

"Could be. Anyway, there are still lots of possibilities; it's early in the investigation," she said.

"When Jeffrey comes out of the coma, I'm sure he'll be able to tell them something," I replied.

"Maybe not," she said, softly. "Prepare yourself, Lorelei. With a head wound like his, there could be memory loss, he might not be able to speak for a while, or be disabled in some other way. Then too, he may not *want* to tell what happened."

Jeffrey disabled? I hadn't considered it. And why wouldn't he want to tell what happened to him? The situation was getting more depressing, I thought, as I said goodbye to Delcie. I pushed aside those thoughts, and immediately dialed the number for Detective Black in Orlando.

"This is Sydney Black, leave a message and I'll get back to you."

For once, I was glad to get voice mail. It was a reprieve from recounting my story yet again. I left a message, and my phone number.

Next, I called the office. Becky answered.

"Lorelei, I'm so glad your back."

"How's Jeffrey," I asked. "I finally reached his sister."

"Oh good. Is she coming?"

"Not yet," I said. "She has to wait until Jeffrey's mom gets there. How's he doing?

"Nothing's changed. I call to check on him several times a day. I think they're sick of hearing from me."

"I'm going to go see him later. In the meantime, what's happening at the office? How's the rally coming?"

"Great! We've got lots of volunteers…it's going to be huge. Are you coming in today?"

"I'll swing by there after I stop at the hospital. In about an hour or so. Tell Diana I'm coming in, and ask her to wait there for me. I've got some news that may lift her spirits."

"What?" Becky asked. "Did you find out something juicy about Valdez?"

"Later. Let me get myself together here. I'll see you in a little while."

I hung up the phone, and fell back onto the bed. Maynard was soundly napping. It would be so easy to go to sleep again and forget everything. But, I thought of the famous a line from Robert Frost's poem: *The woods are lovely, dark and deep, but I have promises to keep, and miles to go before I sleep. And miles to go before I sleep.*

Chapter 15

"Mrs. Crane. What a coincidence. I was going to call you." Detective McBride, dressed in a nicely tailored blue suit and tie, was leaning against the desk at the nurse's station as I approached the intensive care unit.

I concealed my surprise at seeing him, and said, "I'm here to see Jeffrey. What did you want?"

"I've just had a talk with Mr. Waterman's doctor," he said. "There's a chance they'll start bringing him out of the coma in a couple of days."

"Thank God," I said. "That's great news."

"As long as you're here, how about spending a few minutes with me before you go in?" he asked, amiably. "There's something I want to talk with you about."

"Really?" I wondered if Delcie had told him about the incident in Orlando, and quickly dismissed the idea.

He took my elbow, and started walking me toward the waiting room. "It won't take long, I only have a couple of questions. I've got to get over to the courthouse for a trial." Ah, I thought, that explained why he was dressed in a suit, but what about this new friendlier attitude?

We sat down in the empty waiting room; he took out his small red notebook, and thumbed through the pages.

"There are a few points to clarify from our conversation last week. Uh, yes, here it is. You said that you didn't know who Mr. Waterman would be meeting that night."

"Yes, and I still don't know," I responded.

"And when I asked you, you said you heard he was dressed like he was going on a date—with a woman. You pointed out that he was wearing cologne which was unusual for him."

Yes. Jeffrey detested men's colognes. He said they were decadent."

McBride smiled. "And the way he was dressed was the reason for thinking he was meeting a woman?"

I was beginning to feel uncomfortable at the direction of McBride's questions. "Yes, that, and other things, as I've told you before," I said, wondering where he was going with these questions.

"What if I told you that the person Mr. Waterman met on the Prairie that night was a man?" McBride watched for my reaction.

I didn't respond. I had already been reconsidering the situation now that I knew about Jeffrey's lifestyle. Could it have been Eduardo he was meeting? Eduardo said that Jeffrey didn't want him up here. Did he come up anyway, and did Jeffrey insist on meeting him where they wouldn't be seen together?

McBride was still studying his notes, when he said, "Mr. Waterman was wearing hiking boots. The other prints we found at the scene were from men's dress shoes. We also have some fibers from Mr. Waterman's clothing that we've sent for analysis. They may further indicate his contact with another man."

"Okay, so what's your point?" I asked, with my easiest acting…a blank stare.

"If it was a man, it narrows the field by half, doesn't it?" McBride said. "And by the way, we've listened to the 9ll call. It was also a man's voice. In fact, we got a cam shot at the phone booth where the call was made."

"Did you identify the caller?"

"Not yet."

"So, how can I help?"

"You've been working with Mr. Waterman since he arrived back in Gainesville," he said. "Can you think of a gentleman he might have had some kind of relationship with? You know the sort I mean."

I responded with a continuation of my blank stare.

He scratched the side of his face for a moment before persisting. "Let me be frank, Mrs. Crane: Mr. Waterman's behavior prior to the meeting, the secrecy you described, the fact that it was another man with him, and the place they met…taken together they point to a probable homosexual tryst. So, who did he meet there?"

"I don't know," I said flatly, returning McBride's scrutinizing look. "I really don't know." I was not going to shed suspicion on Eduardo.

He looked down again at his notebook, remained silent, and finally said, "Mrs. Crane, you don't seem as shocked by what I've suggested as you were when I first interviewed you. Why is that? Is there something more you can tell me?"

I didn't respond.

"According to others I've interviewed, you two spent a lot of time together, and you were once married," he said. "Surely he confided in you about the man or men in his life," McBride insisted.

I shook my head. "No, I have no idea who Jeffrey met or why."

"Hmm," he murmured, looking unconvinced by my response.

"I do have something I wanted to talk with you about," I said. "That is, if you're finished with your questions." I saw him frown, and realized my irritation at his persistent probing was becoming apparent. I didn't mean to deceive him, but I needed time to think it all through. I had to be very careful not to implicate Eduardo, nor violate his confidences.

"Yes, that's all for now," he said with an official's coolness. "What is it you have to tell me, Mrs. Crane?"

"Yesterday, when I was in Orlando, a friend of someone I know told me that Keezer might be involved in a major fraud related to his development activities. It hasn't come out yet, but it will be a big scandal when it does." That was vague, but enough to further suspicion about Keezer."

"Tell me more," McBride said.

"That's it. Right now, it's only a rumor. I'd like to have the details myself," I lied, and momentarily was aware that I was lying a lot lately. "If it were public knowledge, we could use it to discredit him, and maybe stop the Prairie development."

McBride gave me a hard stare, but said nothing. I didn't know if he expected me say more, or if he was considering how to value what I had just told him.

"Another thing," I said. "When I was in Orlando, I was threatened—abducted actually—because I knew about it."

"Abducted? By whom?" he asked, obviously startled.

I told him about the men who had picked me up. Once again, I refrained from implicating Eduardo or Louisa. I said that I was in the process of reporting the incident to the Orlando police, and I gave him the detective's name. He wrote it in his notebook. I omitted mention of Delcie. I wasn't sure he knew about our friendship, and I thought it best to keep it private.

"Why do I have the feeling that you're leaving something out?" he asked. "You do want us to find Mr. Waterman's assailant, don't you?"

"Yes, of course I do," I replied.

"So you heard a rumor about Mr. Keezer, from 'a friend,' and you were warned to keep it quiet. Is that right, Mrs. Crane?"

"Yes, that's right."

"Why were you in Orlando in the first place?" he asked.

"To track down the rumor. Jeffrey was supposed to go down there, but..." I gestured meaningfully toward the doorway to the SICU. "I thought I could get information to discredit the developers."

"But you say you didn't get anything specific."

"Right," I said.

"Did anyone else know that Jeffrey or you were going to Orlando for this purpose?"

"I guess a few of us at the Center. But it was always just about a rumor. Now, of course, the fact that I was threatened says something about the truth of it, don't you think?"

"Maybe, but you haven't given me enough details to be helpful. I'll have to check into it myself." He made a few notes in his notebook, and looked up at me with a stern yet somewhat bemused expression. "Thanks for the lead, Mrs. Crane—and I glad you weren't harmed—but you should really leave the detective work to us."

"I'm only trying to help. Is there anything else? I really want to see Jeffrey now."

"That's all," he said. "But Mrs. Crane, if you do think of anyone that Mr. Waterman might have met that night—someone he's mentioned, an old friend, or anyone you've seen him with—be sure to call me. The same with the so-called rumor about Mr. Keezer."

"I will. I promise." I said, and I started walking toward the intensive care doorway.

"I guess I'll see you at the rally on Saturday?"

"What?" I asked, turning back.

He was standing in the doorway, legs apart, and looking at me with a half grin on his face. He seemed pleased by my surprised reaction. "You know, you may think of me as an adversary, but I'm really on your side. In more ways than one."

"What do you mean?" I asked, warming to this man.

"I once worked as the law enforcement officer, with the Department of Environment Protection, on Prairie detail," he said.

"I didn't know there was a law enforcement officer on the Prairie. I thought there were only park rangers," I said.

"Most folks don't know it, but there's criminal activity out there. Not just crimes like firearms, or animal rustling, but theft of valuable artifacts. Things like that. Anyway, I love the place. I don't want to see it ruined any more than you do."

Well, well, I thought, so much for stereotypes. Nature lovers show up in all kinds of occupations and uniforms.

"I'd like to hear more about that," I said. "Maybe you can tell me some of your stories when I see you at the rally."

I pushed open the doors to the SICU, and felt a little guilty about lying to McBride. I walked into Jeffrey's cubicle, and found him much as I had last seen him. He was inert except for the slight rise and fall of his chest, and still connected to numerous machines; like a man in a sci-fi movie.

I sat down near him, and whispered close to his ear, "Jeffrey, who did you meet that night on the Prairie? Was it Eduardo? Keezer? Or are there even more secrets that you've kept from me?" He didn't move. I sat back in the chair, closed my eyes, and began a visualization with a fully recovered Jeffrey sitting up on the edge of the bed, smiling happily, and telling me who he met the night he was shot.

"He looks a little better, don't you think?" The nurse's voice broke into my meditation.

I stepped away from the bed as she approached and took Jeffrey's pulse. "I don't know. He still looks like he's embalmed, if you know what I mean," I said, staring at his lifeless tanned face. "By the way, I was finally able to reach his sister. She should be calling."

The nurse replaced the bag on the IV pole and said, "Oh she's already called, and got the doctor's number."

"Good." I watched as she flicked her fingernail on the IV line and checked the monitors around his bed. "When will he be out of the coma?"

She glanced at her watch and said, "It's just Thursday. He's scheduled to be sedated for a full week. I'd say maybe we'll start bringing him out by Monday."

"How does that work? Does he wake up right away or what?"

"Oh, no, the doctor will decrease the drug dosage until he's almost conscious. Then we'll continue to gradually reduce it till he's awake." She moved his hand closer to his body, and surveyed the arrangement of the bedding as though she were simply tidying up in her living room. Walking around to the other side of the bed, she tapped a monitor, and added, "After that, we wean him from the ventilator until he's ready to be extubated."

"Extubated?" I repeated the unfamiliar term, and then understood it to mean removing the tubes. "When can I talk to him?"

"The detective asked that same question," she said. "It'll take anywhere from 24 to 36 hours to get him off the drugs. Then, if he's able to talk..."

"If he's able?" I repeated. Delcie had warned me about this, yet the nurse's words gave me a sense of foreboding. Despite the tube in his mouth and all the equipment surrounding him, Jeffrey looked safe and peaceful. It hadn't occurred to me he wouldn't return whole and alive, like his old self.

"We can't determine much at this point," she said. "He may or may not be able to talk. There could be memory loss, dysarthria..."

"What's that?"

"Difficulty speaking," she explained. "It's one of the possible outcomes. It all depends. The doctor will have to assess the amount of damage to the brain."

"Okay, I get it. You don't really know what he'll be like, do you?" I said, not unkindly. I felt a cold chill, and was eager to leave before I learned anything more.

"Yes, that's right." She gave me an apologetic smile. "Brain injuries are tricky. It will take time to know how much damage has been done."

I nodded, and left the SICU feeling depressed about the problems that awaited Jeffrey's reawakening. Would he ever be the same, I wondered. Denial had always served me well, and I brushed aside my feeling of sadness. I replaced it with a renewed determination to pursue whoever did this terrible damage. I've played revengeful characters on the stage, but now I was getting a deeper taste of this bitter emotion.

I drove to the office, and when I stepped through the front door the sounds of laughter, shouted questions, and loud banter assailed me along with the blast of frigid air. It lightened my spirit to see the room filled people of all ages, who were enthusiastically engaged in preparing for the rally. About thirty volunteers were making posters and signs, and bundling flyers. The desks were occupied by those who were making phone calls and trying to be heard over the din.

The door to Diana's office was closed. I knocked, and opened it a crack. She was sitting behind her desk looking out the window.

"Can I come in?" I asked.

She turned and looked at me blankly for a moment before responding, "Oh yes, of course, Lorelei." She rose from her desk and came over to greet me with a hug. "I'm so glad to see you, please sit down. How was your trip to Orlando?"

"Interesting," I said, noting how pale she looked.

"Just interesting?" she replied. "Were you able to get any information that we can use against the Valdez company?"

I heeded Delcie's warning to be careful, and gave Diana an abbreviated version of my Orlando trip. There was no point in getting hopes raised if I was not yet able to verify and use the information about Keezer. I omitted the abduction incident entirely. She had enough going on without worrying about my safety.

"So you weren't able to get anything definite that we can use at the rally or in our law suit? Too bad." She rose and stood staring out of the window.

"Law suit?" No one had mentioned it to me.

"Oh, I'm sorry, of course you don't know about it," she said, returning to her desk. She looked preoccupied. "The coalition agreed to join with the Nature Conservancy in suing the county over allowing the development permit to stand in violation of the current land use plan."

"But that could take a long time," I said. "The land could be cleared and building started before..."

"That's right, but we're hoping either to get an injunction, or that the threat alone might act as a deterrent. Anyway, we're trying to stall them. It's our strategy of last resort."

The door to Diana's office opened and Becky told her boss that she was needed in the main room.

I sat there feeling frustrated by not being able to tell Diana all I had learned about Valdez. It was the one thing that could probably blow them out of the water immediately if it were known. Their financing would be impaired, and the scandal might motivate the commissioners to find a way to invalidate their permit without a lengthy law suit. I knew I had to find a way to expose the Keezer-Sparks connection without implicating Eduardo. I hoped when Bill came home we could brainstorm a solution using his business connections.

Diana returned, looked at her watch, and took her handbag out of her desk drawer.

"Sorry, Lorelei, but I've got to pick up Hank." She started toward the door.

I followed her, and asked, "How is Hank?"

She stopped at the doorway. "Hank's fine. We got through the teen court relatively unscathed."

"But you thought he was in some other trouble. Didn't you tell me Detective McBride was going to come to your house?"

"He did come. It turned out he thought Hank had some information about a guy they're investigating. It's someone who hangs out at the garage where my son sometimes works after school. They go hunting together." She hugged me, now I've really got to leave."

She left the office. I stood there puzzling over this new piece of information. Could Hank's friend be the night guard for the Valdez site? No, that's too much of a coincidence. Lorelei, you're beginning to see suspects behind every tree. I'll ask McBride about it when I see him at the rally.

"Chester called you," said Becky. "He called a few times while you were gone, but today he said it was urgent and you should call him right back."

"Okay," I said, shut the office door to dim the noise, and sat at Diana's desk to make the call. Chester picked up the phone.

"Lorelei, where have you been, for God's sakes? I've been trying to get you for days."

"It's just been two days, Chester, calm down."

"Well, the costume fitting and the publicity shoot are today. You've got to be over here at three."

"Okay, don't worry. I'll be there." I hung up the phone, and started to leave the office.

Becky stopped me. "You still haven't told me what happened in Orlando. What about it, Lor. Are you going to tell me or not?"

"I'm afraid there's not much to tell at this point. I did get some information about Valdez, but until I can verify it, it can't be used."

"Can't you give me just a hint? Is the IRS after them, or what?"

I laughed, and knew that Becky wouldn't be satisfied until I gave her some inside information.

"Okay, there's nothing to tell about Valdez right now, but I did run into Detective McBride at the hospital this morning."

"Oh him," she said with a look of distaste.

"He said they're certain that Jeffrey was meeting a man that night on the Prairie. And they seem to have some promising evidence about a potential witness."

"A man? Why would Jeff have been meeting a man out there?" she asked.

"Why, indeed, Becky. You know everyone who hangs out on the Prairie. Think about it."

I had my hand on the door knob, ready to walk out, when she rushed up to me, and grabbed my arm. In a hoarse whispered voice, she said, "Give me a break! Don't tell me those a-holes think Jeff was having some gay thing going on?"

"Don't know, but I've got a hair appointment. I'll talk to you tomorrow." I opened the door and fled before she could bombard me with protestations about Jeffrey's sexual orientation, and more questions about what I had learned in Orlando.

Chapter 16

At almost every stop light on my way home, I pulled down the vanity mirror to look at my new hair color. The lustrous black highlighted my hazel eyes, and gave me a sultry look that might appeal to Bill. If he protested I'd slap on my best Lauren Bacall voice, in southern drawl, and say, "But darlin', I kinda thought you might be turned on by my new, ever so sexy do." On the other hand, I thought, Jeffrey would object since he always loved my red hair. Finally, at one light, I tried pulling my hair back to see how it will look when I fix it for my role as Varya—I concluded the more severe style suited her chaste character.

At home, I did a quick change of clothes, microwaved a frozen dinner, and took it and a glass of Merlot out onto the patio. Maynard joined me, and sat in my lap, purring up a storm.

I sipped the wine, watching the light fade in the woods, and listening to the sounds of night fall. A dog barked in the distance, a nighthawk croaked its evening song, and a neighbor called her children into the house. Their arrival was punctuated by the slapping sound of a screen door. The air was redolent with a thick earthy aroma emanating from the rain soaked woods behind the house. My experience in the sinkhole gave me a new awareness of rich earthy smells.

Fatigue, hastened by the wine and dimming daylight, set my thoughts adrift. Pictures of Jeffrey floated across my consciousness: the motionless figure I had been visiting in the hospital, the energetic man who reappeared in my life with such audacity that morning at the Center office—I could almost feel the electricity generated by his familiar charm as he tried to get me to go out with him for lunch. The picture shifted to the impulsive hot-head who taunted Keezer to the point of danger that day on the Prairie, and the Jeffrey, remorseful and tender, who opened his heart to me on Sunday evening at Charley's.

My dreamy state was shattered, recalling the image of the man who was tense and secretive about his relationships. The Jeffrey who surprised me the most—the one who had secrets.

"Secrets!" I said, startled by the thought of a new connection. I lifted Maynard from my lap to the floor, and I stood up...suddenly alert. Was that it?

I started pacing, as I recalled the commission meeting where Jeffrey and Commissioner Judson Sparks had such a puzzling reaction to one another.

Maynard left the patio, startled by my sudden activity.

Incredible, I thought. Could it have been Sparks that Jeffrey met on the Prairie that night? What did those two have in common? Despite Jeffrey's denials, it was apparent that they knew each other.

I considered the possibilities aloud, walking from one end of the patio to the other, as if I were presenting facts before a jury:

"Did Jeffrey have business dealings with Sparks in Orlando?"

"Yes, Sparks had real estate interests all over the State. Maybe he hired Jeffrey as a consultant."

"But," I said, countering my own argument, "if it was just business, why would they both be so secretive and nervous?"

I paused, and stood staring into the dark night as another idea surfaced: it seemed a bit more far fetched.

"Could Jeffrey and Sparks? An affair?" It would have to have been in Orlando, I thought. And where did Eduardo fit into all of this? A public figure like Sparks would never chance a homosexual encounter on his home turf.

"Or would he? Sparks wouldn't be the first man, or woman for all that, to risk everything because of a passion."

"Bingo. That must be it. If it wasn't Eduardo who came to town, it was Sparks who Jeffrey met on the Prairie that night."

I was excited at the possibility that I had finally solved the puzzle about Jeffrey and Sparks.

I left the patio, and walked back into the kitchen to refill my wine glass.

"That must be it," I said still presenting my case. "Jeffrey met the commissioner to talk him out of his support for Valdez. He had hinted about the importance of the meeting to Becky. Yes, the pieces fit, and it feels right."

Next, I thought about Sparks. It must have been he who made the 911 call.

"He must have realized his whole political life could be blown up in a flash!"

I felt a wave of sympathy for the nervous commissioner, and imagined his sheer panic when Jeffrey was shot.

The doorbell rang, and startled me out of my speculations. I opened the front door, and was surprised to see my friend, Delcie.

"Lorelei, do you realize you just opened the door without checking to see who was there?" she scolded as she walked in, stopped, and looked closely at my hair.

"Do you like it?" I asked.

"I do. Looks a lot better than that Dracula wig you wore last week."

"I'm so glad to see you, Del. Come out back to the patio. Would you like a glass of wine?"

"Nope, I'm on duty—can't drink," she said. "I was in the neighborhood, and just came by to check up on you. And I'm glad I did. You really have to be more careful about who you let into your house."

"I do?" I said, surprised at Delcie's sudden concern about my home security.

"You bet you do. Don't just go opening the door like that again. In fact, I'll feel a lot better when Bill gets home, and you're not out here by yourself."

"Delcie, honey, you don't need to worry about me. But it is sweet of you to be concerned."

As I led the way through the kitchen, she looked at the plastic tray that had held the remains of my frozen dinner, and shook her head in disapproval.

"Your mama would have a fit if she caught you eating like that."

"It's the only way I can keep my weight down," I said opening the French doors. I flipped on the patio lights and fan, and she followed me out. She quickly glanced around, neatly folded her jacket on the back of a chair, and sat down.

"Did you call Detective Black?"

"I left a message on her phone mail," I said, and remained standing. I was too excited to sit down.

"How about McBride?"

"I ran into him at the hospital this morning, and filled him in, as you suggested."

"Good," she said.

"Can't I get you some water, a soda—something?" I asked.

"No thanks, I just finished dinner in town. You know they're following up on the guy who was out on the Prairie when you and Becky went hiking—more like trolling, I'd say." She flashed me a look of mock reproof.

I stood at the table, grasping the back of a chair, and wondered if I should share my theories with Delcie. As a sheriff's deputy, it could be an awkward situation for her to hear what I had concluded.

"What are you so jumpy about, Lorelei?" she said, studying me.

I sat down. "Oh nothing. Have they talked with him? Did he admit anything?"

"Not yet," she said. "But there's a pretty good chance that he may be the same guy who shot the deer. That places him at the scene when Jeff was shot."

"I thought so. Can they prove it?"

"Before they interview him, they want to talk with some acquaintances of his. Then, if they can positively link him with the deer head, he might start to open up."

"Good," I said, and remembered that Diana's son was one of the boys McBride had already talked to.

I felt so agitated, I was sipping my wine too fast, and I began to feel dizzy. Slow down, Lorelei, I thought. Your mind is going in twenty different directions. Delcie was staring at me with a look of curiosity. Like she was waiting for me to tell her something unusual.

"Now just don't go talking about any of this if you see McBride," she said. "We're not supposed to be giving out information about an ongoing investigation, you know."

"Don't worry, Delcie. I haven't even told McBride that I know you."

"Let's keep it that way. What else's on your mind? I know there's something."

Okay, I decided. I'm going to talk to her about the Jeffrey and Sparks connection. I needed a sounding board. I stood up again, walked around the table to where she was sitting, and said, "Delcie, can you take off your cop hat, and just hear me out for a minute? Off the record?"

She looked at me with the same curious expression she gave me a few minutes ago, and replied, "Yeah, I guess so. As long as you don't tell me you've committed a crime," she said with a quick smile.

"Okay. Look, I have a hunch about something." I started pacing the room again. "But before I tell anyone else about it, I need you to tell me if I'm way off base."

"What's your hunch?"

"I told you that Jeffrey has a gay lover in Orlando."

"Yeah, that was a shocker."

"Well, I'm beginning to think he also had a relationship with someone here in Gainesville—someone he was meeting the night he was shot."

"And I'm sure, Ms. Marple here has an idea just who that someone was."

I stopped pacing and turned to face her. "Bingo! How about commissioner Judson Sparks," I said flatly, and waited to see her reaction.

"You got to be kidding," Delcie said, sitting straight up in the chair, and letting out a low whistle. "Commissioner Sparks and Waterman? How'd you come to that wild conclusion?"

"I'm not kidding," I continued, and plopped down in my chair. I took a slow slip of wine to let her digest the shock, and continued, "Jeffrey and Sparks had a very bizarre response to one another at the commission meeting. The way it all happened makes sense to me now."

"Holy Lord Jesus. Sparks? Wait'll McBride hears that one."

Now, Delcie was the one who stood up. "I think I will help myself to a soda," she said, walking into the kitchen.

As she came back to the patio with a can of soda, she stopped to examine the French doors, and operated the sliding bolt lock a couple of times.

I resumed my scenario as she returned to her chair. "If my hunch is correct about the two of them, and I think it is, what I've been trying to figure out is who else knew about it?"

"I see where you're going with this," Delcie said, and leaned back, looking away for a moment as she considered my suggestion. "You're thinking the shooter was someone who found out about their relationship, and didn't much like it?"

"Yes, enough to take a shot at one of them."

"You're getting to be pretty good at this detecting business," she said, with an amused look. "I suppose you have an idea about the shooter, too?"

"Well, my first thought was Eduardo. That's the guy Jeffrey's involved with in Orlando. He didn't want Jeffrey to come up here in the first place, and I think he's intensely jealous."

Delcie leaned forward, and I could tell her mind was beginning to it work over. She was hooked. "So he comes up to Gainesville, finds out about Sparks, follows them to the Prairie, and takes a shot at his boyfriend?"

"What do you think?"

"I don't know, Lor," Delcie said. "It wouldn't be the first time a jealous lover whacked his cheatin' partner—or the one he's cheating with."

"Yeah, but I'm still not sure about it," I said. "For one thing, I can't imagine Eduardo shooting anyone. Although I suppose it's possible he could have meant to scare them, and missed."

"I'd sooner bet on the commissioner's wife," Delcie said. "Didn't you tell me she was involved with Keezer in the money scam?"

"Of course! I didn't think about that angle."

I had completely forgotten about Chelsea Sparks and her role in the embezzlement of Valdez funds.

"Maybe she wants to get rid of her husband," Delcie said. "The Prairie would be an ideal place to do it. No witnesses, easy to hide, and have evidence messed up; what with all the rain."

She stood up, and walked over to Maynard who had returned to the patio. She gave him a pat on the head, and looked out the patio screen door.

"I'm not sure she would have missed though," I said. "You know Chelsea Sparks is part owner of an Army and Navy surplus store. She has to know something about guns, doesn't she?"

"True enough," Delcie said, continuing her survey of the area around the patio.

"Don't you have some motion lights for out here?" she asked.

"No, they'd be going on all the time with all the critters around," I replied, beginning to feel annoyed by her preoccupation with my patio. I wanted her full attention on the subject at hand.

She bent down and poked at a corner of the screen near the handle to the outside patio door.

"How long has this screen been torn?"

"Delcie, now stop it!" I said, "You're beginning to make me feel paranoid with all this security snooping."

She made a gesture of surrender, and returned to her chair.

"I really need you to hear me out," I said. "What if Chelsea Sparks just wanted to scare her husband and it truly was by accident that she hit Jeffrey?"

"Well, I'll tell you one thing I do know," Delcie said, putting her hands down flat on the table. Her college ring made a sharp clang when it hit the glass top. "Where there's murder involved, the spouse is always a good first suspect."

"That's what McBride said." I began to mull over this new thought. Could it have been Chelsea Sparks who shot Jeffrey? The woman's name kept coming up in the most surprising ways. I looked up to see Delcie staring at me.

Soda in hand, she pointed at my head, and said, "You know, the more I look at you, the more I think black hair suits you. I never would have guessed it."

"Me neither. Actually, you're the first person who's seen it since I left the shop. I'm kind of taken with it myself."

We sat in a thoughtful silence for a few moments. The hum of the katydids filled the night air. I felt it was providential that Delcie stopped by, and helped me to air my thoughts about Jeffrey's shooting.

"Okay, let's work on a motive for the commissioner's wife," she said, raising her hand to tick off each motive on her fingers: "First, there's the money thing; second, she has another lover and wants out of the marriage; third, she's pissed about her husband's sexual preference. It could create a scandal, she'd be publicly humiliated, and since she has some lucrative contracts with local law enforcement, her business could be at risk." She clapped her hands together. "That's a bunch of motives, I'd say."

"And a good case for at least wanting to scare him," I said. "All things considered, I'm going to have to talk to McBride."

"Be prepared. He's not going to like it one bit," Delcie replied. "What you're talking about is a political nightmare. Investigating a county commissioner? Oh, no. Don't expect him to thank you for that one, Lor."

"Well, I'll think it over a bit more before I tell him."

"Don't wait too long," she warned. "I think you're on to something, and he'll need to know about it."

"I'll talk it over with Bill when he gets home tomorrow night. The rally is Saturday. If I talked to McBride now, he might think I was just trying making more trouble for Valdez. Sparks is one of their big supporters on the commission."

"Like I said, don't wait too long to talk to McBride."

"I won't. Thanks Del, it's really been helpful to talk with you."

She got up, put on her jacket, and we started walking to the front door. I picked up my wine glass, and dropped it off at the kitchen sink.

We stood at the door, and she stared at me.

"What?" I said.

"Just wondering, you think you're gonna keep the hair color after the play? You're making me think about doing something with my own." She ran her slender hand across the side of smoothly plaited black hair.

"But I love your hair!" I protested.

She shrugged, gave me a quick embrace, and stepped out the front door.

"At least you got some good lighting out here," she said, looking around at the front of the house. A floodlight, on a tall pole, cast a bright glow around the entire parking area. I didn't tell her we turned off the light at night to keep the darkness around the Prairie.

She turned, and gave me a serious look. "Lorelei, old friend, I know how you Micanopy folk like to think you're living in the country—old-time friendly and all—but I want you to lock all your doors and windows, and call 911 if you hear anything. Anything at all, you got me? You're sittin' on information that a few folks probably wish you didn't have. You've locked in on the big ones: money, sex, and reputation; they're some powerful motives for murder."

"Yes, Deputy Wright," I said, in a playfully mocking voice. "I promise. I'll be careful."

I stood at the door, waving to her as she backed her car down the driveway. I locked the front door, returned to the kitchen, and plopped down on a chair. I had a lot to think about, and my head was spinning with the scenarios we had discussed.

We didn't even talk about Keezer as a suspect, only Eduardo and Chelsea Sparks, not to mention the young security guy. But I couldn't think of any motive for him to shoot Jeffrey, though he was certainly important as a witness to the shooting. I was relieved to learn that the police were going to question him.

I folded my arms on the table, and rested my forehead on them. It was all too much; I had to let my brain relax for awhile. I wanted to get back to *The Cherry Orchard* where life was complex, but less personally urgent. A picture kept floating across my mind: it was Jeffrey, lying frozen in the white cubicle. Jeffrey who, because of a malevolent accident or intention, might never be the same again.

I got up and turned out the downstairs lights. I called for Maynard, but he didn't respond. He sometimes went for an evening outing through the patio cat door. I left one of the French doors slightly ajar so he could reenter the house, and headed up to my bedroom to prepare for tomorrow's rehearsal.

There was thunder in the distance as I climbed the stairs to what I thought of as my tree-top retreat. I stood at the glass doors leading to the deck. The sight of hundreds of lightening bugs filled the woods as though the stars had fallen among the trees. It took my breath away.

As I started to go out onto the deck, there was a crashing noise from downstairs. I stood stock-still. Goosebumps rose on my arms. What the hell was that? I held my breath to listen. Was it a door slamming? No, it was the sound of glass breaking.

I was not going to just cower in fear waiting for someone to show up at the top of the stairs. That would be too scary. My heart was racing as I grabbed Bill's golf putting iron from the closet, and headed back downstairs.

"Is that you, Maynard? Did you knock something down?" I shouted, as I descended, turning lights on as I went.

A loud meowing came from the kitchen. My hand froze as I reached for the light switch. I thought I heard the click of the patio door closing. "Who's there?" I called breathlessly, afraid of an answer. I nervously surveyed the dark room, and peaked out on to the moonlit patio. I couldn't see anyone.

Turning back to face the kitchen, I flipped on the light and saw a red stain on the tile floor where my wine glass lay shattered next to the unbroken wine bottle. Maynard sat nearby, looking up at me with kitty innocent eyes.

Did Maynard come back in through the patio? Was it the wind or he who pushed the French door shut as I came into the kitchen? I'd heard of cats pushing doors closed, but didn't recall Maynard ever doing it. I cleaned up the wine, locked the patio door and left the lights on. I headed back upstairs with Maynard under my arm. I was trembling and still unnerved as I locked the stairwell door to the bedroom. Before getting into bed for the night, I took a sleeping pill hoping to get some rest for the weekend's rehearsals and the rally.

Chapter 17

I slept fitfully, and awakened often to listen for sounds from below. In the morning—while brewing my tea—I looked around downstairs, and finally decided no one had entered the house last night. It was most likely that the violence and intrigue of the past week were beginning to stir my imagination in a dark direction.

Delcie's cautions about security began to sink in...along with a sense of dread. Of course, she was right; I had been mugged once because of what I knew. The same thing could happen again, or worse.

The phone rang.

"Lorelei, did you see the news last night?"

It was Diana.

"No, I didn't watch TV," I replied.

I got up, leaned on the balcony railing, and studied the woods. Shafts of light, like spotlights on the stage, penetrated the shrubs, and illuminated the forest floor. The morning air was still cool, and there was a musky earthy aroma.

They did a segment on the rally," Diana said. "Wiley was interviewed. He was very impressive."

"Great," I said, and I inhaled the light breeze before returning to sit on the chaise.

"They also mentioned the break-in at the Sierra Club."

"What did they say?"

"Apparently the police still think it was vandalism by neighborhood kids."

"What does Mike Smith say about it?" I remembered that Mike took over as head of the Sierra Club after Dalton died.

"Mike and I both think it was more than a coincidence," she said. "Anyway, I just wanted to thank you for the work you did to get us all the media coverage. Everyone in the county should know about the rally by Saturday."

"Good. And how are you doing, Diana—with Hank, and with Dalton's death?"

"Oh, I'm getting along. Thanks for asking. So I won't see you until the rally tomorrow."

"Yes, I'll be there."

After we hung up, I went into the bathroom, and looked at myself in the mirror. My face looked pale and drawn from too little sleep and too much tension.

I might not need much makeup to play the severe looking Varya, I thought, as I turned my head at different angles. I pulled my hair back from my face, and studied it as I assumed a variety of facial expressions. Like most of Chekhov's characters, Varya was filled with complex and volatile emotions.

I left the bathroom, returned to the deck, and resumed my work on the script. I was at the part where the family is about to disperse. The estate, along with its cherry orchard, has been sold at auction to the businessman, Lopahin. Varya's stepmother urges him to make the expected marriage proposal to her daughter.

I put the script down in my lap, and tried to imagine all the things that Varya would be feeling when she enters the room and sees Lopahin for what may be the last time. She is absent-minded, and distant with him. When Lopahin leaves, not having proposed, Varya collapses in tears, but moments later—in a swift resolution of feelings—is ready to join the family.

Finally, I felt I had connected with her. There have been times when I've felt dizzily fragmented, and almost paralyzed by the pressure of change. Times when it was easier just to let things happen, and accept the decision of fate. In a way, it was how I wound up marrying Bill, and abandoning my dream to become a Broadway actress.

As for Chekhov, I now understood the greatest challenge in playing his characters was that they move from one emotion to another with lightening speed. I was eager to get to the theater, and see Renee's concept of Varya's motivation.

I arrived on time for the cast call. Renee was pleased with my new hair color. She said it was "very Varya." She ran us through a couple of scenes: positioning us, and directing the use of actions and props. This blocking and getting the beat of the scene always provided a kinesthetic connection to the script that helped me memorize my lines and cues. It was my first real step into the world of the play.

When Chester called a break, I rushed out to the lobby to phone Bill. It was after five, and I knew he would have arrived home from San Francisco.

He answered the phone after several rings, and said, "Lorelei, it's you. I didn't want to call the theater. I know how you hate that, but I'm eager to see you."

"Me too, Bill," I replied.

"God, I hate coming home to an empty house. Even Maynard is out somewhere. Can you get away during your dinner break?"

"I don't know, it's only twenty minutes," I said, glancing over my shoulder at another actor who was waiting to use the phone.

"Try to stretch it, will you? I really need to see you."

His voice had an unfamiliar pleading quality.

"Okay, I'll persuade Chester to let me cut out for a half an hour. And Bill, bring something to eat, will you?"

"I'll pick up some sandwiches, and meet you in the parking lot. Say 20 minutes?"

"That's good," I said, and added, "Oh Bill, just so you won't be too shocked, I've had my hair dyed black for the play."

"Sounds intriguing," he said, and hung up.

I sat in my car for only a few minutes before Bill pulled up alongside me, and got into the front seat. He leaned over, and gave me a long, arduous kiss.

"Wow!" I exclaimed. "You really were eager to see me."

He leaned back, and inspected me. "I've missed you."

So, what'd you think?" I asked, flipping up the back of my hair. "Do you like it?"

He continued to study my face before responding, "Yes, I think I do. It's different, but sexy, in a way."

We embraced again until the tantalizing aroma from the bag of food he brought got to me. I broke away.

"Food. I need food," I said with in a mock Russian accent.

He handed me a sandwich, and draped a paper napkin across my lap. "Al fresco, Madame."

I laughed. "It's so good to see you. It feels like you've been gone for months. I can't believe it's only been a week."

I took a large bite out of a tender and juicy brisket sandwich. It tasted so delicious I didn't want to speak until I finished it.

Bill just sat looking at me while I ate. "I want to hear everything," he said, and touched my hair. "On second thought, I'm not really sure I like the change all that much."

"It's just temporary," I mumbled with a mouthful of food. "Aren't you eating?"

"No, I'll take it home. Anyway, I was worried about you...what with Dalton, and then Jeffrey."

I finished a couple of more bites, and took a sip from the bottled water he placed in the console.

"Oh, darling, you don't know the half of it," I said. "I've got some fascinating stuff to tell you. But it's too involved to go into now. Tell me about your trip."

He wiped his hands across his face in a gesture of weariness, and said, "Well, I'll give you the short version: I listened to a lot of dull papers, one brilliant presentation, and had some decent dinners with old friends."

"That's it?" I asked, stuffing my sandwich wrappings back into the bag. The aroma of beef and dill pickles permeated the car.

"Oh, I did run into some of my former students; all doing quite nicely."

Bill's tone was flat, he was slumped in the seat, and he kept twisting his wedding band.

I took his hand, and watched him closely as I asked, "So what really went on?"

"I don't know," he shrugged, withdrew his hand from mine, and stared out the windshield. "Maybe I'm getting too old to go to these things anymore."

"Bill?" I said, touching his arm. "You sounded so urgent when you called. What's it all about?"

He turned to me with a remorseful look.

"I don't want to talk about it right now. There isn't enough time, is there?" he said. "I just wanted to be sure you were all right. That's all." He looked away and stared out the car window.

A glance at the car clock told me he was right about there being too little time. "Speaking of colleagues and former students, there's something I need your help with."

"What?" he asked, startled out of his reverie.

"Do you know anyone at the Regional Bank in Orlando?"

"Central Regional?" His eyebrows shot up, and he looked at me quizzically. "Why?"

"I'll tell you why later, but do you know anyone connected with them?"

He took a few moments to consider my question, and then replied, "As a matter of fact, I do. Cody. Cody Robertson's a former grad student of mine who works there. Last I heard, he was made VP."

"Really? That's excellent, darling." I looked at the clock on the dashboard and saw that my break time was up. "I'll talk to you about it later."

"Dammit, Lorelei," he said. "You do love to be mysterious, don't you?"

"Isn't that part of my charm?"

He looked at my hair again, and said, "Hell, I can't even depend on recognizing you after I've been gone for a week."

He bent over, and kissed me hard. The sandwich bag slid off his lap to the floor.

I pulled back from him, and took a deep breath.

"Wow, again," I said. "Let's pick this up later."

I wondered what was making him so impulsively amorous, and so moody.

"Later. Always later," he said, with a sullen quality in his voice.

"Hey, not fair," I said, frowning, and confused again by his sudden change of tone.

Finally, he gave me a tight smile, and bent down to scoop up the mess on the floor. "Okay, go back to your play." He opened the door and abruptly left the car.

I turned back to look at him before I entered the theater. He stood watching me—looking distracted, a little sad—and he didn't return my wave. I realized that Bill and I had just had an encounter similar to Varya and Lopahin's, both immersed in their own preoccupations, and failing to connect except superficially. How Chekhovian, I thought.

Rehearsals hadn't ended until after ten, and I hoped Bill was still awake. I called his name as I climbed the stairs to our bedroom. The room was in semi-darkness; an angled beam of light from the bathroom lay across the foot of the bed. He was apparently asleep, and despite the fact that I was eager to talk, I decided not to wake him. I was dead tired, and eager to simply crawl in next to him.

Suddenly the light on Bill's night stand clicked on, and he pulled himself up against the headboard, rubbing his eyes.

"Lorelei? Sorry, darling. I was reading, and just couldn't stay awake. I knew I'd hear you when you came in. How was rehearsal?"

"Everything went well," I said, taking off my blouse and slacks, and dropping them on a chair as I walked into the bathroom. "Can you stay awake a little longer so we can talk? I'm sorry I had to run off on you like that, but Chester is very strict about being on time. It's a union thing." I was proud of being an Equity actor although sometimes thought it more trouble than it was worth.

"Sure," Bill said. "Maynard finally showed up. I don't know where the hell he was, but as soon as I started to fix myself some dinner, he appeared."

"Oh, yes, that's our boy. Always ready for the food bowl."

I pulled my nightgown over my head, shut off the bathroom light, and sat down on Bill's side of the bed. He moved over to make room for me, and took my hand and kissed it.

"Now tell me, what's been happening here?" he asked. "And what's the business with the bank in Orlando?"

"Well, I guess it's safe to tell you now. I didn't want you to worry until I could really explain everything."

I leaned down to give him a quick kiss, detected the faint scent of a fruity shower gel, and impulsively pulled his arm around me, and cuddled against his chest.

He held me for a moment, and then gently pushed me away from him.

"Why would I be worried? Lorelei?" His tone held a reprimand as if he expected to hear something unpleasant.

"I've gotten into a situation that's become a bit dangerous because Jeffrey..."

"Dangerous because of Jeffrey?" Bill said. "I thought he was in a coma in the hospital."

"I meant I went to Orlando, because of Jeffrey. Oh, and he's going to be out of the coma on Monday. Anyway, I think I told you on the phone that I had to verify a rumor he'd heard about Valdez."

"Yes, and what happened?"

"It appears the scandal is bigger then any of us thought. Keezer's skimming money from a bank construction loan."

I got up, gathered my clothes from the chair, and carried them to the closet.

"Keezer?" he repeated.

"You know, Crawford Keezer, the front man for the Valdez Company on the Prairie development."

"How'd you find out about all of this?"

"That's a long story," I said as I returned to the bed. "The problem is that my source insisted that he remain anonymous. So obviously I can't use the information to our advantage. It wouldn't be credible without a source. Also, there's the danger..."

"Danger? You used that word before." Bill sat up straighter, threw his legs over the side of the bed, and a look of alarm crossed his face. "Lorelei, what in hell have you gotten yourself into? You'd better tell me everything."

I told him about meeting and my informant in Orlando. I gave him a whitewashed account of my subsequent abduction, Delcie's warning to remain quiet about what I learned, and the interactions I had with Detective McBride. I didn't tell him about the previous night's incident with the broken glass and door. By the time I had finished, Bill was up and pacing the room.

"Now, I'm glad I came home when I did," he said, stopping to place his hands on my shoulders. "This has to be resolved, and let the police deal with it."

"Forget the police. It's too early to tell them. It's your help I need."

"My help? But how?"

"You said you had a former student who's an officer at the very same bank that made the loan to Valdez."

He stared at me for a moment, and returned to sit on the edge of the bed. I sat down next to him.

"So that's where the bank comes in?" he asked. "You want me to get my former student, Cody Robertson, to look into this thing for you?"

"Right. Keezer must be guilty of bank fraud or embezzlement or something like that. And the sooner they prove it..."

Bill quickly grasped my plan, but the look on his face was both skeptical and disapproving. "So you hope the bank will make it public, Valdez will be discredited, and somehow decide to abandon their Gainesville project."

"Exactly," I replied. "With any luck it will happen before they do too much damage to the land."

Bill moved to the chair opposite me. He shook his head, as though the idea were preposterous. Finally, he gave me an affectionate smile, and said, "But, my dearest sleuth, have you considered that even if the bank proved there was a Valdez fraud—and that's a big question mark—they may not want it made public? They might even deny it?"

"Why would they?" I asked.

"For the same reason that Valdez obviously wanted to keep it a secret. You say they even threatened you and risked police involvement. Don't you see? It's their reputation, the public trust, and everything that affects their business. Think it through."

"Oh, I didn't see it quite that way," I said in a small voice, feeling deflated and a bit stupid after hearing his logic.

"Look honey, you're really out of your depth here. You're an actress, not a private investigator. And I'm really concerned about you being in the middle of all of this."

"But wait, I just had another thought," I said. "If Keezer's already moved the money off shore—that's what my source thinks he's done—then Valdez will be out a million dollars. That alone may kill their plans here."

"Could be," Bill said. "That's a more likely scenario, especially if they're cash strapped. At any hint of fraud, the bank is likely to call the loan. The company or someone at Valdez will have to come up with the money, and fast."

"That's it, Bill. So will you call your student, and ask him to check it out?"

I watched as he mentally organized the details of the situation. He tilted his head, and his eyes became an almost opaque blue as they always did when he was deep in thought.

"Okay. I'll do it. I suppose the bank could check up on the company that got the loan to see where the money went. If their auditor found cause, they might be able to get a subpoena and go from there. Then again, it might be impossible to trace. I don't know. Accounting isn't my field."

"But you'll do it? You'll call him?"

"Yes, I'll do it. But I can't just go to a bank officer, even if he is a former student of mine, and say 'My wife told me this and that, so you need to check it out.'"

"But my source swore me to secrecy," I protested.

He sat down on the bed. "Nonetheless, I have to have something more specific than what you've told me. Like what is the connection of your source? Is it to the bank or to Keezer?"

"I guess I can tell you that much," I said. "The informant is sort of a Valdez relative. Anyway, he was directly involved in the financial set up so he has first hand knowledge."

"That's a little better," he said. "I'll contact Cody, but only because I want to get you out of this mess as quickly as possible."

"Oh, thank you darling." I gave him a hug. "Have I told you how good it is to have you home again?"

"I'll let you show me." He gave me a leering look, and seeing my reaction, he added, "I know we're both tired, but we can have a date tomorrow night—after your rehearsal. I've gotten rather turned on by the sultry, dark-haired woman in my bed."

I pressed my hand to my heart, looked at him coquettishly, and said, "I am in totally in your power, sir."

We got into bed, Bill reached over for the light, and I thought it might be a good time to ask about his strange behavior when he met me earlier, at the theater.

"Wait a minute before you turn off the light. Look at me. Is there something you want to tell me? Something that happened at the conference maybe?"

I could feel the air between us suddenly grow heavy.

He pulled back from the light, leaned against the headboard, and said, "Okay, if you really want to talk about this now. For one thing, Lorelei, what you've told me about your exploits while I was gone just confirmed something I thought about earlier."

"What's that?" I moved closer and took his hand in mine.

"This might be the last conference I go to without you." He gave me a serious look, and said with finality, "From now on, either you go with me, or I won't attend."

"Really, darling, that's quite a change. Can you do that? Just not attend?"

"Can I?" He let out a mirthless laugh. "Honey, I'm a full professor. I can do anything I want short of fornicating with a student at high noon on the Plaza of the Americas."

I smiled at his answer, though it touched a little too close to my actual suspicions, and he still hadn't explained his odd mood when we met at the theater. "But why? Why would you make such a promise? I know how much you enjoy going to these conferences."

"I don't want to leave you here alone again. You're so…so impulsive."

I looked more closely at him, and knew he wasn't telling me the whole truth. Did I even want to know the whole truth? I was overcome with weariness, and I didn't have the energy to probe his relationships with the parade of young, always beautiful, women graduate assistants. It would have to wait, I thought.

I scrunched down under the covers, and said, "Well, the only impulse I have right now is to sleep! Good night."

Bill turned out the light. He kissed me chastely on the forehead, slid under the covers, and turned his back to me. I pressed my body against his, and drowsily resolved to find out what was going on with my husband.

Saturday morning was already steamy hot when I awoke and went onto the deck for some stretches. I thought of ways to approach Bill about his strange behavior the day before. It would have to be done at breakfast since the rally was in the afternoon, and I had rehearsals right after. When I came down to the kitchen, he was fully dressed, reading the paper, and having a cup of coffee. As I put some cereal in a bowl, and sat across from him, he announced that he would soon be going into the office for the day.

"Bill, aren't you coming to the rally?"

"I don't have the time. I've been away for a week. I've got to catch up before Monday's classes and meetings, and God knows what else that's been going on while I was away. I probably have a hundred email messages. I only scanned them while I was gone."

"But, Bill..."

"Look, Lorelei," he paused, and held his hands out in a helpless gesture. "You don't need me there. When I get to the office, I'll try to find Cody's home number in Orlando, and I'll give him a call. Will that make it up to you?"

"Yes, that'll be a big help." I decided it was now or never, and I wanted to ease into the topic. "Bill, you remember we're having our tenth anniversary this month."

"Yes, I know," he said, still reading the paper.

"Ten years is a long time for two people to share their lives. You get to know someone pretty well in that time, and..."

"And what?"

"You know how important it is to me that we're honest with one another."

"Yes, of course. Lorelei, what are you getting at?" He put the paper down, and looked at his watch.

"I want to know what really happened to you in San Francisco. What made you so sad, and needy yesterday? And that ridiculous promise about not attending conferences without me."

He looked annoyed, and responded, "Lorelei, there-is-nothing-to-tell-you. I guess—at that moment—I was feeling that I just had enough of the academic rat race. I am tired of it, you know...the pomp and pomposity. There's nothing more to tell."

"I don't believe that's all of it, Bill. And, how does my going with you change the rat race?"

"I can't explain it," he said wearily, "it just does." He picked up the paper, and turned the page.

"Bill, please, look at me, dammit! Are you sure there's nothing you want to tell me? I promise I will act like an adult if it's something unpleasant. Does it have to do with another woman?" There, it was out and I felt a mixture of fear and relief.

"Another woman?" He cocked his head and frowned. "You're the only woman for me, Lorelei. I thought you knew that."

I resisted his clichéd dismissal of the subject. "C'mon, Bill, don't think I haven't noticed how those pretty little grad students look at you. It must be very tempting."

"Don't be ridiculous. They just flirt a bit, that's all. Now, I've really got to be going," he said folding the newspaper, and getting up from the table. He came over, kissed me on the top of my head, and said, "Don't worry, darling. Nothing happened, and nothing's going to happen. You're my only love."

As he left the kitchen, I had the fleeting thought that maybe my suspicions were wrong, and his behavior yesterday was just fatigue from his trip. But a watchful little devil-voice whispered in my ear, *Beware*!

"Bill," I called down the hallway to his office, "after the rally, I'm going straight to the theater. Please stay awake till I get home. I want to talk to you some more."

He returned to the kitchen, briefcase in hand, and gave me a stern look, as he said, "Lorelei, I want you to be careful at that rally. Stick close to Diana and people you know."

"What are you talking about?" His warning took me by surprise. "There's going to be a big crowd. Nothing can happen."

He shoved the folded newspaper in front of me. There was an article about the rally and a large picture of the site where it would be held.

"Just watch out for yourself. That's all I'm asking."

Maynard chose that moment to provide comic relief by jumping up, and shamelessly seating himself in the large wooden salad bowl in the middle of the table.

"Guess my boy wants a little attention," Bill said, as we both smiled indulgently at our plump feline.

"Maybe I should take Maynard with me to the rally for protection," I teased.

"I mean it, Lorelei. It's nothing to joke about. Just be careful." He slapped the newspaper down on the table and left.

Chapter 18

Highway 441 resembled streets around the university during a major football game. Cars were bumper to bumper on the roadside as far as the eye could see. At the entrance to the Valdez property, just south of the rally area, an enormous banner hung across the tree line facing the road: "Save The Prairie from People: Go Gators." I smiled at the humor, and marveled at the skill and daring of the tree climbers who had hoisted the banner.

It was a little before noon, the time the rally was to begin, and traffic was crawling. I spotted a parked commuter bus with a crowd of students spilling out of it. The big cardboard sign on its windshield said, "Prairie Rally." Many of the students carried placards with slogans: "Save the Prairie," "Protect Wild Places," "Valdez is Gator-bait."

The pathway that Jeffrey and I had staked out the week before was now festooned with balloons. Cars were crammed into business parking lots, and driveways for at least a mile away from the entrance to the rally. A few green and white Sheriffs cars, which Delcie called "Pickle Suits," patrolled the road; others were parked on the side. Families, some with little children in strollers, walked along the roadside, and bicycle riders cautiously threaded their way among the parade of people heading toward the rally.

I found a place to park, and grabbed my knapsack with water, some fruit, and bug spray. As I walked back toward the entrance, my new hiking shoes squished in the mushy grass, still wet from the previous night's rain. The afternoon sun beat down, and my blouse quickly became drenched with sweat. I thought, only Gator fans would be crazy enough to sit outside in the heat and humidity of this time of year in North Florida.

At the entrance to the rally site there were booths offering water, soft drinks, pastries, and hot dogs, and the usual fundraising efforts by church and school groups. A half a dozen Hare Krishnas sang and danced while some of their minions handed out plates of steamed vegetables and rice from the back of a van.

The sounds of a bluegrass band could be heard as I moved along the path to the rally. It was slow going since there seemed to be a legion of petition gatherers. I signed for a tax increase to increase positions in the county's Department of Environmental Protection, legislation to outlaw the use of live animals by university research labs, and a petition by our own Coalition to Stop Development on Paynes Prairie.

As I completed the last petition near the edge of the clearing, Diana's voice boomed over the portable loudspeakers. She introduced herself and opened the rally.

"Welcome, citizens of Alachua County and friends of Florida land and heritage," she said in a strong and confident voice. "The Coalition to Stop Development on Paynes Prairie represents local, regional, and national environmental and civic organizations, as well as individuals who care about preserving and restoring this special place, the common wealth we enjoy today, and leave for our children and their children's tomorrow. Wild lands, like the Prairie, are not only vital to our well-being, but they contain a diversity of living things whose very existence is threatened by persistent and poorly planned over-development in our State."

Cheers and applause erupted from the large crowd who stood in the shade of the trees, and were seated in lawn chairs or on blankets in the clearing. A group of children were chasing one another among the trees. A well-known reporter from the local TV station, and her camcord operator slowly made their way toward the speaker's platform. "It is our goal today," Diana continued, "to bring attention to the enormous value of this historic Prairie, and to urge—no, *demand*—its protection from development."

There was more applause, loud whistles, and a blast from a battery-operated fog horn as I made my way closer to the platform. I scanned the area, and felt a chill remembering the visit Jeffrey and I had made here only a week ago.

Diana continued, "Today, you will hear speakers from various groups tell you about the many facets of Paynes Prairie. You will learn about the historic, ecological, and recreational significance of this vast marshland. You will hear how development by the Valdez Company threatens its vitality and the very health of our community. Finally, you will be asked to take action to stop this and all future development of Prairie uplands. We urge you to listen, ask questions, even challenge the views expressed, and to join us in saving the little that is left of Florida's wilderness. Thank you."

More applause, and cheers as Diana stepped down from the podium, and Wiley Evans took her place. I moved next to Diana.

"I need you to do something for me, Lorelei," she said, and held my arm while she looked up at Wiley as he began to speak.

Wiley introduced himself as Diana's co-facilitator of the rally, and in his most stentorian voice began:

"We live in a critical time. Political decisions we make about the land today are permanent." Wiley paused, looked around at the audience, and locked eyes with one of the county commissioners as he continued, "These decisions ultimately change the face of Florida for all time. Political policies about water, land use and development, and the invasion of foreign species are the things that call for wise decisions if we are to preserve anything of the real Florida, and protect the quality of life of its citizens—present and future. I want to tell you a story about this land, the real Florida."

Diana said, "He's going to give them a history lesson." She turned to me and whispered, "Listen Lorelei, we've got a big problem."

"What?"

"You've got to find Becky"

"Becky?" I said. "Isn't she here?"

"I'm sure she is. But you've got to find her and see what her little band of eco-warriors is up to. Did you see the banner on the Valdez property? I'm afraid that's just the start..."

"Yes, I saw it," I said, and didn't mention that I admired it.

"Well, it's not appropriate. We're not here to trash Valdez. We're trying to educate people and get them to want to protect the Prairie."

"Yes, I know, Diana."

"If Becky's group does anything like Jeff Waterman pulled at Jonesville, it could ruin what we're trying to accomplish today. You know the media."

"What do you want me to do?" I asked. "They're a rag-tag band at best and—according to Becky—some of them will do their own thing no matter what anybody says."

"I don't expect you to stop them," Diana said. "Just try to persuade them to wait until the rally is over so there won't be any confusion about us condoning whatever it is they do."

"Okay, I'll try," I said, but I remained standing next to Diana delaying the start of my unpleasant assignment, and captivated by Wiley's speech.

Wiley was saying, "...we humans have inhabited this Prairie for about twelve thousand years. If you can think of something that happened in Florida, it happened here. The Prairie looks pretty much the same now as then...with more or less water. From our earliest record, nomadic Paleoindians hunted in this area. Archeologists located one of their sites right south of here, where 441 comes up from the basin, at Bolen Bluff. Those early natives were skilled at killing large mammals: prehistoric mastodon and mammoths, relatives of the elephant, you know."

At the mention of elephants, I saw several boys and girls stop playing on the sandy ground. They looked up and began to listen to his story.

"Do you know how big one of them mastodons got?" Wiley noticed the children's attention, and talked directly to them. "Why one fella found a jaw bone, down in the Floridan aquifer of all places. The aquifer is the underground river below us. It's where our drinking water comes from. Anyway, this diver...well, he guessed the beast was about fifteen feet tall. The Indians probably saw giant ground sloths right up here, too. They were twenty feet long, and tall enough to graze at the tops of trees." He pointed to the treetops, and paused with a look of wonder on his face. "Imagine that!"

Wiley stopped, picked up a bottle of water, sipped some, and waited a few moments before he continued. "Now around 1,000 B.C. we know the Indians were growing melons and gourds on the

Prairie—it might even be the earliest farming on the continent—and, in the area around it, they grew beans, squash, corn, and tobacco. Later, the Spaniards came, and made the Potano Indians, who lived here, work on the Spaniards big ranch. I can walk the trail at Bolen Bluff that leads down to the basin, and almost picture the natives—riding on small Spanish ponies and herding cattle left free when the Spaniards finally abandoned their Rancho de la Chua, 300 or more years ago."

Wiley looked down at the children who were seated in front of the platform, and asked them, "Do any of you know what the word 'la chua' means?"

"Big jug," shouted a girl who looked about eight years old.

"Big jug. Very good," Wiley said, and smiled approvingly at the girl. "The Potano's word for jug was La Chua. Other Indians called the Prairie lake, a-la-chua meaning a 'jug without a bottom' or bottomless lake. The English called it 'alatchaway.'

Wiley paused, and smiled affectionately at the children.

"Well, to finish my story about the natives who lived here…there were Creeks, Yamasees, Oconees, Makasukes, and Muskogees—these names have a familiar sound to them, don't they? Eventually, they and the runaway slaves who lived with and near them, banded together with the Cuscowillas, and were called Seminoles which meant 'runaways.'

"So what happened to the Seminoles and to the chief, King Payne, for whom the Prairie is named? Well, I'll tell you about their sad fate that history records as the Seminole Wars."

Diana turned to me with an urgent and worried look on her face. "Please, Lorelei, go and find Becky. I'm sure Wiley will give you a copy of his speech to read later."

"Okay. Sorry," I said, and turned to look around for anyone I knew who might have seen her.

I moved through the crowd, entered the dense woods, and wove my way through fallen palm fronds, and shrubs, until I neared the Valdez property. I felt sure that if Becky was up to anything dangerous, it would be away from the crowd.

There was a crunch of footsteps behind me. I turned to look back, and a hand clamped over my mouth. A muscular body pressed against me, and pulled me behind a clump of large palmetto shrubs. I recognized the body odor.

Oh no! Not him again. I tried to wriggle free of his grip, and bite his hand, but he held my jaw rigid. His arm was wrapped around my chest and pressed hard. Yes, it must be the same guy who grabbed me in Orlando. His foul-smelling sweaty body was almost more offensive than his breath next to my face. I stomped my hiker on his foot, and he loosened his grip long enough for me to duck down and away from him. He caught me by the arm, and yanked me to him with such force that I slammed back into his body and was momentarily dizzy. His hand went over my mouth again.

"Shut up!" he whispered. "I won't hurt you. I wanna to talk to you."

I tried stomping his foot again but he was wary enough to avoid my reach.

"If I let you go, you gotta promise not to scream, or I'll have your face down on the ground where you can't scream. What'll it be? It's your call."

I had a sense memory of his knee in my back and my face pressed into the grass at Jeffrey's apartment building. I stopped struggling.

"Promise, no screaming? I just wanna talk."

Okay, I thought, he just wants to talk. I was curious. Finally, I nodded. I wouldn't scream. At least not yet.

"We warned you to keep quiet," he said, and dropped his hand from my mouth.

He faced me, and held a tight grip on both of my arms. He wore an olive green tee shirt that was drenched with perspiration around the neck and armpits. A tuft of blonde chest hair curled around a gold neck chain, and I saw a fire-spitting dragon tattoo that ran the length of his right arm down to his wrist.

"I didn't tell anyone—except my husband, of course." I desperately wanted to wipe the feel of his sweaty paws from my mouth.

"Yeah? Him and who else?"

He looked older than when I'd seen him in the dark car. His receding hairline was accentuated by the tight pull of his ponytail, and his face had the look of a boxer after one too many fights.

"Nobody else," I said.

He looked doubtful. "I'll bet. Anyway, we changed our minds."

"What?" I was confused.

"Yeah," he said. "Things change. Ain't that always the way? So now you're gonna to carry a message to Keezer."

"You're kidding."

"You're gonna tell'em you know about the money he took. You're gonna tell'em unless he gets it back into the Valdez account, you're goin' to the police."

"That's stupid," I said, and by the look on his face, regretted my choice of words. "He'd know the police wouldn't believe me. I have no evidence. It's all hearsay."

"If he says that, mention there's a bookkeeper in Orlando who'll tell the police about the little deal with Keezer."

"Why don't you go to Keezer yourself?"

"That's our business."

"And what if I won't do it?"

"Lady, get real. We ain't askin' you. We're tellin'! You want your boyfriend to come out of his sleepy time, don't you?"

"Jeffrey? You can't get near him."

"You do like I say, or else."

"And if I go straight to the police? You realize you've kidnapped me, and now…"

"Kidnapped? You mean the little sightseeing ride we took in Orlando?"

"Some ride," I said, and backed up a few steps.

"Go to the police; we'll know. And then the bookkeeper won't be there to talk. You get it?"

"I'll think about it," I said.

"Yeah, think real hard. We'll be watchin' you." He gave me an appraising look and said, "You get out real late from those plays, don't you? Drivin' alone across that empty Prairie could be dangerous. Just do what I told you, and nothin' bad will happen. Hasta luego," he said, and disappeared through the dense shrubs.

Wow, I thought, shaken by the encounter. I stood there for several minutes, and took deep breaths, while I relived the short and surprising incident.

I hurriedly retraced my path back to the rally. I was still confused by what the Valdez goon asked me to do, and mad that they had apparently decided to use me as a pawn in their scheme to get their money back. Yet, if there was some reason to buy into the crazy plan, the thought of having something on Keezer at last was very tempting.

Chapter 19

I stood at the edge of the clearing and looked around for Detective McBride, hoping he'd kept his promise to attend the rally. I spied a shred of the crime scene tape hanging loosely from a tree, and I recognized where the mobile crime van had been parked the night Becky and I were on the Prairie. It seemed years ago.

Diana was talking with Commissioner Sparks, and I went over to them.

"Oh, Lorelei, you've met Commissioner Sparks, haven't you?" Diana broke off her conversation to introduce me.

Sparks looked more relaxed than when I saw him at the commission meeting. He wore a pair of chinos, and a blue polo shirt with a Florida Gator emblem. It was hard to keep from staring at him now that I suspected his relationship with Jeffrey. He flashed a broad smile and put out his hand to me.

"I don't think we've actually met," I said, grasping his warm hand. "It's nice to see you here, Commissioner."

"I wouldn't miss it," he said. "Despite what you environmentalists think, I care a great deal about our county's land and heritage."

Diana and I gave one another a look.

"Diana, can I see you for just a minute? Excuse us, Commissioner," I said, and pulled Diana a few feet away.

"Lorelei? What in heavens name? Did you find Becky?"

"Have you seen McBride? I need to see him, ASAP."

"Why no, I haven't. Has anything happened?"

"Tell me, it isn't about Becky and that gang of hers, is it?"

"No, no. Don't worry about Becky, there's nothing for you to be concerned about," I said, and hoped I was right since I hadn't actually seen her.

"Then, let's get back to Commissioner Sparks before he gets away."

I debated approaching one of the deputies to tell them about my encounter in the woods, but decided to wait to see Detective McBride. Sparks was engaged in conversation with an elderly couple when we returned. "I was just saying, I hoped both sides of the Prairie story would be told today," he said, beaming with a politicians practiced smile.

"Both sides?" Diana asked.

"Right. You do know the Prairie has always been about business and growth. I'll bet even you didn't know it was probably the first location in the country for commercial agriculture...during the 17th century. Cattle and produce were bought and sold to Cuba and the Bahamas. You'll still see cows being raised around here long after the Camp family sold their land to the State."

"Judson, oh Jud," shouted a blonde who waved to the commissioner as she made her way toward us, stepping around a thicket of lawn chairs and blankets.

"That's my wife, Chelsea. You've met her, Diana." Sparks cheerlessly waved back and beckoned her over.

"Oh, yes," Diana said, and whispered to me with uncharacteristic sarcasm, "Here comes the aging cheerleader."

I gasped as she approached. She looked like the woman who was with Keezer in the parking lot at the Prairie marina! But that woman had black hair. Could she have been wearing a wig? Everything I now knew about the complicity between Keezer and Spark's wife told me it probably was her, and it made me more curious to know what they had been fighting about.

As she hurried to join us, I was amused by her outfit: jeweled sandals, tight shorts, and a revealing halter top blouse. She looked dressed more for a poolside barbeque than an environmental rally.

Judson stopped speaking until she was upon us, and then began introductions. "You know Diana Demeter, and this is Laurie..."

"Lorelei Crane," I said.

The elderly couple had drifted away.

Chelsea Sparks gave me a cursory nod, and spoke to her husband, "Judson, Harris is here and I want you to talk with him." I was startled by the deep, smoker's voice that belied her very feminine appearance. She paused to glance at Diana and me before she continued, "You know, about the thing we discussed this morning."

"Oh, right," he said. "I'll catch up with him in a little while."

"Now, Judson. Before he leaves," she said, raised an eyebrow, and glowered at him.

I was surprised by her commanding tone, and saw an embarrassed, darting look in Judson's eyes.

"Okay, dear," he said quietly. "As you wish. I'll see Harris in just a minute."

She pursed her lips and made an impatient smacking sound.

"Excuse us for a moment," she said to Diana. "There's some urgent business we need to discuss." She put her arm through his and seemed to wrench him into motion. Her attitude was so forceful, I wouldn't have been surprised had she taken him by the ear. They walked over to a large oak tree about fifty feet away.

"Whoa," I said. "That's one tough lady. Who would have thought it by looking at her?" I continued scanning the crowd for McBride as I listened to Diana.

"I know," said Diana. "I've had a couple of run-ins with her over promoting gun shows around here. My son Hank and some of his friends sneak into them. Anyway, she's impossible to deal with; doesn't give an inch. Did you get a whiff of that cologne? I think it made my allergies act up."

"What does Keezer see in her anyway? She strikes me as a little over the edge."

Diana shrugged. "I've often wondered if Judson knows about them, or just doesn't care."

Probably both things are true, I thought. We stood watching the couple. Chelsea Sparks' body language radiated dominance. Her hands were either on her hips or she aggressively pointed her finger in her husband's face. He stood, slightly stooped, with his head bowed, and occasionally nodded. It was painful to watch the interaction. I felt sorry for him.

Diana looked around the clearing with a satisfied smile. The folk music group was leaving the stage, and another speaker was setting herself up at the podium. "I think it's all going very well. What do you think?"

"It's great," I said. I wondered if I should call the Detective, but I didn't have his card with me, or maybe I could ask one of the police to call him for me.

Diana looked at the podium and said, "Excuse me, I see the woman from the county Arts Association is struggling with the mike. I guess Wiley's off somewhere." Diana hurried away to the podium.

"Lost someone, Mrs. Crane?"

He startled me. "Thank goodness it's you, Detective. I've been looking for you."

"What's up?"

"I have to talk to you. Something's happened."

"What'd you do to your hair?" he asked. "I almost didn't recognize you."

"Oh, it's dyed for the play. Listen, you won't believe it. One of the men from Orlando—the one who dragged me into the car and threatened me—he's here. He followed me into the woods, and started making the craziest demand. I couldn't believe it, but…" I had to pause for a breath as the words came rushing out.

"Slow down, Mrs. Crane. Let's get away from all these people, and you can tell me what happened."

"But he might still be around. He's about 5'9", wearing an olive tee-shirt, very muscular build, a large dragon tattooed on his right arm." We both stood scanning the crowd, but couldn't see anyone fitting that description.

The screech of microphone feedback pierced the air, and was followed by a high-pitched voice over the loud speakers: "Paynes Prairie has been a source of inspiration for artists of all kinds, not just musicians, like those you've heard today, but also writers, painters, photographers, and poets. Listen now as I read the poet, Stetson Kennedy's word portrait, *Paines' Prairie.*"

> I stand on the rim of the nut-brown bowl
> that is Paines' Prairie:
> listen as the cat-squirrel chatters and scolds
> the sinking sun.

Clouds in the West
stretched, gauze-like
on the fingers of the wind,
dissolve into soft brown rust
and disappear.

The oaks weep crystalline tears
that drip from mossy beards
into white sand.

A marsh hawk screams,
swooping after the marsh hare that runs
trembling under a log.

Flapping white herons
rise in a long line from the ponds…
it is their wings that sing the finale
to the prairie's evening song.

"C'mon. Over there," McBride said, nodding to a wooded area just beyond where the Judson and Chelsea Sparks were still talking. He took my elbow and guided me in that direction.

As we approached the couple, they were exchanging accusations.

"It's about the money, isn't it?" Judson said in a stage whisper. He looked at her with disgust. "All you ever think about is the damn money."

She had a murderous look on her face as she spit out her words, "How dare you accuse me of greed…you little weasel. Like you don't suck up to the developers to get money from those cozy little land deals?"

"Commissioner," McBride said, nodding to Sparks as we passed.

The two of them immediately fell silent. Sparks looked at McBride without recognition for a moment before a slow flush rose on his face, and his eyes darted like a trapped animal.

"Uh, hello. Excuse us." He took Chelsea by the arm, and they moved away from the tree.

Chelsea Sparks' accusation was provocative, and her aggressive behavior made me think of something Delcie and I had considered. Could Mrs. Sparks have been the one who shot at and missed her husband? Maybe she followed him, knowing the Prairie was once a frequent rendezvous place for gay men.

McBride stopped walking, and said, "Okay, now about the man from Orlando?" We stood in a small clearing near a green duckweed pond. I quickly scanned the pond for alligators. The sound from the podium was muffled. The buzz of afternoon insects became more distinct.

"Yes, it's definitely the guy I told you about. The one who picked me up in the car in Orlando."

"You saw him here, at the rally?"

"Uh huh, he grabbed me again." I saw McBride look me over as though he would find some evidence of my being harmed. "No, he didn't hurt me. Actually, I'm almost getting used to being roughed up."

McBride smiled. "When was this?"

"It's been almost an hour."

"What did he want?"

I walked over to sit on a fallen log. "Before I tell you about the guy, seeing Commissioner Sparks reminded me of something. Diana may have already told you about the incident."

"Which incident?" he asked, looking confused as he walked over to where I was sitting. I observed him more closely, and thought, no one would guess McBride was a homicide detective. Dressed in jeans and a short-sleeved plaid shirt he looked like any other guy at the rally. I concluded he had a kind of rugged good looks; he wasn't exactly handsome, but had a lot of sex appeal like the cowboy hero in a western.

"Did you remember something else?" he asked.

"When Jeffrey and Sparks saw one another at the commission meeting, they both acted strangely nervous. Like they knew each other but were afraid to admit it."

"Suggesting?" McBride asked.

"I don't know. You asked me to try to think about Jeffrey's relationships here and that's something I remembered."

He gave me a skeptical look. "You think the commissioner had something to do with Waterman's shooting?"

"I don't know what the connection is," I said, pretending I hadn't any suspicions.

"What I do know is Jeffrey tried to convince me they were strangers. He seemed very secretive, and Jeffrey's not—didn't use to be—secretive. If he knew Sparks, why would he want to hide such a useful connection?"

McBride started to sit down next to me but I warned him off. "You'll get chiggers. I'm drenched in bug spray, so hopefully, they won't get me."

He nodded, shook his head and rubbed the back of his neck. There was a long silence while he considered a possible relationship between Jeffrey and Sparks. I could feel perspiration running down my back. Mosquitoes buzzed around my face.

At last, he said, "I don't like it. A county commissioner? Nope, I don't like it one bit. We'll just have to wait for the evidence at the crime scene. If it implicates Commissioner Sparks, that's a whole world of trouble I don't want."

He stood up, took a pack of cigarettes out of his pocket, tapped one on the back of his hand, and lit it. He inhaled deeply; the smoke momentarily clouded his face, and drifted away. He noticed me staring at him.

"What?" he asked. He looked down at the cigarette as though he was surprised to be holding it. "I know, I'm trying to give it up," he said defensively. "This thing between Waterman and Sparks is bugging me. Remember I told you I thought Waterman might be having a lover's tryst that night?"

I shook my head. "That's not it. I think Jeffrey may just have been trying to get Sparks to back-off in his support for the development. He even told Becky his meeting that night might fix the situation." That was at least half of the truth, I thought.

McBride took a long drag on his cigarette, and said, as though to himself, "If Commissioner Sparks witnessed the shooting, this Valdez thing sure has gotten a lot more complicated."

I saw that the usually imperturbable Detective looked visibly shaken. I wondered if I should tell him about Keezer and Chelsea Sparks, and my latest thoughts about her—the ones I was exploring when we first arrived at the clearing—but I decided I'd already dumped enough in McBride's lap for now. "What about the Valdez security guy?" I asked. "Did you speak with him yet?"

"Oh, you mean "AJ?" What's his name, yeah, Angus James Hill? We're still interviewing some of his pals. I did talk to his boss at Gator Security…said he was an all right kid."

"We met that Gator Security guy when we went out to the Valdez site. I don't think I'd trust him."

McBride gave me a rueful smile. "The guy you met was probably Randy Ashcroft. He's an ex-cop," McBride said flatly. He snuffed out his cigarette on the log, field-stripped it, and scattered it on the ground. "Now, tell me more about who grabbed you. By the way, did you ever talk to the detective in Orlando?"

"No, we've been playing phone tag. I haven't talked with her. Have you?"

"Yeah, I got hold of her. She didn't know anything, and sounded like she already had enough on her plate." He walked around the clearing, stopped and pointed at me. "You still haven't answered my question. What'd he demand?"

Okay, I thought, the truth. I told McBride exactly what my abductor had told me to do. McBride listened with his head down, until I had finished my story.

"Christ, so Keezer really has made off with a mil. Well, he wouldn't be the first guy to steal from his partner."

"What do you think I should do?" I asked.

"Nothing. Not a thing," he said emphatically. "You don't want to get in the middle of this. These guys are messin' with you. They'll do whatever it takes to get their money back."

"What if he comes around again? He warned me not to go to the police."

"I'll put a tail on you. In the meantime, don't go anywhere by yourself. Come to the office; give me a description of the guy, and a full statement. We'll take it from there."

"I can't do it today. I've got a rehearsal in about an hour."

"You're over at the Tuscawilla?"

"Yes."

"When do you finish up?"

"Rehearsals usually end around ten o'clock. We get a dinner break at six."

"Okay, Mrs. Crane. I'll be there at six. Now, let's go back to the rally. If you spot the guy, get to the closest deputy. Tell'em to call me, pronto. I'm headed back to the office."

As we walked back to the rally, I was glad I had told McBride the truth. I had come to trust him, and it was a relief to have a partner in this bizarre chain of events.

"Are you married, Detective?" The question suddenly popped out of my mouth.

He turned and gave me a quizzical look, "Sort of."

"Sort of?"

"Yeah, she's been gone quite a while. FBI. Trains cops all over the world."

"Oh," I said.

"What made you ask?"

"I don't know. Just wondering."

He took a step back, looked at me with one eyebrow raised, and gave me a funny half-smile. "So, you've decided I'm not such a bad guy after all."

"Maybe, but you do have a reputation to get over, you know," I said teasingly, and regretted it the minute it was out of my mouth. I didn't want to reveal Delcie as my source of inside gossip about McBride.

He shrugged, and said, "Glad I've made an impression on somebody." He touched my arm, and said, "I want you to be aware of your surroundings, and stay close to other people."

When McBride left, I turned my attention to the speaker's platform. Mike Smith, Dalton's replacement at the Sierra Club, had just begun to speak.

"Lorelei, I've been looking everywhere for you," Diana was breathless as she rushed up to me. "We've got a real emergency on our hands," she said with a distraught look on her face.

"What? What's wrong, Diana?"

"Jimmy Valdez. He's here, and he says he's calling the police to stop the rally. And, he's going to sue us!"

Chapter 20

"You're kidding," I said, "Jimmy Valdez is here? Why would he dare to show his face here of all places?"

"I'll tell you in a minute. It's awful." Diana put a finger to her lips, and turned to watch Mike Smith begin his speech.

"We all recognize the State's booming population growth, and the need to provide housing for newcomers," he said. "We know that Florida is a magnet. We have no income tax. Retirement communities are constantly being promoted. And of course, there's the sunshine. You notice none of the ads mention hurricanes, humidity, and mosquitoes!" The audience laughed as he took out a handkerchief and wiped his forehead.

He continued, "Florida's been exploited by real estate and tourism folks, probably since William Bartram first described it as a paradise. It's always been a place of dreams; one nineteenth century writer even coined a name for our area, 'The Eden of the South.'"

Impatiently, I whispered again to Diana, "Tell me about Jimmy Valdez."

She turned back to me; her face was ashen. "He says our people have sabotaged his property. Wiley's trying to calm him down over there, on the other side of the podium. We're trying not to call attention to them." She looked at me with a stern expression, and said, "Lorelei, this is just what I was afraid would happen."

"I'm sure there's a misunderstanding. I'll go talk with Mr. Valdez." I felt guilty for not having found Becky, but was reluctant to tell Diana what happened to stop me. Diana nodded, and led the way around to the back of the podium where we stood, and watched Jimmy Valdez and Wiley in an animated discussion.

Suddenly Jimmy Valdez yelled, "I don't give a God-damn about your rally. You're getting people worked up to destroy our project." He angrily punched his fist into the palm of his hand. Wiley took a step back and eyed Valdez warily. "And I won't stand by and let you do that."

This wasn't the same cool Jimmy Valdez I had met earlier. He was more volatile than I would have imagined him to be. His face was red with heat or anger or both, and his white guayabera stuck to his back with perspiration.

"Now, if you'll just hear me out, Mr. Valdez," Wiley's said, his voice dropping low as he gave us a look that said, don't interrupt.

I honored the request for a few minutes, then stepped forward, and touched Valdez on the arm. He turned with such swiftness I thought he might hit me.

"Remember me, Mr. Valdez? Lorelei Crane." I flashed a smile and put out my hand. He looked confused and didn't return the gesture. "We met a couple of weeks ago, on your property." I suddenly remembered why he failed to recognize me. "I had red hair then," I added.

"I remember you. You were with that man. He's probably behind all of this. You people have given us nothing but trouble," he said with a menacing look.

I felt like responding that it was his people who were giving us all the trouble. Instead, I politely asked, "What's happened?"

"It's those friends of yours," Valdez gestured toward his property. "They have stolen our surveyor stakes. They broke into our construction shack, and vandalized it. God knows what they've done to the architect plans we had there…or the computer."

He wiped his forehead with his hand, adding, "And that preposterous banner hanging in the front of our property. Who do you people think you are? That's private land." He stopped speaking, his outrage apparently putting him at a momentary loss for words.

Oh Becky, I thought, what have you all done? Once again I noticed Valdez's alligator shoes, and for a moment had the insane thought that his footprints might be the match for those taken at the site of Jeffrey's shooting.

Wiley stepped in front of me. "As I said earlier, Mr. Valdez, I assure you we have had no part in any of this. I understand your desire to call the authorities," Wiley said in a conciliatory tone. "What happened sounds terrible. You should report the damage to your property. Be assured, it was not our group."

"No, it is all of you!" Valdez angrily spat the words. "You want to stop us from building on our own property." Valdez pointed a finger at Wiley. "You have not heard the last of this," he said, and abruptly walked away. He took a cell-phone out of his pocket, and had it to his ear as he marched through the crowd toward the road.

"Oh, God," Diana groaned. "There goes the TV crew right after him." She turned to face me with an angry look. "Lorelei, how did this happen?"

"I swear I don't know," I said.

"This is classic Waterman. He probably planned it all before he got shot."

She was right, and, of course, Valdez was right...we did want to stop his development.

"Just wait until I see Becky Haimovitz again," Diana continued, "I won't have someone working for the Center who pulls stunts like this."

I rolled my eyes at Wiley, silently pleading with him to calm her down.

"Here's the next speaker," Wiley said. "Diana, will you take care of her? I'll see if I can catch up with Valdez, and try to reason with him again." He briskly walked in the direction Valdez had taken.

I remained near the podium, feeling guilty, to help Diana. She introduced the next speaker who had a slow, deep, southern drawl that was so intimate it compelled you to listen to what she was saying:

"I talked with Jack Gillen just after his retirement—some of you know him as the longtime manager of the Prairie—anyway, I asked him, 'Jack, I know Paynes Prairie is the richest wildlife habitat in Florida, but what makes it a special place for you?'"

She paused, letting us think about the question before going on.

"He told me he was most impressed with its vastness—he called it an uninterrupted natural system."

She gestured dramatically toward the open Prairie.

"He said he was awed by the complexity of the ecosystem, and how it changes so fast and dramatically. The change isn't just seasonal, it's constant. He told me they once took pictures of certain places on the Prairie at different times of the year, and each picture was different. He said, 'sometimes you can't even tell it's the same place you were in!' "

"Now what would cause such continuous change?" she asked, pausing again, to take a sip of water. She held up the bottle for the audience to see.

"Water," she said. "It's all about water. I see most of you in the audience today have been drinking bottled water. Well, just like us, all the wildlife on the Prairie need water to survive. The trees, flowers, shrubs, and grasses—they all depend upon the water supply. This is a wet prairie: its ecosystems change, adapt, and remain vital depending on the flow of water, and the advent of fire. And when the Prairie's too wet, lots of critters come to the uplands, what we call the rim. Too much water is what drove those old gators up onto 441 to sun themselves last week."

She took another sip from her bottle and paused while she looked down at her notes.

A man wearing a Florida Gator tee-shirt shouted out into the audience, "Speaking of gators, anybody got the score for the game?"

Some people sitting close to the podium turned around to shush him.

"Yeah, we got two touchdowns in the first quarter," yelled a man at the rear of the crowd who held a small radio to his ear. There were cheers that almost drowned out his next words, "Auburn has the ball."

A middle-aged woman, seated on a lawn chair under a moss-draped oak tree, yelled out in a thick Southern accent, "Go War Eagles!"

There were loud boos and hisses. The Auburn fan shrugged it off, and seemed pleased with the mischief she made among the enthusiastic Florida Gator fans.

The speaker smiled with amusement, apparently unperturbed by the brief interruption, and continued. "This is one of the greatest wetland areas in Florida. What does that mean us? The Prairie basin is a major recharge area for the underground aquifer...where we get our drinking water. To make it simple, when we pollute the Prairie, or for that matter, any of our natural springs and sinkholes, we pollute our drinking water. Remember, even the water in your Dannon bottle wasn't manufactured; it probably was drawn from our Floridan aquifer just a few miles up the road in High Springs."

Diana and I were sitting on the rear edge of the podium as a light breeze came up through the trees, and small yellow and rust-colored leaves drifted down at my feet. In contrast to the recent fray with Valdez, everything now seemed peaceful.

The speaker dropped her voice as she said, "And that's why we are here today because the quality of the wetlands—water, the life of the basin—will be directly affected if any development project is allowed to be built on this Prairie rim. It's not about preserving the natural scenery, though itself an increasing rarity in Florida. No, the real harm is from the drainage or run-off from human habitation—chemicals from cars, landscaping, you name it—which will flow from the rim, onto the basin, down the Alachua sink, and into our aquifer. It's that simple."

"She's good," Diana whispered.

I nodded, and continued to be mesmerized by the speaker's soft voice, the place, a feeling of harmony with all the people who were joined by this event.

"So we must protect the rim of the Prairie as a buffer, as a haven for the animals that live on the basin, and for the purity of our water. We need to do this as though our lives depended upon it—they do! Thank you for listening."

There was loud applause. I stood up and stretched.

Wiley returned, and said, "No luck. I couldn't find him."

"Well, you tried," Diana said. "I guess we'll just have to wait and see what happens. Maybe the rally will be over before Valdez makes good on his threat."

Wiley nodded, and stepped up to the podium, tapped the microphone to make sure it was still live, and said, "Now, we've been preaching at you quite a bit. And you've been very patient, especially in this heat."

"Talk a little bit longer," Diana said. "The Woodbridge Sisters haven't arrived yet."

Wiley nodded, "It'll be just a few minutes until our next group of entertainers. In the meantime, I want to read something to ya'll." He reached into the pocket of his shirt, put on his glasses, and looked at an index card. "This is from David Brower's book, *Let the Mountains Talk, Let the Rivers Run*. Brower, as some of you know, was a longtime National Sierra Club President who later started Friends of the Earth. Anyway, what he wrote is especially relevant to the purpose of our gathering today:

We need to tire of trashing wildness. It's not making us happy. It's not making us healthy. It is making us miserable and despairing. Killing trees, habitats, and animals, and separating ourselves from nature is making us all a bit crazy. We need to restore the earth because we need to save the wild. We need to save the wild in order to save ourselves."

Wiley paused, removed his glasses, and looked out at the fanning crowd. "Protecting Paynes Prairie, keeping it a wild place—that's what we all want to do. And now, I see our lovely singers have arrived. If you haven't heard them before, you're in for a real treat."

He stepped down from the platform while the Woodbridge sisters took the stage.

"That was great, Wiley," I said. Diana gave him a weary but affectionate smile. It was time to make my way back to my car. "I've got to get out of here."

"Oh, yes, your rehearsals," Diana said.

I hugged Diana and Wiley. "You guys did a wonderful job today. This rally, with the publicity and all, I'm sure it's going to galvanize people. Don't worry about Valdez. He's probably all bluster," I said, knowing my reassurance was far from the truth.

"I hope so," Diana said. "Thanks for all you've done, too, Lorelei."

I trudged back to the highway, only to find traffic was at a complete standstill. As I edged, through the onlookers, closer to the road, I saw the reason for the stalled traffic.

Guerrilla theater was being performed on the roadway: several people were dressed as trees and enacted being cut down by chainsaw wielding construction workers. They lay in the middle of the road while sheriff's deputies and highway patrol officers converged on them. I wondered if Becky was in one of the costumes, and how she was going to defend herself from Diana's ire.

Another small group in animal costumes dramatically fled in fear across the other side of the highway, pursued by a gang wearing Valdez tee-shirts and brandishing rebar stakes. They looked like the metal stakes Jeffrey had used at Jonesville to defeat the construction vehicles at the site. If Jimmy Valdez was angry about what he had already discovered on his property, I tried to imagine his rage if the earth moving equipment had their huge tires punctured by metal stakes.

I hiked back to my car thinking about Jeffrey. He would have loved being in the middle of things. It was a three-ring circus—a kind of theater of the absurd—but I knew the actors played their roles as much out of a sense of despair as for the fun of it.

It was a challenge to try and harness my high-spirits from the rally, and redirect them into the role of the 19th century Varya. But by the time I neared the theater, I was immersed again in *The Cherry Orchard*, feeling Varya's anxiety about being displaced and empathizing with her mother's despair at the destruction of the orchard. I hoped for a better fate for the trees on the Prairie.

As I slipped into the rehearsal hall, Chester stopped talking, glared at me, and said, "You're late,"

"I apologize. I'm really sorry, but I was at the Prairie rally."

"I heard traffic was tied up for miles," said one of the actors.

"How did it go?" my friend Cassie asked, motioning me to a chair next to hers. "Will you be on TV?"

"It was a hoot," I said, sitting down. "You all would have enjoyed..."

"Sorry to interrupt you girls." Chester's voice dripped with sarcasm as he stared at Cassie and me from the head of the table. "Renee will be here in a few minutes, and she'll want to see everyone working on their parts. So, off you go. Get a partner, and cue one another. We'll be doing a full walk-through this evening. Dinner break at the end of Act I."

The cast dutifully found partners. Some stood face to face, and others moved to chairs spread around the room. Cassie and I paired up. It was natural for us to work together since she played my younger sister, Anya.

"Did Bill get home?" she whispered, pulling up a chair.

"Yes," I whispered back as I joined her.

"And what about Jeffrey? How's he doing?" Cassie's eyebrows shot up to warn me that Chester was moving toward us. She looked down at the script, and recited a cue.

I responded with my line as Chester approached. He nodded approvingly, and moved on to another pair of actors.

"Jeffrey's still sedated."

Cassie frowned, and said, "I guess we'd better stick to our lines, and catch up during the break."

"I'm afraid I'm already booked. Detective McBride is coming to see me then."

"Really? What's the latest, Lorelei?"

"Too much to tell," I replied. "I'll call you for lunch this week, and fill you in. Let's just keep working."

Once Renee took over the rehearsal, time passed quickly. I was fully absorbed in the play and forgot about everything else. When we broke for dinner, McBride was waiting for me in the lobby.

As he approached he said, "You look surprised to see me, Mrs. Crane. I thought I told you I'd be here."

"Oh, yes, I haven't forgotten. I've just been living in another century. It takes me a few minutes to make the switch."

"I guess so," he said. "Can we go someplace to talk in private?"

"Back into the rehearsal hall, I think. Everyone's taking a break."

"I'm sorry to have to meet you like this, during your dinner time. I picked up a sandwich for you. I hope you like turkey."

"How thoughtful," I replied. I took the brown bag he offered and was glad to be saved from the diet drink which I had brought for dinner. I led him into the rehearsal hall, and we sat down in a corner of the room where we wouldn't be disturbed.

"I only have twenty minutes. I hope this won't take long." I said as I started to nibble on the sandwich.

"No, mostly I want to make sure I got the facts right," McBride said. "The way you described them to me at the rally. By the way, were your friends pleased with how it went?"

"Oh, yes. It was a big success."

"I heard there were some arrests made. It obviously got livelier after I left."

"Arrests?" I said, thinking about Becky, and the merry chase her friends had given the police on the highway. "You mean for the highway antics?"

"Antics, huh? An interesting description for vandalism and resisting arrest, but I won't go into that now. Let me check what I've got down, and ask you a couple of questions."

McBride pulled out his small spiral notebook, and read back what I had told him about the encounter with Valdez's man at the rally.

"Is that an accurate account of what happened?" he asked.

"Pretty much, but you didn't mention his not so subtle threat about my driving home late at night and..."

"Don't worry, I got it. I've assigned a deputy to follow you home. Is your husband back in town yet?"

"Yes, thank goodness. He'll be at home tonight."

"Good. What time do you finish up here, ten o'clock?"

"About then."

"Okay. A deputy will be waiting for you. Her name is Delcie Wright."

"What?" I said, and gulped on the bite of sandwich.

I was shocked that Delcie had been assigned. I went to the nearby refreshment table, poured myself a glass of iced tea, and brought it back to where we were sitting.

He watched me with curiosity. "You have a problem with a woman deputy?' he asked with that funny half-smile he had given me at the rally.

"No. Of course not. I appreciate the protection. I'm sure Deputy Wright will be just fine."

"Good," he said. "Now, I want you to think back to our first conversation about the Waterman shooting. Tell me again why you mentioned Mr. Keezer might be a possible suspect."

I described the incident that took place at the Valdez property, in which Jeffrey had taunted Keezer to the point that he had reached for the rifle in his truck, and Jeffrey's response to make trouble for Valdez.

McBride said, rubbed his chin, and sighed. "So Keezer is about as much of a hot-head as Waterman. It's not a strong motive, but he definitely had the means and his alibi for that night is pretty shaky."

I continued eating my sandwich while McBride skimmed his notes. Then he got up, stretched his arms out, and locked his fingers on the back of his neck to stretch. He looked tired.

"I know I'm going over some of the same ground we've already covered, but I've got a pile of suspects. I need to eliminate one or two of them. Sometimes it takes just a word to give me a new insight."

"That's okay. I'm used to repeating story lines."

"Right," he said with a nod. He glanced around the room with interest. "Tell me, Mrs. Crane, as an actress, I'm sure you can size up people, and their motivation. What's your take on Keezer? You think he was mad enough to take a shot at Waterman?"

I thought for a moment before responding. "No, I don't think so. He was furious at Jeffrey all right—the way Jeffrey kept pushing him—but I never got the feeling that Keezer was a vicious man. Jimmy Valdez maybe, but Keezer, no."

"Valdez?" He shook his head. "Hell, right now his alibi looks tight. He's got witnesses that say he was hunting with them out in the Everglades that night. That puts him about 300 miles from the scene."

Meticulously groomed Jimmy Valdez, hunting? Yes, I could picture him enjoying blood sports, war games, or whatever it was some men did out in the Glades.

McBride said, "Just a couple more questions, and I'll get out of here. Tell me again about the meeting you witnessed between Commissioner Sparks and Waterman. Did anyone else see their interaction and comment on it?" He flipped pages in his notebook until he found the one he wanted. "You mentioned Mrs. Demeter was with you."

"Yes, Diana saw Sparks' reaction. But she just brushed it off, saying he was probably afraid of being approached by three environmentalists."

"And later Waterman admitted knowing Sparks? Isn't that what you told me?"

"No, he didn't actually admit they knew one another. He always maintained that Sparks just reminded him of someone he met in Orlando. But I never believed him. I can read a connection between two people, and they had it."

"I'm sure you can, Mrs. Crane." McBride's intonation and the way he looked at me made me feel self-conscious. My face felt warm, and I averted my eyes.

He continued, "You said Waterman's meeting that night was related to the Valdez project?"

I looked up at him again, and was relieved to find him scanning his spiral notebook. The awkward moment had passed.

"Yes, that's what he told Becky before leaving her house that night."

"I guess I'll check with Ms. Haimovitz again."

"Have you talked with Judson or Chelsea Sparks yet?"

"No comment," he said, abruptly standing up. His uneasiness with the subject was obvious. Looking apologetic, he added, "I can't comment about an on-going investigation."

McBride had already violated that rule more than once, but I realized he wasn't going to tell me anything about the county commissioner and his wife. I knew enough about politics to understand that any hint of the Sparks' involvement would land McBride and his superiors in the middle of a political scandal.

"Last question, I promise," McBride said. "About the guy you and Mr. Waterman thought you caught poaching on the Prairie, A.J. Hill, the Valdez security guard. Just how much hostility was there between the two of them? Tell me again what happened."

"It was really a brief conversation." I hesitated for a moment, recalling the scene. "After the gun shots, the man appeared as if from no where. Jeffrey kept his cool. He told him he wasn't allowed to have a gun, or to hunt on the Prairie. He denied that he was hunting—thought it was obvious he was—and told us he was guarding the Valdez property. They had some more words, I don't remember exactly, and then he recognized me."

"From his high school play," McBride prompted, following his notes.

"Yes, he had seen me in *Macbeth*, and we talked about that for a couple of minutes. Jeffrey warned him he could be in trouble with park rangers, and that he—Jeffrey—might report him."

"Warned him? How?"

I tried to picture the scene again. "He was stern, you know, just to let the young man know how serious he was. But, he didn't act like he was going to do it right away."

"Did he report the incident to the park staff?"

"No, at least I don't think so. Wait a minute, there was a pretty heated exchange as we were leaving."

"Tell me about it."

"The young man made some very disparaging remarks about gays on the Prairie. I remember it making Jeffrey very angry."

"Did anything else take place? Did A.J. lift his gun at any time?"

"No. That was it. We just left. When I told Jeffrey I thought the incident was dangerous, he just shrugged it off. That's all there was to it."

McBride made a few more notes, pocketed his notebook, and got up to leave. The scene reverberated in my mind, and McBride's question about the gun sparked a new idea.

"You don't think he shot Jeffrey, do you?"

"You've been very helpful again, Mrs. Crane," he said. "Thanks for taking time to see me." He glanced around the room with the interest people have in seeing what lies behind the scenes of familiar organizations. "Good luck on your rehearsals. I'm looking forward to seeing you in the play."

Before I could respond, he turned and walked away. I watched the self-assurance with which he carried himself, smiled as I heard the click of his hard heels on the polished wood floor, and thought Homer McBride was defying yet another stereotype—no ordinary gum-shoe detective was he. I felt a bit of a thrill thinking of him sitting somewhere in the darkened audience watching me come alive in my world.

Chapter 21

"Was that your detective?" Cassie was standing next to me before I was aware of her presence. "He's not half bad-looking, and I noticed the smile on your face." She wagged her finger at me as though to say, "Gotcha."

"Yes, that was Detective McBride," I said, feeling a blush rise from my neck. I looked at my watch. "God, Cassie, I just have enough time to make a trip to the bathroom before we're due back. I can't be late twice today."

The rehearsal went well. Most of the cast had their lines memorized, which pleased Renee. She paid me a rare compliment: "Lorelei, well-done. Your Varya has just the right amount of repressed passion." I savored her words. Repressed passion? I knew something about that all right.

It was after ten when we finished up. I walked out to the lobby with Cassie.

"Hi, Lor, how's it going? I kind of watched a bit through the doorway."

"Delcie! I thought I'd drop my teeth when McBride told me it was you. Cassie, this is an old college friend of mine, Delcie Wright."

"Glad to meet you, Delcie," Cassie said, and Delcie smiled in return.

"We're going to hang out here for a bit," I said. "See you tomorrow, Cassie. You were great tonight."

She took the cue, waved goodbye, and joined a small group of actors who were slowly making their way out of the theater.

I put my arm through Delcie's, and we moved over to sit on a bench along the side wall. "So you're going to be my bodyguard? How ironic is that?"

"Yeah, not bad duty getting paid to spend time with your girl friend."

"I guess you heard about the confrontation at the rally?"

"McBride told me. Sometimes, he acts like he's a big city homicide detective, NYPD. On the other hand, when he told me you were grabbed again, I agreed you needed protecting."

"I still don't get why they want me in their dirty game of cat and mouse."

Delcie looked concerned, and said, "Remember, I warned you about those guys. We've heard a couple of the same types are up here from Miami. Your guy may be one of them. We don't know what they're planning. In South Florida, they get away with stuff that would make headlines up here."

"Well, that's worrisome," I said. "I'm sure it's Keezer they're after. Funny they don't seem interested in Chelsea Sparks. She's his partner in crime."

A wave of weariness washed over me. I bent down in a rag doll-like collapse to let the blood rush to my head.

"C'mon, Lor," she gently touched my arm. "Let's get going. Do you want to drive with me and leave your car here overnight?"

"No," I said, sitting up, and willing myself to revive. "Just follow me home. Bill will be there. I'll be all right."

"Have you told Bill about all this?" She stood up, grabbed my hands and pulled me to my feet. I caught the slight fragrance of her cologne, Clinique *Aromatics Elixir.* Hardly what your average deputy would be wearing, I thought.

"Have you filled him in or not?"

"Tell Bill?" I said. "If he knew everything, he wouldn't let me out of his sight."

"Maybe that's not such a bad idea for right now. Wish I had a man who'd care for me that way." A wistful note had crept into Delcie's voice.

"Are you kidding? I can almost hear you complaining about how he was smothering you, and how you be needing your space. When it comes right down to it, we're both damn strong…you've even got a badge to prove it!"

She put up her hands in defeat, "You got me there, Lorelei. Still, every now and again…"

"I know, sometimes we all yearn to feel safe and cared for like little girls."

The lobby lights were being dimmed in sections, signaling us to leave the building. As we walked out to the parking area, Delcie stayed so close I could feel the tension in her body. She quickly glanced from side to side, and seemed alert to every sound. Her unmarked car was parked next to mine.

"Be sure to lock your car door, and don't worry. I'll see you home safely."

"I'm not worried," I said. "I'm too tired to worry."

The drive home was uneventful. Contrary to what the Valdez creep had implied, the darkened Prairie held no terrors for me. I found pleasure at the sight of a full moon pasted onto the dark sky, and covering the vast expanse in a gray, smoky haze. It made me remember that the Prairie was so vast, it could be seen from a satellite. And, as I passed the observation platform, I looked at all the cars parked there. Because it was also uninhabited, it was the best place to observe the night sky.

Delcie was right behind me as I pulled into our driveway and got out of my car.

"You want to come in for something to drink?" The invitation was made more out of courtesy than desire. I was eager to be alone with Bill, and pursuing last night's conversation.

"No, thanks anyway," she said, leaning out of the car window. "Got a call while I was driving over here. I need to check out some activity on NW 13 Street. I'll be by in the morning."

"Great," I said. "Come around ten, and have coffee with us. I want to discuss a new theory I have about Jeffrey's shooting. McBride made me think of it."

Delcie made a face. "Now, Lorelei, stick to your Russian drama and stop tryin' to do our job."

The front door opened. Bill came out holding a sheath of papers. His glasses were pushed atop his head, and his hair was ruffled like it got when he was frustrated. For some reason, grading student papers always seemed to make him irritable.

"Lorelei, it's late. I was beginning to worry about you." He walked over, put his arm around my shoulder, and kissed my cheek. He peered at the car behind mine, and said, "Delcie? I haven't seen you in a long time. How did you two meet up?"

"Long story, darling," I said. I blew a kiss to Delcie. "See you tomorrow, Kevin." I challenged Delcie to remember Kevin Costner in the movie, *The Bodyguard*.

"You ain't no Whitney Houston, girl, no matter your black hair." She gave me a thumbs up. "See you guys."

Delcie backed the car out, and disappeared into the night.

I inhaled the almost cool night air as we walked into the house, arm in arm. "Doesn't it smell good, Bill? Do you smell it? There's just a hint of fall…and listen."

The katydids' song still dominated the night sounds, but I knew their season was ending as summer was coming to a close. A hooting owl made known its presence in the woods nearby.

"C'mere, you," Bill said, after he had locked the door behind us. He took me in his arms. "I don't want to talk about anything: not the rally, or rehearsals, or the way the dean screwed us on our budget while I was gone. I just want us, you and me, to take a couple of glasses of wine, go upstairs, and get reacquainted. There'll be plenty of time for the serious stuff tomorrow. Okay?"

"Yes, Bill," I said, and was grateful for a reprieve. There would now be no need to explain Delcie's presence or anything else that happened in my day. I was also too spent to further probe Bill's possible infidelities at the conference. That would take time when we were both more rested. "A glass of wine and a nice back rub is what I need about now."

"You've got it." He kissed me gently. I went upstairs to shower while he went into the kitchen for the wine.

"I'm sorry I fell asleep on you last night," I said as I walked out to the sunny patio. Bill had already set the breakfast table with a bowl of fruit, some rolls, and a carafe of coffee. "I was totally exhausted, what with the shower and your back rub…"

"You were like a dead woman." Bill got up, and gave me a hug before he pulled a chair out for me. "I must have been reading in bed for at least an hour, and I never saw you move a muscle."

"Well, I'll take seconds on the back rub." I hunched my shoulders and did a few neck rolls. "I still feel so stiff. Did we get any calls last night? I'm expecting to hear from some friends of Jeffrey's who said they'd be here this weekend."

"Your mother called, and wants you to call her. Nothing urgent. There's a message on the machine from a Janine in Oregon. Something about flying in to Gainesville. You'd better listen to it."

"Janine? That's Jeffrey's sister."

The front door bell rang; Bill went to get it, and returned with Delcie.

"Look who's here. Our new paper carrier," he said, alluding to the fact that Delcie had obviously picked up our Sunday paper from the driveway, and was carrying it in under her arm.

Delcie didn't look in a playful mood as she dropped the paper onto a chair. She was all business.

"You guys have the TV on yet this morning?"

"No, did they cover the rally, or just focus on the demonstrators?" I asked.

"Oh the rally got good coverage, but there's a bigger story than that. Lorelei, you're not going to believe it." She paused dramatically. "Crawford Keezer's dead."

"Keezer? Oh, my God." I stood up, and stared at her in shock as Bill reached for the newspaper.

"Yup... apparent suicide." Delcie stood next to the table, legs apart and hands on her hips. "It's not in the paper yet. Next of kin were notified early this morning."

I was speechless as I watched Bill sit down, and compulsively start scanning the front page as though he hadn't heard her say it wasn't in the paper.

"I'll take that cup of coffee now," Delcie said.

On my way into the kitchen for a cup, I said, "I can't believe it. What happened? Wait..."

"There's nothing in here, about it." Bill was still rifling through the first section of the paper when I returned to pour Delcie's coffee.

"She said it's not in the paper. Delcie, how did it happen? I'm in shock,"

"Forty-five pistol to the head. Nasty. Blood all over the place, and believe me it wasn't orange and blue," she said grimly. "They found him early this morning. The Medical Examiner's guess is that he died sometime last night."

"And they really think he killed himself?" It seemed too improbable.

"Forensics has a lot of work to do before we get cause of death," she said. "McBride's been assigned the case, of course."

Suicide. I still couldn't believe it as I recalled Keezer's optimism and energy at the commission meeting. "It's hard to imagine a man like that taking his own life," I said.

"Yeah, well his wife didn't believe it either," Delcie replied, sipping her coffee. "That's what the Boca detective told McBride after breaking the news to her."

"First Jeffrey, and now Keezer," I said. "And Dalton Ames before them."

The three of us were silent as we seemed to be digesting the surprising turn of events caused by Keezer's death.

"Delcie, more coffee?" Bill said. "I can make a fresh pot."

"No thanks, I'm already tanked up."

"Did you say where it happened?" I said.

"At the property…in the construction trailer."

"Was there a note? Any explanation?" Bill asked.

"I shouldn't be tellin' you any of this, but I guess it's all right given everything."

She looked at me questioningly, as though to ask how much more to say in front of Bill.

"Please, tell us everything," I said.

"There was just a sheet of paper that said 'sorry' with his signature. Not much."

"But suicide doesn't make sense," I said. "With all that money, Keezer could have left the country if he was worried they were on to him. Yet he's been hanging around here—with Chelsea cheerleader—doing business as usual."

"Chelsea who?" Bill asked looking from me to Delcie.

"I'm sure it was her we spotted in a little rendezvous with Keezer at the Prairie marina," I said to Delcie.

"Lorelei, what is going on here?" Bill asked. "You apparently haven't told me everything. If you're in any danger, I deserve to know about it. I am your husband."

I put my hand on Bill's, as I waited for Delcie's response to what I told her. He pulled his hand away, sulkily folded the newspaper, and leaned back in his chair with arms folded.

"Be sure to tell all that to McBride," Delcie said. "If it turns out to be something other than a suicide, it'll be a real mess all right. Old Homer McBride'll be in his glory, of course. Though he already has his hands full with the Waterman case."

Bill got over his sulk, and said, "I'm serious, Lorelei. I demand to know what's going on. You're both keeping things from me, and I don't like it."

I looked at Delcie; she shrugged and stared out at the woods.

"Okay, Bill. I'll tell you, but you have nothing to worry about. Delcie's been assigned to watch out for me."

I had his full attention as I described being confronted by the Valdez thug at the rally, and my conversation with McBride afterwards. I also told him about seeing Keezer and his girlfriend at the Prairie marina, and later discovering her to be Judson Sparks' wife.

When I had finished he said, "I don't like any of this. I just hope McBride, and your friend here, get you out of the picture as soon as possible."

"You can count on it, Bill," Delcie said, and gave me a cross look. "I've been telling her to stick to her stage drama, and leave the police work to us."

He looked at her doubtfully, and said, "I guess it's time I told you about my conversation with Cody Robertson."

I turned to Delcie to explain, "Cody is a former student of Bill's who's a VP at the bank that made the loan that Keezer ripped-off."

"Anyway," Bill continued, "he was naturally very interested in what I told him. I couldn't answer many of his questions, but he got the idea. He said he'd have one of his auditors start checking first thing Monday morning. The funny thing was that he didn't seem all that shocked by it."

Delcie nodded. "You'd be surprised how much white collar crime flies under the radar," she said. "Bill, you better call Detective McBride and tell him about this Robertson guy. I'm sure he'll be checking that angle, and will definitely want to interview your bank guy himself." She slid her business card across the table to Bill. "Just call the Sheriff's Office, and ask for Detective McBride."

I sat there, still trying to come up with some common thread that would explain all of the violence that had taken place since the Valdez project had been announced.

I looked at Delcie and said, "Before when I mentioned it to you, I thought it might be crazy. But I'm becoming convinced there must be ties here with Dalton's heart attack, the ransacking of the Sierra Club offices, Jeffrey's shooting, and now Keezer."

As I expressed the idea, the connections clicked: all the events could be related to one man, Jimmy Valdez, and his thugs; or maybe even Judson Sparks.

"Whoa, Lorelei," Delcie spread her hands out on the table. "Let's not get ahead of ourselves here. Right now, Keezer's death is classified as an apparent suicide. As for the others? Time will tell."

"Well, whatever happens, Delcie, I'm counting on you not to let this woman out of your sight until the whole thing is over."

Delcie grabbed my hand, and said, "We're going to be like Siamese twins, Bill. Don't you worry."

Bill stood up, absently patted my head in the way he knew I hated, and left. I heard him call to Maynard as he walked through the kitchen to his office.

"I've got to check the answering machine to see when Jeffrey's sister is coming in," I said. "Wait for me, Delcie, I'm going to run upstairs and get dressed." I got up, cleared the table, and on my way into the kitchen, I asked, "Do you mind if we stop by the hospital on the way to rehearsals? "

"The hospital's okay," she replied, stretching out her long legs, and leaning back in the chair.

When we passed the SICU waiting room, I saw Louisa Monterosa sitting hunched over, and idly thumbing through a magazine. "Louisa," I called out as I stepped into the doorway of the waiting area. "I've been thinking about you, and wondering if you and Eduardo were in town."

Louisa looked up, put her hands to her cheeks and rolled her eyes, "Ay, Lorelei." She came over and gave me a hug. "I called you at your home a little while ago and left a message. You dyed your hair?"

"Yes. When did you get in? Is Eduardo with you?"

"Yes, he's in with Jeffrey right now. We didn't get here until late yesterday. Eduardo had some work to finish before he could leave Orlando."

"Oh, excuse me, Louisa Monterosa this is my friend, Delcie Wright."

"A pleasure," Louisa replied.

"Come sit down," Louisa said, and patted the seat next to her. "I need to talk with you." She glanced at Delcie with a doubtful look as though trying to decide about including her.

Delcie picked up on Louisa's discomfort. "Lor, I'm going to check in at the nurse's station. I'll be back."

"What's happening Louisa?"

"It's Eduardo. Since we arrived here he's been…like a little crazy."

"What do you mean?"

"When we came here yesterday, we took turns going in to see Jeff. Every time Eduardo came out, he was more agitated. I tried to calm him down, and reassure him that Jeff would recover. Then he got it into his head that he wanted to see for himself where the shooting took place, and he started asking around here until he found someone who had attended your rally yesterday, and gave him directions."

"Did he go?"

"I don't know for sure where he went. I didn't see him again until this morning. Lorelei, he's an absolute wreck. I don't know what to do for him."

Eduardo appeared in the doorway to the waiting area. He looked nothing like the well-groomed, handsome man I had met in Orlando. His whole appearance was disheveled. He wore jeans and a wrinkled white shirt that looked as though he had slept in it, and he kept nervously running his hands through his hair.

"Eduardo, it's me, Lorelei…with black hair." I stood up to greet him. As he approached, I saw his eyes were red-rimmed.

"Lorelei, have you seen him?" He tightly grasped my shoulders. "Did you see what he's become? They've made him into a vegetable." He stepped around me, dropped down to the seat next to Louisa, and put his head between his knees. "My Jeffrey, he's a zombie." He looked up at me with a mixture of hurt and anger.

"But, Eduardo. I'm sure they told you he'll be coming out of the coma starting tomorrow."

"And then what? Maybe still a vegetable!" He shot back in a raspy voice. He stood up, and began to pace the room.

Louisa gave me a worried glance. I noticed Eduardo's sand-caked shoes, and concluded that he probably did go out to the Prairie.

Delcie came back into the room, looked curiously at Eduardo, and said, "I was talking with the nurses. They seem pretty optimistic about Jeff's recovery."

Eduardo stopped pacing. He scrutinized Delcie as if evaluating her authority to make such a statement. "Nurses," he spat, "they're always positive. What does it mean?" He returned to the chair across the room.

Louisa heaved a deep sigh, and looked at me helplessly.

"Delcie, this is Eduardo. He's a close friend of Jeffrey's in Orlando. Eduardo, this is my friend Delcie Wright." They glanced at one another without any greeting, and Delcie sat down next to me.

"Have you heard the news?" I asked, looking at Louisa and Eduardo, and hoping to break the tension that had filled the air. "It's about Crawford Keezer."

"The man who might have shot Jeffrey?" Louisa asked.

Eduardo's face drained of color at the mention of Keezer. He slumped down with his head in his hands.

"He's dead. They think it's suicide. It happened in the trailer at the Valdez construction site," I said.

"Because of Jeff? Did they accuse him of the shooting?" Louisa asked.

"No, I don't think that was it. My friend, Delcie here, she's a sheriff's deputy and…" I stopped in midsentence as Eduardo jumped up from the chair. His face was now the color of chalk.

"I think…" he put his hand to his mouth. "Excuse me." He rushed from the room.

"What's with him?" Delcie said.

"Louisa?" I asked.

She shrugged. "He seemed fine driving up here, but he started to get crazy as soon as he saw Jeff."

"But it wasn't the first time he'd seen him since the accident," I said. "Why would he be so agitated now?"

"I don't know," Louisa responded. "This morning—he was such a nervous wreck— I tried to get him to tell me about going out to where Jeff was shot, but…"

"He went out there?" Delcie became suddenly alert. "When?"

Louisa looked puzzled at the abrupt change of tone, "I don't know. Sometime last night."

I looked at Delcie. "You don't think he had anything to do with…"

"I don't know. But, I'm calling McBride. Be right back."

Delcie left the waiting room, and Louisa turned to me. She looked panicked. "She doesn't she think Eduardo was involved with this man Keezer's suicide, does she?"

"She is a deputy sheriff, and just the fact that Eduardo was anywhere near the scene last night. I'm sure they'll want to interview him as a possible witness."

"Oh, poor Eduardo." Tears welled in Louisa's eyes. "Excuse me, Lorelei; I'll be back in a few minutes. When Eduardo returns, please try to comfort him. I don't know what to say anymore."

Delcie walked in as Louisa left.

"They're not leaving are they?" she said. "I put a call out to McBride. I'm sure he'll get over here when he gets the message."

"No, I think she just went out to the ladies room, and Eduardo should be back soon. Look, I'm going in to see Jeffrey."

"Uh, before you go in there, did Louisa tell you where they were staying? Do you know what kind of car they're driving?"

"I don't know. Ask her when she comes back."

"And you're sure they're coming back?" Delcie said suspiciously.

"Hey, lighten up, Delcie. These people are friends of Jeffrey's; they aren't criminals."

"Yeah, you're right. I just wouldn't want to have to answer to McBride if this guy, Eduardo, kind of disappears on us."

I left Delcie standing at the entrance to the intensive care waiting room anxiously monitoring the hospital corridor.

Chapter 22

Eduardo's behavior was disturbing, but I quickly forgot about him as I entered Jeffrey's cubicle. I sat at his bedside, and described the highlights of the rally as though he could hear me. I left out any mention Jimmy Valdez's threats, or the arrests of some of Jeffrey's buddies in EcoSave!, and I didn't say anything about Keezer's death. I simply told him about the enthusiastic crowd—named some of the politicians and speakers who were there—and described the scene on Highway 441.

"You would have loved seeing your old gang in costume, and staging their guerilla theater across the highway. Traffic came to a standstill, and the police chased after them was like an old time Keystone Cops movie. It was hilarious."

I suddenly was struck by the sharp contrast between my cheery monologue and Jeffrey's still, lifeless figure.

"The only thing it lacked was you, Jeffrey, I said softly, and leaned close to his pillow. "I missed you. Your sister and your mom will probably be here tomorrow. It's going to be a big day for you. They'll be reducing the drugs that have allowed you to heal. So please, dear, start gathering your strength to return to us." The bandages had been trimmed and I was able to kiss his cool forehead before leaving the room.

I walked out of the unit, and Delcie, McBride, and Louisa were standing in a tight knot in a corner of the waiting room. They stopped talking when they saw me at the door. Louisa sat down. Her face was flushed, and she gave me a pleading look.

Delcie greeted me, "How is he?"

"The same. I'm anxious for him to be out of this coma. I miss him." There was an unexpected catch of emotion in my voice.

McBride gave me a curious glance, and said, "We seem to have lost one of your friends."

I looked at Louisa. "Eduardo? He hasn't come back yet?" Louisa shook her head and clasped her hands together.

"We were just talking to Ms. Monterosa, and she seems baffled by her friend's disappearance," McBride said.

"I told them he probably went back to the hotel," she said. "You saw for yourself he was sick."

Delcie looked skeptical. "And maybe a little scared," she said, speaking to McBride. "He got agitated when Lorelei—Mrs. Crane—mentioned that I was a deputy, and that's when he left the room."

"Can you explain his behavior?" McBride asked Louisa.

"Eduardo and Jeffrey are very close," she replied. "He was naturally upset to see Jeffrey in this condition, and I think he didn't sleep much last night. I don't know why your deputy is so suspicious. He probably just went back to the hotel to get some rest. I'm sure you'll find him there, Detective."

"Okay, we'll see," McBride said. "How long will you and Mr. Sanchez be staying in Gainesville?"

"I have to be at work tomorrow, but Eduardo mentioned he'd stay here for another day or so. Until Jeff had regained consciousness."

"What kind of car is Mr. Sanchez driving?"

"We drove up together. In my car."

"What's the color and make?" Both McBride and Delcie had their notebooks out.

"It's a brand new dark green Volvo sedan," she said, and looked at me with a worried expression.

"The license number?"

"Just a minute." Louisa dug into her handbag, pulled out her registration, and handed it to McBride.

I pulled Delcie away, and whispered, "Believe me, the man you saw here today is nothing like the one I met in Orlando."

"I hate to tell you, but he acted guilty as hell about something. You know revenge can cause even nice people to do some very ugly things."

"Deputy Wright," McBride spoke brusquely as he approached us, his notebook in hand. "Since you know what this guy Sanchez looks like, I want you to get over to the Holiday Inn, and see if he's there. If he is, hang on to him. Call for a backup to meet you. Here's the tag number for the car. Don't lose it. We might need to call in an APB."

Delcie rolled her eyes at me. "Yes, sir," she said to McBride.

He grabbed her arm. "Just tell him I want to talk to him, and for Pete's sake, don't scare him. We don't need a possible eye-witness bolting on us again." He turned from Delcie to me. "Mrs. Crane, if you could hang around for a few minutes, I want to talk to you."

Louisa was sitting across the room. Her face was now pale, and expressionless.

"Yes, I'll stay, but Louisa needs a ride back to the hotel."

"Deputy Wright can take her back," McBride said turning to Delcie.

"Sure," Delcie agreed.

"But, Wright," he lowered his voice, "see the lady to her room before you check on Mr. Sanchez. I don't want them talking to one another. Got it?"

"Of course," Delcie said, walked over to Louisa, bent down and gently took her by the arm to leave. Louisa looked and acted like she was in shock.

"Call me as soon as you find out if he's there," McBride added as they were leaving the room.

I followed McBride's brisk pace to the end of the hallway where, just a week ago, Becky and I had stood while she emotionally confessed her love for Jeffrey.

"We got our shooter," he bluntly announced.

It took me a moment to grasp what he was saying, "You mean?" I looked back toward the SICU. His news was so direct and unexpected. "Who?" I asked.

"Turns out to be your admirer, one "A.J." Angus James Hill."

"Really? He didn't seem the type," I said thinking of his shy response to me.

"We confronted him after a couple of his friends told us about the deer head he'd bagged last week. By the way, your boss' son, Hank Demeter, was real helpful. I had to press him a bit, but he finally admitted that A.J. had bragged to him about the deer. That put him at the scene. We got a search warrant, found his rifle—pretty sure it'll match up—and he confessed."

"Just like that?" I said astonished at simplicity of it all.

"It's sometimes like that when you get some hard evidence to show them. They just give up," McBride said.

"But why did he shoot Jeffrey?"

"Said he didn't know why."

"That doesn't make sense."

"Apparently, he accidentally came upon the two men: Waterman, and the other man. A.J. was hauling this deer rack on his back, in a kind of sling, when he looked up and says he saw them too close to just be talking…maybe he thought they were going to be kissing. He said he'd seen queers out there before, and it always made him angry. When he recognized Waterman—the same guy who hassled him about hunting—he took a shot at him. Thought he aimed over Waterman's head, but said the load on his back must have thrown his aim off. He didn't mean to hit him; just wanted to scare'em."

"Good Lord. Where do all these vicious homophobic young men come from?"

"I don't know about vicious," McBride said. "Poor kid, I kind of felt sorry for him. He was bawling by the time I finished with him. Course, his parents were in shock. Hardworking people; father's a butcher at a market in Alachua, and the mother works in the cafeteria at the elementary school. When his father heard what A.J. had done, he seemed more upset about the deer carcass the kid left behind than he was over the shooting—'waste of good meat,' he said.'"

"You felt sorry for A.J.?" I asked, suddenly feeling indignant. "What about the man in there?" I pointed down the corridor. "He's been in a coma for a week. We're not even sure he'll be all right when he comes out. This was an evil hate crime, and Jeffrey's life was nearly taken by this so-called 'poor kid'?"

"Aw, c'mon, Mrs. Crane. You gotta see it from my perspective. I've seen a lot of people you'd call evil, but here's a boy with a name like Angus—probably been teased all his life—he was just being impulsive."

"Impulsive? Then how come a guy with a name like Homer became a cop, not a killer. He must have taken some teasing without shooting anybody."

McBride stepped back as if I had thrown water at him. Delcie had warned me that H. "Mac" McBride would skewer anyone who addressed him by his first name. His eyes narrowed, and he cocked his head. I thought he was going to respond with some angry retort, but instead his face broke into a smile.

"I take your point. But hopefully, your friend will recover. This boy's looking at doing a mandatory 20 years for attempted murder. He'll be middle-aged before he gets out."

"Well, maybe he'll learn some anger management in prison," I retorted.

"You're kidding, of course," he said. "Prison's going to shape the rest of his life. Like too damn many A.J.'s just stupid or too impulsive. They should be working or in college. When they do get out, there's precious little done to help them reenter society so a lot of them will wind up going back. Here in the so-called land of the free, we have more people incarcerated than any country in the world, more than two million and rising! And Florida's leads the pack, did you know that?"

I admired McBride's outrage at the criminal justice system, but it didn't make me any more sympathetic toward the man who shot Jeffrey.

McBride's cell phone rang; he turned his back, and walked a little way down the hall. Despite his low voice, I could hear what he was saying.

"Yeah, I thought so. Okay, call in an APB. You've got the tag number. Stay there with the woman. I'll be over in a few minutes."

He returned to where I stood. "Sanchez isn't at the hotel."

"Oh, dear." It was all I could think of to say."

"Do you have your own car, or did Deputy Wright drive you into town?"

"No, she followed me to the hospital. I've got my car."

"Where are you going now?"

"To the theater. Oh, I almost forgot to tell you," I said as we started walking toward the elevators. "My husband had a message from a former student at the bank that made the loan to Valdez. Their auditor will be checking on it tomorrow. Deputy Wright told Bill to call and tell you about it."

"Good. Is he home today?"

"Yes, but you may have to leave a message. He often doesn't answer the phone." My thoughts flashed to Eduardo. "He couldn't have gone far, Eduardo I mean. What do you think?"

"Don't worry, we'll find him," he said, dismissively.

We stood waiting for the elevator in silence. I kept thinking about Eduardo, and wondering where he would turn in his panic.

"Say, when's your opening night?"

McBride's suddenly light tone surprised me. "This Friday," I replied. "I couldn't believe it when you said you would attend. A theater-going homicide detective—like a character right out of a British mystery novel."

He looked slightly embarrassed. "I don't usually go to plays, but you're the first actress I've gotten to know. I'd like to see how you do."

The elevator arrived, and we got in. "I get extra tickets for the opening. I'll leave one for you at the box office?"

"I'd appreciate that," he said.

"Will you need one ticket or two?" Did I sound like I was fishing for personal information, I wondered?

"Just one, thanks."

"Good, and please join us after the play for a little celebration at our house."

"I'll do that, Mrs. Crane. Now, please do me a favor. Don't stop off anywhere on your way to the theater. I'll have Wright over there in a little while. She'll follow you home again tonight."

"Do you think it's necessary?" I asked. "Now that Mr. Keezer is dead, it's over, isn't it?"

We were walking out into the parking lot. McBride stopped, stepped directly in front of me, and said in a low and very firm voice,

"Mrs. Crane, we haven't yet confirmed how Keezer died. My own suspicion is it'll turn out to be a homicide. Unfortunately, you have critical information about some of the suspects. Yes, you do need to be protected, trust me. Please be very careful, and do as I say."

I appreciated his warning, but didn't understand his comment about my having critical information. Everything I knew was known to a number of people, including Valdez's own operatives. Besides, with a sheriff's deputy as my bodyguard, I couldn't imagine anyone attempting to harm me.

"C'mon, I'll walk you to your car," McBride said, and took my arm.

Driving away from the hospital, I realized that I was hungry. McBride's warning not to make any stops still struck me as overly cautious. I wanted something to eat that would be healthy, and tide me over till our dinner break, when the theater would provide food. It couldn't be anything fattening, like fast food, now that the measurements had been taken for my costume. I drove to my favorite supermarket.

The front lot was crowded so I pulled into a space on the side of the building. I was reflecting on the whole scene at the hospital, and especially upon McBride's news about A.J. Hill. I tried to imagine what triggered his deadly impulse. Was he abused as a child? Did he suffer from the homophobic's threatened sexual identity?

Thinking about the young man's motivation, reminded me how surprised people are when I play some evil or dysfunctional character. They often ask, "How can you be so convincing?" "It's called acting," is my brief reply. But if they're really interested, I explain that—given the right circumstances—all of us have the potential for every human trait and behavior. Over the years, I've simply learned how to connect with those places within myself. Despite my understanding of human behavior, a part of me still felt unforgiving toward Hill.

I turned off the ignition, and out of the corner of my eye I saw a black limo pull into the space next to me. I glanced at it to see a man in dark pants and shirt emerge. I stepped out of my car, and the man appeared next to me so suddenly I bumped into him.

"This way, please, Mrs. Crane," he said, forcefully taking my arm and moving me to the now opened limo door.

"Hey, what's going on?" I sputtered, stunned by the speed and power of his movements. I attempted to cry "HELP!" but it came out more like a weak squeal. My abductor's gloved hand was over my mouth, before I could utter another cry, as he quite swiftly shoved me into the darkened interior. I landed on a side bench seat.

The door slammed shut, locks clicked, and we were moving. Good God, I thought, I'm being abducted again. Right here in Gainesville.

I banged on the smoky window separating the cab from the driver's compartment, to get the men's attention, and to see if I recognized them. I suspected it might be Mr. Muscles at the wheel, but couldn't be sure because the man wore a chauffeur's uniform complete with cap.

I picked up my handbag, from where I had dropped it on the floor, and started rummaging through it.

"Please, let me find the damn cell phone," I said, as my eyes became accustomed to the dark interior.

It was then I saw I was not alone.

"Mr. Valdez?"

He sat in the far corner of the back seat. His slight frame and dark clothing had kept him shadowed by the black leather interior. It was the small gold chain around his neck that had caught my eye, and I was aware of the faint aroma of lime. He held a drink glass in his hand.

This obviously was not the same enraged man I had talked to at the rally, but one who was cool, in control, and much more like when I had first met him with Jeffrey and Becky. His cold, dark hooded eyes appraised me in a way that gave me the creeps. If he had been an actor, Jimmy Valdez would have been typecast in the role of a suave villain.

"Yes, Mrs. Crane. I apologize for the roughness of your arrival. I wanted to see you earlier, but you always seem to be surrounded by your friends or the police, and I wasn't sure you would voluntarily meet me for a little talk."

"Talk? Why don't you and your men ever just ask to speak to someone?" I said, with more bravado than I felt. "These strong-arm tactics are outrageous, not to mention illegal. I've already reported one of your thugs to the police, and now this..."

"Yes, of course, Mrs. Crane you could report me as well. But under the circumstances, I don't think you will. Besides, no one has actually harmed you, have they?"

"It was harmful scaring me out of my wits, and threatening to hurt me. What circumstances? What do you mean?"

"Why don't you relax," he said, carefully placing his glass in the armrest holder. "It isn't my intention to scare you, and I promise no harm will come to you."

I didn't believe him on either count, but I said nothing.

"I think we can be mutually helpful to one another."

"Helpful? If you really want to be helpful, tell your goons to drive me back to my car."

"Give me a few minutes, and I'll tell you what I want. Would you like something to drink?" He motioned to a small bar. "We have..."

"Look, Mr. Valdez, I want out of here, right now!" The limo had stopped in traffic, and I pushed on the door handle. It didn't budge.

"Have it your way," he said. "I'll get to the point."

He leaned forward, and eyed me with that penetrating look I recalled from our first meeting. It disconcerted me now as it did then. McBride's advice that I drive directly to the theater echoed in my mind. I silently chided myself for my naiveté. Or, was it arrogance that had put me in harm's way?

"What is your point?" I asked. I pushed on the window button in hopes it would open, and I could scream for help. It didn't move. I was totally locked in.

"I understand Eduardo Sanchez left Gainesville in a hurry today," he said. "And by the way, I know all about him and your former husband. I also know it was Sanchez who told you about the theft committed by my partner and his mistress. And now, unfortunately, my partner has been murdered."

"Murdered?" I was shocked by his certainty. "The police think it was suicide."

I stared at him, and his eyes darted nervously away from me. He's very uneasy about something, I thought. Oh great, Lorelei, now you're locked in a car with a murderer!

There was a long pause before he resumed eye contact and spoke again. "I know my partner," he said, and absently started to play with the chain watch that hung loosely on his wrist. "He would not have taken his own life."

"If not, who do you think killed him? Maybe someone like you who he cheated out of a million dollars?" I said, surprised at my own boldness. I studied Valdez, waiting to see his reaction.

"That's just what I want to talk to you about, Mrs. Crane," he said, seeming to relax. "Why do you think Mr. Sanchez left town so hurriedly? Especially since his boyfriend is still in a coma?"

"I don't know. Maybe he just panicked." I know the feeling, I thought, as I was aware that all my old body aches had returned.

"No, it's more than panic," he said. "What would you say if I told you Mr. Sanchez and my partner had a fight last night in the construction trailer?"

I was momentarily speechless.

"Eduardo…with Keezer?" I knew Eduardo had gone to the Prairie, but it never occurred to me he would have gone there to seek out Keezer.

"Yes, it is a surprising twist, isn't it?" It was his turn to study my response.

"But wait a minute," I said. "How do you know all of this? Have you told the police?"

"No, I haven't told them. I wanted to talk to you about it."

"Talk to me? Why?"

He uncrossed his legs and leaned forward. Instinctively, I recoiled.

"I decided to talk to you, because they probably won't believe me, Mrs. Crane. You see, when they discover that it was murder and not suicide, I will be the most obvious suspect...as you yourself pointed out. The headlines will read, *Business Partner Suspected of Murder*."

"You still haven't told me how you know Eduardo fought with Keezer." I said, heedlessly pushing him for some revealing admission.

He sighed, and bent his head in thought before responding. "I called the construction trailer last night. Crawford answered, and sounded very drunk. I could hear someone talking to him in the background; it was a man's voice. Crawford told me he'd call right back, but he never did. And then..."

"And you think Eduardo was with him?"

"Yes, who else? I know he thought it was my partner who shot his friend."

"Oh yes, the revenge motive. I still don't get what you want from me? You've not exactly endeared yourself."

"Yes, I know. I'm the enemy. But if you care about Mr. Sanchez at all, I can forget the phone call to Keezer."

"Is that a bribe? For what?"

"I want your husband to persuade Cody Robertson to give me time to repay the money that was stolen. If the bank calls in the authorities and demands immediate repayment of the loan, it could ruin me—my reputation—and harm a lot of other people. That's why I wanted you to persuade Keezer to return the money. If he thought others knew about it...anyway, I couldn't approach him myself. He would have just denied it, or worse. Now, of course, it's too late for any of that."

This was crazy; yet, it at least explained why his muscle man had made the strange demand that I approach Keezer about returning the money.

"How do you know my husband's connection with your bank?" I asked.

"I have my sources."

I wondered if his sources included a tap on my telephone. Which led me to reconsider the possibility of a break-in on the night before Bill returned: the night when there were sounds downstairs, and I found the broken wine glass, and the patio door that had been mysteriously shut.

Valdez studied his manicured fingernails, and then looked up at me, and said, "So what do you think of my proposition, Mrs. Crane? Get your husband to talk with his friend at the bank, and everyone wins. If not..."

The limo air was icy, and I felt myself starting to shiver. But it was more than just the temperature; it was also a reaction to his veiled threat, and the ominous stare that accompanied it.

"What I think is that I want you to take me back to my car. Right now! This is very confusing: first you terrify me with your abduction tactics, and now you want me to cooperate in a scheme to save your reputation."

"And that of your friend, Mr. Sanchez. Here's my card. Call when you've thought it over." He slipped the card into my handbag.

The car stopped. I peered through the window, and saw we had pulled up next to my car.

Valdez pushed a button, and softly said a few words in Spanish to the driver. The door locks clicked, I opened the door, and stepped out of the limo.

"Think about it, Mrs. Crane. You'll find it's in our mutual best interests."

I slammed the door, and the limo backed out, and pulled away. Still stunned by the startling encounter with Jimmy Valdez, I momentarily stood in the hot sun next to my car, rubbing my arms. I was trying to get relief from the goose bumps I experienced in his presence.

Driving to the theater, I examined Valdez's motives. He knew of my close relationship with the sheriff's office. Was he playing mind games? Did he count on me telling them about the phone call, and thus diverting suspicion from him to Eduardo? Unless there was a record of it, there was only his word for the call. Maybe he knew Eduardo was there because he, too, was at the trailer with Keezer. Did he really think I wanted to protect Eduardo enough to withhold evidence from the police, and get Bill to influence his banker? And how did Valdez know that Eduardo had left town?

My head was spinning with questions, but the one thing I did know was that I didn't trust Valdez; he was shrewd, desperate, and probably weaving a complex web using me as bait. I pulled up to the theater, and knew I would have to wait until later for help in trying to sort out this plot.

Before getting out of the car, I called home on the cell phone, and reassured Bill that I was all right.

Delcie was standing at the door of my car just as I got out. "Where the hell you been, girl? I was about to put out a bulletin on you."

"Delcie, you won't believe it. Valdez picked me up at the supermarket."

"Jimmy Valdez? McBride's been callin' all over town for him."

"That's interesting. Let's go. I can't be late," I said, putting my arm through hers as we climbed the steps to the theater. "Did they find Eduardo yet?"

"No, but they'll catch up with him. He couldn't have gotten far. So what's this about Jimmy Valdez? How'd he pick you up?"

"In a black chauffeured limo. Mr. Valdez had a most interesting proposition. I'll tell you about it later."

"Proposition? Was he in his own limo or a rental?"

"C'mon Del, I'm really rushed. I guess it was his," I said, not knowing exactly why I thought so.

"I'm relieved to see you safe and sound. I was ready to call McBride, and tell him you weren't here yet. He wouldn't of liked that, and he'll definitely want to know about your encounter with Valdez. Let me see if I can reach him."

We had stopped in the lobby, and other actors hurried by us into the theatre. "No, please don't Delcie," I pleaded, grabbing hold of both of her hands. "I've got to get into the theater. I promise it wasn't anything that can't wait a few hours."

She frowned, and said, "I shouldn't let it wait, but okay let's pretend you didn't tell me anything just yet."

"Oh, thanks, you're a trooper! No joke intended. Look, we probably won't be finished until 10:30 or later. You know we open this Friday night."

"I know. I already bought a ticket."

"You did? I could have gotten one for you. Anyway, don't wait around for me. I'll call you when we're through."

"Oh no, I'll be over around ten. And I'll want to hear all about your encounter with Valdez."

I gave her a quick hug. "Okay, your call. See you later."

I fell in step with a couple of fellow actors, and gave Delcie a royal wave. I was aware that, at this moment, I had roles in two absorbing plots; Chekhov's, and the real life drama whose ending was as yet unknown.

Chapter 23

"We found him," Delcie said, as I walked out of rehearsals into the theater lobby. She was sitting on a bench near the box office, and got up to greet me. It was almost eleven o'clock.

"Found him?" I repeated, momentarily surprised to see Delcie, and confused by her assertion.

"You know, your friend, Sanchez. Picked him up on I-75, at the Plaza, just outside of Orlando. Highway patrol officers identified him."

"Is he…is he all right?" I asked, picturing Eduardo's extreme distress at the hospital, and feeling thrust back into real life by Delcie's announcement.

"Oh yeah. He didn't even resist. They said he was dazed. Anyway, he willingly drove back to Gainesville with them. McBride's been interviewing him."

"What's his story? No, don't even try to tell me right now. I'm exhausted, and incapable of comprehending anything. Renee worked us so hard my brain is mush—too much Russian emotion. I'm glad Eduardo's all right. He's not in jail or anything?"

"He wasn't charged," she said. "I guess McBride hasn't made a real connection between him and Keezer's murder."

"So it's definitely murder now?" I asked, thinking about Jimmy Valdez's prediction.

"Not officially, but McBride's operating on that assumption. The information he's gathered, and initial evidence at the scene makes suicide less certain than it first appeared. The crime scene guys are still working it, and McBride's checking possible suspects, getting toxicology, and all that."

"Toxicology? I thought he died from a gun shot?"

"True, but apparently they found a couple of Roofies lyin' around. The M.E.'s thinking he may have been under the influence at the time he died."

"Roofies? The 'date rape' drug?"

"Yup."

It didn't make sense, but I was suddenly distracted by experiencing a wave of nausea. The lack of food, an accumulation of stress from the day's events, and rehearsals were taking their toll.

"I've really got to get home, Delcie. Let's get out of here."

"Are you sure you're up to driving? I could take you home, and pick you up in the morning."

"Maybe that's a good idea. My reflexes are probably shot. I must have walked miles back and forth across the stage; I repeated one scene alone about a dozen times. Did McBride ever talk to Jimmy Valdez?"

We walked out of the theater to Delcie's car.

"No, and he really wants to. But the way I heard it, Valdez already has local counsel, and nobody's talking to the police."

"He's slick all right," I said remembering his observation about being first in line as a suspect.

"And rich. Now remember, you promised to tell me about Valdez picking you up before you went into rehearsals. What happened? McBride'll want to hear every little detail."

"It's complicated, and I need to sort it out. Basically, he wants Bill to persuade Valdez's banker to keep everything under wraps and let him pay off the missing money. "

"Why'd he think Bill would do that?"

"Like I said, it's complicated. He offered a bribe."

"What could Jimmy Valdez possibly offer to bribe Professor Bill Crane? Building a new Business College with his name on it?" She laughed.

"It was me he was bribing. He thought he could get to me by promising to protect Eduardo."

Delcie looked totally confused.

"I know," I said, getting into her car. "I told you it's confusing, and frankly I can't even think about it right now."

"Okay, I won't push, but you've got to tell McBride first thing in the morning."

I nodded, and tried to slump down in the seat as much as the seat belt would allow.

To her credit, Delcie didn't ask me anymore questions. She did most of the talking. She described her surprise at the drug found near Keezer's body, and went on about it. She explained that Rohypnol, also known as "Roofies," had a bunch of other street names. My attention drifted in and out, and I tried to imagine Crawford Keezer using a drug like the one she described.

"What's it like?" I asked, "Cocaine, marijuana, or what?"

"It's a heavy duty tranquilizer—much more powerful than valium—but it's not prescribed by doctors, at least not in the States. It's mostly high school and college kids who are using it. Combined with other popular drugs, it gives a quick, intense high. It's popular in gay bars, too."

"Oh no," I muttered, hoping that wouldn't be another connection with Eduardo.

"What?" Delcie asked, glancing at me.

"I'm confused," I said. "Do they actually think Keezer used Roofies?"

"More likely, someone doped him."

"But why?"

She shrugged, "That's what McBride's got to find out."

We rode in silence until she drove up to my house.

"What time do you need to be in town tomorrow?" Delcie asked.

"Oh, you don't have to pick me up. Bill will drive me to my car. He goes to campus late on Mondays."

"I shouldn't let you loose after what happened today."

I nodded sheepishly. "But I'll be with Bill. Honestly, I've learned my lesson."

She cocked her head, raised one eyebrow, and then laughed. "Jesus, Lorelei, you make it sound like I'm your mama. Okay then, as long as Bill's with you."

"I'll call you and McBride when I get to town. Promise," I said crossing my heart, and getting out of the car.

I entered the house, and leaned back against the closed door to gather my strength for the climb upstairs. Except for the hall light, it was dark on the ground floor. I heard the TV in the bedroom, and called to Bill as I went up. He didn't answer.

All the lights were on, Bill was in his pajamas, and sprawled on top of the bed. A half-open book lay on his chest, and he was asleep. We really need to get day jobs, I thought, as I sat down next to him. I leaned over, and kissed him.

"Bill, I'm home," I whispered as I tickled one of his feet.

He jerked awake and said, "Lorelei? Are you finally home?" He pulled himself up against the headboard, and rubbed his eyes. His sleepy look and the lock of hair that hung over his forehead made him look boyishly vulnerable.

"I miss you, dammit," he said.

"You must have been desperate to turn to the TV for company," I said, getting up to switch off the television.

"Just turned it on for news," he replied. "There are a bunch of new tropical storms brewing in the Caribbean. They say we could get one of them. How did rehearsals go? Ready for the big opening night?"

I sighed, "As ready as can be. The technical is Thursday. We'll be in full costume—sets, lighting, and music. I'm sure it'll be another long day."

"Well, brace yourself; I have some dramatic news for you for a change," he said.

"What's that?"

"Your friend Louisa called." He glanced at the clock on the nightstand. "It was about an hour ago. She asked me to recommend an attorney for her friend, Mr. Sanchez."

"What?" I stopped undressing, and stood at the foot of the bed.

"Apparently the police have been questioning him for hours about Keezer's death."

"And? Go on."

"Louisa said he admitted to being near the scene around the time."

I felt a shiver as my mind flashed back to the conversation with Jimmy Valdez. Was he telling the truth after all? Could Eduardo have been there with Keezer? "But, Delcie just told me that they didn't arrest him."

"They didn't. But Louisa thinks he should have a lawyer. I agreed."

"Did you give her a name?"

"The only criminal lawyer I know is a guy at the UF Law School. He takes a case from time to time. I told her if he can't handle it, he'll refer her to someone else."

"Good. Delcie told me McBride now thinks Keezer was murdered."

"Murdered? I didn't hear anything about it on the news."

"They don't have proof yet."

Bill got out of bed, and stood in front of me. "So, are there any other dramas that you've gotten into today? I hope Delcie stuck with you like she promised."

"Bill, they arrested the man who shot Jeffrey!" I sat on the foot of bed. I was barely able to stand anymore, let alone be subjected to any critical questioning.

"I didn't hear about that either, but then I've been dozing on and off."

"I met Detective McBride at the hospital. He told me it was the young man who Jeffrey and I encountered when we were scouting the rally site."

"No kidding," he said, sitting down next to me. "Why in heaven's name did he shoot Jeffrey?"

I told him the story McBride had recounted to me, and reluctantly included the part about Jeffrey and the other man in a near embrace. I didn't intend to "out" Jeffrey, but it was time for Bill to get the whole story.

"So Jeffrey's gay now?" He shook his head with an amused look on his face. "Did you know?"

"Not until recently."

"Who's the other guy? Anyone we know?"

"They don't know yet," I said. I found myself unable to name the sleazy Judson Sparks as someone with whom Jeffrey could be involved.

"Well, I guess I don't have to worry about the competition, do I?"

"Bill!" I said, and slapped his leg. "What a flippant thing to say. I'm very worried about Jeffrey."

"And the kid just took a shot him?"

"He's claiming he it was an impulse, and he only meant to scare them."

Bill rubbed his foreheaed, a gesture he used whenever he felt tired and stressed. "Dammit, Lorelei, this is just what I've been afraid of. Ever since Jeffrey's been back in Gainesville, you've allowed yourself to get into one risky situation after another. It's not like you to get so dangerously involved in something like this."

"It's not Jeffrey's fault," I said. "It's this whole Valdez project; it's gotten so weird."

"What else happened today?"

I told him about the scene at the hospital in which Eduardo panicked and disappeared when he learned that Delcie was a sheriff's deputy. Next, I recounted my encounter with Jimmy Valdez. I made it sound friendlier than it felt at the time. I told him what Valdez had proposed, that he would forget about hearing Eduardo's voice at Keezer's, if Cody Robertson could be persuaded to deal privately with him.

"Where in hell was Delcie when this happened? I thought she was supposed to be protecting you?"

"Don't blame Delcie; she had to take Louisa back to the hotel. McBride warned me not to stop. It was entirely my fault."

"This just keeps getting worse," Bill said. "Your Russian drama pales in comparison. Anyway, why did Valdez think I could make all that happen? Was he being straight with you, or do you think he wanted something else? "

"I'm not sure," I mumbled, falling back on the bed.

"Lorelei?"

"I said, I don't know. I'm confused, and exhausted. Let's just go to sleep and discuss it in the morning. Maybe you can help me to sort it all out."

Bill returned to his side of the bed. I watched him as he took a sip of water, crawled under the covers, and turned off his reading light. I, too, got under the covers. We lay silently, side by side. I was overtired, and my eyes felt propped open. I watched the moonlight, filtering through the trees into our room, and draping across the foot of the bed like a light summer blanket. It was a soothing sight, and I began to feel sleepy at last.

Bill gripped my hand, and said, "Something still doesn't make sense to me. Why would Valdez be foolish enough to compromise himself with that proposal? Withholding evidence is illegal, and everyone knows it."

"I think he's desperate," I said. "He sees nothing but ruin if the fraud becomes public, and the bank calls the loan."

"Desperate enough to kill his partner? I guess it happens."

"I don't know. I asked him that point blank to see how he'd react."

"You did?" He released my hand, and turned on his side to face me. "Darling, you're either very brave or very foolish. How did he react?"

"Hard to read. He admitted he'd be an obvious suspect. That's probably why he got a lawyer right away."

"He took such a chance confronting you the way he did. Then again, sometimes very smart people can do some very stupid things. Anyway, promise me you'll call Detective McBride first thing in the morning, and tell him everything. And I mean everything, Lorelei. Promise me."

"Yes, dear, I will."

He emitted a grunt, snuggled against me, making me feel warm and completely protected. "Love you," I murmured dreamily, but was swept into a troubled sleep picturing myself in the limo with Valdez. My last conscious thought was: who really could have been with Keezer when Valdez called him—if, indeed, he called?

I awakened early Monday with a feeling of urgency to learn about Eduardo's encounter with the police, and what he told them about his activities the night Keezer died. I called Louisa and arranged to stop by the hotel to see her and Eduardo.

At breakfast, Bill reminded me of my promise to talk to McBride about my encounter with Jimmy Valdez, and he agreed to drive me into Gainesville. I didn't mention the stop I planned to make before going to see McBride. I figured it best to avoid another confrontation about my being "dangerously involved," as he had described it.

He dropped me off at the theater; I picked up my car, and drove to the Holiday Inn. On the way, I continued to puzzle over Jimmy Valdez's assertion that it was Eduardo's voice he heard in the background when he talked to Keezer. The more I thought about it, I concluded that several other people could have been there, including Valdez himself.

The elevator let me off at the 3rd floor; I found Louisa's room, and knocked at the door.

"Lorelei, please, come in," Louisa said, in her silken voice, ushering me into the sunny room. I walked past the bathroom, with its pleasant perfumed aromas, and saw Eduardo hunched in a chair facing the window. He was wearing sunglasses and staring outside. He seemed oblivious to my arrival.

"Eduardo. Lorelei is here," Louisa said, and gently touched his shoulder.

He turned slowly, stood up, and shook his head as if to clear it from what he had been thinking, "Lorelei, I'm so sorry. Please." He gestured me to the other chair.

Though I was unable to see his eyes through the dark lenses, Eduardo looked even worse than the day before. He was unshaven, his slacks and long white sleeved shirt looked like he had slept in them, and his entire posture communicated defeat.

"Eduardo. The glasses?" Louisa said.

Eduardo shrugged, and slowly removed his sunglasses. His eyes appeared more deep-set then I remembered, and he held my gaze only briefly.

Louisa sat on the edge of the bed near us. “Eduardo, tell Lorelei what you told the detective last night. She’s here to help.”

He put his hands up to his face before he spoke. “I don’t know how you can help. The detective…he didn’t seem to believe me.”

“Tell me what you said to him. I know Detective McBride. He’s not a bad guy, and I’m going to see him later.”

“Please, Eduardo,” Louisa said. “Give her a chance.” She reached over and touched his hand.

“Okay. I’ll tell you. God, they made me repeat it over and over again.”

“They drove him back from Orlando,” Louisa explained

“I came back willingly,” Eduardo responded with a flash of defensiveness. “I want to cooperate. I have nothing to hide.”

“Of course you don’t,” Louisa assured him in a soothing tone, and turned to me. “He called me from the Sheriffs office when he arrived back in Gainesville, but then they questioned him for hours.

I continued to study this man who had undergone a transformation since our first meeting at the Candlelight Club in Orlando. He wore two small band aids, one on his cheek and another on the side of his neck. It struck me as odd since he obviously had not shaved. I watched patiently as he leaned forward in his chair, massaged his temples, and took a deep breath before speaking.

“I told them after seeing Jeff just lying there in intensive care—looking like a vegetable—I kind of went crazy. I needed to see for myself where he was shot. I couldn’t understand how such a thing could have happened. So I asked around until I got directions. It wasn’t hard to find the spot because there were stakes with ribbons at the entrance.”

He got up from the chair and stood facing the window before turning back to me. “I walked around for awhile—looking for where Jeff might have been standing—trying to picture the whole thing, you know? I must have wandered around for maybe a half hour or so. It was dark by that time, and I got lost. I didn’t have a flashlight or anything. At one point I even tripped and landed on something sharp…a piece of glass, I don’t know, but I was bleeding.” He lightly touched his left arm, but it was covered by his shirt sleeve.

Ah, I thought, does that also explain the band aids on his face?

"Then I saw light through the woods, and headed toward it." He walked over to the desk, took a drink from a glass of water, and returned to the chair. He slouched down before continuing, and stared ahead as though visualizing the scene. "It was coming from a trailer in a clearing. I walked toward it, and was going to knock on the door to ask for directions to the road, but when I got closer I heard shouting inside." He looked up at me, "I didn't want to get into it, so I moved around until I saw a truck parked near the trailer. I found a path it had made, and walked back onto the highway to Louisa's car."

"And then you came back to the hotel?" I asked.

"No, I was still real upset. I stopped at some bar—Charley's I think it was called. I got cleaned-up, had a few drinks, and came back to the hotel." He stopped talking, and dropped his head as though the telling had exhausted him. He took the sunglasses from his shirt pocket, and put them on again.

"And that's what you told them?" I said.

He nodded.

"Did you know it was the Valdez construction trailer, and that Crawford Keezer might be inside?"

His head jerked up defensively. "No. How could I know that?"

"Could you hear what the argument was about?"

"The police kept asking me that. I told them I didn't hang around long enough to listen to the argument."

"Was it two men you heard?"

"I don't know. I think so. Maybe."

"Did you see another car there?"

Eduardo squirmed, and looked at Louisa. She reached over, put her hand on mine, and nodded at me as though to say "enough." I realized that my questions must have seemed to him like another interrogation. I stopped talking, sat back, and watched Eduardo. I was thinking about his story. I understood why the police had questioned him so thoroughly. He was clearly a witness at the scene of Keezer's death. But did they also suspect him of being involved in it?

Louisa, as though reading my mind, broke the silence. "I haven't been able to reach the law professor your husband recommended.

When I called the Law School, they said his office hours start at nine thirty. I'll call again in a little while. I think Eduardo should have had a lawyer last night. Your husband agreed."

"Eduardo, how did the Detective McBride react to what you told them?" I asked. "Surely, they don't think you had anything to do with Keezer's death."

He looked at me with doleful eyes. "I'm not so sure. The way they kept at me. I don't know what they think. They weren't hostile or anything. They just kept asking the same questions over and over again. The detective told me it may be a homicide." He shook his head, and looked stricken. "And then he asked me to let him know when I planned to return to Orlando. He said they would want to interview me again." He paused, and gave Louisa a pleading look.

"Eduardo," I said, leaning closer to him. "I'm certain they'll be interviewing other people: Keezer had a partner with plenty of reason to be angry, and he also had a girlfriend who's married to one of our county commissioners, so don't think you're the only one."

"I didn't do anything wrong," he murmured. "I just wanted to see where Jeff was shot, that's all. I just wanted to understand." He turned his chair to face out of the window again, shrouded in despair.

Louisa and I got up, and walked to the door.

"I'm going to see McBride right now," I said. "By the way, did Eduardo drive back here?"

"No, they had my car towed back from the Plaza where they picked him up. It's somewhere in what the detective called 'secure storage.' I don't know when I'll get it back. I guess I'll have to rent one to get home."

"Oh, Louisa. I am so sorry about all of this. I just hope it will all play out soon." I looked back into the room at Eduardo's forlorn figure. "I wish I could offer more consolation to him…to both of you."

She raised her shoulders in the universal shrug of helplessness. "I appreciate your help, Lorelei. And your husband's. He was very sympathetic last night, and it helped to talk to someone. I want to believe Eduardo when he says he had nothing to do with that man and yet…"

"What is it, Louisa? Surely you don't..."

"No, no. Nothing." She gave me a wan smile, and hugged me before opening the door to the hall. "I'll keep calling the lawyer. Go now, Lorelei. Will I see you later at the hospital?"

"Yes, of course," I said, puzzling over the doubt expressed in her last statement about Eduardo. What are they keeping from me, I wondered?

Chapter 24

I entered the visitor's area at the Alachua County Sheriff's Office. I was directed to sign in, after I asked to speak with Detective McBride. The reception officer made a phone call, and told me he would be out in a few minutes. I picked up the phone that hung on the wall near the glass enclosed reception area.

"Hi, Becky. This is Lorelei."

"Lorelei? Diana and I have been trying to reach you forever. Where are you? Are you coming in to the office? There's…"

"Whoa. I'm at the Sheriff's Office. I'll be there in about an hour."

"Sheriff's Office? What's going on? Is it about Mr. Keezer?"

"Can't talk now, Becky. I'll see you in a bit." I hung up before she could ask more questions.

I sat on a plastic chair in the small but attractively furnished reception area, and glanced around at the collage of public relations photos of deputies in action. It was the first time I had ever been inside ASO headquarters on Hawthorne Road. I felt a kind of excited fascination watching the various people walking through the area, and except for those who were uniformed; I tried to imagine why they were here.

This is a whole other world, I thought, as a parade of young people, boys and girls, came through with adult relatives or friends. I asked the man sitting next to me if he knew what they were here for. "Teen Court," he said. It made me think about Diana's son, Hank, and I tried to picture the two of them in a group like this a couple of weeks earlier.

"Mrs. Crane?" Detective McBride emerged through the crowd of kids, and stood in front of me. "I left a message on your machine about twenty minutes ago. I thought you might still be sleeping. Actors always sleep late, don't they?"

"Good morning," I said. "Yes, I could have used a late sleep-in today, but I wanted to see you first thing."

"I want to talk to you as well. Come on into my office," he said.

I got up and followed him though a locked metal door, down a long, brightly lit hallway with many offices. The air conditioning must have been turned down to 60 degrees, and I was freezing. We entered a small office with a metal desk, a computer atop it, and a file cabinet in the corner. There was an Ansel Adams print on the wall opposite the desk, and a bulletin board, overflowing with notices and photographs, on the wall alongside it. I sat in front of the desk.

"So what brings you here? Hey, are you shivering? Do you want some coffee?"

"No thanks" I said, crossing my arms and briskly rubbing my hands over them. "I had a curious encounter with Jimmy Valdez yesterday."

"Valdez?" He stood up, took the coat jacket from the back of his chair, and walked around the desk to drape it over my shoulders. "Here. This should help."

"Oh, thank you," I said. "He forced me into his limo when I stopped at a supermarket. Then his henchmen drove me around while he talked to me."

"I'll be dammed. 'Henchmen,' you said?" He seemed entertained at my choice of words, and then his tone grew serious. "Why didn't you call me? Did you tell Deputy Wright about this?" He started looking through the messages on his desk, and without looking up said, "Do you want to press charges?"

"No. They didn't hurt me. But I think you'll be interested to know about his proposition."

He looked up, with an amused smile on his face, and said, "Proposition? Don't tell me…?"

I knew it was an intentional misunderstanding. Detective McBride's flash of humor made me feel more relaxed. "He proposed I persuade my husband Bill to talk to his banker. He wants Bill to convince Cody Robertson to make a deal with Valdez not to go public with Keezer's fraud."

"Did he now? How interesting. Your husband never returned my call."

"He said he thought it would be better if I talked to you first."

"Okay, back to your encounter with Valdez, and I do want you to consider pressing charges. What was the bait? Or, should I say who?"

I paused for a moment, struggling between my promise to Bill to tell McBride everything I knew, and my feelings of loyalty to Eduardo. I didn't relish implicating him further.

"Mrs. Crane? Look, you've got to tell me everything," he said, as though reading my mind. "In fact, one of the reasons I wanted to talk with you is because I learned you haven't been leveling with me."

"Oh? What haven't I told you?"

"How about your discovery that the woman you saw with Keezer was Mrs. Sparks, for starters." He leaned back in his chair, and studied my reaction.

"Oh, that. I guess I just forgot about it until..."

"Yeah, until Keezer turned up dead?"

"How did you find out?"

"Deputy Wright told me about it after I talked with Mrs. Keezer."

Oops, I thought. I guess Delcie's loyalties finally collided, and her professional responsibility won out.

"Now, let's sort this out," he said. "First, tell me what Valdez had to say to you. Then, I want you to tell me again about the incident with Mrs. Sparks."

I told him what Valdez told me, including his call to Keezer, what he heard in the background, and that he believed it was Eduardo's voice. McBride was taking notes as I talked.

"Did Valdez tell you why he thought it was Mr. Sanchez he heard? Did he indicate he had known Sanchez before?"

"I don't know," I said. I suddenly realized that the two men could have known each other since Eduardo's brother-in-law worked for Valdez. It was the family connection that put Valdez and his thugs on my trail in the first place.

"Mrs. Crane? What are you thinking?"

"I guess they could have known each other," I admitted. "Eduardo's brother-in-law works for the Valdez Company in Orlando."

McBride looked at me crossly, and said, "You seem to know a lot more about this case than you've told me. So there's a good chance the two men know one another?"

"I'm still not certain," I said. "When I asked Valdez why he thought it was Eduardo's voice he heard, he didn't specifically say he recognized it. It was more like he assumed Eduardo wanted revenge for Jeffrey's shooting."

"And you bought it? Valdez would know better than to think Keezer had anything to do with Waterman's shooting. But let's forget that for the moment. Anything else I should know about your conversation with Valdez? Anything at all?"

"No, I've told you everything."

"Good. Now, let's get back to the incident between Keezer and Mrs. Sparks. Tell me everything you can remember, please."

"Well, at the time, I didn't know it was Chelsea Sparks in the truck with Keezer. It wasn't until I saw her at the rally on Saturday that I began to suspect she had disguised herself for their rendezvous by wearing a black wig."

"Black hair seems to be in vogue at the moment, doesn't it?" he said, briefly looking up at me. "Go on."

"Jeffrey and I brought lunch out to the Prairie, where the pavilion and the boat ramp are, near the camp grounds. When we were getting ready to leave, I spotted Keezer's truck. We had just seen it at the Valdez site. He was with a woman, and I was curious, so I snuck in as close as I could get to see who it was."

"And you're sure it was Mrs. Sparks?"

"As I said, I didn't know who it was at the time. I've never really met her; just seen photos, you know."

McBride nodded, "Then what?"

"Keezer and the woman were obviously in some kind of argument. I couldn't hear them because they had the windows up with the motor going, but I could tell by their body language it was a fight. She was making a lot of aggressive gestures toward him, and their faces looked angry." I paused trying to remember any other cues that made me believe it was a fight.

"Then what?"

"Then they spotted me. The woman turned away so I couldn't see her. Keezer got out of the truck, and started yelling at me. He accused me of stalking him. I guess he thought it was because of the fight that he and Jeffrey had had earlier at the construction site."

"What happened next?"

"I ran. Back to the car. We pulled out of there before Keezer could do anything. You know he has a gun in the truck, and had threatened Jeffrey with it that morning."

"Was that the end of it?" McBride was looking down, and scribbling furiously on his notepad.

"Yes, except when I met Mrs. Sparks at the rally—saw her up close—I realized she was the woman in the truck. Diana had told me the gossip about their relationship so it wasn't hard to make the connection."

"I wish you would have told me all of this when we saw Mrs. Sparks at the rally."

"I'm sorry, I just didn't think about it at the time. I was so distressed at being grabbed again by the Valdez thug, and the rally. There was just so much going on."

"Okay, I forgive you." He stood up, and sat on the edge of the desk near me. "But this thing's looking more and more like a homicide investigation, and unfortunately you seem to be in the middle of things. So it's critical that you tell me everything you know or learn that's related to the case."

It seemed a good time to try and find out what Eduardo's status was with the police. "What about Eduardo Sanchez?" I asked.

"We've met with Mr. Sanchez."

"Yes, I know. I saw him this morning and he told me about it."

"Did he tell you why he fled town, and that we found a shirt with blood stains on it in his car?"

"Blood stains?" I repeated, momentarily shocked by McBride's disclosure until I recalled Eduardo's description of his fall in the woods.

"We don't know whose blood it is yet. It's being analyzed."

"He did explain the blood, didn't he?" I said.

"Said he fell down, and got a lot of scratches trying to find his way out of the woods. He did have some minor injuries, but we can't make any assumptions as to how they occurred."

I wondered why Eduardo didn't tell me about the police confiscating his shirt, and if Louisa knew about it.

"Anything else, Mrs. Crane?"

"No, I guess that's all. But you've told me before that I'm a quick study. So for what it's worth, Eduardo Sanchez doesn't strike me as someone who would murder anybody. In my opinion, you have some more likely suspects." I stood up, shrugged the jacket off my shoulders, and handed it to him.

"Thanks," I said, watching him carefully hang it on the back of his chair.

He stood next to his desk, and said, "People who commit murder don't exactly walk around with a scarlet letter, Mrs. Crane. On the contrary, they often come in very ordinary packages. But you are right about one thing: there are other people who might make better suspects than Sanchez. At this point, no one's being ruled out."

"Good," I said, getting up ready to leave.

He took my elbow and led me out of his office. As we walked down the hallway to the reception area, he said, "Do me a favor, Mrs. Crane. The next time Valdez, or anyone connected with this case, tries to talk to you, please call and let me or Deputy Wright know about it, immediately. Will you do that?"

"Yes, I promise."

"And I want you to think again about filing a complaint against Valdez."

"No, I don't need to get anymore involved with him than I already have. But I will report anything and everything to you. Frankly, my husband insisted I do the same thing. I didn't intend to get into the middle of things. I've got a play opening to think about."

"Right. Stick with Chekhov, and leave the investigating to me. Will you be going to the hospital today? I'm told Mr. Waterman may be alert enough to talk by afternoon."

"Yes, I'll be there."

He opened the metal door leading out to the reception area, and we exchanged goodbyes.

I left the building, feeling the pleasurable warmth of the hot morning air, but still unsettled about the status of Jeffrey's friend, Eduardo Sanchez. Too many questions remained unanswered: Why did Louisa hesitate in asserting his innocence? Did Jimmy Valdez and Eduardo know one another? And what about the blood stained shirt found in Louisa's car? Why didn't he mention it?

I drove back across town, to the Center office, thinking about Detective McBride. I had a feeling of satisfaction about the way our relationship was developing. He had turned out to be a decent guy, and his willingness to joke and share confidences with me made me feel special.

I also had a growing respect for what his job entailed. When crimes were committed, there were so many missing pieces to the puzzle, half or untruths to sort out, and conflicting agendas among everyone involved. In a way, my process as an actress was not dissimilar from his. We both had to delve into people's intentions and motivations; we both needed to be disciplined about the unfolding of our discovery process, and not give away too much too soon; and we both participated in a collaborative endeavor to uncover the truth. Yet, in my profession, I had the distinct advantage of knowing, in advance, what the ending would be. It was a scripted finale.

Becky rushed me as soon as I entered the office. Her energy was explosive. "It's amazing isn't it, Lorelei? First Jeffrey and now Keezer. Did you read the article in the paper? Why were you at the Sheriff's office?"

"Hold on, Becky, one thing at a time. Let me get in the door first." I brushed past her on my way to my desk. She followed closely behind.

"The paper described the guy who shot Jeffrey. He had some cock and bull story about why he shot at Jeff. Thank God his aim wasn't worth a damn."

"Yes, Jeffrey might have been killed," I said. "I know, Becky. I know." I eased into my chair, looked at the papers heaped on my desk, and wondered where to begin.

Becky sat down next to my desk, and continued talking in an excited rush of words. "Diana said Hank helped the police identify him. Said he's actually a friend of Hank's. But the thing about Jeff and the other guy he was with, you know, what they implied in the paper. I still can't believe that Jeffrey's gay. Is he?"

"You'll have to ask Jeffrey," I said, pretending a preoccupation with my mail.

"Naw, I don't believe it for a minute," she said. "Anyway, we'll get to talk with him today. Do you think he'll be like totally normal when he's off the drugs?"

"I don't know," I said, and stopped shuffling papers to look up at her eager face. I felt a sudden burst of sympathy for Becky. Was I ever that intense, I wondered? "I'm going over to the hospital after I deal with all this stuff. I got a message from his sister, Janine. They may not be able to get here until late tonight or tomorrow, which suits me fine. I'd just as soon not run into them."

"Oh, I want to meet his sister," Becky said, and returned to her desk.

I wanted to get off of the subject of Jeffrey before Becky started to press me for more information about his personal life. "Has Diana been in? What does she think about Keezer's death?"

"It's so totally weird. We didn't know what to think. Anyway, she and Wiley are in a meeting at the University with a guy from the Nature Conservancy. She told me Keezer's death may change everything."

"I hope so," I said, sorting through newspaper clippings about Saturday's rally.

I studied the picture of the troopers and Gainesville police pursuing some of the costumed protesters across the highway. "Hey, Becky. That was quite a show you and your gang put on. Did any of them get put in jail?"

"Only a couple. As usual, it was the stupid ones that got caught. But we made bail for them right away."

The phone rang and Becky answered, "It's for you."

"Lorelei, it's me, Delcie. Rumor has it you were in to see McBride this morning."

"Yes, I told him about Jimmy Valdez picking me up."

"You didn't let on that I've been feeding you information about the case, did you?"

"No, Del, don't be paranoid."

"Can't help it, goes with the job. How about if I pick you up at work? I assume you'll be going by the hospital, and maybe we could grab a sandwich in the cafeteria before you go up to see Jeff."

I laughed at her suggestion. "Are you still my guardian?"

"More or less, and I think you can use some support. You know, in case he isn't a-okay."

She was right, I felt a jolt of fear at the mere suggestion that Jeffrey might not be the same as he was prior to the shooting…denial was such a soothing state of mind.

"Anyway, McBride wants me to stay in contact with you," Delcie added. "That incident with Jimmy Valdez worried us."

"It did me, too," I said, letting out a long breath of air. "Okay, you know I never turn down a chance for a meal. Come by around one. And, Delcie, thanks."

"Hey, that's just what friends do."

We walked through the hospital cafeteria line, and commented on all the seductive carbs we weren't going to eat.

"So you had a cozy talk with McBride?" Delcie said, taking her salad and coffee off the serving tray. "Was he his usual rude self?" she asked.

"Not at all. In fact, he was rather thoughtful. I think I'm beginning to like him."

"Like McBride? That's an oxymoron."

"I was surprised to hear you told him about my discovery that it was Mrs. Sparks with Keezer at the Prairie pavilion. I thought you didn't want us to have any connection?"

"Had to do it, Lor. It was a critical piece of information, and I couldn't hold it back from him. Especially since he had just learned that Keezer recently asked his wife for a divorce, and she had refused to give him one."

"How interesting," I said, feeling unaccountably slighted that McBride hadn't shared that information with me. "It does explain why Chelsea Sparks might have been so angry when I saw her that day."

"And it gives her a motive for murder," Delcie added, stabbing a piece of chicken in her salad.

"The cheerleader, a murderer?" I considered the idea for several minutes as I finished my sandwich. I pictured Chelsea Sparks at the rally when she was viciously berating her husband. "She's the hair-pulling, groin-kicking type all right, but I can't picture her killing Keezer because of a divorce. They've been in a relationship for years. Why now?"

"Depends. There might be other things involved."

"Oh, like the money," I said.

"Yeah, that's always a good motive," Delcie replied. "Secrets are another good one."

"Secrets, as in a scandal?" I could only think of one candidate to fit that description. "You're thinking about Jimmy Valdez?"

"Not just him. What about the commissioner?"

"Judson Sparks? Why suspect him? He and Keezer were buddies."

"Think about it," Delcie said. "If Keezer promised to get a divorce, Mrs. Sparks might have felt confident enough to rub her husband's nose in the affair, or maybe she flat out told him she was leaving. Aside from any antagonism she could have triggered, he's also up for re-election next year."

"And politicians don't like scandal," I added.

"You got it. It could sink him if it got to be a dirty divorce. Remember, she's got some juicy stuff on him, too."

"But murder would be the worst thing."

"Yeah, but Keezer's death was set up to look like suicide."

As I sipped my tea, I reflected on the growing list of suspects and motivations involved in Keezer's murder. The intricacies of this plot were becoming more intriguing than most of the plays I'd been in.

"You know, Del. This would make a fascinating drama. For the first time, I can understand why you chose police work over acting."

"Only the homicides," she said. "Most of the rest of what I do is flat out boring."

I gathered our plates and cups onto my tray. It was time for the inevitable meeting with Jeffrey. As we were walking out of the cafeteria, I put my arm through hers, and said, "Delcie, I really appreciate your being here with me. You're a good friend. After all of this is over, I'd like us to see one another more often."

She looked at me with a surprised but pleased expression, and said, "I'd like that, too, Lorelei. I really would. Who knows, maybe you could even talk me into giving up my high paying civil service job, and going back into the actin' and starvin' business." We both laughed, but there was a hint of seriousness in her statement.

At the nurse's station, they told us Jeffrey's drugs had been reduced last evening, but it was too early to tell about any brain damage. The nurse mentioned that Detective McBride was in with Jeffrey, and the surgeon had restricted the frequency for all visits during Jeffrey's first day of recovery.

Delcie and I stood outside the waiting room. Minutes later McBride emerged through the doors of the intensive care unit.

"Mrs. Crane," he gave me a half-smile as he approached. "Your friend is awake, and I'd have to say he's a bit cranky."

"Did he tell you anything about the shooting?" Delcie asked.

"No. He's confused. Doesn't remember much about that evening. The doctor came in while I was there. He told me it'll be a while before Mr. Waterman recovers his short term memory."

"I want to see him," I said, and left McBride and Delcie standing in the hallway.

"Lorelei?" Jeffrey was sitting up. His head was still bandaged, but the respirator tube was out of his mouth, and he was alive!

"Jeffrey, we were so terrified." I bent down and kissed him.

He looked at me with a puzzled expression. "Lorelei, what happened to your hair?" His voice was hoarse and raspy, and I could see it was painful for him to speak. "They won't tell me anything except that I had a head wound. Some detective was in here a few minutes ago asking me questions, but I can't remember anything."

"Don't try to talk too much right now. And don't worry. You're memory will come back in time. The important thing is that you are going to be all right."

"Aaah, my head feels like someone took a crowbar to it. I feel like barfing, so it must have been some brawl."

"You've had a serious injury. Actually, you look like you've lost some weight. Have they given you anything solid to eat?" I looked around to see if there was anything to eat.

"I hate hospitals," he said. "Get me out of here."

"I can't do it. You need care."

He frowned as though trying to form a thought. "But the rally. I'm supposed to be doing something."

"The rally's over. It was a great success." The doctor had mentioned that his short-term memory would be gone for a time. He didn't appear shocked by what I told him; he just looked a bit confused.

"Well, dammit," he said, and pounded his fist on the bed.

"Calm down, Jeffrey. Everything is fine. Your sister and your mom should be here today or tomorrow."

"Janine? I don't understand. She lives in Oregon."

"Jeffrey, we thought we were going to lose you. You don't realize how very seriously injured you were."

He cocked his head, looking as though he were trying hard to remember something.

The nurse came into the room and said, "I'm sorry, but Mr. Waterman needs his rest." She looked at me sympathetically, and I took the cue.

"I'll see you again tomorrow, dear," I patted his hand, and began to leave.

"Red!" he shouted.

I swung around at his plaintive cry. "What is it, Jeffrey?"

His face was gripped with consternation. "Your hair—what did you do to it?"

"I'm in a play. It's just dyed. Don't worry." I blew him a kiss and left.

When I went back out into the corridor, McBride was standing apart from Delcie and talking on his cell phone.

"How is he?" she asked.

"Alive, thank God! Confused, irritable, but otherwise he's okay. He thinks he was in a barroom brawl." I looked over at McBride.

"He's taking a call from one of the crime scene guys," Delcie said.

McBride flipped his phone closed, and joined us. He looked unhappy. "I've got to get over to the county office. Deputy, keep tabs on Mrs. Crane."

"Any new information about Keezer?" I asked.

He scowled at my question. "Oh, I've got plenty of information, Mrs. Crane; too much, in fact."

"Can you tell us anything?"

"Us?" he said, looking quizzically at Delcie. Her face was impassive. He addressed his response to me. "Let's just say that Mr. Crawford Keezer had a number of visitors the night he was killed, and it's now my distinctly unpleasant duty to investigate each of them." He turned and left.

"What?" I looked at Delcie waiting for an explanation.

Her gaze followed McBride, as he strode down the hall to the elevators, before she spoke. "I think he means, some powerful people have definitely become suspects, and now he's the one who has to rub their noses in some deep shit—a cop's worst nightmare."

Chapter 25

It was almost three o'clock when we left the hospital, and Delcie dropped me back at the office. I was eager to see Diana. A lot had happened since we last talked. I found her absorbed in paperwork at her desk, and quietly humming some old familiar church tune. In contrast to the last time I'd seen her, she looked surprisingly calm.

"Lorelei dear, how is Jeffrey? Sit down," she said, gesturing me to a chair. "Tell me about him. Then I have some exciting news for you."

I told her about my visit with Jeffrey. We talked a few minutes about the newspaper version of his shooting, and I mentioned her son Hank's assistance in identifying A.J. Hill.

Her face darkened as she said, "A.J. Hill has always been trouble. I've been warning Hank about him ever since they were together in the sixth grade."

"Well, I'm just glad Hank was willing to help the police," I said.

There was a long silence as she frowned, and looked out the window.

"What's wrong, Diana. You seemed so peaceful when I came in and now…"

She gave me a long, thoughtful look. "Lorelei, can I tell you something in absolute confidence?"

"Of course," I said, thinking it might be some confession about Dalton. I was still curious about their relationship.

"It's about my son, Hank." She took a deep breath, and pressed her hands to her lips before speaking. "After Detective McBride talked with him and left, Hank made a terrible and tearful confession to me." Her voice choked with emotion. "Apparently, my son was involved in the Sierra Club office break-in the day Dalton died!"

"Oh, my God, Diana. I'm stunned!"

"It was all A.J.'s fault, of course. He was put up to it by his boss…"

"The owner of the Gator Security Services?" I asked with a sense of excitement at the implications…it was beginning to click!

"Yes, can you believe it? Anyway, A.J. talked Hank into going along with him. Hank said he didn't realize what would happen. He only stood look-out, and didn't help A.J. trash the place. You can imagine how upset he was when he later found out about Dalton. That's why he finally admitted it all to me."

"What are you going to do about it? A.J.'s already going to prison, but Hank…"

"My son's basically a good boy. He needs some counseling, and time to mature. Of course, I agonized over what to do. Finally, I decided to talk to Mike Smith about it. He was very understanding—he has teenagers of his own. We agreed that I would pay for the damages to the office, anonymously, and he wouldn't press charges or tell anybody else about it. I think it was a real wake-up call for Hank, and it's made us closer than we've been since his daddy died."

"I'm glad you told me, Diana. It explains some connections I've been trying to make in this whole Valdez saga. Anyway, don't worry, I won't tell anyone about it."

"Thank you, Lorelei. I know I can trust you not to say anything."

Yet, another secret, I thought, and this one had Jimmy Valdez's handwriting all over it. It was a repeat of the Miami Sierra Club arson that Jeffrey told us about.

Diana stood up, and stretched. "Apparently Mr. Keezer's demise has changed the Valdez saga, as you call it. Wiley and I met with some folks from the Nature Conservancy this morning."

"Yes, Becky told me," I said.

"They're making an offer on the property." She looked at me with eyebrows raised in wonder, and said, "Isn't that a miracle? Of course, the rally and the death of Valdez's front man had a lot to do with it. Not that anybody is happy about that, by the way. It's quite tragic for his family."

I nodded. There was a respectful pause in our conversation before I spoke again. "So you're counting on Jimmy Valdez being ready to throw in the towel on the project?"

"Yes," Diana said. "We think he'll be glad to cut and run if he's offered a fair price for the property."

I thought about it for a moment. I was sure Valdez would jump at the offer, and it meant he wouldn't need me or Bill anymore to get the bank to delay action. The sale of his property would solve Valdez's financial and public relations problems; that is, unless his real problem was going to be a murder charge.

"That's exciting news, Diana. I'm sure the coalition members will be thrilled. Actually, it will solve a number of problems."

She looked as if she expected an explanation, but I checked my watch and realized I had to get to the theater. My final costume fitting was at four o'clock.

"I've got to run," I said, rising from my chair. "Remember I'll be off this week—for the play—but call if you need me for anything."

She pointed to a stack of papers on her desk. "I've got the letters you wrote to the coalition; I'll just have Becky add a postscript about the Conservancy offer. And, Lorelei, please tell Jeffrey I asked about him. We do have philosophical differences, but I know his heart is in the right place."

"I'll tell him," I said, and as I was leaving, invited her, Wiley, and Becky to the party at our house on Friday night.

The next several days flew by in a blur that was typical for me during the week before a play opening. I was thoroughly absorbed in preparing for my role, polishing it during the day for each evening's rehearsal.

Sometimes, especially while I was doing long yoga sessions, my real life bled into my life as Varya. I looked out, through her eyes, at the chain of events in which I had become embroiled. I sometimes pictured Varya spending endless hours at the hospital, alternately weeping for Jeffrey, imposing herself in his care, and berating the staff for their inattention. Varya was, after all, a diligent caretaker. It made me feel good to contrast my behavior with hers. I liked the Lorelei who, unlike Varya, had the curiosity and, frankly the guts, to risk going off on her own to investigate dangerous situations.

During the week, I saw Bill only briefly before he left for the office and when I returned home late at night. I talked to Jeffrey on the telephone, and he told me his mother and sister arrived Monday evening. Every day he sounded more and more like his old self.

Neither of us mentioned Eduardo. I knew he was still in Gainesville. When Louisa called me on Tuesday morning, she said he felt too depressed to do anything. She added that while his attorney urged him to return home, he stubbornly refused to leave the Holiday Inn.

"Lorelei," she said. "All he does is sit in the hotel room and watch TV all day and all night. He orders room service, and leaves half of it. I'm really very worried about him."

"I guess he's been traumatized," I said. "It might help to get him out of the hotel room, at least. You know my play is opening Friday night. If you're both still here, why don't you come? Afterwards, I'm having a little party at my house."

"I don't know. Maybe. I'm going to Orlando for a couple of days, but I'll be back up on Friday."

"Please come, and bring Eduardo. It'll be good for him to be among people." I hoped that Eduardo would still be a free man by Friday.

Delcie checked in on me at the theater each day. She professed to know little about the progress of McBride's investigation. According to her, there was evidence at the crime scene that placed each of the suspects there, but McBride was not discussing the results of his interviews or any other matters related to the case. I asked her again about it on Thursday afternoon right before the technical rehearsal.

"What did McBride find out from the banker in Orlando? Do they know how Keezer got the money?" I asked.

"McBride mentioned talking to him, but said the guy was tight-lipped. Wouldn't fess up to any problems with the Valdez Company."

"I'll bet Jimmy Valdez already got to him," I said. "By now the Nature Conservancy probably made their offer on the property. Jimmy will guarantee replacement of the stolen money, and the bank will avoid a scandal."

"I didn't know about a Conservancy offer," Delcie said. "But you're right, it does explain why McBride's getting stonewalled by the banker. I'll have to let him know."

"Is there anything else happening with the investigation?" I asked. "I spoke to Louisa a couple of days ago. She's very worried about Eduardo; he's despondent. You think he's still a suspect?"

"Don't know. Like I said, McBride's playing it pretty close to the chest. I guess he's trying to keep an open mind. Doesn't want anyone else second guessing his case. Then again, I'm pretty sure until toxicology and other test results come through he won't have any definitive proof that it was murder."

Delcie left as soon as the technical rehearsal began. We were in full costume. I wore an ankle-length flared black skirt and a white long sleeved blouse with a high neck and lace bodice. A large ring of skeleton keys hung at my waist. When I moved about quickly, the jangling of the keys was distracting, but the costume designer had fixed the problem by pinning the keys from inside my pocket.

I got chills walking into the theater and seeing the completed set. Despite the many glitches, I loved the technical. It was the first time all artistic components of the production were brought together. It was artistry, not unlike a fine painting to which multi-colored layers of acrylics made a richer, more dimensional work of art. The costumes, props, lighting, music, set design, and special effects always enhanced my performance, and allowed me to enter more deeply into the world of the play. During the technical rehearsal, I became Varya; speaking and moving in her time and place.

When rehearsal was over, I stayed to talk to Chester about a concern I had with the actor who played Epihodov, a comical character referred to as "two and twenty misfortunes." I felt he tried to upstage me, and wanted Chester to watch for it. Renee had already departed; beginning with the opening night, it was the stage manager who was in charge of the production. Chester agreed to give the actor a note about it. By the time I changed back into my clothes, and exited the theater, the parking lot was almost empty.

I looked around for Delcie, but apparently she was running late. I got into my car, started the engine, and put the AC on while I waited for her. I began searching through my handbag for some mints. My mouth felt I'd been chewing on cotton balls. A distant vapor lamp shed barely enough light for me to see what I was doing.

I jerked around when I heard a metal tapping on the window behind me. The shadowy figure standing next to the car turned out to be Delcie. I lowered the window, and my heart was still racing.

"You scared me," I said. "I'm so tired, I thought it might be Jimmy Valdez again."

"Sorry. I'm late because of a fracas in Newberry…why'd you think it was Valdez? He hasn't contacted you again, has he?"

"No, I guess he's just got me spooked."

"I'm sure that's been his intention all along. Anyway, don't worry, I'll follow you home now."

She drove behind me all the way home. I reviewed my encounters with Jimmy Valdez, and added the new information I had learned from Diana. It was his man behind the Sierra Club break-in. I agreed with Delcie that scare tactics were his basic strategy for getting what he wanted.

I had encountered Jimmy Valdez three times: at the project site when Jeffrey had confronted Keezer, at the rally when he threatened Wiley, and in the limo when he picked me up. I learned enough about him now to expect the unexpected. Jimmy Valdez could be highly emotional, cool and cunning, or as genial and contrite as my gentlemanly neighbor when his dogs tore up my wildflower bed. In short, he was as good an actor as any I'd known, and that alone was unnerving.

Finally, I banished him from my mind, and returned to my thoughts about Jeffrey. Though I knew he was being well-cared for by his family, it had been several days since I I'd visited the hospital. I wanted to see how he looked, and since his memory was starting to return, to ask him some questions...face to face. What did he remember about that night on the Prairie when he was shot, why hadn't he told me about his relationship with Eduardo, and did he believe his friend capable of murder?

It was early, and I entered the hospital just as breakfast trays were being delivered to patients. The corridor was fragrant with the aroma of bacon and coffee. It was especially tantalizing since I had skipped breakfast to get to the hospital first thing, before Jeffrey's family arrived.

He was sitting up in bed, and looked almost fit except for the bandages which still covered a portion of his head. A tray of half eaten food had been shoved to the side.

"Lorelei, you're an early bird, aren't you?" he said in a hoarse voice. "What are you doing here at this hour?" I looked around. His monitor wires had been removed, and it was strangely quiet without their bleeping sounds and the steady whooshing of the respirator. "Yeah, they're moving me to a regular room today."

"Oh, Jeffrey, that's wonderful." I kissed him lightly. "Can I finish your toast? I'm famished," I said, still scanning his features, looking for any subtle changes, as I scavenged the remainder of his breakfast. "Tell me, how do you feel today?" I sat down, and reached for his hand.

"Well, they warned me the old memory would be pretty flakey, and I still have the world's worst hangover. Other than that, I guess I'm in okay shape. That is, for someone who's been shot in the head!" He motioned for me to pour him some water from the bedside pitcher. He took several gulps and said, "God, my throat's killing me. The damn tube, you know." He pointed to his mouth.

"I'm sure that'll go away. Maybe you shouldn't be talking too much," I said.

"Have they told you when you can leave the hospital?"

"Maybe in a few more days. Then back for therapy and tests for awhile."

"Will you be staying in Gainesville? Anymore thoughts about making it permanent?"

"No, that'll have to wait a while. In the meantime, I'll be at Becky's. She wants to play nursemaid, I guess." Jeffrey winced and put his hand to his throat.

"She'll take good care of you," I said, and thought Becky would be in her glory having charge of Jeffrey. "You shouldn't be talking so much if it hurts."

"Nah, it's okay. Janine and mom are leaving today."

"I've been too busy to see them. It's Friday, and our play opens tonight."

"I guess there's no love lost between you guys anyway."

Jeffrey gave me a quizzical look, and his face darkened. "They say I was almost killed?"

"Yes," I said, squeezing his hand.

His mood unpredictably lightened, and his eyes held that teasing look of his. "You almost got me out of your hair for good. How'd that feel?"

How did it feel knowing Jeffrey might die? His question took me aback. I had had so many different feelings since I had first learned of the shooting. It was hard to sort through them to give him an honest answer, and his searching look told me he wanted something true.

"I don't know," I said. "It seems like a hundred years ago since you were first brought in here. I guess I was terrified. Then, after the doctor made me believe you would recover, I still felt scared, but kind of remorseful, too."

"Remorseful? Hell, Red, life's too short to have regrets." He looked around the room, and gave a bitter laugh as if to prove his point.

I knew he was right, yet I mentally recalled the subjects I had talked to him about while he was in the coma: our passions, the accident, his drinking, and the miscarriage. Had he heard me? Would he remember?

"You probably weren't aware of it," I said, "but I've been here at your bedside many times since you were brought to the hospital. I guess the calamity made me reflect a lot about us."

"I hope you remembered the good things. Cause that's what I've been thinkin' about. Our camping trips, the all night philosophy sessions…the sex! You still look like that hot older woman I married, except for that god-awful black paint on your hair!"

"It's just for the play," I reminded him, touching my hair self-consciously. "My memories aren't as lighthearted as yours are, Jeffrey. What I've been remembering is how unfairly I've treated you, and how important you've been in my life. The rally made me think about a lot of things, and you're right about one: we had a lot of passion then, didn't we?"

"Yeah, in the bedroom and out," he said, and grinned. "Hey, about the rally, Becky's told me a lot. I hate that I missed all the fun. But contrary to what you might think, I haven't been sitting here just drooling like an idiot. I've been trying to figure out some stuff about my life. Like what do I do next? Cause I've decided for sure that I'm not going to drift along anymore. I've been thinking about the lab job, my old professor, Dr. Curtis, offered. Maybe I'll stay here and finish my Ph.D."

"And what about Eduardo?" I blurted it out without intending to sound so confrontational, and added more softly, "I've met him, you know. What about him if you stay?"

He gave me a rueful smile, and took in a slow deep breath before responding. "Oh yes, Eduardo. And you probably also want to know why I never mentioned him, don't you?"

"Among other things."

Jeffrey breathed another deep sigh, and averted his eyes.

I sat still, no longer touching him, and saying nothing to ease the silence.

"Well, it's too long a story to tell you now. Maybe another time, over a few beers."

"And Judson Sparks?" I asked. "What role does he play in your life?"

Jeffrey squirmed a little, furrowed his brow, and set his lips. "Sparks is nothing to me. I thought I could use him. You know, to stop the development project."

"How? By blackmail?"

"Oh, c'mon, Lorelei. Let's not pretend to be so saintly. You yourself said you'd do anything to stop the project. I knew Sparks from Orlando. He showed up from time to time at a bar I used to go to. We'd have some drinks together is all. He was kind of an odd bird.

I was shocked when I came up here, and learned he was a big wig in Gainesville."

"Yes," I said, "a county commissioner complete with a wife."

"Some wife. She's a piece of work. Jud told me how she was fooling around with an old boyfriend—that Keezer jerk of all people. She even told him about the affair, flaunted it. He was furious, but didn't think he could do anything because she threatened to expose his 'little secret,' as she called it. She asked for a divorce, but he told her no way. He wasn't going to let her off that easily."

"Sounds like they were locked together in marriage like one of those awful movies where the husband and wife try to kill one another. Ugh, how terrible."

"I actually felt sorry for the guy. He was practically getting hives over the whole situation. On the one hand, here's Keezer screwing his wife, and on the other hand, he's getting a piece of the action on some of the Valdez projects. Honestly, when we talked that night on the Prairie he seemed to be on the verge of…I don't know what."

The nurse came into the room, took Jeffrey's pulse, and told me that I had to leave in a few minutes.

"Did you tell Detective McBride what you just told me about Sparks?"

"No, why would I? He was only interested in what I knew about the kid who shot me. I still can't believe it was that dumb-ass kid we met."

I realized no one had told Jeffrey about Keezer's death, so he wasn't aware of any reason for McBride's interest in the Sparks' marriage. Now wasn't the time to explain how both the Sparks' had become suspects in a possible murder investigation.

"I guess there's a lot we don't know about people, even when we think we know them," I said dryly, and got up to leave.

"C'mon now, Red, sarcasm isn't your style." He looked up at me with such a sweet and loving expression that I suddenly felt light-headed. I had to steady myself by holding onto the foot of the bed.

Our eyes locked in a silent communication, and after several moments he said softly, "You know Lorelei Waterman Crane, I've been thinking. Maybe you and I gave up too soon—there was so much love—maybe we should have tried harder. I hate to think there's no hope at all for us."

No hope at all? Was that true, I wondered, still feeling shaken and confused by the sudden eruption of feelings.

"I don't know, Jeffrey. All I do know is that since you've come to Gainesville, I've started taking risks again. I feel more alive than ever, and it feels damn good."

He smiled. "See, there's still some spark alive, isn't there?"

"Who knows? You just work on getting better." I nonchalantly blew him a kiss, and left the room. My legs felt rubbery, and when I walked out of the unit, I had to sit in the waiting room for a few minutes to catch my breath. If Jeffrey did decide to remain in Gainesville, I knew I'd have to confront my feelings about him. It was all so complex.

The rest of the day was filled with activities related to opening night. From the hospital, I went to the gym for a workout, had my hair done, and arrived home around noon. Thoughts of Jeffrey had subsided as I focused on the evening ahead.

A call to the caterer reassured me that the bar and snacks would be set up before Bill and our guests arrived home after the play. I left a voice mail message for McBride, telling him I had more information about the case, and reminding him to come to my house after the play.

By late afternoon, I had completed my yoga and breathing exercises, a final run-through of my lines, and left home for the theater. I felt ravenous, but knew it was just stress hunger. I never ate anything before a performance.

Backstage was chaotic as usual. Some of the actors cued one another on their lines while the costume and make-up assistants made hurried finishing touches. The properties manager frantically searched for the governess' gun that had mysteriously disappeared from the props cabinet. Chester seemed to be everywhere at once: giving directions to his assistants from the sound booth, on stage monitoring arrangements, and joking with some of us, via wireless headsets, in the green room. Finally, we were hushed as the theater filled, announcements were made, and the first actors cued to move on stage.

For the next two hours, I was Varya. At the start of the play, I joyfully welcomed my stepmother and her entourage home, after a five year absence from Russia, in which she had squandered her fortune on the continent. I cried and laughed with her as she reminisced about returning to her childhood home, and its beloved cherry orchard. Alternately, I was the shy and highly emotional woman who, with painful awkwardness and ill timing, kept running into the rich businessman to whom everyone expected I was to be engaged, and ended my last scene sitting alone and sobbing.

Once off-stage, I watched from the wings as the play ended with the family's mournful farewells. Finally, there was a poignant monologue by the ancient servant, Firs. He had been thoughtlessly locked out of the house, and left behind by the family he had served for his entire life, a victim of an old era.

I shivered as I listened to the final sound on stage: the strokes of distant axes. The beloved cherry orchard was being felled. It evoked a desolate feeling. The feeling I had already experienced hearing chain saws on the Prairie at the Valdez site.

We took our bows to a standing ovation. Curtain calls always made me feel schizoid: I was still in role, but also myself, the actor, being applauded. Added to that confusion was the feeling of relief and sheer elation at the audience's reaction. It was an emotional kaleidoscope as complex as any Chekhov could have written.

During the second curtain call, I scanned the audience and saw Bill, Delcie, and Detective McBride standing side by side, and applauding enthusiastically. In the upper corner of the theater, I was surprised to see Louisa and Eduardo. He was on his feet, and gave me a two "thumbs-up."

I changed clothes quickly, and had a glass of wine at the cast party that was set up in the rehearsal room. Everyone seemed pleased with their performance and the audience's energy. There was a lot of talk about how the production would be reviewed.

I left the cast party and drove home. Delcie had waited for me in the lobby, and followed in her car. Crossing over the Prairie, a full harvest moon illuminated the ocean-like vastness. My heightened state of excitement collided sharply with its absolute serenity.

Chapter 26

Delcie and I parked our cars, and entering the house, heard Bill call out, "She's here. "Hail the queen of the theatre." He greeted me at the door with a peck on the cheek, and put a glass of wine in my hand as he led me into the living room.

"Remember, I'm just the housekeeper, not the queen," I said, and moved around the room receiving kisses, hugs, and congratulations from Diana, Wiley, and members of my neighborhood fan club. Becky, Louisa, and Eduardo stood in the doorway to the kitchen. Detective McBride was leaning against the fireplace mantle, holding a bottle of beer, and watching me with an amused grin on his face. I walked over to him, and he extended his hand. I took it, kissed him on the cheek, and caught the faint aroma of a men's cologne that I loved. As I drew away from him, McBride's face reddened.

"We have to talk," I whispered.

"I know. I got your message," he said.

Bill reappeared at my side, "Darling, you were wonderful tonight."

"I have a question," McBride said. "Whatever happened to the gun? I kept waiting for somebody to get shot."

I laughed, thinking, of course, McBride would spot the one thing in the play a cop would be interested in. "You mean the gun the governess was wearing?"

"Yes. Why have a character packing a gun unless there's going to be shooting?"

"No one knows," I said. "Some say it's a typical Chekhovian twist to make you think something's going to happen, and then nothing does. Like real life, you know?"

Bill turned away and started talking football to one of the neighbors, and I excused myself to go into the kitchen and check on the caterer.

When I walked into the room, I found Becky, Louisa, and Eduardo—standing in a corner with drinks in hand—laughing at Maynard. My cat had apparently purloined a canapé from the counter, and was pushing it around the kitchen floor as though he expected it to come alive.

"Lorelei, you were wonderful," Louisa said, rushing over to give me a hug. "I'm so glad we came to the play."

Eduardo nodded shyly and said, "I love the theater, and it was fascinating to watch you act." He appeared remarkably like the well-groomed and handsome man I had first met. What a recovery, I thought.

"I forgot just how amazing you are as an actress," Becky said. "I actually got chills at the end; the sound of axes was awesome."

"Thanks. I'm so pleased you came…especially you, Eduardo." Louisa and I exchanged happy looks. "Have you seen the caterer?"

"She's out on the patio, I think," Becky said helpfully.

"Excuse me," I said, and walked through the French doors to the patio.

The caterer and I talked for a few minutes, and Detective McBride came out to find me.

"You said you needed to talk with me," he said. "This might be a good place."

"Yes, the food isn't quite ready so we'll have a few minutes."

We moved away from the table, well out of the caterer's way, and I asked, "I hope it isn't awkward for you that I invited Eduardo Sanchez here tonight?"

"No, he's told us everything we need to know, and agreed to come back up as a witness when we need him."

"So, he's in the clear then?"

"Yes. I spoke with him this week. Now, what's the important information you have for me?" he asked.

"I visited Jeffrey today, and he told me something I thought you should know."

"He remembered something about the shooting?" McBride asked, suddenly becoming more alert.

"No, it wasn't that. He told me Judson Sparks was enraged by his wife's affair with Keezer. He said Sparks was frustrated by his wife's threat to expose him if he tried to do anything about the affair. He also mentioned that Sparks was involved in some of the Valdez projects."

"Hmm," McBride said, rubbing his chin. "That fits."

"What do you mean?"

He looked at me thoughtfully before responding. "You know, Mrs. Crane, you're not only a hell of an actress, but you've got a lot of spunk. Not to mention a keen nose for getting information."

"Thank you for the compliment," I said.

"I've been thinking. I might be able to use your help sometime…some freelance undercover work. It might even lead to a more interesting part-time job than you have now. You'd make a good private investigator. Think you'd be interested?"

I was completely taken aback by his suggestion, and must have showed it in my reaction.

"Well, just something to think about," he said, as he walked over to the buffet table, and seemed preoccupied with popping shrimp into his mouth.

Something to think about? My first impulse was to jump at the chance. I had found the last three weeks exciting—a tonic I had desperately needed. I recalled a recent TV interview I had seen with the actor Brad Pitt. His comment struck a deep chord in me when he said, "actors spend a lot of time pursuing interesting characters, and forget to pursue an interesting life." I desperately wanted to have an interesting life. And maybe McBride's offer was a ticket. Yet I knew I'd have to think about it. Lorelei Crane, Private Investigator? And, of course, I'd have to consult with Bill before deciding, though I was certain he wouldn't like it.

McBride put his plate down, and slowly walked back. "Took you by surprise, didn't I?"

"You did that," I said. "Now, since you trust me enough to want my help in the future, how about telling me about your investigation? What's happening?"

He seemed to expect my question. "Okay, you've been so involved in the case; I'll let you in on where we stand."

"I'm all ears," I said.

"Mind if I sit down? I'm really beat." He sat down, picked up his beer, and rolled the bottle between his hands before taking a sip.

I pulled a chair next to his, watching him take a swig of his beer. His square jaw, and tanned face seemed more relaxed than usual. The sultry sounds of a Diana Krall CD, and the hum of conversations in the adjoining room were reminders that I had guests, but for the moment, my attention was riveted on McBride.

He leaned forward and whispered, "The M.E.—Medical Examiner—is pretty sure that Keezer was heavily drugged and would have been incapable of shooting himself. But we still need the tox report to prove it. The DNA tests will take quite a while longer."

"So it was murder," I said, thinking Jimmy Valdez may not be off the hook just yet.

"Valdez's lawyers admitted to us that he was at the scene with Keezer that day, but they say it was in the afternoon. So far his alibi checks out. That leaves the spotlight on the commissioner and his wife. There's evidence that both of them were there…probably at different times.

"Eduardo heard shouting that sounded like a man's voice," I said. "So did Jimmy Valdez when he called."

Delcie stuck her head out the patio door, and said, "Is this a private session or can I join you?"

McBride looked annoyed, but waved her in. Delcie pulled up a chair causing us to form a tight threesome.

He said, "I was just going over some things with Mrs. Crane. Since you two have been spending so much time together, I'm sure she already knows some it. Right, deputy? Girl talk's hard to resist."

Delcie stiffened, and I had a flash of anger at McBride for his taunts. "Actually, Detective, I have to come to Deputy Wright's defense here. In all fairness, she hasn't told me anything more than you have, and she often gathers information for you rather than gives it out."

"Thanks, Lorelei, but I can defend myself," Delcie said, still sitting straight-backed in the chair. "The only thing I'm guilty of is not telling you that Mrs. Crane, Lorelei, and I have known one another since college."

"I guessed as much," he said, slowly taking another sip of beer. "Your mutual interest in one another made me suspect you were friends. I guess it's okay, now that we all know about it."

"Good," I said. "Please continue. So both Mr. and Mrs. Sparks visited the trailer that day?"

"Yes. And they both have impressive motives for killing Keezer. The commissioner is the betrayed husband. That made him a prime suspect right off the bat. But his alibi seems to hold up for the time of the shooting. He's got a half a dozen or more witnesses saying he was at an Elks Club initiation or some damn thing."

"I'll bet you're relieved about that," Delcie said.

"You bet I am. I was looking at a political nightmare for a while," McBride said.

"So, that leaves Chelsea Sparks?" I asked. "Cher chez la femme."

McBride snorted, "Yeah, the femme or someone we haven't turned up yet."

"Like a hit man hired by Valdez?" Delcie said. "He has the motive, and he's the kind of guy who doesn't like to dirty his own hands."

"Could be," McBride said. "Wouldn't be the first time a guy with Valdez's connections got revenge. But this murder has the mark of an amateur. My bet is it's the girlfriend, and maybe a helper. Keezer asked his wife for a divorce to marry Mrs. Sparks. The wife says she refused."

I nodded. "That could be what they were fighting about the day Jeffrey and I ran into them at the marina." I felt excited as I put together pieces of the story I'd personally witnessed.

"Possible," he said. "So we've got a disappointed girlfriend who probably has access to a million bucks stashed away in some off-shore bank."

"The money they stole from the Valdez Company," I said.

He put up his hand while he continued, "And who has recently got a hold of some Rohpnol."

"How'd you find that out?" I asked.

Delcie said, "We interviewed her student employees, and one of them owned up to getting it for her. Like I told you, Lor, it's easy for college kids to get the stuff."

"Darling?" We all jerked around at the sound of Bill's voice. "When were you planning on inviting our guests out to the buffet?" He stood in the doorway, and pointed at the food table. He looked annoyed at the sight of the three of us in a huddle.

"Just a few minutes," I said. "This is important." I waved and flashed him a look that said please-do-not-interrupt-me-right-now.

He lifted his glass, said "Cheers!" and left.

I turned back to McBride, "I guess the 'man's voice' that Eduardo and Valdez heard shouting at Keezer could have been Chelsea Sparks," I said. "Remember what a deep husky voice she had when we ran into her at the rally?"

"There could have been a show-down that night," McBride said. "She had to have planned in advance to slip him that Roofie. It was probably the only way to set it up to look like suicide. That, and the note which, by the way, was cut from some other sheet of paper…a letter maybe."

"Clever. But how clumsy to drop some of the pills."

McBride cocked his head and frowned, "How did you know about that?" he said, giving Delcie a sideways glance which caused her to stare down at her lap.

"So have you arrested Chelsea Sparks?" I asked, trying to change the subject.

"No," he said, emitting a stoic sigh.

"Why not? Do you need more evidence? Does she have a tight alibi?"

"I've interviewed her once, and you can be sure I tried to bring her in again. Trouble is we can't find her!"

"What?" Delcie blurted out the question before I could.

"Chelsea Sparks has disappeared. She's gone." McBride said.

"You're kidding. She just vanished?" I asked.

"We've got a BOLO out on her."

"'Be-On-The-Look-Out,'" Delcie explained.

McBride continued, "We're pretty sure she's left the country by now. Her husband says their safety deposit box has been emptied, and her passport's gone. Interpol has been notified. It'll all be in the papers tomorrow."

"How very astonishing," I said, and sat back, feeling suddenly exhausted.

McBride slumped in the chair and stretched out his legs. He looked discouraged.

I leaned forward and touched his leg. "Don't worry. You'll find her."

"Not if she's half as good an actress as you are," he said and smiled. "Now, you'd better get back to your guests. This is my, uh, our problem," McBride said, looking at Delcie with something akin to respect. He stood, and picked up his beer.

We walked back into the living room, and I invited everyone to visit the buffet on the patio.

"Lorelei, isn't it great? They're moving Jeffrey to a regular room in the hospital." Becky came up and locked her arm in mine.

I followed my guests out of the living room onto the patio. Diana took Wiley's arm as they left the room, and he glanced at her with affection. Oh my, I thought, this evening is just filled with intriguing events—not the least of which was McBride's startling idea that I enter the field of private investigation.

Chapter 27

It was long after midnight when Bill and I finally said goodbye to the last of our guests, put the food away, and went upstairs to bed.

"That was a success, don't you think?" Bill said, while we were undressing. "What in the world were you and McBride talking about for so long?"

"McBride was catching me up on the Keezer investigation. You'll read about it in the paper tomorrow."

He followed me into the bathroom, and stood alongside me while I brushed my teeth. "While you had your tête-à-tête with McBride, I had to carry the party by myself all night. I'm sure our guests thought your disappearance a bit odd."

"Sorry, darling," I said, walking back into the bedroom. "I'm sure it was fine, but I'm almost dead. Let's just go to sleep." I got into bed, and turned off my light.

Bill stood at the foot of the bed, staring down at me. "I don't understand why McBride wants to involve you in this stuff anyway. It's police business. I've repeatedly asked you to stay away from it. It's too dangerous."

"Yes, dear."

"And we really need to make a date with one another," Bill said, getting into bed. "It's been too long since we've spent any real time together...we're like those proverbial ships crossing in the night."

Unable to respond, I fell asleep as soon as he turned off his light.

I awoke to the sound of the television, and peeked at the clock. It was almost nine o'clock Saturday morning. I held my arm across my eyes to keep out the light, hoping to sleep some more.

Bill said, "Sorry to wake you, darling, but I wanted to see about those storms in the Caribbean. I'm supposed to be going to a conference in Miami next week."

"Miami? I didn't know you were going to Miami," I said, wondering if he would be taking his grad student along with him, and if his earlier resolution to forego conferences had vanished.

"You didn't? I thought I mentioned it a few weeks ago." Bill climbed back into bed, pulled me to him, and whispered, "I wish you were free to come with me. You know, I really got turned on last night seeing you on stage."

"I'm glad you find me so desirable, but I still feel a bit sleepy."

"C'mon, Lorelei, you don't have to be at the theater till the afternoon, and I'm free all day. At least we can spend some time together this morning," he said, caressing my back.

"Please, Bill, give me a chance to wake up. I feel like I've been drugged," I said. I pulled away from him, and propped myself up against the headboard.

He sat up next to me, and began kissing my neck.

My attention was suddenly caught by the picture on the TV screen. Passengers were hurriedly moving down the gangplank of a cruise ship docked in some Caribbean port. There was a close-up shot, and I gasped.

"Oh my God. I don't believe it," I said, straining sideways away from him.

"Lorelei? What's the matter?" Bill asked, turning to see what I was looking at. As he did so, I wriggled away, jumped out of bed, and rushed over to the TV.

"What the hell?" he cried.

I stood mesmerized in front of the screen, but the scene had already changed. I was certain I had spotted Chelsea Sparks leaving that ship. She was wearing the same black wig I had seen her in that day at the marina, and she was engaged in an animated conversation with a man wearing a University of Florida Gator cap! It had to be the hunky Gator Security guy whom I'd seen the first day I'd met Keezer and Valdez.

"Honey, I can't explain right now, but I've got to get in touch with McBride. I'll have to go see him, right away!"

"Lorelei, are you crazy? What's this all about?" Bill got out of bed, and followed me into the closet where I pulled on a pair of jeans and a shirt.

"Bill, I promise, I'll be back in a couple of hours, and I'll tell you everything."

When I walked into the bathroom, he edged in beside me and glared while I splashed some water on my face, and combed my hair.

I grabbed my handbag and started downstairs, but Bill tried to block the bedroom doorway.

"You can't just jump out of bed like that and leave me with no explanation," he said.

"Please, Bill. It's important. It's about Keezer's murder," I said, and pushed my way past him.

I hurried downstairs, got in my car, and headed into town. I pulled my cell phone and McBride's card out of my bag. He answered immediately.

"Mrs. Crane? What's up?"

My heart was racing with excitement.

"Homer, I need to see you right away. I'm on my way into town. I think I know where you can find Chelsea Sparks."

There was a moment of silence, and he said, "I'm in my office. I'll wait for you."

I felt like I was hyperventilating, and I forced myself to take deep breaths. As I started across the Prairie, it was glimmering in sunlight, and I saw the majestic green tree canopy at the far side of the basin. I experienced a wave of gratitude knowing that, unlike Chekhov's cherry orchard, no axes would sound at this pristine site. It was a perfect moment, and I shouted, "Go Gators! C'mon Gators, let's go!"

McBride met me in the Sheriff's office waiting room. "You got here fast," he said leading me back to his office. His clothes emitted a new aroma—tobacco smoke. He's stressed, I thought.

"Sit down, Mrs. Crane, you look like you're about to burst," he said, shutting the office door.

"They're in the Caribbean somewhere. I'm sure you can find them."

"Slow down," McBride said pulling his chair around to the side of the desk. "What'd mean 'them'? Tell me everything from the beginning."

I gradually caught my breath, and calmed down. "It was this morning—right before I called you—Bill had the TV on to watch the weather news. It was then I spied Chelsea Sparks. She was getting off a cruise ship."

"Did you get the name of the ship? The port?"

I shook my head. "She was with the man who owns Gator Security, your friend, the ex-cop. Remember? I met him when I first met Keezer and Valdez. It was the Gator cap that caught my eye."

McBride's eyebrows shot up, "I'll be dammed. So it was the two of them. That explains a few things. I've been trying to reach him, but his secretary will only say he's out-of-town. She really doesn't seem to know much."

"I'm so sorry I didn't get the ship's name or anything. I was just so shocked to see them."

"Don't worry," McBride said. "We can get the video." He looked thoughtful for a moment. "I just hope it's a country we have an extradition treaty with, and…" he looked at his watch, "that they haven't already flown off somewhere else. Excuse me a minute."

When he left the room, I tried to relax, but realized I was both perspiring and freezing cold.

McBride returned a few minutes later. "Okay, we're getting the tape." He sat down and looked amused as he said, "So Randy Ashcroft finally struck pay dirt. He's been knockin' around at one thing or another ever since he was kicked off the force at Gainesville P.D."

"You think he was in on Keezer's murder? You said it looked like an amateur job." I kept my promise to Diana, and didn't tell McBride it was Randy Ashcroft who had also ordered A.J. Hill's break-in at the Sierra Club.

"Randy wasn't the sharpest cop—that's why he was fired—he had a weakness for the ladies that got him into a lot of jams. Now he finally got himself a rich one." McBride smiled and shook his head.

"What is this, Homer...every police officer's dream? You actually sound envious."

McBride's face took on a wistful look, "Envious? Maybe a little. Think about it, living at the top of the food chain on some beautiful Caribbean island. But, hell, he's gotta know we'll be hunting for him. It might take awhile till one of them gets homesick."

"Anyway, I wanted to let you know about them as soon as possible." I stood, ready to leave.

"I appreciate that, Mrs. Crane."

"Please, call me Lorelei. I think we know each other well enough."

He smiled, put out his hand, and I took it. "Have you given any thought to my proposition last night?"

There was that word again—'proposition'—proposals on both sides of the law, and oddly enough made by two very different men: Jimmy Valdez and Detective Homer McBride.

I withdrew my hand from his, and replied, "I'll be honest with you...the idea fascinates me, but I think—for the sake of my marriage—I'll wait a bit before responding.

"I understand. Anyway, thanks for all your help. Maybe we could have lunch together some day soon. You can tell me more about the theater."

"I'd love it, Homer. In the meantime, will you let me know if you catch up with them?"

He nodded. "I'll do it...Lorelei."

I walked down the long brightly lit hall glancing into the various offices with a new interest in the activities going on in them. But on the way home, I felt a sense of let down.

The dramatic events that had begun several weeks ago had come to a conclusion, of sorts. The loose ends yet to be resolved were both my suspicions about Bill's fidelity, and my own feelings about Jeffrey. And then there was the matter of Detective McBride's most intriguing proposal. I shivered at the sudden realization that I had passed a watershed, and was well on the path of a new beginning—and that, after all, had been my deepest desire.

Afterword

More About The Prairie

During my college years in the 1950's, Paynes Prairie's only significance to me was that on the long drive up from Miami, it signaled we had almost arrived home, to the University of Florida campus. In 1970 the state of Florida purchased the land now designated as Paynes Prairie Preserve State Park and has been attempting to restore it to the way it was when naturalist William Bartram first saw it in 1774.

Today, most people experience Paynes Prairie at speeds in excess of 70 mph, on one of the two roads that bisect it: State Road 441 and Interstate I-75. To the car-bound observer, it appears as a sometimes greenish, sometimes brownish open grassland peppered with a few small trees. In the fall, a blur of yellow marsh marigolds, goldenrod, and lavender tinted dog fennel may be seen lining the road. Overall, however, the view appears to be as unremarkable as when I traversed it about 50 years ago.

In 1990 I returned to live in Gainesville with a heightened sensitivity to place and a passion about ecological issues. I began work with Florida Defenders of the Environment and famed environmental activist, Marjorie Harris Carr. It was her advocacy to protect the Prairie in the 1960's, through the Gainesville Garden Club, that ultimately led to its status as a state park. I discovered that its seemingly bland landscape was actually rich—diverse and teeming with as much life and drama as a human city!

The Prairie contains more than 350 non-plant species including such large animals as alligators, American Bison, white-tailed deer, and descendants of 16th century Spanish horses and Florida range cattle. I've come to appreciate that the fearsome large alligator population—top predators on the Prairie—helps to sustain other life around it.

During the wet season, gator holes, which protect their newborn, provide homes for other species which in turn rejuvenates the marshland.

The amount of rainfall directly affects the quantity and diversity of species, and water flows are a continuous source of contention among Prairie management, the regional water utility, and surrounding towns. During various seasons, water in its many lakes and ponds influences the number of fish and the up to sixteen species of long-legged migratory wading birds—including large flocks of raucous sandhill cranes. The marsh marigold and other plant species die or replace one another when there is too much or too little water. And so it goes—a vast grassland that is ever changing in a continuous ebb and flow of life.

The impact of human populations is also a part of the Prairie's story. Exhibits in the Visitor's Center, in Micanopy, provide a trip through time in which humans have inhabited the Prairie for 12,000 years. Today, there are many pieces of privately owned property on the Prairie rim which have, as in my story, development potential. Despite political issues surrounding this privately held land, there are efforts, by such initiatives as Alachua County Forever, to purchase the most strategic uplands, and to place them in preservation status.

In their publication, *The Great Alachua Savanna: A Visual History of Payne's Prairie*, O'Connor and Fradkin (1997) write, *Paynes Prairie reminds us of our past, our history, and our origins. It represents the Garden before the Fall, the primordial home for which we long...a refuge that we must somehow preserve to save not only our planet but ourselves* (p.183). All that and more is why I chose to write about this unique and splendid place.

Printed in the United States
53075LVS00003B/31-81

9 781591 136651